HEAVEN SHOULD FALL

HEAVEN SHOULD FALL

REBECCA COLEMAN

HARLEQUIN®

entertain, enrich, inspire™

Recycling programs
for this product may
not exist in your area.

ISBN-13: 978-0-7783-1389-2

HEAVEN SHOULD FALL

Copyright © 2012 by Rebecca Coleman

For questions and comments about the quality of this book please contact us at
CustomerService@Harlequin.com.

www.Harlequin.com

Printed in U.S.A.

First printing: October 2012
10 9 8 7 6 5 4 3 2 1

To Breckan

Through the open door I could see my husband hard at work just outside the shed, a column of sweat staining his T-shirt in the June heat, his solid arms shedding flecks of grit and sawdust as he twisted down the metal vise. He wore a ball cap with the brim tightly rolled and heavy leather work boots, and when he stepped back and held his small, lethal project up to the light, the ease of his broad shoulders and smoothness of his belly made him lovely in spite of his efforts. Truly, Cade could have been anything. With his passion for his country and whip-smart intellect, he could have been the congressman he had once aspired to become. He could have been a pastor or a diplomat, a marine, or, thanks to his sincere charm and beautiful eyes, a very successful womanizer. But instead he stood alone outside this shed in northern New Hampshire, loyal and angry and probably not entirely sober, building a pipe bomb.

I caught his eye, and he waved and commenced to shake powder into the pipe from a narrow-topped bottle.

"Lunch is ready."

"Be there in a sec. Is the baby awake?"

"Yeah, he's in the high chair. Candy's watching him."

"How's he feeling?"

"Better. I put some drops in his ear and they seem to be helping."

"Good. Poor kid." He slipped in a fuse, and then, with a cautious hand, slid a palmful of nails down the center. "You know what we need, Jill?"

I could think of many answers to that question, but Cade answered it himself.

"A weekend away," he said. "No whining kids, no animals to feed, no parents in the next room keeping things all quiet and inhibited. No sitting watch at three in the morning like we're the goddamn Branch Davidians. Just you and me in a motel room someplace, getting friendly." He set the other end of the pipe into the vise and tightened it down.

"There's an alumni weekend at our alma mater next month. We could go to that, if you haven't blown yourself up by then."

He laughed. Carefully he set the completed bomb into the box with the others, then came over to kiss me. Not to my surprise, he tasted like beer.

"'Let justice be done though the heavens should fall,'" he quoted, low voiced, smiling.

I smiled back stiffly. "Come eat. The family's waiting."

He turned on the garden spigot and crouched to wash his hands in the crashing water. It flowed away from the house in a narrow river, carrying away steel dust and explosive powder, the grime of farmwork and sloughed dry skin from his calloused hands: the slow erosion of my husband.

Chapter 1

JILL

The signs for Baltimore–Washington International Airport began to appear above the highway ten miles out. "Keep right." Cade shot a glance at my side mirror, then shifted two lanes over in one graceful, if reckless, maneuver. I braced the dowels of the two miniature American flags against my lap, but they barely shivered. Cade and his little white Saturn coupe were like a boy and his dog. He spent half his life in the thing, and there was no reason to doubt his skill at handling it.

"I bet he's dying to get off that plane," said Cade. "It's a fifteen-hour flight from Kabul to Baltimore. That's a crapload of Nicorette."

I grinned. "So if he seems really cranky, I shouldn't assume that's his normal personality."

"Nah. He's a cool guy. Getting shot at for three years probably makes a person a little edgy, but he'll mellow out fast enough." He felt around in the console and, finding it empty, said, "Pass me the mints, will you, Jill?"

"You've got one in your mouth already."

"Yeah, but it's almost gone."

I reached into the neatly arranged "auto office" box at my feet and retrieved the Altoids tin from a side pocket. "Cade, you're a mint addict."

"Usually you're not complaining."

"The first step is admitting you have a problem."

His brow creased above his sunglasses. "I thought it was believing in a higher power."

"No, that's the second step. That a higher power can restore you to sanity."

A white sign appeared above our heads, marked with a rainbow of coded indicators. Cade turned down his Dave Matthews Band CD, as if quieter music would help him see the signs better. "'Arriving Flights,'" he read aloud. "We're coming to get you, bro."

We navigated the labyrinth of the parking garage and emerged into the airport. Once through security, our gate passes in hand, we joined the crowd gathered around the walkway cordoned off for the soldiers. The air was electric with anticipation. We could see, through the window, the plane pulling up to the gangway, setting off a noisy cheer and the waving of handmade signs drawn in red and blue marker. Young mothers strained to see through the glass, leaning heavily on the handles of their strollers, as if exhausted by the journey. Senior citizens stood patiently alongside, the men wearing trucker caps embroidered with the names of units and platoons, the women in sweatshirts hand painted with cheerful flag themes. Cade passed his American flag off to a little girl, then unclipped his sunglasses from his T-shirt collar and shifted them to the back pocket of his jeans. When I gave him a funny look he explained, "I don't want to stab Elias with them when I hug him."

Then the door opened, and a great wave of a cheer rose up as the first soldiers started down the walkway. Among the colorful crowd, their tidy uniforms—buttoned and tucked, the digital camouflage in subtle shades of sage and moss—gave them gravitas and dignity. *So many hands to shake,* I thought, *so many people to work through,* when surely each one must want nothing more than to collapse in a recliner with a beer. One soldier after another worked his jaw around a piece of gum, and I thought about what Cade had said on the highway.

At last Cade's searching gaze snapped into recognition, and he uncoiled his arms from their crossed position against his chest. "Hey, dude," he said, clasping Elias's extended hand, then pulling him into a hug unimpeded by the flat ribbon of the walkway marker wedged between them. "I missed you, man."

For a year now—ever since Cade and I began seeing each other—I'd been looking at the same photo of his brother, a glowering soldier bulked out by body armor and carrying an M-16, standing on a patch of sand with an American flag pinned to the tent behind him. The image was tacked to the corkboard above Cade's bed in his dorm room, among the various bumper stickers from campaigns he had volunteered on—local representatives, congressmen, state senate—and a postcard of Teddy Roosevelt's Rough Riders portrait with the quote "Aggressive fighting for the right is the noblest sport the world affords." Elias almost never wrote letters home, so on one rare trip back to their farm in New Hampshire, Cade had commandeered the photo sent to their sister, Candy, as a thank-you for her church fundraising the money to buy him the body armor. "Thanks" and "Elias" were scrawled on the bottom in a sloppy cursive that looked as if it belonged to a twelve-year-old schoolboy, not a twenty-four-year-old army infantry specialist, but it looked as if Elias had bigger things on his mind than good penmanship. Sometimes when Cade and I were making love, I caught sight of that scowling image and felt a wave of guilt. Here Cade and I were in the ivory tower of academia, casting aside our textbooks to spend an afternoon at play in his bed, while seven thousand miles away his brother was making a diligent effort not to die. But the fact was, we had each chosen our own path. And now here we all were, together.

As Elias extracted himself from the hug and made his way out of the line, I watched him. He was shorter than Cade by a couple of inches, and stockier; his face offered none of the animation that lit Cade's, but his blue eyes, like his brother's, were piercing. His expression was more or less the same as the one he wore in the photo. When he looked at me I felt as if he had been watching me all this time, all these months I'd been with Cade, a witness to my secrets. I felt embarrassed when he shook my hand.

"This is Jill Wagner," Cade told him. "My fiancée. She's the one who's been sending you all the care packages."

His hand was warmer than my own. Holding my gaze, he indicated Cade with a cock of his head and said, in a tone that was barely jesting, "You're actually going to marry this asshole?"

"Not for a while yet. We both need to finish school first." Amusement lit Cade's face, and so I joked back, "I still have plenty of time to reevaluate."

"Smart thinking. Thanks for all the packages. You make a mean chocolate chip cookie." He turned to Cade. "I need a smoke so bad I'm ready to go on a shooting spree."

"I don't think you can say that in an airport."

"If they throw me out I can get to my smokes faster."

We separated while the soldiers all regrouped to turn in their government property. Cade and I retrieved the Saturn and pulled it around to the pickup lanes, idling as we watched Elias make his way through baggage claim. As soon as he was outside, he stopped in front of the open automatic doors and lit a cigarette. Other travelers moved around him, casting shy reproachful glances in his direction.

"Eli," Cade shouted. "Over here."

Elias nodded and meandered over. In spite of the cool November breeze he unbuttoned his uniform jacket and folded it into his duffel bag, revealing just a thin sandy-brown T-shirt. He turned his face toward the sun, closed his eyes and pulled in a deep breath of air. "No dust," he said. "Nice and cool. Fuck, yeah, it's good to be home."

"Still got five hundred miles to go, bro."

"Yeah, but not until tomorrow. This is close enough. No question."

He dropped his bag into the trunk and climbed into the back passenger seat. As we turned out onto the highway he gazed out at the landscape, squinting, blowing thin cyclones of smoke out the window. After his initial friendliness, he'd gone quiet.

"Did they debrief you?" asked Cade.

"Yep."

"How'd it go?"

"Fine."

Cade glanced at him in the rearview mirror. Elias set his boot against the center console and flicked ash out the window. After a minute he said, "It's good to see green again."

"Well, you'll see all the green you can stand back home."

"Have you talked to Mom and Dad?"

"Not in a while. I avoid it whenever possible." Elias chuckled, and Cade added, "Anyway, I've been busy. I've been working on this damn campaign for five months that only *just* ended. We won the election, at least."

"What do you do, Jill?" he asked, and in surprise I glanced back over my shoulder at him. "You run around doing all this election stuff, too?"

I shook my head. "No way. I couldn't care less about politics."

"Well, *that* sounds like a match made in heaven."

I smiled, and Cade said, "She hangs out with farm animals all day. So we both deal with a lot of bullshit. It works out."

"We both run, too," I told him. "I ran track in high school, and Cade's always training for some half marathon or another. So we go running together a lot."

"I bet Cade tries to outrun you," Elias said, "competitive son of a bitch that he is."

"And you wonder why I don't bring you home to meet my family," Cade said to me. "You hear the stuff they say about me?"

Elias laughed low. "Just speaking the truth, bro. She's got to learn it sometime."

It wasn't long before we made the turn back into College Park. Cade and I lived in the dormitories on campus—he in a single room, me with a snooty roommate—but on the weekends he often crashed at the apartment of his friend Stan. Up until the previous year he and Stan had been roommates, but now Stan had his own place, at which he held frequent parties. He was generous in offering his futon—or a patch of carpet—to whoever couldn't drive home. Cade, whose ambition for an elected office made him ultraparanoid about getting a DUI, spent so much time on that futon that he actually kept a toothbrush in Stan's medicine cabinet. It hadn't seemed like much of a stretch, then, to ask to borrow the place for the night when Cade got the call that his brother was coming home and wanted to spend a day hanging out before making the trek back to New Hampshire.

Cade unlocked the door, and Elias stepped inside. He set his pack down on the floor beside the futon and looked around: at the mannequin head with the dart stuck in it, the poster of a trio of blonde girls in bikinis posing on a beach, the dry-erase board above the old metal desk that was the central piece of furniture in the living room. He caught sight of the photo clipped to Stan's computer monitor—of Stan in a black suit and tails, popping out his lapels with his thumbs and flanked by two transvestites in full regalia.

"What in the hell is that?" asked Elias.

"That's Stan," Cade explained. "The guy you've heard me talk about a million times. This is his place. He's dressed up like Riff Raff from *The Rocky Horror Picture Show*."

"*That's* Stan?" He walked over and peered closely at the photo. Then he looked over his shoulder at Cade, his upper lip curled in the first grin I'd seen out of him. "Does Dad know you've been living with a black guy?"

"What do *you* think?"

Elias laughed and straightened up again, still looking at the picture. "That's Stan," he repeated.

"He'll be in and out this weekend. You can take the futon and I'll sleep on the floor. Stan's got enough blankets in the closet for an army."

"Nah, I'll take the floor."

"No way. You just got back."

"All the more reason. Floor's still better than what I'm used to." He looked at the girlie posters on the walls. "Some black guy, huh?"

"He only dates white women."

Elias chuckled again. "Dad would shit a brick."

Cade shrugged. "Back in his glory days. Since the stroke, not much pisses him off."

"If you say so. Bet that'd still get a rise out of him on a good day."

I looked quizzically at Cade, but nothing in his expression acknowledged the glance. Elias quit looking around and sat on the edge of the futon, opening up his pack and pulling out a clean T-shirt, socks and boxers. "Don't bother me none,"

he said. Then, almost as if pulled down by sheer fatigue and
the comfort of the mattress, he lay back and rubbed his hands
against his face, letting out a long, tired groan. "Mother*fuck*,"
he added. "God, it's good to be back."

That was the last I saw of him for a long time. For all those
months, that was the image I held of him: supine against the
futon, his body all muscular and stocky and hard as a nail. The
smallest details stuck in my mind. How neatly the waistband
of his BDU trousers lay against his stomach and circled his
hips. How the bulk of his shoulders seemed barely contained
by his shirt's thin fabric. It was not attraction I felt, exactly,
so much as awe. Here was a soldier, honed like the edge of a
blade, yet stretched out before me like a cat on a windowsill.
His beauty was not like Cade's, but it was still beauty.

I still try to remember him that way, sometimes. I think
he would want me to.

It had been only a couple of months before that Cade and
I had had a similar reunion. On that day—the last Saturday
in August, just a few days before the dorms reopened—I had
run down the hill in front of the lodgelike main building of
the camp where I'd spent the entire summer, racing to meet
Cade as his Saturn churned slow clouds of dust along the dirt
road. He'd stopped and gotten out of the car, opening his
arms to me, and I had thunked against his chest with a force
that made him stagger back against the car. "Missed you,
too, babe," he murmured against my hair. We had meant to
see each other every other weekend, but he'd gotten so busy
working on Bylina's campaign for Congress, and time had
plodded along until it was two months since he had visited me.
I understood. With my jeans and stubby, plain fingernails, my
total disinterest in ever again living in a city and my sketchy
family history, I had little to offer as a partner to someone

who wanted to be a congressman one day. But I did possess patience and devotion, and the very reason I loved Cade was that he could find his passion and follow the prize of it like a polestar. I couldn't very well fault him for being himself.

All summer I had lived at Southridge, the camp I'd attended every year since I was thirteen—although now I was a counselor and teacher, no longer a little camper kicking around in the woods. My mother had first signed me up for the annual retreat for Alateen, the support group for teenagers with alcoholic family members: She was the alcoholic in question, although she had twelve-stepped when I was young enough not to remember it. Still, she thought it would be good for me to spend a couple of weeks in the woods with other kids whose families spoke the peculiar language of recovery, making friends, trying out rustic crafts and learning how not to turn out like any of my close relatives.

Once I outgrew the retreat, I signed on to become a counselor, and for three summers now I had lived at Southridge full-time. I loved being outdoors in the piney air at the foot of the Allegheny Mountains, teaching people much older than me how to survive in the uncharted wilderness. All kinds of people passed through—packs of Boy Scouts and troubled foster kids, hipster folk intent on learning to garden organically and brew their own beer, paranoid survivalists seeking the skills to live off the grid when the people finally rose up against the government. I'd learned to cheerfully tolerate all kinds, and did my work so well that Dave—the head guy at the camp and, next to Cade, my favorite person in the world— had tried to persuade me to stay on through the fall and do my semester online. I'd had to patiently explain to him, again, that online classes aren't an option for agriculture majors.

Later that very day—the one on which I had run down the road to greet Cade, loaded my stuff into the trunk of his

Saturn and sped back toward College Park—he had taken me down into D.C. and proposed to me in the nighttime glow of the Jefferson Memorial. The bronze figure of Thomas Jefferson loomed overhead, his knee bent as if to take a step forward; the lettered quotes from the Declaration of Independence curved all around and above us, giving me a sense of vertigo, but beyond it the Tidal Basin lay blue and softly rippling. I knew what it meant that he had chosen this place: that he was drawing me into the pantheon of the things he loved most, showing me that nobody less than his personal hero would be called upon to witness it. Of course I accepted, even though I knew an actual wedding would be a long time coming. We were only twenty-one. We had all the time in the world.

On the day Elias came back, after Cade had dropped me off at my dorm and driven off with his brother for a night of revelry, I flicked on the TV and settled onto my bed with a bag of Starbursts to watch *Lockup: Raleigh*. My mother had been a huge fan of the show, a lurid reality program that followed six women held in a North Carolina prison for various violent offenses. Our favorite was a woman named Kendra, a former pill addict who had attacked her boyfriend with both ends of a rake. Kendra wore one side of her hair in cornrows most of the time and used expressions like "be breezy" and "tell me what's poppin'" and "life ain't all peaches and cream." I think my mother liked the show so much because the women were a caricature of what she might have become had she not joined Alcoholics Anonymous, and like most successful twelve-steppers she took a dim view of people who wanted to hold their old lifestyle close to their hearts. Kendra was an easy target. As a gentle reminder of how good I had it, when I complained about the pressures of school and SATs, my mother would sometimes pat my hand and say, deadpan, "Just remember, Jill. Life ain't all peaches and cream."

Midway through the program, the door swung open and my roommate waltzed in. I chewed a candy and braced myself for the inevitable comments. Erica and I had been living together only since September, and already she had a finely honed skill for needling me at any tender spot she could identify. As she stuffed her makeup into its little quilted bag, she looked over at me with one arched eyebrow. "How can you eat that stuff?"

"They're Starbursts. Who doesn't like Starbursts?"

"They're pure sugar."

"Yes. I know."

She squeezed the makeup bag into her purse and turned toward the TV. "What is this, *White Trash Wonderland* again?"

"Lockup: Raleigh."

"Is your boyfriend still at the office?"

"Nope. He went out with his brother."

She smiled tightly. Her face was a mask of makeup. "Well, have a great Saturday night."

I sighed through my nose as she left the room, failing to let the door close all the way. As I got up to shut it myself, I scanned the room and tried not to see it through her eyes: the small, chattering TV; the crumpled bag of candy on the bed; my phone, plugged in to its charger because I had no use for it tonight. Before self-pity could creep in, I picked up the landline phone and called Dave.

"It's Blackbird," I said as soon as he answered with a hearty "Dave Robinson here." I had been using my camp name for so many years, and had developed such a good reputation around the place, that normally it was a point of pride. I was the semi-legendary Blackbird, the ragtag little city kid who had blossomed into a trail-guiding, scat-identifying swan.

But alone in my dorm room it sounded a little goofy, like a kid playing spy.

"Hey, kiddo! Good to hear from you. I just found a sweatshirt you left here. Pretty nice hoodie. Want me to mail it to you?"

His face appeared in my mind's eye with an expression to match his voice: warm brown eyes and easygoing, energetic smile, shaggy dark hair brushing his shoulders. He shaved maybe every couple of weeks, and then with haste and indifference. I smiled and tugged the phone closer to my wooden desk chair. "Sure. I was wondering where it went. Thought maybe I left it behind at Cade's friend's place."

"I'll send it out on Monday. How's the semester treating you?" His dog began to bark, and he made a noise to shush her. "How was October?"

"I made it through okay. Kept busy."

"You think about your mom a lot?"

"Yeah, but I tried not to dwell on it. It's been three years now. I need to keep moving forward. One day at a time, and all that." I shut off the TV. "I finally got to meet a member of Cade's family today. His brother. He just got back from Afghanistan."

"All this time and you *still* haven't met any of them?"

"Nope. They live pretty far away, you know. I think he finds them embarrassing. He says they're nothing like him."

Dave laughed ruefully. "We all think that about ourselves. Never as true as we want to believe."

"His brother seemed fine. I'd been sending him all these care packages with snack food and Little Debbie cakes and stuff like that, and he thanked me for them. It has to be overwhelming when you first get home after three years, so I thought that was sweet that he remembered."

"Gonna be a hell of an adjustment, I'm sure. I remember those days."

I frowned and slouched lower in my chair. "I thought you got kicked out of Ranger school."

"I did, but then 9/11 happened and they sent me to Afghanistan anyway. Coming back wasn't much of a party. Why do you think I ended up living in the woods?"

"I never heard you talk about that."

"Nope. One day at a time, right? Keep moving forward."

I twisted the cord around my fingers, a strange cat's cradle. "No fair using AA lingo against me."

"Go easy on the guy, that's all I'm saying. Around the holidays is the worst time to come back, with everybody wanting you to be all cheery when you're not feeling it at all. What was he, a grunt?"

"Yeah. Infantry. He did roadside patrols and things like that. He got a Purple Heart for a leg wound a couple years ago—something exploded in a car that was driving up to them, or something like that."

Dave gave a low whistle. "Get that guy into therapy, stat. I'm not joking."

"Oh, he's just a normal soldier. There must have been a hundred other soldiers who got off that plane with him. I'm sure they don't all need therapy." I let my voice slide back into a less serious register. "Be breezy, Dave."

At the razzing sound he made, I broke into a grin. "The wisdom of Kendra," he said. "Words to live by. So, hey—are you coming down here again for Christmas this year? Easier if you tell me in advance instead of just showing up."

"Not this time. I'm going to New Hampshire. Embarrassing or no, Cade can't escape it this year."

"*That* sounds like a threat."

I laughed, but there was an edge to it. "You know what,

Dave—I need to get through to him that even if his family is a little crazy, at least he's got one. When I was a kid, I envied the kids who had aunts and uncles and big noisy households. And these people live in a big old farmhouse in the country with three generations in it. It sounds *great* to me. I think he just doesn't appreciate it."

"Or maybe they really are nuts. Maybe he's the only sane one of the bunch."

"I doubt that. This is Cade we're talking about. To him, everything's got to be on a grand scale. I hate to say it, but he's a drama queen."

"Well, you'll find out."

I smiled. "Yes. I will. Finally."

He offered a short laugh. "Love ya, kiddo. You know it. And if they all turn out to be a pack of lunatics, I'll still be here with the dog."

Chapter 2

CADE

Street hockey was the first thing to go. Up until Jill came along I'd spent every Sunday afternoon on my Rollerblades on the closed-off section of Pennsylvania Avenue that fronted the White House. The other guys who showed up for the pickup games were mostly young Capitol Hill staffers, people I'd worked with in previous political campaigns or knew from my internship the summer before. There was a rare glory to battling it out with hockey sticks in the shadow of the White House, skates clunking and whirring, our shouts and cheers carrying into the air that rose to the surreal blue D.C. sky. My body felt strong then, my spirit light. As a kid I'd spent every winter ice-skating on the frozen quarry lake, so I was a pro on skates, and aggressive on the court besides. Girls watched from the sidelines, rooting from the spectator space along the tall iron fence. When I scored a goal, they cheered, and I loved it. Arrogant as it might be, I was a junkie for adulation.

And then, for Jill. Jill who had no interest in power, who did not find the city exciting. Jill who had crash-landed in my life during a season when the crush of school, the constant lack of money and the pressure of that season's campaign were all conspiring to make me snap. I needed fewer obligations, not more. The consolation for being a campaign vol-

unteer, working like a cult member with the stakes so high
they made wealthy men break out in a cold sweat, was the sex.
Late nights stapling signs together in a small office get really
monotonous. Trudging around neighborhoods knocking on
doors, working the phone banks. You want to blow off some
steam. These opportunities crop up for very hot, very random sex in interesting locations. I looked forward to it every
year. And yet there I was, giving all that up, even giving up
street hockey to spend more time with Jill, because I ached
to be with her *all* the time. It was dumb love, and I knew it,
and I didn't give a shit even remotely.

In any campaign, if you're aspiring to be a legislator yourself one day, you do it in part for the connections. In life you
can never, ever underestimate the power of networking. Same
goes for making enemies—make a good-faith effort not to
piss people off any more than absolutely necessary. This was
a lesson I sure didn't learn at home. My father was the Coos
County Regional Grand Champion in pissing people off. He
was a farmer—one who did sorely little to network with the
locals, the way farmers ought to—but mainly he just picked
fights with the people who rented storage units from him at
the U-Store-It owned by my family, and gradually he sold off
his other commercial real estate holdings because his business
relationships got too contentious. He and his brother, Randy
ran a shooting club. When Dad's friends there started acting
like a bunch of drunk jackasses Randy objected, and instead
of working it out, Dad just told him to go suck it. From a
political-science perspective this is not the kind of thing we
call "effective collaboration." But then a few years ago Dad
had a stroke—brought on by smoking, yelling at everybody, or
maybe the locals putting a hex on him—and he's been pretty
docile ever since. He'd mellowed somewhat even before that,
mainly because my sister married a similar asshole and so my

dad handed over the crown to him. Dad kind of took the role of Queen Mother Asshole, so after that he just showed up at special events to wave and be an asshole for old times' sake.

I learned a lot from that example. If you want to break bad with people and determine your manliness by how many people avoid you, then you get to live in a pile of disintegrating lumber a stone's throw from the Canadian border, eating the saliva of everyone who prepares your sandwiches locally. The life I wanted was not that one.

What drew me to Mark Bylina's campaign was not strictly the connections or the networking. It was the fact of him being an environmentalist Republican. In my opinion that's where the future of the country is headed. This country has seen enough of the nice-guy Democratic bleeding hearts who make as good a commander-in-chief as my mother would, and enough yahoo Republicans making it look as if Americans can have brains or values but not both at the same time. What we need is a true statesman in the tradition of Teddy Roosevelt himself. Somebody who can set a hard line economically but not make it sound as though he plans to burn polar bears for fuel. Bylina is a fiscal conservative but a social moderate, supported initiatives to reduce industrial waste and the carbon load on the atmosphere. He had a great message, and I believed in it. And in him.

The master plan had it that I would graduate with a master's degree in economics the following spring. It was a five-year program, and it was an honor to have gotten into it in the first place. I graduated high school summa cum laude. Even for a hick school, that was still an achievement. The magna cum laude grad was a girl named Piper Larsen, who could solve formulas in AP chemistry as fast as most people could calculate a tip. I dated her for a while.

In any event, the goal was that the work I did on Bylina's

campaign would be enough to propel me into a job in his administration, if he won. I wanted to assist with creating policy, develop some connections, move into the private sector for a while and then run for Congress in about ten years—once I had some money and was old enough to be credible. In the meantime, in between working my crappy bursar's-office job and hanging out with Jill, I was spending every spare minute at Bylina's office, helping out with fundraising.

The main challenge to my policy of making as few enemies as possible was Drew Fielder, this pasty-looking peckerhead who lived on my floor in the dorms and who volunteered with me on Bylina's campaign. The guy had a gut, and acne on his neck. Twenty-two years old and already he had a gut, and yet his favorite thing was to give everybody else, and me in particular, shit about how we looked. This coming from a guy who liked to dress up for *The Rocky Horror Picture Show* with a whole group of people, including my buddy Stan who was otherwise normal, and prance around the Student Union in drag. He wasn't a good-looking guy and he sure as hell was even uglier as a woman.

"It's The Most Handsome Bastard in the World," he always announced when I entered the room. This was a joke Stan had started. Fielder knew it because back when we were roommates, Stan liked to shout it down the hall when he saw me walking back from the bathroom in a towel. But it was funny when Stan said it. Fielder just shouted it at random, and it was annoying as all hell. He was also fond of constantly asking if I'd just gotten back from vacation, which was his way of mocking me for tanning. Try to suggest to him that a little vitamin D might clear up some of that acne, though, and he'd pout for hours. But around Bylina he brought out his pro game, using the energy he had saved by acting like a dick to everybody else. I'd worked on political campaigns since my senior year of high school, and never had I seen an ass-kissing sycophant on the level of Fielder. The ridiculous part was that he wasn't even a Republican. He was registered as a Democrat. It was killing me, wondering if the staffers closest to Bylina already knew and just didn't care at that point, or if they had no idea. Nobody wants to be the snitch, but God, did I ever hate that guy.

Normally I was glad to be in the office—model volunteer, always—but on the day Elias came home I was counting down the hours from the minute I got there. Fielder was in, too, but everybody knew my brother was coming back from the war, and for once he kept his mouth shut so as not to sound like a jackass. At three o'clock sharp I left to pick up Jill and rush over to the airport, then as soon as we got Elias settled in I took Jill back to her dorm and he and I went out to get cheesesteaks. That was his singular focus: it was as if he'd spent three years in the Middle East mainly missing that specific food product. Other than the cheesesteak talk, he was pretty quiet. Unnaturally quiet. Elias was one who, in his ordinary life, would talk until your ears fell off. You had to get him started first, but if you said to him, say, "Elias, tell us again about that time in high school when you tripped and fell on your face on the track while the cheerleaders were practicing," he'd stretch out the story to twenty or thirty minutes even if he knew you'd already heard it a dozen times. But today he couldn't be provoked by that kind of stuff. He just wanted the cheesesteak.

So I filled the silence by talking about myself instead. After dinner I told him there was a place I wanted to show him. I drove west on the parkway until the hospital appeared above the trees. Took that exit, then the one onto a road that seemed to go nowhere, then an access road. With every turn we climbed higher up the hill. At the top was this gigantic blue

water tower shaped like an upside-down teardrop. The sun
was setting and the clouds were blazing pink, like radioac-
tive cotton candy or a scene from *Fantasia*. Under the tower
was a parking lot made out of rough construction sand, no
painted lines. Nobody ever parked there except maintenance
workers, but damn, was there ever a view. I got out, and Elias
slammed his door at the same time I did.

We walked to the crest of the hill, that blue bulb looming
above our heads. Electrical cables looped up and then down
the hill, past some sort of concrete-block structure surrounded
by razor wire, an electrical substation probably. But past that,
way down in the distance where the land was low, there was
D.C. Staggered roofs, a thousand lights—*ten* thousand—glowing like fireflies, double headlights cutting through the dusk.
The memorials, white marble all lit up, made a compass rose:
the Lincoln Memorial a cube, the one for Jefferson curved
like a lens and farthest away, the needle of the Washington
Monument pointing at the sky.

"God*damn*," said Elias. "Terrorists' wet dream, this little
crow's nest here. Can't believe they don't have it secured."

"Nothing you can do from here."

"You can look." Elias took a few steps closer, then stopped
and crossed his arms. A siren blazed down the parkway; the
sound, from where we stood, was lonesome.

"That's my city," I told him. "Someday, man, that's gonna
be my fuckin' chessboard. Not a room I can't get into or a
rope I can't get past."

"You planning on getting elected king?"

I laughed. "No, I'm gonna be like Ted Kennedy. Not right
away. Not even real soon. But eventually, over time." I pointed
toward the Jefferson Memorial. "That's where I proposed to
Jill."

Elias nodded. He slid a box of cigarettes from his pocket

and clenched one at the side of his mouth, then asked, "You want one?"

I hesitated. Sophomore year I'd worked late nights on a contentious campaign for state delegate. That season, I'd picked up the habit from the other staffers. I told myself I'd quit as soon as the election was over, and I did. But goddamn—was it ever a murderous struggle. I didn't have the money to support the addiction—that was the bottom line. Otherwise I would have kept it up forever. It gives you something mindless to do when you're sitting around waiting for things to happen, and there's a lot of that in politics. It helps you focus and relax at the same time. In no time flat I had gone from being a nonsmoker to the guy who rolled out of bed and lit up before he peed. I'd stayed away from the stuff ever since I quit, because it was so hard the first time I figured I couldn't quit twice. But this was Elias. That's the other thing smoking does—it helps people bond.

"Yeah, sure," I said.

He handed me a Marlboro and his lighter. As soon as I lit up, the pleasure of it was visceral. Tasting the smoke in my mouth was like sex after months of jacking off. Sex with the wrong person. Right away I knew this had been a bad idea.

Elias exhaled through his nose like an angry bull. "Mind if we sit down?"

We sat on the bristly grass on the curve that overlooked the city. For a few minutes neither of us said a word. I asked, "So how was Afghanistan?"

"You don't want to know."

"'Course I do. Not like you ever wrote."

He shrugged. "It sucks. It's hot. Sand shits up everything you brought with you inside of a month. And the *people*. It's still the Stone Age over there. Trying to fix anything's like pissing in the wind."

"So what do you think about how the president's allocating troops? Do you think he should have gone with Congress's recommendation instead?"

Elias gave a slow shake of his head. "Man, politics is your bag, not mine. I don't give two shits."

"How can you not care? It was your *job*."

He shook his head again. I rested my arms against my knees and looked toward the city. From the roof of a building near the Washington Monument, a flag flapped like crazy in the wind. The dark and the distance obscured the details, the stripes and the stars, the color. It had to be American from the soil it was on, but in the dark you'd never know.

I tried to change the subject to get him talking again. "What did you think of Jill?"

"She's cute." He paused and looked out over the city. "I'd do her."

I grinned. "Yeah, she's cool."

"How long have you been with her?"

"About a year. She was friends with somebody Stan was dating, so they introduced us."

"White chick?"

I snickered. "Of course. As soon as I started seeing her I deleted all my booty-call numbers from my phone, changed around my work hours to spend more time with her, you name it. It was crazy. I was eat-sleep-and-breathing her."

"You felt the same way about Piper."

I crushed out the smoke against the earth. "Not even close. Anyway, Piper's long gone. And I was in high school then. That doesn't count."

Elias gave a scornful laugh, exhaling hard, clouding the air between us. "Man, don't ever say it didn't count. Don't fucking insinuate it wasn't worth your while. I'm not sure which one of us would get a bullet in the head over that one."

"All right, all right. Sorry."

The silence pulled tight. Elias said, "I'm just messing with you."

"I know," I said. But it sounded unconvincing. "Hey, want to get a beer?"

Elias laughed again. "Man, I don't want to get *a* beer. I want to get *hammered*."

"All right, then." I held out my fist, and Elias bumped it. "This one's on me."

The next morning I drove Elias to the bus depot. I felt hungover as all hell. Elias, though, had put back twice as many and still looked okay. He had changed back into a tight brown T-shirt and fatigue pants that tucked into his boots. With him slouched in the seat, one foot resting on the opposite knee, it was more obvious than ever: dude was *ripped*. In my mind my brother was still the fat kid, the one everyone teased about his jelly-belly gut and man boobs, but now I felt out of shape next to him. He must have done nothing in the desert except lift weights.

When we pulled into the drop-off lane, Elias didn't get out right away. He just tapped a finger against the window frame and stared at the low concrete building.

"Tell Mom and Dad I said hi," I said to him. When he didn't respond, I added, "And take it easy, all right?"

He grunted. After another few beats of silence, he said, "Bus isn't here yet."

"It doesn't leave for twenty minutes. People say they usually run pretty tight. I'm sure it'll get here in time. If it doesn't, give me a buzz and I'll come get you."

He took his cigarettes out of his pocket and lit one. Then he set the lighter on top of his pack and passed them over to me. I held up a hand to decline, but my willpower misfired. I shook one out of the box and lit up.

"Back to reality," said Elias.

"You don't sound too pleased."

He exhaled lackadaisically. "I don't even know what reality looks like anymore."

I turned just slightly in the driver's seat, twisting around so I could see him better. Elias's voice seemed to have gotten much deeper, maybe as a side effect of smoking like a chimney. His soft-edged New Hampshire accent was gone, replaced with sharp r's and a flat intonation. If I didn't look directly at him, it was hard to reconcile the voice with my brother.

"You could always reenlist," I said.

Elias snorted a laugh. "No way. My body's too jacked up for it. I probably couldn't even pass the physical."

"Are you kidding? I've never seen you in better shape."

He shook his head, scornful. "My leg never really healed right. I get migraines. My shoulder's fucked up. You name it. I'm done playing in the Sandbox."

"So what are you gonna do instead?"

Silence fell again. He held his cigarette out the window and gave the filter a few soft flicks with his thumb. He paused, dragged and finally said, "Man, don't ask me that question."

"Sorry. I'm just making small talk."

"Yeah, I don't know how to make small talk. It's not what we do in my line of work."

"*Sorry.* Jeez."

Elias exhaled with a frustrated sigh. The vibe between us felt tense. I smoked nervously, glad to have something to do in the dead space. In the distance a silver bus appeared, driving slowly toward us down a long, curving road.

"Good luck with your girl," said Elias. "I envy you that."

I grinned. The tension vanished like a wave pulling back from the sand. "Thanks."

He leaned into the backseat and wrestled his duffel bag over the console. Probably I would have hugged him to say goodbye, but the bulky bag wedged into the space between the seats. He reached across and bumped my fist.

"Fuck her brains out, man," he said. "It's what I'd do if I were you."

Chapter 3

JILL

My mother believed in signs. Not in a superstitious way, really, but from the belief that sometimes an event catches your attention and brings to the surface of your mind, all of a sudden, a truth about yourself that you ought to pay attention to. When I was twelve she told me about the moment she knew she needed to get sober. She was driving north of Fresno, California, with me in the back of the car, and I asked her about the trees growing in the orchards alongside the road. I was four years old, she told me—she knew the date exactly—and I wanted to know what sort of fruit they were growing that was round and fuzzy and green. So she pulled the car over onto the shoulder, and we got out to take a look, because she wasn't sure. We were in town to visit her parents for what would prove to be the last time. It was a lovely day, but she was feeling sad and angry, because her parents' health was poor and they were mean. *A couple of old, sick drunks,* she said. *The most pathetic type of creature in the world.* All she could think about doing was getting back to our hotel and opening up a bottle of wine, to make the day go away.

We got out of the car and pulled one of those fuzzy things off a tree. She thought perhaps it was a kiwi, so she split it open for me, and inside there was an almond. *I was just so amazed,* she told me. *And so were you. Thirty-two years old and I had no idea almonds grew that way.* We both laughed, and during that moment she didn't think about anything except the wonder of almonds.

Then she said we needed to get back in the car before we got caught by the farmer, and when she turned around she could see that we were on a hill that looked down over the entire city of Fresno. And this was what moved her—even though the sky was beautifully blue and fluffed with white clouds where we stood, the city was covered by a deep gray cloud that was pouring down torrents of rain. From that distance she could see it easily: the storm that appeared to have singled out the city, like a biblical punishment. *I'd never seen anything quite like it,* she said, *and that's when I knew. That's how my parents were and that's how I would become, walking around a beautiful world with a storm pouring over just us. I had to change. It didn't happen right away. It took me a while. But that was the moment I knew.*

Long after she was gone, I tried to remember every part of that story, to think hard on it so I could understand every aspect of her revelation. It had changed my life and hers, after all. When I stood there in the almond orchard I hadn't any idea of what was going on in her mind just then, but in the end it had made me who I am. I wasn't sure if I believed in signs the way she did, but I believed in the truth the sign had taught her: that it was never too late to start over, no matter where you came from, no matter who you had been or how daunting the path appeared. Her own mother had taught her what kind of a life she didn't want, but mine taught me what kind of life I did.

Thanksgiving passed quietly—Cade and I camped out for the long weekend at Stan's, house-sitting while Stan made the rounds of his grandparents' homes—and suddenly it was December, with Christmas carols playing in the campus bookstore and greenery strung in lopsided loops around the dining hall. This was the time of year when depression started stalking me, and I had to fight it back the way you might hold up a stick against a rabid dog. It was the same thing every year: I'd play the tough girl through October, the month in which my mom had died, and just when I was congratulating myself at having muscled through another anniversary, the holidays would be upon us. Last year, when Cade and I were still newly an item, I had packed my car and driven out to Southridge once he left to visit his family. It hadn't been difficult to cover my disappointment at not being invited up to New Hampshire, because our relationship was still so new that it seemed excusable. This year, though, his silence on the subject was causing my case of the holiday blues to arrive at double speed. When I had told Dave I'd be going home with Cade for sure this year, I had thought there was no chance he wouldn't ask me. But as December meandered on, I grew less and less sure.

I chalked it up to distraction, at least at first. Ever since Mark Bylina had won the election, Cade had grown obsessed with whether he would be offered a job on his staff. For months he had attended to the menial tasks of electioneering with slavish diligence, all in the hope that his good work would be rewarded with a permanent job once the election was over. Now his excitement was tempered by his suspicion that Drew Fielder, his least favorite fellow volunteer, was being groomed for the assistantship Cade had hoped for.

"I've put in twice as many hours as that asshole," he said, late on a Sunday afternoon as we lay in bed. "That guy knows how to show up and *look like* he's been working, then vanish as soon as the paid staff's out of sight. And then I leave early one day this week so I can come see you, and the manager's calling, 'Leaving early, Cade?'"

"That sucks. I'm sorry."

"It's not on you. My sister's already pissed that I didn't come home for Thanksgiving, as if I could leave when Bylina had community service stuff going on all that week. I told her I'll be back for Christmas, but she doesn't get it. None of them do. The whole idea of climbing the ladder is just beyond them."

I draped my arms loosely across my eyes and took a cleansing breath before I replied. It was time to address this. "At least you've got a place to go," I pointed out.

He frowned at the ceiling. "No, all I've got is guilt and pressure to go someplace I don't want to. If you were in my shoes, you'd hate it, too."

"Not living on a farm. That part would be amazing."

He snorted a laugh. "Amazing. Yeah. Picture this, okay? It's minus five degrees outside. You're sleeping in a hundred-year-old house with drafts out the yin-yang. The roof leaks, and two smokers spent all day putting the smoke from four packs of Marlboros into the air. You're getting up at four-thirty to milk cows in the bitchin' cold because hey, you're home, they expect you to pitch in like you always did before."

"I don't mind milking cows. Or the cold."

"You'd hate it. Hate it like death."

"I wouldn't. It's no different from what I've done every summer since I was thirteen."

"You don't know cold until you've lived in New England. And spending the holidays with my family would be hell. Believe me, Jill. Especially my brother-in-law. He's King Jackass of the Universe." He got out of bed, still wearing nothing but his watch and his boxers, and took a Mountain Dew out of the minifridge.

"I've got to meet them sometime," I said. "And it's depressing to be alone over Christmas. It really is, Cade."

"You can go visit Dave, right? That's what you did last year."

"I could, but I was hoping to spend it with you. It seems kind of lame to go hang out with my old camp counselor while my fiancé is off with his family." I sat up and pulled my T-shirt over my head. "It's not normal."

Cade laughed again. "Neither is my family."

"Nobody's is. Everybody thinks that."

Still holding the soda can, he made a gesture with his arm that said, *I'll give you that one.* But along with it he added, "Let me put it differently, then. I don't want you to come."

I glared at him. "Wow."

"Don't start yelling at me. I'm doing both of us a favor. You and I don't need to be trapped in a farmhouse on the Maine border with a bunch of crazy people. You think it's going to be some cozy Christmas reunion, but really it's going to be like a Stephen King movie. I know it, and you don't, and so it's my job to spare you."

"How are we supposed to get married if I don't ever meet your family?"

"That's not the question. The question is why you'd still want to marry me once you *do* meet them."

"Oh, Cade."

I rolled over and crumpled the pillow beneath my chin. Against the cheap little side table his BlackBerry vibrated— once, twice, three times. It never stopped for long. I swallowed hard and tried to force myself to believe he meant well. He wasn't hiding anything, except whatever it was that he found embarrassing about them. It was at times like this that I wished my mother were still around. I could ask her whether it was right to trust that he would come around to it on his own time, or if he was treating me poorly and I needed to call him on it. But in her absence it all hovered in my mind as a formless question. When she died, the one small consolation had been that at least I was eighteen, an adult, not the child I had been just eight months before. But the longer she was gone, the more I knew I needed her now as much as ever, and that there was nothing merciful in losing my mother just as I was trying to figure out how to be an adult woman myself. I'd thought it would get easier over time, but three years later, I was still waiting.

As soon as he finished his last final exam, just days before Christmas, Cade left for New Hampshire. He insisted on going alone to face his parents and siblings and King Jackass of the Universe himself. Thanks to my arrangement with the university—necessary, given that I didn't have a home—I had permission to stay in my dorm over winter break, but I moved into Cade's room for the week anyway. Sleeping in his bed made me feel less alone, and the quad in which he lived was noisier, making me feel less like a straggler left behind on Christmas.

Technically I wasn't supposed to be there. The resident director of Cade's dorm, Hagerstown Hall, tolerated my presence because she knew about me and figured that since I could sleep in only one room at night, it didn't matter whether it was my dorm or Cade's. The only other person staying on the guys' side of the floor was Drew Fielder. Cade always treated the guy with barely repressed hostility, but around him I tried to be friendly—after all, Stan seemed to like the guy well enough, or at least tolerated him as part of the regular *Rocky Horror* group. Cade's attitude toward him struck me as a little childish, and it seemed to me that a guy with social skills as strong as Cade's would know that it doesn't pay to make enemies.

On Christmas Eve, Hagerstown 6 was deserted. I sat on Cade's bed with my laptop balanced on my knees and *Lockup: Raleigh* on low in the background, a cup of powdery hot cocoa leaving a wet ring on the table beside me. I was musing on whether to email Dave and ask him if I could drive down to see him the next day; the thought of his judgment of Cade inhibited me, but the loneliness made it tempting even so. Down the hall the elevator door thunked open, followed by the *squee squee squee* of loafers on tile. A shadow fell over me, and I looked up. It was Drew, of course, leaning one shoulder against the doorway in his shirtsleeves and pinstripes, top button undone. He looked at me with his weird uncertain smile, a petulant curl of his upper lip. His hair, misted by the rain, curled toward the crown of his head like a cool-cat lounge singer's.

"Did your boyfriend abandon you?"

I shook my head. "He's up in New Hampshire with his family."

"Sounds like abandonment to me."

"I'm fine."

He jiggled his knee through the awkward pause. Then he asked, "You want to order some Chinese or something?"

I blurted a laugh. "Chinese? On Christmas Eve?"

"Sure. My family does it every year. Nothing else is open, after all."

"Why don't you guys just have ham and sweet potatoes and whatever else everybody eats on Christmas Eve?"

"We're Jewish."

"Oh." I tapped a finger against the side of my laptop, considering. It wouldn't be difficult to make an excuse to get rid of Drew, but if I spent some time with him, maybe I could get some insight that would help Cade learn to deal with him. And the fact was, I was bored and lonely. And I *did* feel abandoned, after all.

"Sure, yeah," I said. "Do you have a menu?"

We set up the cartons on the table in the lounge. Drew set the TV to a *Seinfeld* rerun. "Jewish Christmas," he said. "A little bit fun and a little bit depressing."

"Tell me about it."

"Don't you have family or anything?"

"Not really." I watched him root around in the carton and produce a piece of shrimp. "I thought shellfish weren't kosher," I added.

"I don't keep kosher."

I offered him a slow grin. "You're a Jewish Republican who doesn't keep kosher. That's original."

"I'm not a Republican. God, no."

"But you work for Bylina."

"Yeah. I'm an opportunist."

Seinfeld broke to commercial. A jangling advertising tune came on, several notches louder than the regular TV volume. Drew cracked open his soda, watching me as he drank from it. Whenever I'd been around him in the past, Stan's friendliness toward him had led me to see Drew as harmless, if slightly arrogant, with a mild case of social awkwardness. But here, alone with him, the vibe he gave off had more of an edge to it. The arrogance was still there, but it felt creepier.

"Well," I said when the volume died down, "why don't you go to work for somebody who shares your views? Somebody who's working on issues you believe in? That's the point of being in politics, isn't it? To make a positive change in the world."

He eased back in his chair and set down his soda can. "Are you asking me to pull out so Cade can get the job?"

"No, I'm just asking why you'd even want it when you could get the same job working for somebody whose convictions are in line with yours."

"I might pull out. It's possible."

I nodded. "If you don't believe in it, you ought to. Don't you think?"

"I don't know," he said. He spun the can in circles with his fingers. "I'm not sure I have the right motivation."

For a few moments I puzzled over the strange response, my attention still cocked toward *Seinfeld*. Then all at once it clicked. I looked him squarely in the eye. *"Drew,"* I said with disgust.

He shrugged.

"I'm not even going to dignify that with a reply." I snatched the delivery bag from the table and stuffed it into a garbage can. As I bustled around angrily he watched with a bemused detachment that unnerved me.

"You know why I admire Cade?" he asked.

My shoulders twitched. "Because unlike you, he has principles?"

"No. That's not why." His voice disdained me. "Because he's so fucking ambitious."

"Thanks," I said icily. I saw now exactly why Cade detested the guy so much, and felt shamed by my naïveté. "I'll pass that on to him when I tell him about this whole conversation."

"If you want. He'll be sorry you didn't take me up on it. He wouldn't admit it, of course. But he'll wish you'd just done it and kept your mouth shut about it."

"You have no idea what you're talking about. Cade's not like that at all."

"As if you'd know," he said, "when it's all been sunshine

and rainbows and snuggle sex for the two of you. I've been on the campaign trail with him, and I know a little different. Let me tell you, Jill. You don't know a guy until you've seen him under pressure. Cade's like everybody else. He only cares about one thing." He held up a single finger.

"That's the stupidest cliché ever." ·

"Not sex," said Drew. "Recognition."

I hurried back to Cade's room, dressed quickly and headed back across campus to my own dorm. The sidewalks were deserted. I thought of Cade sitting around his living room with his parents, his brother and sister, and seethed at both him and Drew. Here I was alone on Christmas Eve, hurrying away from the leering creep to whom I had afforded benefit of the doubt, all because Cade wanted to avoid the embarrassment of me meeting his brother-in-law. My messenger bag beat against the side of my coat, and I breathed into my hands to warm them. I knew what would sneak in just behind this anger: self-pity. That was how I would spend Christmas, and the next year I would dread the holidays all the more, remembering how miserable this one had been.

It doesn't have to be that way, I thought. I jogged up the steps to my building, tossed a few things into my overnight bag, tugged on the hoodie Dave had just mailed back to me and headed out to my car. I thought about calling him, but it was late already and I didn't want him to feel he needed to wait up for me. I had a full tank of gas and a key to my old cabin, and I would find him in the morning. He wouldn't mind. Dave never did.

In the few photos I have of my mother and me together, it's easy to see we don't resemble each other at all. She was fairly tall, with honey-blond hair that kinked into unmanageable curls when the weather grew the least bit humid. Despite her coloring, she had an Italian face—a regal nose and long eyes, a smile that appeared to store a secret. Sometimes I wondered if she had hoped for a miniature version of herself, rather than the baby daughter she received—one destined to be fine haired and button nosed, with eyes so round as to seem perpetually surprised. Even as a teenager she had looked like a *woman,* while long into college I still had to pull out my driver's license to be allowed into R-rated movies.

She never voiced the truth we both knew: that I looked like my father. It had to be true, because I resembled her family not at all, and yet she would never tell me who he was. Around the age of eight I entered a stage of nagging her with questions: what was his name, his job, where did he live, did he know about me. She brushed them off or changed the subject, until finally, when I was twelve and began asking again, she gave me her first sort-of answer.

"If you want to know the truth, Jill," she said, using that wry monotone that never meant anything good, "I wasn't in a very good place when I found out I was going to have you. And once I knew you'd be joining me, I wasn't about to go back to that place to see if anybody wanted to tag along."

I understood her meaning—that she had abandoned him, not the other way around. I stopped asking her after that; I knew enough about addicts by then to grasp that whoever he was, wherever he was, he was sure to disappoint me. And it had to be bad for him, because my mother was not one to assume someone was beyond hope. Padding around in her panty hose, her curly hair up in a messy bun from a long day at the office, she would pull the extra-long phone cord into the one bedroom and shut the door when one of the women she sponsored in AA called. If the call went on for a long time I would turn out the lights, make up the futon and try to sleep. Always I would overhear her calming and definite

voice, and even though I knew she was handling a crisis—
someone's sobriety on the brink of failure—the sound of it
would lull me easily to sleep. She was a sure guide, knowing
the route through every situation. Eventually she would slip
back out, hang up the phone in its cradle and lie down softly
on the other side of the futon, because this bed was technically
hers. Some nights I would move to my bedroom, but usually
I feigned a deep sleep so I could nestle near her warmth all
night, like a chick beneath her mother's wing.

Sometimes now, when her absence became less bearable,
I would imagine those moments with her until the line between reality and memory seemed almost to disappear. In a
warm bed, with my eyes closed, it was so easy to imagine.
But even then there was a bittersweet edge to it, because for
all my belief that she and I were inextricably connected to one
another, at the critical moment it proved not to be true at all.

On that day, the day it happened, I was rushing to class—
I had lingered too long over my lunch in the Student Union,
browsing through my notes for the midterm that was now
only ten minutes away. As I hurried up the stairs, I pressed
through a crowd gathered around the two televisions suspended from the ceiling in the entryway. They were riveted
on some news broadcast. For only a second I glanced up at
it—a stretch of red desert, the wreckage of two small planes,
an excited voice-over—before squeezing between two students and pushing out the door. It would be hours before I
checked my voice mail and found the message from the police
in Las Vegas, requesting that I call immediately.

I had spoken to my mother only the day before. I knew she
was in Las Vegas, finally taking a well-earned vacation now
that her only child was away at school—a girls' weekend with
a couple of friends from AA. When I'd called her she sounded
breezy and excited, telling me about the shows and the buffets,

the tour of the Grand Canyon they planned to take the following day and how she should have done this years ago. I'd
caught the glow of her euphoria and mirrored it back to her,
enthusiastic on her behalf and envious, in a good-natured way,
of the fun. She told me that the next time, she'd take me with
her, and wished me luck on my midterm before dashing off to
what sounded suspiciously, from her vague description, like a
Chippendales show. If she had mentioned the Grand Canyon
tour would be by small plane, I hadn't paid attention. And
so when I saw the flash of the television screen, heard them
say Las Vegas, I had only the briefest moment of thinking *my
mother is there* before the thought followed, *but that's not her.*

Before it all happened I would have been certain that, in
such an event, I would *know*. A sudden feeling would arrest
me, a sense of disturbance or perhaps even a premonition,
and I would scramble to call her to discover what was wrong.
Never would I have believed that I would sense nothing, that
I would look up at the very scene of my mother's death and
hurry along to my next class, utterly ignorant. The guilt that
came along with it stalked me, uninterrupted, for a year. I'd
pushed on through the semester believing that it was what
my mother would want me to do, but even then I nursed
the suspicion that I had a lot of nerve to assume I knew what
my mother would think or want. The image of those two
wrecked planes, having clipped each other and fallen simul-
taneously to the earth, lingered in my mind like the flame of
a vigil candle. Even now it remained there, flickering in the
background somewhere, always. It was as if I believed that by
holding it in my mind, I could make amends for my indifference to it at first sight.

That year, Dave had insisted I come to Southridge for the
holidays rather than spend them alone. It had turned into a
tradition-by-accident, as every year circumstances dropped me

there, and this year was no different. When my car emerged
from the trees that pressed closely against the road I saw a single light on in the main lodge, in spite of the fact that it was
two in the morning on Christmas Day. I thought I would slip
past, drive up the side road to my cabin. But then the storm
door swung open and Dave stepped onto the porch, looking
wary at first, then smiling.

On Christmas Day, Dave and I strapped on snowshoes and
hiked out into the forest. The gray clouds sent down an occasional riot of flurries, and between that dark sky and the
blanketed ground the world seemed to be holding me like a
firefly between two hands. In silence I followed Dave down
the trail we both knew. His green jacket and dark hair collected a dusting of flakes that melted slowly, and his hiking
pole made a steady *chunk* against the buried ice as we moved
ever deeper into the woods.

He stopped in a clearing I knew well. Hidden under a drift
was a campfire ring; the fallen tree was a place to sit, as were
the two slabs of stone nearby. In the summer months the staff
came out here to spend time together, away from the fire pit
closer to the lodge that was used nightly by our guests. Nearby
was a waterfall that created a pool to wade in on the hottest
days, but in the winter it ran dry, and the silence of its absence
confused my ears like a distant hum. Through a break in the
trees I could see the mountains—the ski trails twisting down
the north face, the march of the lifts uphill, the little buildings dotting the peak. But this place felt a world apart from
the comfortable resort life. The longer I stayed in college, the
more I suspected that I belonged out here instead—not just
as a summer job until I earned a degree that could secure me
something better, but for good. When I had agreed to marry
Cade, even as I said yes to him, this was the thought at the

back of my mind—*but how will I live in the place I love?* I told myself it was a petty concern, but the truth is there's no way to talk yourself out of the concept of *home*. I loved the quiet here, the distant sight of sailboats drifting on the lake in the summertime, the way the mountains framed the sky. The little log cabins were easy on my eyes, and the framework of life felt so simple and unencumbered by a tiring menu of choices. I'd believed, in the romantic, girlish way, that it was worth giving up anything for the sake of real love. But even now I sometimes wondered, *which* real love?

Dave pulled off his gloves and flexed his fingers, then blew into his hands. He nudged me with his elbow and lifted his chin to indicate the woods beyond. Two does stared back at us, their ears alert and tails high. The smaller one eased and nudged a patch of brush for a moment, then followed the other as she bolted into the forest.

"Jill, I'm going to be honest with you," said Dave.

The sound of my real name spoken by him jarred me to attention.

"I think you ought to think hard about Cade," he continued. "I know—you're giving him a pass on this one because you understand about somebody being embarrassed by their family. I remember how your mom felt about her folks, so I know where that comes from. But if Cade felt like he had to choose between them and you, I think he made a bad decision."

"That's not it. He doesn't want me to have to deal with all their drama, is all. He means well."

He turned his head toward me and squinted, as if trying and failing to see things the way I did. "He's been with you a year now. You told him you wanted to go, and he knew you didn't have anyplace else to go, either." Dave shook his head. "In my opinion he failed a loyalty check, and that means something. You deserve to be with somebody who has more empathy for you. Somebody who's always on your side."

I shook my own head slowly, but Dave wasn't saying anything that hadn't already crossed my mind. I didn't want to hear him speaking it aloud, and so I said nothing. Because for over a week now I had been waiting for my body to give a sign that everything was ordinary—that our long Thanksgiving weekend at Stan's had left us with a romantic memory and not an immediate problem. I'd postponed taking a pregnancy test because I feared the answer, and dreaded the possibility that Cade would receive the news and leave me behind on Christmas anyway. That would be more than I could bear. My mother had taught the women she sponsored about taking a searching and fearless moral inventory of themselves to figure out who they really were; it was the Fourth Step officially, and a good idea for anybody, she often said. *Know what you are capable of. Know what stands in the way of your moving forward.* I had done that, and found myself sorely lacking. I wished I had my mother's courage, but when I looked inward all I saw was the fear of finding myself in her situation, alone.

"It's getting darker," I said. The temperature was dropping and the air felt sharp and clear, with the smell of new snow enlivening it. "We should go back."

"Don't be mad at me. I'm just trying to look out for you."

"I'm not mad," I told him, and it was true. After this week, once Cade was back, we could let the situation unfold in an organized way, unimpeded by his brother-in-law. I wasn't afraid that Cade would shirk his responsibility. I only feared that I would decide he was unworthy of it, and if that was the case, I didn't want to know.

Chapter 4

CADE

It's not as if it was the first time this had happened to me. Senior year of high school, barely more than a month after I lost my virginity, my girlfriend Piper pulled me aside during open lunch in the courtyard and told me she was pregnant. She always wore a lot of eye shadow that made her eyes look huge, and so all the fear in them came right at me. *Do something, Cade.* There was some accusation in there too: *you promised.* But what did I know? I was seventeen. Of course I'd thought it would be fine to have sex. I would've sworn to her I could beat Lance Armstrong in the Tour de France right then if I'd thought it would help me close the deal, and I would have believed it, too.

I'm not sure what my excuse was at twenty-one. Over-confidence: it's a problem. It's probably why, when Jill came to me and told me *she* was pregnant, I took it in stride. Part of me was definitely freaked, but by then I'd spent so much time knocking on doors, talking up candidates, that my gut reaction in an uncertain situation was to project total confidence. Here Jill was caught in this fight-or-flight response between hightailing it to some camp in the woods or else to the abortion clinic, and I'm all, hey, it's gonna be great! I'll teach the kid to play hockey!

It definitely wasn't like that when it happened with Piper, when for the first few days I was in denial, mulling over all the reasons it wasn't even possible, along with these spikes of cold-sweat, hyperventilating panic. I'd envision this show-down in the living room with my folks, my dad grabbing me by the collar and shoving me up against the wall like he used to do with Elias, my mom all stoic, but radiating utter disappointment. After about a week I couldn't take it anymore. I drove down to the U-Store-It to talk to my brother alone. I didn't know who else to go to.

When I got there the parking lot was empty except for Elias's green Jeep, which was a relief. If he'd been driving the van I would have suspected my brother-in-law, Dodge, would be there, too, but the Jeep was Elias's own, and he didn't want Dodge Powell to so much as breathe in the smell of its air freshener. I parked next to it and went around back to find him. The storage units were basically garages, three sets of four arranged in a U shape around the little office building. We had this one customer who kept a weight bench and a full set of weights in his. Lately Elias had taken to driving down there and letting himself into that unit with the master key so he could lift weights. It went against policy, and if he ever got caught either by Dad or Dodge or the customer, he would have been in trouble. But Elias was nineteen and kind of in a "fuck it" stage at that point. He'd graduated high school a year before and had been working with Dodge ever since, managing the U-Store-It, and since then he'd gotten a lot quieter—part Clint Eastwood, part serial killer.

Sure enough, I found him in the last unit on the right, lifting. He was lying on his back on the bench, with an impressive amount of weight on the crossbar. His shirt was hiked up and under it, his gut was jiggling with every pump of the bar. Elias's body was like one big temper tantrum. If Dodge brought home doughnuts one Sunday, Elias would eat as if his own execution was the next day, and I swear he'd go up by five pounds overnight. But now that he'd taken to secret weight lifting, in no time he was bulking up like the Incredible Hulk. Unfortunately it still had all the doughnuts on top of it, so mostly he just looked fatter.

He clunked the bar back in place and sat up once he noticed me there. It's not as if I ever dropped by just to say hello, so he knew something was up. He fanned out his shirt at the front—it had a big V of sweat down it—and asked, "You need something?"

"I got a problem, man."

Now, Elias was a good guy. He was the guy you called in the middle of the night if you snuck out to see your girlfriend and then inadvertently locked yourself out of the house, or if you needed an emergency ride back from, say, Massachusetts, or had to borrow fifty bucks. Stuff like that didn't shake him. He'd just go. And so it surprised me when he shot me this *glare*. The kind where a person's eyes look to be two different sizes and one of them is twitching underneath. He got up and started yanking weights off the bar.

"I'll bet you do," he said. "I sure as hell bet you do."

For the life of me I didn't know what was up his ass. Mentally I went over anything I might have done wrong to him lately, but nothing came to mind. Whatever it was, I figured he had to be on the wrong track, so I said, "Piper's pregnant."

"Oh, *I* know."

That was unexpected. "No, you don't. How would you know that?"

"A friend of a friend told me."

"Who?"

"None of your business." He clunked the weights back on the storage bars.

Asking more wasn't going to get me anywhere, so I gave up. "I don't know what to do. I'm completely freaked."

"Shoulda thought about that before you nailed her, shouldn't you?" The bench was between us now, and even though he was standing normally his bigger arms made the stance look threatening. I stood there feeling all sheepish, and his face shifted to this look of total disgust. "Fuck you, *Cadey*," he said, using Dodge's asshole nickname for me. "Fuck you sideways."

By then I didn't know what to say anymore. I'd sort of figured out what his reaction was about, but I didn't know where to go with that. I didn't know where to go at *all*. There were a lot of boxes lying around, and I sat down on the closest one behind me and planted my elbows against my knees, dropped my head down and started to cry.

"Jesus Christ," said Elias. No chance was I going to look up at him, but I could feel him standing there looking at me, stuck on what to do. When he was much younger, eight or nine at the most, our father used to come down *really* hard on him for crying. He'd shove Elias down into a chair and bend over him, screaming himself hoarse, one fist up all threateningly, like someone about to beat a dog with a newspaper.

Elias came around the bench and sat on the box next to me. All I could see were his shoes, beat up sneakers stretched all wide at the bottom. I was still making little gasping, sniveling noises and wiping my nose against my shoulder. It was bad. Years later the memory still makes me cringe.

"What am *I* supposed to do about that problem?" he finally said. "I can't unfuck her for you."

"Don't tell Mom and Dad."

"I won't."

"If Dad finds out—"

"He isn't going to do shit to you. I'll knock him out if he does. But you're his favorite anyway. He won't."

"I just ruined my life."

"Naw. Least it's Piper. Worst thing that happens is you're stuck with her—that doesn't count as ruined."

I didn't say anything back, and kind of awkwardly he put his arm over my shoulders. He never hugged anybody, so that was a stretch for him. He didn't have any real answers for me. There wasn't anything he could do but sit there and assure me Mom and Dad weren't going to kill me and bury me in the backyard. But he did that. And for a really, really long time I felt like shit about all that, because I knew—I *always* knew— that he loved her.

When I was home for Christmas, almost right away I noticed the hacked-up tree in the backyard. It was over by the barn. What had still been a giant oak when I'd last come home was now a four-foot-high pile of splintered wood, with these long raw shards sharp enough to kill a man sticking out in all directions like some kind of lethal haystack. I asked my mom, "What happened—that tree get hit by lightning?"

She shook her head. She was standing at the stove with the teapot, raising and lowering a couple of tea bags into it to steep them. "That's Eli's."

"That's Eli's *what?*"

"His tree for when he's mad." She closed the lid, letting the tags and strings dangle down the side of the teapot. She nodded toward the back-porch windows and said, "Your father and Dodge cut off most of the limbs a few years back anyway, you know, because it had a disease. When Elias needs to blow off some steam he goes out there and he chops at it. Doesn't bother me any. I wanted that tree gone years ago."

I looked out the back window again and saw the ax wedged in a hunk that used to be a branch, off to the side, almost buried beneath the snow. We'd tried to build a tree house in that oak years ago when we were kids. "That's a lot of steam to blow off," I said.

She shrugged. "Olmstead men," she said. Then she poured a cup and drank it black, without any sugar.

A little while later Elias came downstairs. He'd been locked up in his room all day, sleeping off a migraine. When he saw me he said, "I need your help with something."

I glanced up at a motion behind him. My mother was pushing a big cellophane-wrapped plate piled high with Christmas cookies across the kitchen island. It had an oversize red bow on top.

"Need to run over to the Larsens' real quick," he said. "Be good if you could ride with me."

The Larsens were Piper's family. "Sure," I said, and he shrugged on his coat and picked up the plate of cookies. The cellophane was bunched up so high it got in the way of his face.

"Take your car," he said. "I don't like driving anymore."

"Why not?"

"Too many distractions."

That seemed like a weird reason. In Frasier, New Hampshire, there's really nothing but woods and fields and the occasional rotting house here and there. But whatever, I didn't mind driving. It was only a couple of miles to Piper's. When the house rose up along the road, a boxy white Victorian at the end of a long drive that curved uphill, Elias said, "Pull up on the shoulder a sec, all right?"

I parked on the gravel, right behind the family's old fruit stand. The wood was gray, like driftwood, with a darker slush slopped up against the decaying boards on the bottom. You could still see the shadows of the painted watermelons, and the yellow letters, faded almost invisible but not quite, that read Fine Fresh Lemonade.

"How come you didn't bring Jill up here for Christmas?" he asked.

"Dodge."

He nodded. Looked out at Piper's house, squinting. "You're still engaged and all that?"

"Yeah. What, did you think I was going to try to move in on Piper?" He made a face but didn't answer. "That one's dead, junked and sold for parts, man. She's all yours."

"I just want to say hello."

Sure you do, I thought.

"You're not going to feel awkward about seeing her, are you?" he asked. "After that stuff that happened?"

I shook my head. "'Course not. Maybe if she'd had an abortion I would. But a miscarriage isn't anybody's fault."

"Maybe she was never even really pregnant in the first place."

I shrugged. Sometimes I'd wondered that, too. One day she had a positive pregnancy test, and then another three weeks went by and all of a sudden she told me not to worry anymore, she'd had a miscarriage. I'd gotten used to living in despair over it and then ta-da, the whole problem was gone. It was as if someone had kidnapped me at gunpoint and driven me all over town with their boot against my neck and then, without warning, dropped me off in my own front yard. Except that the whole experience made things so weird between us that we broke up over the phone and never really talked much after that. It had made everything too heavy, too fraught.

"Probably not," I said, for my brother's sake. I knew it was what he wanted to believe.

I turned the car back on and pulled up into her driveway, and we crunched through the snow and up onto the porch. Elias rang the bell with one gloved finger, trying to hold that huge plate of cookies in both arms like a squirming calf.

When Piper opened the door she saw me first, because the cellophane was blocking Elias, and smiled.

"It's the Olmstead boys," she said, noticing my brother under there and taking the plate out of his hands. "Aww, thank you. Come on in."

We stepped inside and Elias unzipped his coat. The woodstove pumped out blazing heat that shimmered the air in front of it like a mirage. I stomped the snow from my boots onto the rug. Piper crossed the room to set the cookies down on the dining table. She still had a fine little ass, but not for me.

"Elias, you must have just gotten back," she said. "How was it?"

"Not too bad," he said. I cut a sideways glance at him. He'd had his thigh torn open down to the muscle by a piece of shrapnel, seen friends die, killed people. But around Piper it came out like an underwhelming vacation.

"Slimmed down a little, didn't you?" she said, and he looked at the ground and chuckled even though getting her to notice that had been the sole reason he'd opened up his coat. I gave him a bemused sort of look, because this was as close as Elias got to pulling out his A-game. But then something in his face changed and when I looked over I saw a guy had come in from the back porch with his arms full of firewood. As he arranged it in the fireplace, Piper asked Elias about where he was working now (he wasn't) and if he thought things had gotten better for women now that the Taliban was gone. *Latch onto that one*, I thought, *c'mon, dude,* because Piper was a curious person, the type who really wanted to know about international politics and women's issues. I could see in her eyes that she was hoping for a substantial sort of answer. But Elias had shut down. He just shrugged and said, "Nothing's ever going to get better there. They all just want to kill each other. Far be it from me to stop 'em."

The guy got done kindling the fire and came over. Piper introduced us. His name was Michael. I was going to ask where he went to school, but then he wrapped his arm around Piper's waist and said to my brother, "Army vet, huh? Thanks for your service."

Maybe all siblings have this problem, but sometimes with my brother I might as well consult a Magic 8 Ball to figure out what's going on in his head and other times it's like I know everything. These tiny cues of his, they become like a code. As soon as that guy touched Piper I glanced at Elias, saw him looking at the guy's hand for a split second before he zipped up his coat. "It wasn't for you personally," he said, and Piper laughed uneasily while Michael shot Elias an offended glare.

I didn't say anything during the drive home. Nothing about him smoking in my car. We stomped back into the house, right into the kitchen where my mom was washing dishes and my sister, Candy, was fussing around with a jelly roll cake. She had a big bowl of frosting on the island and was spreading it onto the cake in the pan. Mom asked, "You give the Larsens those cookies?"

Elias grunted a yes.

Candy licked her thumb and looked at Elias with reproach. "Well, you're not giving them my Yule log cake."

"Nobody wants your Yule log cake, Candy."

"I'm just making sure. Since three-quarters of the Christmas cookies in this house just went down the street and now my boys hardly have any."

"Don't worry about it, Candy," Mom scolded, low voiced. To Elias she said, "Did she like the cookies?"

"*She,*" Candy blustered. "Is there only one Larsen now?"

"Goddamn it, Candy," said Elias. "Lay off."

She shrugged and sucked the frosting from her index finger. "Don't bark at *me,* Eli. Cade's the one I'm surprised at, getting engaged while he's off at school and then coming home to visit a girl he had a relationship with."

I set my gloves on the table and didn't dignify that with a reply. She hadn't brought it up for any other reason except to imply to Elias that he was pursuing my sloppy seconds. Elias, though, took the bait like a raccoon to a tin of cat food. He kicked out the chair he'd been unlacing his boot against so it skidded across the kitchen floor just past Candy. His voice projected in a straight line. "What part of 'lay off' don't you understand?"

"Eli," said our mother in her soft voice, soothing, imploring. She said it again, and for a second I flashed on the time he fell out of that oak tree while we were building the tree house, knocked himself unconscious. She had pulled his head onto her lap then, whispering to him while we waited for the ambulance.

"She doesn't know when to quit," he shouted, still looking at Candy. "Mind your own damn business, will you? Bake your stupid cake and shut your freakin' mouth for once."

He shoved another chair across the floor for good measure, then stormed off through the back porch, his bootlaces ticking against the floor. The back door slammed. A minute later we all heard the whack of that ax slicing into what was left of the tree. Then again, and again.

It was things like that that made me leave Jill back in Maryland for the second year in a row. And it wasn't even Christmas yet, and Dodge hadn't even showed up.

I still remembered the day Elias announced he'd enlisted in the army. It was during that whole Piper pregnancy scare. Mom looked really startled, and Dodge gave him this peeved-off look and said, "What the hell'd you go and do that for?" That was the giddiest I've ever seen Elias look. I knew what he was thinking: *I'm finally getting out from under your thumb, you redneck motherfucker.* He and I had both left home for damn good reasons. We didn't belong here in this house. It was like the year Dodge built Candy a garden edged with pressure-treated lumber—it didn't look too bad from the outside, but all season the chemicals leached in and leached in, poisoning everything that grew there. And here we all were again, boxed in by the same dirty lumber. But not for long. Not together.

Maybe half the reason I was so smooth about it when Jill broke the pregnancy news to me was that last time all my histrionics had turned out to be nothing. Maybe I felt that this time would have the same outcome, because the panic with the Jill situation was more of a slow burn. But this time it wasn't going away, and in addition to that, after a few weeks she was *so* sick. She couldn't even go to class anymore, and her stupid roommate was complaining. I called up Stan, and he said it was fine if she crashed at his place for a little while until we figured out what to do next. At first it was a good solution. Stan was out a lot and worked weird hours, so when I came by after work every day we usually had the place to ourselves. We'd cook dinner, watch TV, try to work out a better plan. She kept talking about going to live at her camp around Deep Creek Lake, and I wouldn't have anything to do with that idea. I couldn't stomach the idea of her calling in that kind of favor from her camp friend Dave—a man I'd barely even met—and asking him to carry us until we could get on our feet. Even her living with Stan galled me every single day—seeing her purple toothbrush in the holder with his, watching him walk in the door with a bag of candy for her mixed in with his groceries, and worst of all, getting a call from him late one night and hearing him say he'd taken her to the emergency room because she looked dehydrated. The *little while* that Stan and I had agreed to wore on into two months, then three, and I hated feeling as if I was turning into a third wheel in the coming of my own child.

And then exams ended, and it was nearly summer. Ever since I left home to go to school, I'd found a way to stick around College Park between semesters. There was always someone whose apartment I could crash at. But this year I looked at Jill, who was pretty damn pregnant, and at my job, which paid about the same as a shoe factory in India, and knew the old plan wasn't going to work anymore. The baby was due August 24. If I wanted there to be any chance of me going back to school in the fall, my life between now and then needed to be as cheap as possible. So I had no choice. This summer I was going back to Frasier, and Jill was coming with me.

My hero, then and now, was Teddy Roosevelt. He was all about the qualities that make a man a real man and how to be admirable and noble and all that stuff. Right there on my wall, on a postcard Jill had seen a hundred times, was his Rough Riders portrait with my favorite quote underneath it: "Aggressive fighting for the right is the noblest sport the world affords." I wish I could say the situation with Jill brought out the best in me, but in all honesty that would be a lie.

You wouldn't believe how thin the line is between gratitude and resentment. The more you owe somebody, the more you hate them for all they can afford to give you when you don't have shit. After all those months he sheltered her, Stan had given us more than I could ever repay. And I knew when we got to Frasier, Elias wouldn't think twice about how he had stood by me through a stupid mistake years ago and now, 112 college credits later, I still couldn't figure out how to operate my own dick. I should have felt really thankful about all that, but somehow it just made me want to punch somebody in the face.

Chapter 5

JILL

Seeing Stan's futon folded up and pushed against the wall finally drove the point home: Cade and I were leaving. Up until then I hadn't even realized I had developed an attachment to the thing, as if it were a large teddy bear given to me during a hospital stay. In a way, it had been. The worst of my pregnancy-related illness—hyperemesis, the medical term for puking too much—had lasted only a month before Stan got spooked one night and dragged me to the hospital. *Dead white girl in my living room would not look good for me,* he had joked on the way. They hooked me up to a bag of rehydrating solution, kept me overnight and sent me home with a prescription for antinausea drugs. It's possible I *would* have been a dead white girl if it hadn't been for him.

During those weeks and the few that followed, I spent most of my time curled up in a nest of pillows with a bag of Starbursts and my mother's copy of the Big Book from AA, reading inspirational quotes and stories from people who had turned their lives around. Stan thought I was nuts. Sometimes, propped up on a stack of pillows beside me and channel surfing as I read, he would glance over and shake his head before commenting about how wrong it looked to see a pregnant woman reading an addiction-recovery book. *You remind me of those people on that show you always watch,* he said. But it was pure comfort, all of it. Starbursts seemed to be the one thing I wouldn't throw up. And from the Big Book I could cobble together a pep talk for myself, something that held an echo of my mother's voice.

But as comfortable as I had been there, now was a good time to leave. As I grew heavier, the futon had grown less comfortable; I'd taken to napping in Stan's bed when he wasn't home, and it was awkward when he came stumbling in the door with a pack of half-drunk and cross-dressed friends after *Rocky Horror* to pass them in the hallway as I made my way back to the living room. All of them knew Cade and I were together, and I lived in fear that somebody in the group would voice a suspicion about me and Stan to him that would cause drama. I wasn't concerned about Drew, because Cade was above listening to anything that came out of his mouth, but Stan had other friends Cade respected, and their judgment worried me. I could feel only relieved when, at the end of May, Cade admitted defeat with the summer-job hunt, told Bylina's head of staff to call him the minute any job opened up and we packed our bags for New Hampshire.

The drive up to Frasier took twelve hours. The farther north we drove, the quieter Cade grew and the more grim his expression became. When he filled up the car in Massachusetts and I went inside to use the bathroom, I came out to see him resting his head against his arms on the steering wheel, like a child at a school desk.

I didn't force the conversation. For all that Cade treated each toll road as another coin for the ferryman into hell, I was happy to spend the summer in New Hampshire. Dave had been so disappointed when I called to tell him I wouldn't be back this year, and that I'd be graduating late on top of that, but there was no sense in brooding over what couldn't be helped. I'd thought about my mother a lot in those past few months, trying to coax my confused mind to produce a little of her wisdom, and I was at peace with this decision. *Don't be afraid to ask for help when you need it,* my mother would have told me. At Southridge I would have just been a burden, too ungainly to perform my usual tasks, and any help I requested would have saddled me with guilt. But among family—and Cade's family counted—it would be natural to ask and receive, because this baby was their own.

We crossed the border at the southern end of the state and drove through the Lakes Region, where Lake Winnipesaukee glittered between the trees and tall-masted boats clustered at docks that stretched far into the water. Cade looked singularly unimpressed with the scenery and drove along the gray highway in silence. His music selections grew darker as we crept farther north. The mountains loomed closer and closer; the woods grew more dense; the towns became farther apart and abandoned 1950s-era motels cropped up by the side of the road in numbers I had not imagined possible. We saw moose-crossing signs and the sheer faces of cliffs. Cade made a left turn onto a smaller road that passed through a faded town of Victorian structures; we passed a gas station and a sandwich shop, then a boarded-up bed-and-breakfast with a charred roof, then two miles of nothing. Then a house.

It was set far back from the road and flanked by trees, a sprawling and ancient white farmhouse with two lichen-flecked boulders marking the entrance to the long driveway. At first glance it seemed ordinary enough. The wooden siding was badly in need of paint, but the large kitchen garden at its side was neatly kept, and a gray barn was dilapidated but stable. An American flag flapped from a pole attached to the front porch, with a frayed yellow bow waving beneath it. A much smaller house built of cinder block stood a slight distance away at the edge of the forest. If the Olmsteads owned thirty acres here, I guessed at least twenty of them were wooded. The driveway turned from asphalt to gravel, then hard-packed dust, and here Cade stopped and jerked the car into Park.

Inside the house, two beagles began howling. Cade tossed his sunglasses onto the dash and twisted his body sideways to face me. For a long moment he said nothing, but the muscles in his jaw looked tense enough to snap. Finally he said, "Jill, tell me you love me."

"Of course I do."

"Just say it. Say, 'Cade, I love you.'"

"Cade, I love you."

"I love you, too."

He unclasped his seat belt and got out of the car. From the porch came the sounds of a banging wooden screen and general commotion, and then a woman stepped toward us, heavyset and in her thirties, wiping her hands on a dishrag. Her hair fell to her waist, and she wore a dress of smocklike calico.

"Cadey's home," she cried. I looked at her with some confusion. Too young to be his mother, too old to be his sister, I could not identify who this woman was in the scheme of the Olmstead family. She hurried to Cade and threw her arms around his neck, enveloping him in a powerful hug. "Praise God," she said. "You made it here safe."

He extracted himself from her arms and cocked his head toward the car. "Jill, Candy," he said. "Candy, Jill."

So this *was* his sister. I extended my hand, but Candy used it to pull me into her embrace. "We need another woman around here," she said over my shoulder. "We're outnumbered."

Cade watched us with long-suffering patience. A trio of small boys, all shirtless, rushed out the front door and into the side yard, circumventing their mother. Cade mounted the porch stairs and I fell in step behind him, into a living room crammed with objects and looking as if it hadn't seen an update since 1979. A faded sofa and matching recliner, strewn with multicolored crocheted afghans, bracketed a grungy braided rug. The television rested on a discount-store corner stand with several dust-flocked ceramic figurines on top. Above the sooty fireplace hung the mounted head of a deer, elegantly alert, surveying the poor scene before him. And despite a small fan in one corner of the room, the air was dense with the smell of cigarette smoke, both fresh and stale. Right away I could see that it would be a lost cause to try to keep clear of secondhand smoke. If I wanted that, I'd have to stay in the barn.

Cade's mother, Leela, blonde like him and, like Candy, looking older than I expected, rose to meet me as I stepped into the room. She shook my hand and greeted me warmly, then hugged Cade before quietly following Candy out to the back porch, where they seemed to be in the midst of assembling an egg incubator. The bright light of a clear bulb flashed on and off.

"I'm home, Dad," Cade said to a man seated in a leather recliner in front of the television. The words sounded more ceremonial than anything else; his father, after all, could not have missed him coming in the door. But Cade had warned me that his dad, Eddy, had been foggy since his stroke, and he looked at his father with a gauging eye, as if to determine whether he had gotten worse since Christmas.

"So you are." But his father looked at me, not Cade. A cigarette burned between his index and middle fingers, the long ash on the end lingering precipitously. He wore a long-sleeved plaid shirt despite the warmth of the room, and his hands bore dark red patches, the color of dried blood, that seemed to originate beneath his skin. Cade had told me Eddy was in his late fifties, but to my eye he looked much older, and his voice was thick. His gaze traveled from my feet to my eyes and back again. "That's your girl, huh?"

"That's my girl."

"I'm Jill," I offered. "Nice to meet you."

He nodded unevenly but didn't offer his hand. Cade asked, "Know where Elias is?"

"In the den. Same as always."

Cade circled around the back of the recliner and led me into the room behind it. The space was larger and airier—an addition that encompassed a modern-looking kitchen-and-dining-room combination, as well as a nook that contained another TV and a couple of chairs. In one of these sat Elias, whom I recognized by his features and haircut but who was otherwise strikingly changed. Gone were the hard stomach and muscled chest that had flaunted themselves even from beneath his sandy-beige T-shirt. In their place were a significant gut and soft pectorals, and he carried the weight in his face, as well. When I had met him in the fall, his forearms were notable only because of their strength and deep golden tan. Now both were covered in tattoos. I blinked at him and tried to match the image I remembered with the one in front of me.

Cade took my hand and guided me to follow him. He stepped directly into Elias's line of vision before he spoke. "Hey, bro," he said. "How's it hanging?"

Elias looked up from the television. "Hey," he grunted. He met my eye and said, "Hi, Jill."

. I threw him a warm smile. "Hey, Elias. Great to see you again."

"Did Mom and Dad tell you?" asked Cade.

"Yep. You knocked her up." He half grinned and flicked a glance toward Cade. "Good job there, buddy. You ever heard of Trojans?"

"Yeah. They don't work if you leave 'em in the box."

"They sure don't. Jill, hope to God it doesn't come out looking like me or acting like Candy's kids. If it has to be an Olmstead, at least its dad came from the deep end of the gene pool."

"If you say so," I said, and Cade threw me a joking scowl that made Elias snicker. "He's got endurance, that's for sure. I can't believe he makes that drive all the time. It's *long*."

"Not long enough," Cade said under his breath, and his brother chuckled again. I followed Cade up the stairs to a bedroom sandwiched between two others. He closed the door, then lay down on the full-size mattress and rubbed his eyes. "I'd like to go home now," he said.

"You *are* home."

He groaned and threw both arms over his face. I glanced around the room, taking in the white walls decorated only with a large American flag, the plain childish furniture, the windows shaded by artlessly stitched homemade curtains. I peeked out between them and saw the three little boys running around in the yard. "So those are Candy's hellions, huh?"

"Yep. Wait till you meet their dad. Hoo boy."

"They look pretty wound up. Bet she'll be glad to get them off to school on Monday."

"They don't go to school. They're homeschooled. By Candy, no less. The girl who spells *religion* with a *d* in it."

"At least it's not part of the curriculum."

"If you're Candy, it *is* the curriculum. Wait and see."

I let the curtain drop. "Where's your parents' room?"

He tapped the wall beside the bed.

"Wonderful."

"You're telling me. Elias sleeps on the other side, but he isn't going to care, so we can move the bed to the opposite wall. Of course, that would probably scandalize my mother.

But it's not like she can pretend otherwise, with you pregnant and all."

"True. Hey, what's happened to Elias?"

"What do you mean, what's happened to him?"

"He's gained a lot of weight. And the tattoos."

Cade shrugged. "Yeah, he's gotten pretty chunky. But to tell the truth, that's what he looked like before he joined the army, more or less. The shape he was in when you saw him before—that's not normal for him. Hey, speaking of food—follow me. You've got to see this."

I followed him back down to the first floor where he pulled open a hallway door that led to the basement stairs. Candy peered over from the kitchen and called, "Hey, Cade, you going down cellar? You want to bring me up a can of black beans? I need 'em for tomorrow."

"Sure thing." He sounded almost gleeful. As we descended the dark steps I could tell by the smell of it that this cellar must be finished and not earthen; that much was good, because low dirt cellars gave me the creeps. Then he pulled the chain for the light, and what I saw made me pull in my breath.

The entire wall that faced me, running the length of the house, was filled from floor to ceiling with shelves stacked with giant-sized cans of food. Each bore a dusty yellow label printed with a cornucopia spilling out with produce. Only the black lettering differentiated their contents. PEAS. BLUEBERRIES. CHEESE POWDER. POTATO PEARLS. ROAST BEEF FREEZE-DRIED. Six fifty-five-gallon drums, in a cheerful shade of blue, sat along the adjacent wall beside a chemical toilet and a stack of military-green sleeping cots. An old television sat on a wooden crate, and next to it, a camp stove and a large gasoline-powered generator.

"What is this, a bomb shelter?" I asked.

"Kinda-sorta. You see the gun safe over there?" asked Cade.

He waved a hand toward a wall holding the brackets for at least a dozen hunting rifles, and to the side, a tall brown metal safe that must have held the rest of their collection. "If the army ever runs short, they know who to call. Actually, they don't. Which I think is half the point."

I turned and looked around the room in wonder. The walls and floor were finished with clean concrete. An entire section of wall was devoted to evaporated milk. Several shelves contained varieties of vegetables and fruits, while another seemed to contain only baking mixes: BUTTERMILK BISCUIT MIX, CORN BREAD MIX, FUDGE BROWNIE MIX. There were even cans labeled GARDEN SEEDS.

"Jesus." I exhaled. "You guys are ready for the apocalypse."

"Sixty thousand dollars," said Cade.

I looked at him. "That's how much all this cost?"

"That's my best guess. Freshman year of college, when I was short on money, I got pissed off and sat down to work out what I figured they'd spent on all this shit. That's the number I came up with. How screwed up is that, huh? I'm working my ass into the ground to pay for school, getting nothing from these people, and here's where it all went instead." He pulled a giant can from a shelf and held it up like an infomercial salesman. "So when Jesus comes back, we can all eat precooked bacon."

"I can see why that would piss you off."

"You better believe it." He chucked the can haphazardly back onto the shelf, then walked the length of the unit until he found one labeled BLACK BEANS. "Three goddamn months and we're going home. And by that I mean home to D.C. Because by then I'll be ready to strangle somebody, and when that happens their nuclear bunker won't do them a damn bit of good."

"It's kind of funny, though."

He turned to me with one eyebrow up. "What, *this?*"

"Yeah, all of it. Storing up food, homeschooling the kids. We had people like that at Southridge—the ones who were convinced the government was going to come after them personally. We called them the PSNs. It stands for 'paranoid survivalist nut jobs.'" He laughed, but I cringed inwardly at my bluntness. "Not that I'm calling your family that. Sorry."

"No—fair enough. In my mom's defense, I'm pretty sure she thinks this is as stupid as I do. But she's not one to make waves."

"So whose idea is it?"

"Mostly my brother-in-law's. We always had a lot of food stored up, but it didn't turn into a bunker until Candy married him. My dad thought it was perfectly reasonable."

"Uh-*huh.*"

"The longer you're here, the more sense it'll make. Which is why we're only staying for the summer. Hang around much longer and it starts to eat your brain."

"Well, we could set up our bedroom down here, in the meantime," I said. "Wouldn't have to worry about noise coming through the walls, that's for sure."

He laughed wickedly and slapped me on the backside, and we hurried back up the stairs, the can of beans rattling all the way like a children's toy.

The whole family was already assembled around the dinner table when Cade and I walked in. Leela, sitting at the opposite end of the table from Cade's father, threw me a shy smile, and the family fell silent as Cade and I took our places. Cade bowed his head for the prayer, and I followed suit. The man who was evidently Candy's husband, a tall and sturdily built man I had immediately pegged as a PSN like the ones I trained at camp, intoned a singsong blessing. This was Dodge, the King Jackass of the Universe who had caused me to spend Christmas fending off Drew Fielder's slimy attempts at flirtation. The mere memory gave me a shiver.

"Tell your father about what you learned today, Matthew," said Candy, breaking the awkward silence that followed the blessing.

Dodge loaded his plate with chicken casserole and passed the dish across the table to Cade, who looked at him with thinly veiled contempt. Matthew's reedy little voice replied, "The Declaration of Independence."

"What about it?"

Matthew squeezed his fork between both hands as he rolled his eyes upward in thought, crushing noodles and sauce through his fingers like Play-Doh. "Um…that it was wrote by President Thomas Jefferson to tell the world that we had gotten independent from all our enemies."

"That's right," said Dodge. He forked in a mouthful of chicken. "Enemies like who?"

"Tyrants. Like the British and judges and foreigners, and the merciless Indian savages, and the Muslims."

"Very good." He nodded to Candy. "Nice work there, Momma."

Candy beamed.

Cade took a long drink of his iced tea. Then he said, "I don't think the Muslims were a big threat to the colonies at that time."

"There were Muslims back then," Dodge said.

"There certainly were," agreed Candy. "The Muslims have been around since the time of the Jews. Ask Elias—he was just over there fighting them."

"You want to straighten her out on that one?" Cade prompted his brother. Elias looked up, and Cade tipped his head imploringly. "Who are we fighting over there? The Muslims. or al Qaeda, or what?"

"The Taliban," Elias answered. He picked around in his dinner with his fork and added, "And ignorance."

"Ignorance?"

"People not knowing any better way."

"See," said Cade, "now, *that* makes sense. Let's hope we're making progress on that one."

"We aren't," said Elias.

"You want to talk about enemies," Dodge said, and jabbed his fork in the direction of the front window. "Drove down to the rental property today to fix the dishwasher, and they wouldn't even let me in. Gonna put those people out on their ass, first of the month."

"You can't do that," Cade told him. "There's a process. They've got a lease."

"Lease that says I'm the landlord. I can go in whenever I feel like."

Cade nodded toward his father. "*Dad's* the landlord."

"Doesn't matter."

"Legally, it does."

Cade's mother stood up and lifted the iced tea pitcher from the center of the table. "Stop your arguing. Let's not turn a nice supper into one of those TV programs where everybody bickers at each other."

"So as I was saying," Dodge continued, "they wouldn't let me in. Girl there said her father told her a man has to be home before she can let me in. Don't think I don't know what *that's* all about."

Leela's brow creased. "Nothing wrong with that, really. They're religious, remember. Don't they belong to that church down the road apiece? The nondenominational one?"

"Uh-huh. Randy's church."

I looked from Cade to his father and back again. Randy was the uncle they never spoke to because of some old argument about a gun club. But Cade only said, "What does that have to do with anything?"

"I'm betting Randy's been saying things. They never had any issue with me coming in before, and now all of a sudden they need the father home. Sounds to me like there's been some trash-talking and murmuring going on. I don't take well to that at all."

Elias mumbled something, and Dodge looked over at him sharply. "What'd you say?"

"I said that's goofy."

Taking on an exaggerated posture of shock, Dodge leaned back and shot Elias a squinty glare. "*Beg* your pardon?"

"Chill out. It isn't all that." Elias chopped his fork around in his casserole, looking up just enough to catch Dodge's eye with his own placating gaze. "That's not Randy's style, is all I'm saying. He wouldn't go around gossiping about people. You don't need to worry about it."

Dodge shook his head. "You picked a strange place to stand up and defend that individual. But it's a free country, right, Matthew?" His son nodded adamantly. "You can defend that cockwad if you like."

"*Dodge,*" Leela scolded. "For goodness' sake, *stop* it. First time we ever have Cade's wife at our table, and what's she going to think of us, with you speaking like that at supper? I'm sorry, Jill."

"She's not his wife," Dodge pointed out. He didn't bother to look at me when he said it. I glanced at Cade and he lifted his eyebrows in a silent *I told you so*. I might have felt irritated by the look had it not been so obvious that he was right about the guy. I could handle him, but Cade's embarrassment made all the sense in the world now.

"She's his wife in the biblical sense and that's good enough for me," Leela said. She caught my eye and wagged her head up and down. "You hear me, Jill? It's good enough for me."

I smiled. "Thanks."

"Well, far be it from me to argue with the Bible," said Dodge. "Pass the green beans over here, will you?"

The bowl sat in front of me, but he hadn't addressed me directly, so I made no motion to pass it to him. For several moments he sat in expectant silence; the family continued to eat, and at last he stood and reached down the table to retrieve it himself. When I glanced up to see the shadow of Cade's smile I felt Elias watching me, but when I looked at him he turned back to his dinner and said nothing at all.

Chapter 6

JILL

The baby didn't like the casserole. In the middle of the night I awoke with a raging case of heartburn—not the first of my pregnancy, but by far the worst. I tossed and turned for a while but eventually gave up and ventured down the stairs, hoping the Olmsteads kept antacids somewhere in their Armageddon pantry.

As I entered the addition I heard the television in the den turned down low and saw a column of cigarette smoke rising from the easy chair. I knew it had to be Elias, and when he caught my eye I offered him a polite wave. Other than the television, the kitchen's only illumination came from Candy's incubator on the back porch, a glass-and-wire box holding twenty parchment-colored eggs under the warmth of a sixty-watt bulb. It threw a shadowed light across the kitchen, and as I opened a cabinet and began poking around, Elias asked, "Whatcha looking for?"

"Tums or something."

"I've got 'em over here."

I padded over to the easy chair, and he pulled open the side-table drawer. "I've got a whole little field hospital over here. Tums, Tylenol, nail clippers, allergy pills, you name it. Keeps everything handy."

"Is that a *gun* in there?"

He handed me the Tums and slid the drawer shut. "Hey, if I'm gonna be up at night, at least I can provide a little security."

"Yeah, I've noticed your family's pretty big on emergency preparedness."

He chuckled. "Yep, we're ready for World War Three over here. You see that cabinet there?" He pointed to one above the refrigerator. "It's got potassium iodide pills in it, in the event of a nuclear explosion. If anybody drops a dirty bomb on Lake Winnipesaukee, your thyroid is safe and sound."

"Are you serious?"

"Dead serious. Did you get a good look around the cellar? They've got enough water stored up to float the house to Canada."

I chewed two of the antacid tablets, then asked, "What do you think of all that?"

"I think it's not a bad idea." He dragged on his cigarette, held the smoke in his lungs for a moment and exhaled out his nose. "If we learned anything from 9/11, it's that when the shit goes down, you're on your own. And that goes for normal stuff, too. Out here, if it snows real bad, good luck getting out of the house for a week. If somebody breaks into your house, by the time the cops get here, all your stuff'll be in a truck en route to Canada."

"You guys ever get break-ins all the way out here?"

"It's not unheard of. And there's a lot of people still got grudges against my dad, even now. Pissed-off renters especially. Dodge usually deals with them these days."

I replied with a rude little laugh. "Yeah, *that* must calm them down."

"Seriously, right? He's got a special kind of charm. So what'd you think of that dinner party?" He flicked ash from his cigarette into the beer can beside him. "Dodge is lucky one of us didn't come across the table and choke him."

"Seemed like most of the family agreed with him about your uncle Randy."

"They do. People around here need a hobby. Scrap with somebody one time and then you can milk ten years of conversation out of it. God forbid you just let it go."

I handed him the Tums bottle and he dropped it back into the drawer. The three empty beer cans lined up on the side table rattled as he pushed it shut. I asked, "What happened ten years ago?"

Elias leaned forward a little and, with his cigarette still wedged between his fingers, cupped his hands as if to explain that this story was a whole little world. "You have two extremists. One wants to create a citizen militia with five hundred guns and a whole army of trained-up guys ready to turn Maine into its own republic if they get pissed enough. The other one wants to drink beer, shoot guns, grill burgers and fuck your daughter. There's only room for one of them at the supper table."

I raised an eyebrow. "So which one is Dodge?"

"The second one, obviously. He couldn't organize a sock drawer, let alone a militia. You haven't done the math on him and Candy?"

I shook my head.

"He's forty-one. She's twenty-six. Their oldest kid is nine."

I thought about that for a moment, then wrinkled my nose. "Ew."

"Dad had to sign off on the marriage license, she was so young."

"I'm surprised he agreed to that. If some creep wanted to marry my teenage daughter, I sure wouldn't."

"If the creep is one of your friends, you would. But it's a

stupid squabble if you ask me. Randy's not so bad. He just had a different goal for the group. It's nothing to start a blood feud over, but people have to go and take things personally. You gotta let stuff like that go or you'll drive yourself over the edge."

I sat on the arm of the chair beside his. "Cade's like that about this guy named Drew who's been competing with him for the same job. At some point he stopped being a rival and turned into the enemy. Except that guy really *is* a jerk, and I gave him the benefit of the doubt, too. Over Christmas, when I was stuck at school, I got take-out Chinese with him and he tried to get in my pants."

Elias stopped in mid-drag and, laughing silently, coughed out smoke. "Weren't you already pregnant then?"

"Yeah, but I didn't know it yet. Don't say anything to Cade about that. He'd kill the guy."

"Scout's honor. Pretty funny that anyone would try to cock-block Cade, though." In an ominous voice he quoted, "'Now witness the firepower of this fully armed and operational battle station.'"

I laughed. "What's that supposed to mean?"

"Nothing. Kudos to that guy for thinking he stood a chance. With my brother—just make the son of a bitch work for it, that's all. Make him buy you a big honkin' diamond, at least. You look like you've earned it."

I laughed and stood up. "Thanks, Elias."

"My pleasure."

I reached in to hug him, and at the first touch of my hands against his upper arms he stiffened so violently that I nearly jumped back. But I hugged him anyway, my hands light and the pressure soft, and patted him on the shoulder.

He nodded and scratched above his ear, and I trudged back up the stairs to bed.

★ ★ ★

By the following Sunday Cade had found a job as a shift manager at a hotel seventeen miles down the road, in Liberty Gorge, the first real town south of us. The pay was menial and the job a joke compared to what he was capable of, but work was scarce in the area and it was the best he could do. On Monday, after his morning chores, he donned the cheerful blue-green uniform shirt and headed off to field complaints about broken showerheads, unpalatable food and groups of noisy teenagers.

I wished for an escape as pleasantly menial. It hadn't taken long for me to realize that "the Powell house"—the peach-painted cinder-block cottage tucked in the side yard of the main house—was little more than a formality, a place Dodge and Candy could claim as their own without ever spending any waking time there. Candy homeschooled her sons from the dining-room table of the main house, beginning with the Pledge of Allegiance each morning at 8:00 a.m., followed by prayer, followed by unqualified chaos. It amazed me that Elias managed to spend every day around her and remain so preternaturally calm all the time. Seven days and I felt ready to snap.

Late one morning, when I couldn't handle listening to one more minute of Candy's creationist science lesson, I gathered up the heap of garden peas from the kitchen island and took them out to the front porch. As soon as the screen door slammed, two deer bolted away from the vegetable garden on the house's eastern side. I clucked my tongue in annoyance and sat down to shell the enormous pile, already feeling better just to be out in the fresh spring air, away from the cloud of smoke that blanketed the house's interior. Out front, the Olmsteads' rooster, Ben Franklin, strutted in a slow circle around the yard like a one-bird security detail. He was a strikingly beautiful creature. His comb and wattles were

bright fuchsia, and from the top of his head down to his sad-
dle feathers his coloring shifted from orange to pale yellow
to deep red. The luxuriant tail was peacock-green and shimmered in the light. I admired him from a distance, knowing he was probably territorial. I'd spent the whole previous
summer as Dave's chicken-class teacher, teaching others how
to feed and raise such birds, castrate the males so they could
be raised for meat, and at the end of it all, slaughter them hu-
manely. I knew how to manage birds like Ben, but I wasn't
foolhardy enough to walk into his space right away.

A green Jeep slowed in front of the house and abruptly
pulled into the driveway, driving all the way up to where Cade
normally parked. The door opened with a metal-on-metal
screech. The kid who stepped out of it looked to be about
eighteen, with spiky auburn hair and wire-rimmed glasses. I
knew right away—based on his resemblance to a certain Mup-
pets character—that this must be Scooter. I'd heard Elias mention the guy who rented a room from the Vogel family one
farm over and helped out Dodge with the self-storage place.
He nodded a greeting and smiled at me.

"Good morning, ma'am," he called. "Is Elias awake?"

"I don't think so. He usually sleeps till about one."

The guy nodded again. His earnestly good-natured face
looked comical above the rest of his body, clad as it was in
baggy woodland camo pants, a white crew-neck undershirt
and black combat boots crusted with mud. He held out his car
keys and, a little bewildered, I accepted them. "Just tell him
his stuff's on the front seat, along with his change."

"Okay. Don't you need your keys?"

"They're his. It's his Jeep."

He raised a hand to say goodbye and began hiking back up
the road toward the Vogel farm. I started to walk back into
the house to put away the keys, but then considered that I

should probably bring his loose change inside, too. It hadn't taken long for me to determine I didn't trust Candy's Matthew. Among the end-of-the-world rations in the Olmsteads' basement were cans of something called "carbohydrate supplement," which appeared no different from cellophane-wrapped hard candy. It seemed as if every time I sat down those cellophane wrappers crinkled between the sofa cushions, and I was 90 percent sure Matthew was the one doing the sneaking. Any kid who would brave the basement bunker for a piece of hard candy would have no problem palming someone else's car keys to intercept their spare change.

I opened the side door of the Jeep and retrieved the coins and bills, grabbing the plastic shopping bag while I was at it. Inside was a crisp white pharmacy bag. Curiosity got the better of me, and I peeked at the label. Beneath Elias's name was the word *Prozac*.

I turned and looked up at Elias's bedroom window, almost guiltily, as if I'd been nosing around on purpose. It was dark, the shades drawn, but it always looked that way. For a few moments I debated with myself whether to leave or take it, but in the end I tied together the handles of the plastic bag and carried it inside. Quietly I hung it on his bedroom doorknob. And an hour or so later when he awoke, the bag disappeared without a word. For the rest of the day he stayed in his chair in front of the TV, watching *Rachael Ray* and smoking cigarettes one after the other, as if they were a natural part of breathing.

That evening I walked into our bedroom with a basket full of laundry and found Cade sitting on the side of the bed with his laptop open on the quilt. "Done and done," he announced. "Registered for my fall classes. Now the countdown begins."

"How's that going to work, exactly? I mean, the baby's due

at the same time the semester starts. I could go into labor any-time, and then neither of us is going to be getting any sleep."

"We'll make it work. The alternative is being stuck in this dump for three more months, so trust me, I'll find a way." He shut the laptop and smiled. "*Ahhh.* Feels good just to set up the escape plan. *Always* chart your course, and you'll win every time."

He still didn't have an escape plan, just a fall schedule, but I didn't care to point that out to him. "I wouldn't mind get-ting away from Dodge, that's for sure. He won't shut up about that stupid dishwasher and what he'd like to do to Randy. It kind of freaks me out."

"He makes noise. Him and Candy both. You can't take them seriously. I didn't even realize just how crazy-assed their ideas are until I got away from here."

"No kidding. She keeps trying to talk to me about how we should leave our family planning up to God."

He snickered. "Thought it was obvious we already had."

"She means from here on out."

He pulled off his uniform shirt and nodded. "Yeah. My idea is to use six forms of birth control from here on out."

"Well, you know I'm not on board with her plan, either. She calls it 'quiver full' or something, though I'd like to know why she's only got three kids if she's leaving the whole thing to the Lord."

He cast a bemused glance on me. "They've probably only had sex three times. Or else Dodge can't get it up. He sure acts like he's compensating for something."

I leaned back against the bed, and Cade gave my belly an affectionate pat as he walked around the room collecting chore clothes. "I need to figure out a way to get prenatal care for this one. There's got to be some program through the state."

"No way, we don't want to mess with any of that. Just find

a doctor and we'll figure it out. Ask Candy. She's pumped out enough kids to know."

"Maybe. Hey, speaking of doctors—am I supposed to know that Elias is taking Prozac? Or should I keep pretending I have no idea?"

He popped his head out of the top of a paint-splattered T-shirt. "He's on *what?*"

"Guess I should keep pretending, then."

Cade squinted in confusion. "Why would he be on *that?* He's not depressed about anything. He's fine."

"Cade…he loads a gun every night and keeps watch."

"Well, I can't throw stones at anybody who takes work home with him. But see, that's what I hate about those military doctors. It was the same shit when he got that leg injury. They pumped him full of pain pills and put him back on active duty. What he needs is some physical therapy for that leg and someone to make him get up off his ass. And I bet you he'd sleep better at night if he did something to make himself tired during the day. Watching the Food Network doesn't tire you out. It just makes you hungry, and we can all see that's the last thing he needs."

"Maybe it's all of those things together," I suggested. "Maybe you're right, but he's depressed, too, and just not talking to you about it."

He balled up his hotel shirt like a basketball and tossed it into the hamper. "You know what the cure for depression is?" he asked. He began ticking off items with his fingers. "Running. Spending time with people. And getting laid. That's my therapy plan for Elias. I'll write him a scrip for it."

"I miss running. I can try to get him to come walking with me during the day, though. Maybe you can get some old friends together over here so he can socialize a little."

"I can try, yeah. We'll see what goes. He needs to make an effort, too. He's got everybody's phone numbers, same as me."

"It's a start. Guess he's out of luck on the 'getting laid' part, though."

Cade snickered and pulled open the bedroom door. "Story of the poor guy's life."

Chapter 7

LEELA

The mistakes I made with Cade, in the measure of things, are small next to the other two. Someone who wanted to criticize me—Randy's wife, say—would look at that boy and mutter, oh, he's a spoiled one, he got too light a hand, too prideful a mother. However Cade turned out, whether a body can say he came to be like that on his own, or by me, well—if the worst can be said is I loved him too much, then so be it. So put it on my tombstone.

I wasn't a young mother when I had Candy, but I sure was naive. Always I'd had it in my mind I'd have six children. Three boys and three girls: that was how I pictured it, and I always felt most likely it would come to pass just that way, because I knew the Lord wants to grant us our righteous desires. Candy came, then Elias and Cade, and I had the next three already named: Eve, Emma Lee and Christopher. But after Cade, with Eddy the way he was, I decided no more. Eve, she almost came twice, but that was not to be.

Among the three who did come, it's only natural to be most pleased with the one I got right. That was Cade—the child who got good marks, who could hit nearly every ball pitched to him, whose grin could melt your heart. Any mother can tell you which of her children strangers smile on the most.

It doesn't make a mother love that child any more, and yet a body can't help feeling the pride of it. But Elias was deep and earnest, and I loved him and fretted over him in a special way because of that nature of his, and for being the most like me. I protected him from Eddy's rages in a way I didn't with Cade, even though Cade was the baby. Elias cared, and his brother just didn't. Cade knew from the day he spoke his first word that he was smarter than his father, and he carried himself in a way that showed it. But Elias always had that something deep down, that unsureness that he was all right as a person. So when Eddy yelled at him that he was a fool or a failure, something inside Elias nodded at it like it was a truth, and I couldn't abide that at all.

Yet it was Candy who most rattled my nerves. Even as a tiny thing, there was something sly about her. She was the one who'd take a cookie from the jar, who'd pick up a penny off the sidewalk, and then deny it seven ways from Sunday even if you told her you wouldn't be angry. She'd do you a kindness—bring you toast and tea in bed, say, or iron your church dress you'd set aside—but every time you'd get the uneasy feeling she had a secret motive for it. Like she had a backhanded idea and wanted to make it up to you ahead of time.

Honest or no, it was her nature, and that grieved me something terrible. Before I ever had children I wanted sons for my husband, for certain, but with all my heart I wanted a daughter just for me. I dreamed of the things we'd do together. Years before I married Eddy, when I was carrying the first of my babies, I pictured our heads bent over a quilt together— her with long hair in a clip and a skirt I'd made for her— pinning up the squares. That baby wasn't for this world, and when she left me I grieved not only for what had happened, but for all that never would. Later, with Eddy at my side and the second child in my belly, I didn't allow myself those same imaginings until Candy was born safe and in my arms. And even then, I was wary. Maybe she felt it through her skin, the way I didn't give myself all up to her from the first. See, there are worse things you can say about me, where Candy is concerned, than that I loved her too much. Shameful things I don't dare to think.

One day the three of them decided to build a tree house in the oak nearby to the barn. I suppose Candy was fifteen then, because Dodge was hanging around the place too often and I suspected he had designs on her, so it pleased me for her to have a task that got her away from the house. My children were born two and a half years apart, just about, so Cade would have been ten and Eli someplace in between. Candy had appointed herself a kind of supervisor, which was sensible because she was always a dresses girl and you can't very well build a tree house if you won't wear pants. A couple times a day, when I had business in the barn, I'd walk past and see what they were up to. Usually Elias would be up the tree working, and Cade and Candy would be shouting at one another, because they were too alike in being headstrong. Cade was just a little skinny thing then, and Candy such a tall girl with hips on her and everything else, that it was funny to see those two squabbling.

It was easy to see why Cade had such a temper over it. Candy had some foolish ideas, like she was making Cade paint the tree house board by board before sending the boards up to Elias to be nailed in place. I let them do their thing and stayed out of it. In life, once you're grown, there isn't anybody going to step in between you and the other person and make you work together to straighten it out. God rest my mother, she was so fair that she always stepped into every argument and helped us see one another's sides, and so once I was grown I didn't know how to assert myself in any disagreement. I always kept on waiting for the fairness to become apparent to the other person, and that just isn't the way people are.

Then one afternoon I heard Cade running up to the house yelling, yelling, yelling. His voice carried clear into the kitchen, and I came out in a hurry. He took me to the tree, and there was Elias lying on the ground curled up like a snail, his eyes closed and his arm at an angle that wasn't right. I grabbed him and shook him, not even thinking how that was the wrong thing to do. If a body falls down from a tree, their back could be broken, their neck—you don't go and shake them. But I did, because seeing my Eli in that state made my wits just disappear.

"She told him to go up to that next branch to make a lookout," Cade said. "I told her it's too thin, but she said if it sits just one person at a time it's all right. Then it broke—"

"Where's Candy?" I demanded of Cade. He said he didn't know. I could see, then, that Elias had knocked his head on a rock that was embedded deep in the dirt, and that scared all the warmth right out of my body. I looked Cade dead in the eye and I said, "You get the phone and you call 911."

His mouth got a nervous look about it, like a grimace, and he hesitated. I knew what was going through his head—that foolish line Eddy always said, that *we don't call 911,* which was meant to say if a burglar tries to break into our house, he'd better count on being shot dead before we fiddle around with calling the police. So I said, "Cade Daniel, you pay no mind to that nonsense your father says. You call them right away and tell them your brother's hurt bad."

He ran to the house, and then I started shouting for Candy. I needed an explanation from her, but more than that I couldn't move Eli on my own. He was thirteen or thereabout and he weighed more than I did. But she wasn't anywhere—it was as if she'd vanished into the air, like vapor. Finally I managed to get him conscious, and then the ambulance arrived and took him to the hospital. He had a concussion and a broken arm. I sent Eddy out that night to tear down the half-built tree house, and I told those kids my nerves couldn't take them ever trying a project like that one again.

Candy, though—when I got back from the hospital with Eli that night, she was standing at the kitchen sink pretty as you please, washing dishes. I got her brother settled into his bed and then I came down and, standing very close to her, said, "You ready to give me some explanation for why you disappeared when your brother was about half-dead?"

She said, in this very light voice, "I was praying for him."

"Come again?"

"I found me a peaceful spot over by the garden and I knelt down in prayer for him. And the Lord delivered."

For at least a full minute I was real quiet. Then I said, "I think you know whose fault it is he got hurt, and you were running away to hide from me. He needed you and you abandoned him."

She kept washing, but gave me a sidelong look that was reproachful. "He looks okay to me now, so I suppose it's all fine."

I felt angry at her then, wicked angry, but I felt frightened for her, too. I wondered where I'd gone wrong to make her turn out the way she was. But here I'd brought up Cade just the same way, and while one of them was stepping up to be his brother's hero—overriding even his fear of his father— the other one was strolling off to pray for him or hide from me. I wish I knew how it is one mother can raise two children to be complete opposites. So it was too easy, you see, to feel so proud of Cade that I didn't better keep him in check, and so nervous of Candy that maybe I held back some of the love she needed and deserved. Every little girl has the right to a mother who thinks she's the most wonderful girl in the world, and God forgive me, I don't think Candy ever had that. God forgive me.

Chapter 8

JILL

My mother's cesarean scar was a jagged little ridge that ran from her navel to the top of her underpants, a slim vertical line that divided her abdomen in two. When I was very young she explained to me that usually the surgeon cuts the other way, in a crescent slung low beneath the belly, but when I was born the doctors needed to work quickly. They didn't have time to be neat or to work with the contours of her body. *I nearly lost you,* she said. Now, as I stood on the children's step stool before the Olmsteads' bathroom mirror and regarded my rounding belly through the fading steam from the shower, I wished I had known to ask her more questions. What had caused the emergency? Had her life been in peril as well as mine? How had she felt, waking up after the chaos and trauma of an emergency birth, to find herself without a partner to worry over her and rejoice with her, without a mother to help her recover?

I yearned to hear her voice reminding me how lucky I was that Cade was with me. To counsel me on how to get through this without her. But then, if she were here, I wouldn't need to know.

Be a girl, I thought, an order directed at my unborn child. *Please be a girl.* I ran both hands across my belly, strangely solid and newly convex beneath my taut skin, and imagined a daughter who would link the chain between me and my mother, helping me to understand who she had been, to repeat the wonders she had done for me and honor her for them. I wouldn't know how to raise a boy; I would have to defer to Cade on everything I didn't understand, and that encompassed so much that I wondered how the child would even feel like mine at all. Cade and I had already decided that I would choose the name for a girl and he for a boy; without any hesitation I chose Miranda, after my mother. It was a fair agreement, but secretly I wished to choose the boy's name, too, so that no matter how much he emulated Cade, he would still turn his head at a name I loved.

I stepped down off the stool and pulled on my clothes—the jeans that still fit if I pushed the waistband down beneath my stomach, the radio station T-shirt that had once been relegated to the sleep-shirt drawer before its roominess gave it a new appeal. At least I had Leela now—not my own mother, no, but a woman who had raised sons as well as a daughter, who knew the pain I would be facing and might hold my hand through it. I had only a few months to build a relationship with her before the baby arrived, and since she was a farm woman I had a guess at how best to do that: to share her work. That would mean something to her.

I tied back my hair and tramped upstairs to Leela's attic craft room. The large folding table was strewn with items Dodge had sold on eBay—oddly sized, often fragile knickknacks he'd collected from clean-outs of storage units the family owned. Once a year they seized the contents of any unit that was far enough behind on its rent and sold off the items one by one. In a larger community they would have held an auction for the entire lot, but here Dodge believed it more lucrative to sell things off one at a time. This year they had declared two of the twelve units abandoned, and so the craft room was cluttered with Hummel figurines, ceramic eagles, shot glasses and gaudy lamps. I'd offered to pack it all up for shipping, and I definitely had my work cut out for me.

But I didn't mind. The craft room was a tall, vaulted space, with a ceiling fan to stir the air and open windows that looked out on the front and side yards; it felt like a refuge, and all the more so when I considered the smoky air and dark rooms downstairs. The walls were painted sky-blue, and all around the room, at the height I could reach on tiptoe, hung metal barn stars painted like American flags. These stars—large, sturdy and full of dimension—Leela painted, packaged and sent along with Dodge as he made his trips to the post office, mailing them off to customers around the country who bought them online. Most bore mottoes painted on strips of wood suspended between the stars' two lowest rays—Glory Glory Hallelujah, or God Bless America, or Sweet Land of Liberty. If the customer requested, she attached a wired yellow ribbon, looped into a bow, no extra charge.

In the beginning Leela had seemed shy of me, giving me a wide berth and speaking to me only about what was necessary, but gradually she seemed to be warming to my company. After each morning of packing up eBay items, I began helping her with the craft orders by painting the mottoes across the stars she had otherwise completed. *Candy sometimes doesn't get them quite right,* she told me in a conspiratorial tone, and I had to suppress a giggle; it was no big secret that her daughter wasn't much of a speller. I was glad to have an easy way to make myself useful.

One warm afternoon I carried my box of stars downstairs and settled into the chair beside Elias, who didn't acknowledge me. He was watching his usual fodder: a game show made up of contestants trying to cross a water-based obstacle course using small foam rafts, lengths of PVC pipe and giant rubber balls, narrated in crude double entendre. I had never once seen him crack a smile at it.

"You and Cade need to have a guy's night out one day soon," I said. "I think you both could use it."

Elias gestured toward my chair as if it were a throne. "He could always come over here and watch *Wipeout* with me. Not like I'm a tough person to pin down."

"Yeah, well, that's the thing. You could both stand a little change of scenery now and then. And hey, you could do worse than to go someplace with Cade. Dodge is always saying he wants to get you to come out to the woods with them one day. Said he'd like to see you shoot."

He chuckled. "Homeboy does not want to put a gun in my hand."

"You load one every night."

"That's for security. If Dodge handed me one, I might take it as an open invitation."

"No, you wouldn't, Eli."

He cut a glance in my direction, his eyes conveying a shadow of a challenge. Smoke drifted around his face like an apparition. "Try me. You know what I did over there?"

Over there was his term for Afghanistan. He referred to it often enough, but had never said much about the specifics of his role. "You were infantry, right? You went out on patrol and stuff like that?"

"Yeah, trying to keep the roads secure. Doesn't matter whether you're at the checkpoint or on the road—where we were, there's IEDs all over the place. You might drive over 'em, or else a car comes up to the checkpoint with a suicide bomber in it, either way you're fucked. You wouldn't believe how many of us end up in little bits the size of jelly beans blown all over Afghanistan. And people like Dodge and Scooter want me to come back from that and go out and shoot beer cans while they grill burgers. If that isn't the stupidest shit on the planet, I don't know what is."

"Then you and Cade should go out somewhere. Maybe over to the quarry, right? Hang out there. Isn't that what you always used to do?"

He cast a rueful gaze on the TV and dragged on his cigarette. "Ahh, the quarry. Good times were had by all."

"They're doing another clean-out tomorrow. I'm sure they'd be glad to take you along. I think it's the last one for a while."

He sipped from a can of beer, then shook his head slowly. Round one had begun, with an overweight young man in a life vest jogging in place and shaking his arms, getting ready to tackle a pendulum swinging high above the water.

"It'd be something to do. Break the monotony."

"Spending time with Dodge isn't breaking the monotony."

"Oh, c'mon. They found some interesting stuff yesterday. It's like a treasure hunt."

At that, he snorted. I looked at him with surprise, and he said, "Grave robbing is more like it."

"What do you mean?"

"Profiting off others' misfortune is dirty business. Somebody saved that stuff for a reason." I opened my mouth to speak, and he held up his hand. "I know, I know, they're in arrears, they ought to pay their bills. But when you go and sell somebody's grandma's antiques because they lost their job and put priority on feeding their kids, I think that's dirty. Life's hard."

"Your family wouldn't have been able to feed *their* kids if people didn't pay their rent."

"Sure. Some people deserve to have their shit sold off. Some people don't care. I'm telling you what I think, is all. Just because it's fair doesn't mean it's right. There's such a thing in this world as mercy."

Dodge thumped into the room, and Elias drained his beer. Once Dodge had left, he glanced at me and said, "You know he kicked out the renters, right?"

"The ones with the broken dishwasher?"

"Yep. Gave them forty-eight hours to pack their shit and leave, and now they're gone. Completely illegal. All because he thinks Randy warned them that he likes 'em young. The truth hits you at the core."

My paintbrush was sinking into the jar of blue, untouched. "You said you didn't believe Randy said anything."

Elias waved a dismissive hand. "Dodge's looking for an excuse for a confrontation. He isn't going to get it, not from Randy. What those renters ought to do is sue his ass, but they never would. People from Randy's church aren't too big on getting the government involved. Don't think Dodge doesn't know that."

"That's terrible."

"Yes and no. They want to live that life, then this is a part of it. Maybe they'll turn the other cheek. Maybe they'll stick up for themselves, and we'll get a knock on the door one day. It's their call."

"Can't go on like this forever, though."

"You'd be surprised. Some things can go on an awful long time."

He clicked up the volume by a notch and said nothing further. I sat beside him with my paintbrush and stars, keeping company. On the television, the chunky kid raced headlong toward the climbing wall, then was knocked from his perch by a boxing glove flying out on a mechanical arm. His arms pinwheeled in the air on his way down to the water. The announcers shouted, *Ohhhhhhhh!*

"You fat fucker," Elias muttered.

Cade

The quarry was at the end of a long road barely wide enough to hold a car. When they approached it back then—Cade and Elias, Piper and whoever else could fit into Elias's converted bread-delivery van—broken chunks of asphalt rattled the tires. Now and then low-hanging oak branches brushed the windows, the leaves like aggressive hands. Then the land opened, the quarry lake came into view and Elias parked the van in the scrubby grass in the shade of the tree line. Ragged chunks of granite—some softball-sized, others large enough to stretch out on—littered the ground. A yellow knotted rope hung from a solid branch next to an outcropping of rock, high above the water.

They stripped down to their swimsuits in the shadow of the trees. Just past them lay the shimmering surface of the water, reflecting the treetops in a dark and lacy silhouette. Against it, the squealing teenagers in trunks and bikinis transformed into Indonesian shadow puppets. Treading water, slapping the surface in joyous half-drowning, then flipping like a dolphin and going under into the sudden thick silence. Cade moved through it like an eel. He loved the feel of his own physical symmetry, his resistant strength. Through some primitive sonar he sensed an edge, a wall, and he reached out and grabbed the narrow hip band of Piper's bikini bottom, tugged. Her shriek penetrated the water, and he came up laughing, already ducking the swat of her hand.

On the ledge stood Elias, brown as toast from the sun, the Hawaiian flowers on his swim trunks blotched yellow and orange. *Go, go.* He heaved his arms back and then threw himself forward onto the rope, chest and stomach jiggling, and they loved him for it. The fat-kid smash into the water was epic. When Cade jumped in, nobody cared, but Elias drew a crowd. And then Piper scrambled up the rock, her body angular, a knife edge, her hair blunt-cut and threaded with summer blond. On the rope she was an acrobat. She flipped back and around, tucked and rolled, until she cut through the water long and lean and disappeared.

Disappearing: that was what Piper did. She lived down the road but left for months at a time on mysterious trips with her family, to summer camp, to ski. Once, when they were younger, she left for a year. She was never taken for granted. Elias loved her first. But her preferences were beyond Cade's control, and Elias seemed to bear him no ill will when she singled out Cade for another kind of disappearing. Sometimes, together, they straddled the line between present and gone: on the shaded end of the quarry where a high subsurface ledge made the water shallow, there they could kiss and be ignored. But below the surface her hand worked down his trunks, and she plied him steadily, purposefully, until he came into the water in full view of every one of his friends, his brother, but of course they could not see a thing.

That summer they spent nearly all their free time with one another. Often they bought fireworks and, after building a campfire in the dirt-swept circle of the Olmsteads' shooting range, set them off above the trees. On more than one occasion Elias singed his fingers and would hold them out, black tipped and smarting, for the girls to soothe with ice from the cooler. The range, deep in the woods as it was, hid everything. They drank whatever alcohol they could steal from the back of their folks' top cabinets, then played squealing games of Duck Duck Goose, like little kids, around the fire. On one occasion, one of the other guys found a gun someone had left behind on the range. A box of ammo sat beside it, as though the owner had intended to target shoot but forgot about that particular weapon. Cade found a paper target without too many holes in it and clipped it to the pole. Then the whole group persuaded Elias, who was the best shot among them, to try to shoot out the bull's-eye. He didn't shoot out all the red in the center, but he hit it on the second shot.

Except Elias, they were all drunk on Jim Beam. Elias was heavier and could hold his liquor better. Cade got up and, jerking the sneaker from Piper's kicking foot, climbed onto the stump between the two target poles. "I am William Tell," he announced. He set the shoe on top of his head and added, "This is my apple."

"It doesn't smell like an apple," someone shouted.

"Shut up," Piper said.

"I cannot tell a lie," he said, confusing his fruit legends due to the effects of the Jim Beam, and held out his arms for balance. "My brother Eli will shoot the apple from my head and we will all be saved."

"From what?" Piper yelled.

"From the smell of your feet," answered the guy who had brought the booze.

"Drum roll, please," called Cade.

Someone thumped a rolling up-tempo against the cooler with his hands.

Cade looked at Elias, who stood, legs braced apart, at the shooter's mark. He held the gun pointed at the sky, elbow bent, at the ready. "Aim true, brother," said Cade.

Elias shook his head.

"Aw, c'mon," Cade called, dropping character. "Straight through the middle. You can do it."

"Didn't say I couldn't."

"Hit the *R*," suggested Cade. "Make it say, 'eebok.'"

Elias shook his head again.

Cade stumbled backward and fell off the stump, and they all laughed. Piper scampered over and collected her shoe. After a little while someone threw up in the bushes, and then they all went home.

There were more afternoons at the quarry lake, more nights that summer at the shooting range, although they never saw that gun again. One evening, driving home, Elias spoke up in the silence. The van was empty except for the two of them. The Eagles played low on the radio, and the fan's gentle rattle thrummed from the deep interior of the dash. Cade, barefoot, watched the clouds cast moving purple shadows against the mountains. He felt thoroughly content.

"I really wish you wouldn't do that," said Elias.

Cade looked at him. "Do what?"

"You know. With her. In the water."

Cade absorbed that thought. He exhaled through his teeth, scoffing. "I'll do anything I want with her, anywhere I want," he said. "You would, too, if you could."

Elias said nothing. Kept on driving home.

Everyone knew Elias had loved her first.

But Cade felt no remorse. Not then. Not later. *May the best man win.* And the best man always did; that was why he was the best.

And Elias said nothing because he knew this about Cade, and loved him in spite of it.

Chapter 9

JILL

Only a few days after Elias told me the renters were gone, on a Sunday morning when Candy, Eddy and Leela were off at church with the boys, Dodge pressed the rest of us into service painting and cleaning the rental house. He even managed to bully Elias into coming along, handing him a paint roller and putting him in charge of the room that, judging by the crayon scribbles on the wall, had been the province of the now-evicted children. Cade was put on carpet-cleaning duty, while Scooter and I were sent to the porch to paint trim and lattice. I didn't mind; the air outside was light and clear, more like spring than midsummer, and the view of the mountains from the porch of the shabby little place was breathtaking. From the corner of my eye I watched Scooter as he painted— he was a skinny caricature of a man, with giant work boots and a barbed-wire tattoo around his biceps that appeared sized for someone much larger. His thin wire glasses would have given him a scholarly look were it not for the cigarette he clenched between his lips like a cowboy, puffing as he worked. In a different town, coming from a different family, Scooter might have been another person entirely. The people I loved most—my mother, Cade and even Dave—all took pride in standing in defiance of their families' expectations for them, and Scooter was the opposite of that. Yet something about him hinted at the raw material of a different sort of man—someone he might never become, but could be. I wondered what it was inside a person that set them on one path or the other, and if they chose it, or if it chose them.

We worked all morning. Around eleven, Dodge drove off to buy lunch, and a few minutes later Elias wandered outside for a break, obviously pleased to be free of his brother-in-law for half an hour. He walked out to the mailbox that stood at the edge of the road and leaned against it with his back to us, smoking and looking at the mountains. His shorts and sneakers were spattered with paint, and dabs of it spotted his hands and his forearms, obscuring the shapes of his tattoos. For once, he looked at ease.

"You been talking to Elias much?" Scooter asked me, low voiced. He had worked his way over to where I sat painting a section of lattice, and now hovered above me painting a support beam. I looked up at him, squinting at the light.

"Sometimes," I said. "He's not very talkative when other people are around."

Scooter nodded. "He tell you anything about how he's doing? Or what's going on?"

"What do you mean, 'what's going on'?"

"In his head, I mean. If he's getting any better." I didn't reply right away, and Scooter tossed his cigarette into a bush with a grudging sigh. "I took him to the doctor a while back. He hasn't said anything to me about whether any of it is working."

"I didn't realize you were that close with him."

"I'm not, exactly. He used to give me rides to the bus stop all the time, when I was in middle school. It was almost two miles. He'd see me walking up the side of the road and pick me up in the van. Practically every day." He gestured toward the road, pointing north. "My grandparents live in the senior care home now, but we used to live down that way, near the turnoff. They raised me."

"That was sweet."

"Yeah, it was really cool of him. Especially in the winter. I never forgot it. After he got back from the Middle East, when he saw I was working for Dodge, he asked me who my tattoo guy was, so I took him out to the shop and introduced them. This was maybe three weeks after he got back. The next week he wanted me to take him there again, and the one after that. I felt weird about it, but I didn't really want to say no. I mean, I can't tell this guy what to do, even though the tattoo-a-week program feels strange to me. That and the fact he wouldn't drive his own car."

I set down the brush and shielded my eyes with my hand so I could watch him as he spoke. "So what did you do?"

"I just tried to get him talking. Asked him what the new tattoos stood for, whether he was frustrated with living in Frasier, stuff like that. I kept telling him I owed him for all those rides and I'd take him anywhere if he ever needed me to drive. And then one week he asked if I'd mind driving him to the doctor. It was a huge relief for him to ask. I was starting to get real worried he'd do something bad to himself. He had that vibe, you know? Like right before a kid sweeps his hand across the Chutes and Ladders board and knocks all the pieces on the floor. Spring-tight."

I looked through the lattice at Elias. He seemed unaware that we were talking about him, and even on his best days he had a habit of cocking his left ear toward whoever was speaking. He looked watchful, eyeing the road, but if he was anxious or tense I couldn't tell. Whatever was going on with him lived inside his mind, and there it stayed.

"If you could maybe talk to him," said Scooter. "Try to

suss out if he's doing any better. He never wants to go anyplace anymore, so I hardly talk to him. Dodge thinks he just
needs to work, and Cade—well, I don't really know Cade.
And I wouldn't feel right going to him and telling him how
to look after his own brother."

"I'll see what I can do. He seems to trust me."

Scooter nodded and gazed toward him. "Thanks. Probably he's fine now, but I gotta ask. There aren't enough decent
people out there as it is."

"Too true," I said, and he shot me a halfhearted smile before taking up his trim brush again and retreating into his
deferential silence.

The chickens hadn't come out as they were supposed to.
Once the chicks in the porch incubator hatched from their
neat little circle of eggs, Candy was indignant. The Vogels,
who had traded them to Candy, had told her they were Rhode
Island Whites—standard white chickens with a red comb, the
kind from cartoons and Corn Flakes boxes. But almost as soon
as they had hatched, it was clear that some were not like the
others. They came out with a fine ash-colored sheen across
their backs, and at six weeks some were heather-gray all over,
while others—the males—kept the color on their necks and
tail feathers even as their backs and bodies whitened. They
were Brahmas, I could see, and Candy was annoyed. Despite
their beauty, she felt swindled. She had been promised Rhode
Island Whites, same as all the others.

As soon as they reached the age where they could be sexed,
she wasted no time in separating the male chicks from the fe-
males. On the morning when I saw her in the poultry yard
rounding them up into a tall-sided box, I felt sorry, but I knew
she would care nothing for the pleas of a city girl who thought

the roosters too beautiful to kill. They weren't needed, and so they had to die.

On that morning, when the back door slammed, Candy came in from the yard carrying a cardboard box with half a dozen chicks in it. She set it on the table and got started filling up her mop bucket with water from the sink. Her youngest boy, John, peered over the edge of the box and made clucking noises. He reached in and scooped up one of the chicks, holding it to his chest. I looked from the boys to the bucket and then at Candy. I asked, "You want me to take the kids outside?"

"No, no. They're farm kids. They know how it is."

John was holding the little white chick right up to his face, almost beak to mouth, and making kissing noises at it. Even for a farm kid, I thought he was a little young to watch his mother drown small animals. I knew Candy's choice wasn't unusual, but it wasn't strictly necessary either, especially when we were dealing with only a few. I decided to try my one idea that might resound with her.

"You don't have to kill them," I told her. "You can castrate them and raise them for meat."

She chuckled and turned off the water. "If I knew how to castrate a rooster, maybe."

"I do."

She stopped in the middle of moving the bucket closer to the table and looked at me distrustfully. I continued, "I learned to do it at the camp I worked at. It's not difficult. Then you can raise them alongside the hens and they don't compete with the rooster. They're called capons. The meat's really good. It's expensive, too. A gourmet thing."

She laughed again. "Gourmet chickens."

"I can do it in no time."

Matthew, who had been circling the table as though looking forward to the spectacle of his mother drowning the chicks, looked from me to Candy. "Well, okay," Candy said. "If you kill them by accident, who cares."

The conditions weren't ideal, but I gathered up the supplies I needed and got started. I tried to shoo the boys away, yet they were all rapt at the idea I was going to cut into living birds, and Candy did nothing to discourage them. I was fairly adept at the process. Halfway through, Dodge walked in. He took one look at the bloody towels on the kitchen table, the stunned chicks and his gawking sons, and asked, "Now, what in the blue hell is Jill doing?"

"She's deballing the chicks," offered Candy.

Dodge leaned over my shoulder, close enough that I could smell him. He was the only man who lived here, not counting Cade, who didn't smoke. Dodge smelled of sweat and light cologne and the leather seats of his SUV. The overall effect was a weird combination of manual labor and vanity.

"I didn't even know you could do that," he said.

I explained to him about capons and how they would behave more or less like the hens, and he nodded with approval. He looked at his boys and asked, "What do you kids think of that?"

"It's cool," said Mark. "There's blood."

"Blood and balls," said Matthew. "Except they don't look like balls. More like little bitty lima beans."

Dodge shook his head. "I'll be damned. Lived on a farm all my life and I never seen that. Not once."

I smiled, in spite of the gory scene in front of me. I wasn't *afraid* of Dodge, exactly, but nobody wants to get on the wrong side of someone who wants to go to war over a broken dishwasher. Elias stayed quiet now during Dodge's dinnertime rants, but sometimes he would pause in midmeal, his fork forgotten in his hand, and look at Dodge with a steady, unblinking glare that, in a more magical land than this one, would have reduced his brother-in-law to ash.

At dinner that night, Dodge regaled the family with the story of the day's rooster surgery. "Now, there's a woman who can do everything," Dodge declared, and I glanced up uneasily at the unexpected praise. "Can use hand tools and power tools, knows how to split a log and neuter a rooster, and can still cook a decent meal. She's got you outclassed and outgunned, Cade. I bet she can shoot worth a damn, too."

"If I'm in the right mood," I conceded. Dave always claimed there were bears in the woods around Southridge and had made sure every member of his staff could hit a target with both handgun and rifle. I had never seen a bear or any sign of one around the place, but I was pretty confident I could shoot one if it ever proved true.

"See, she's one up on you," Dodge told Cade.

"I know how to shoot a gun," Cade argued. "Dad taught me when I was Matthew's age. I just don't want to hang out in the woods with you and your compadres, shooting up beer cans."

"You should come along one day anyhow. Spend some time outdoors. You're lookin' pretty pale these days. Getting that desk-jockey look about you."

Cade scowled at Dodge across the table, and I knew he had hit a nerve. Back in Maryland Cade had run at least five miles every morning, but here the farm chores left no time for that before work, and in the evenings he was too tired. He couldn't go tanning here either, and made self-conscious remarks to me about his increasingly wintry complexion. A few days before, I'd caught him looking at himself in the bathroom mirror, peeling down the waistband of his boxers to check for contrast, then rubbing his stomach as if to reassure himself it was still flat.

"Jill, you can come out, too," Dodge said magnanimously, in a tone that made me suspect I was the first female he had ever invited into the boys' club. "The two of you can compete. Make whatever bets amongst yourselves, like a good husband and wife."

Candy giggled. Cade looked at me and rolled his eyes. In spite of my distaste for Dodge, the idea sounded like fun. It would be something to do at least, an interesting break from the monotony of our day-to-day routine. It might be good for Cade, too, to get his head back into the kinds of things people did up here instead of all the things he felt he was missing. I smiled and said, "Sure, I'm up for it. Why not?"

He narrowed his eyes at me before focusing down on his plate, stabbing at his potatoes as if it was personal.

"He needs to just relax and take a breather," said Leela, wrapping a barn star in bubble wrap and slipping it into a shipping box. "Dodge has some funny ideas about things, and goodness knows that shouldn't be any shock to Cade. And he's always got to get all worked up anyhow."

We were standing in Leela's attic workroom, me with the roll of bubble wrap and a pair of scissors, Leela with the priority mail packing labels and boxes and a pen. On the desk the laptop was open to the eBay screen so Leela could get addresses, and indeed it did have a slip of electrical tape over the webcam's camera lens. I cut off another length of wrap and rolled it around a star as she addressed the label in her spidery handwriting.

"You wouldn't think they would dislike each other so much," she went on, her voice a little distracted, "Dodge and Cade, two of a kind as they are. Both of them are men of strong opinions. Both have the stubborn idea that anyone who doesn't agree with them must just be flat stupid. And their opinions aren't so different, but I suppose it's enough that each thinks the other is a dummy. Of course, Cade's only twenty-one. He's got lots of growing left to do. Dodge, I don't know what his excuse is."

"Maybe that he never expanded his horizons."

"Maybe. It does a body good to get out and see the world. Elias sure is better off for it. Did you see what he brought me back?"

I shook my head, trying to make sense of her idea that Elias was better off. She patted a piece of tape onto the box, then walked over to a cabinet and pulled out a small rolled rug. Letting it unfurl to the ground with a flourish, she said, "It's a real Muslim prayer mat. They kneel down on it and do that thing, bowing toward Mecca and all that business."

"That's pretty neat."

She smiled. The delicate metal hooks of her bridgework showed. "Bet you it's the only one in Frasier. I thought it was a bathroom rug when he first gave it to me. Wonder what the Muslims would think of *that,* if I'd put it out for people to drip-dry on."

I grinned back, and she rolled up the mat and put it away. "Cade seems excited about the baby coming," she said. "He's going to be a good daddy. You don't know, Jill, what a lucky thing that is to see a man who cares about all that. Eddy, God bless him, he hardly paid our kids any mind until they were walking and talking. Cade'll be different, I can tell."

I nodded, thinking back to the night before, when Cade had rested his palm against one side of my belly and his ear against the other as if trying to pull the baby closer. *Sometimes I just wish I could hear its heartbeat,* he had said. *I know it's there and all, but sometimes I just want to hear it.* I told him I wished I knew whether it was a girl or a boy, and he'd shaken his head. *I wouldn't want to find out, even if I could. The anticipation is better than knowing.*

"I was always terrified of being a single mom," I admitted. "I didn't want to have to struggle like my mother did. And if I couldn't do as good a job, I knew I'd never be able to forgive myself."

Her smile was tight as she peeled a label and smoothed it onto a finished package. "But that's all mothering is. Whatever your own parents got wrong, you absolutely will not do, and whatever they got right, you'd darned well better get right, as well. That's the disadvantage to those of us who had good mothers. We spend our whole lives trying to match them and can't ever quite shake the feeling that we're falling short."

My voice was teasing. "Maybe it's better to have a bad mother, then. Gives you higher self-esteem in the long run."

"Maybe it's better to know that your children love you regardless," she said. "They don't care how your mother was. They just want their own."

I thought about that. During my first summer at Southridge, all the kids in the Alateen group had gathered around the campfire and told stories about their families. In the typical manner of girls my age I'd started to butt heads with my mother; her mere presence embarrassed me, her nagging about my room and my grades threw me into explosive tantrums and I looked forward to the chance to vent about my life at home. But I never got the chance, because the stories that made their way around the circle alarmed me into silence— tales of parents in denial, parents who couldn't stay sober, or flew into rages, or passed out on the floor in puddles of their own bodily fluids. I understood then why my mother had sent me there, and my heart ached for the kids whose lives had become the collateral damage of their parents' addictions. But it was true—they loved them even so. Admiration and love, I learned, are two entirely separate things.

"You're going to be a good mother," Leela said. "I can tell you're a strong person. You've got the mama lion inside you. You haven't seen her yet, but she's there."

Her praise warmed me. If she had been my own mother I would have rested my cheek against her arm as she worked beside me; but I knew she was Cade's, not mine. "Hopefully nothing will happen to bring her out anytime soon," I replied.

She laughed. "Oh, Jill," she said, and her voice was rueful. "Peace never lasts long enough. That's what's true."

Chapter 10

LEELA

Sometimes during the day Candy will have that TV on, showing those court programs where people air out their dirty business in front of a judge. I don't like to hear that stuff. Some things other folks just aren't meant to know. Why I would ever care who's the father of that baby or whether someone's husband had a lady friend on the side, I can't even imagine. You tell me what you want me to think about your circumstances, and I'll take you at your word. It's none of my business to go guessing at what you've got under the carpet.

My mother and father, they taught me not to stick my nose in the affairs of others, and thanks to that I never felt as though it was a lie to let folks go on believing their presumptions about me or my family. Even my own children never knew I had a husband before Eddy. It seems like a different person's life now, that for four long years I had a different name and lived in a different state, sleeping in a bed every night with a man who was not Eddy. Of course it was so long ago now it doesn't matter one bit. Children assume so many things that it isn't hard to make an old life go away. At one point in each child's life, when they realize what's possible, they'll look you in the eye and ask, "Did you ever have a boyfriend besides

Daddy?" And you shake your head no, and just like that it's gone. None of them ever asks again.

I'd been so lonely, living in Maine. The house Harold promised me had turned out to be a trailer, with secondhand curtains that didn't hang right. These days I wouldn't care too much, but a new bride is picky about those things and she has a right to be. She's making up a home. As it was, all the women my own age, there at our church, had babies already. When they met up it was for coffee and to let the babies play, so they never thought to include me. And then finally I was expecting, and for a while they included me some. I was embarrassed about my house, so I didn't invite people over too much. That was a mistake, I suppose. It made me look inhospitable, but I didn't realize that in time. I should have just bought some real curtains.

But then, before I got any chance to get to know anyone real well or fix the place up any better, the baby—my daughter Eve—was gone. After that I went back home to my mother and father, because I couldn't take living among those women and their babies, nor with a man who thought we could replace Eve like buying a new dog. I couldn't just come back to that trailer, pack up the baby things and get to work decorating as if a new rug and some wallpaper would ever cheer the place up. It was like that life had gone sour in the refrigerator, and there was no choice but to throw it out.

For years I hardly thought about all that. I'd cast it off, and it went away like it was supposed to. But then, once Candy got so concerned with her religion, started passing comments about true marriage and God's plan for families, I felt the sour taste of my departure in my mouth again. I knew that if she really knew me—my own daughter—she would think I was a sinful person. I wanted to say to her, life isn't so simple as all that. If ever there was someone who understands how hard it is some days to be a family, it's the Lord. I kept quiet in spite of Candy's ramblings, and I knew that in this life I'd poured all I had into the measure, and let the Lord fill up the rest of it with grace. That's the main thing with her—she'll spout off with her God-talk about rules and regulations and forget everything about the mercy. The whole blood-flow system she's got all mapped out, with no heart at the center.

But even though I didn't need for my children to know about my first husband, or about their lost sister, having lived inside that loneliness for so long made me anxious for my children to have better than that. Candy I wasn't so concerned about, because she had that hardness in her that, for all its worrisome qualities, made me sure no man would break her. And as Cade came into his own, I stopped fretting over that for him, too. He had a big heart, but if he had a falling-out with a friend or got a snub from a girl, he knew how to close himself off against further hurts from that person. He wasn't like me, where I'd keep bleeding out the feelings like a wound that just won't clot. Neither Cade nor Candy was the type who would ever just pack their things and abandon a life, the way I had. But when I left Harold, I hadn't done it because it was the easy thing. It was just the only way I knew to stop the pain.

Elias, though. I confess that when he was little, his father and I worried that he was a soft boy. He was a sulker, the kind to go off kicking the dust to sit under a tree all alone, licking his wounds. Mostly people didn't try to fight with him, because he was big and if he *did* get a notion to fight back, he'd have that person flat on the ground in one strike. But he couldn't shrug things off, and he never did those peacock-y things boys do to get girls' attention. For a while we worried whether he liked girls at all. His father made some noise

about that, and as much as I shushed him I admit I fretted
over it myself.

And then, not too long before he graduated high school,
he started bringing home Piper Larsen from down the road.
She came from a funny family—her mother and father were
archaeologists or something of that nature, and they'd go
away for months at a time to dig up old pottery and bones.
The house she lived in belonged to her aunt and uncle, who
farmed that land, and I suppose her folks found it convenient
as their home base in between trips to wherever they ran off
to. Well, it's hard for me to trust people like that, but I was
just so pleased to see Eli interested in a girl at all. He always
had some excuse for bringing her around—that she wanted
to see our new baby chicks, say, or to try the rhubarb pie I'd
made because she'd never had rhubarb, or wanted to stay for
supper because it was leftover night at her place. It was cute
to see him trying to court her that way, and she was a pretty
thing, too, like a foal: all bones, big eyes. She had pale, pale
hair. My mother had always told me to make a wish when I
saw a white horse, and every time I saw Piper walk in that
door with Eli, I felt like making a wish on her. I couldn't
have picked a better choice for him, either. She was smart,
grounded, good-hearted. Even though her people were from
away, her family didn't seem so bad, just a little odd. I couldn't
help but picture where it all might lead. And I confess, too,
that since I'd set aside my imaginings about that sweet daughter who would sit beside me quilting, I started inventing new
ones for how I would teach Piper to make a piecrust, or listen to her tell me some things about the strange places she'd
visited. I hoped she would like me.

One night we had her over for supper and she helped me
fix up the biscuits and a salad. Oh, she had the nicest manners, that girl, and a good, open way about her for learning

new things. I showed her how you peel strips down the cucumber, then slice it lengthwise and scoop out the seeds with a spoon before you slice it in smaller pieces, and then you get pretty little half-moon slices with no seeds to bother with. She acted like I'd taught her something really special. She had a manner of touching your shoulder or arm in this affectionate way, like family almost. I was so fond of that girl, I couldn't hardly contain it.

We all sat down to supper, and I'd made sure to put in the extra chair next to Elias, so he and Piper could sit right beside one another. Eddy and I sit at opposite ends of the table, so I made sure to put Piper's seat closest to mine, because now and then Eddy gets off on some tirade during the meal and I didn't want to risk the girl getting spooked.

Elias pulled out her chair for her, all gentlemanly. It made me smile. In all that time I'd never once seen him touch her, but that was just how he was. Elias wasn't a hugger, but none of us were, really, except for Cade. Cade was fifteen then and I had to watch him like a hawk when he brought a girl over. First floor *only,* that was my rule. They could watch television or play a game or what have you, but there would be no going upstairs or, heaven help us, down cellar. At least upstairs I could have overheard if he had anything funny going on, but that cellar was so solid you could hold a party down there and, so long as you had the door shut, nobody would ever hear a thing. Plus Eddy'd stored up enough wool surplus blankets and army cots to tide us over through a nuclear blast, which was about how angry I'd be if I found out my son had gotten some town girl in trouble.

At first supper went fine, but then I got to noticing a strange feeling around my legs, like there was a mouse beneath the table or something. I felt my heart flutter a little—embarrassment was why—and real quietly I slid my foot forward to see if I could stir it up, to confirm whether we had some kind of rodent running around. And what do you know but my calf knocked right into Cade's. At first I thought, now why in the world is his leg all sticking out under the table like that, and then I looked from him to Piper and I figured it out. He was stroking on her leg with his own, right across from his own brother. I didn't have any idea right then if she was offended by that and just too polite to say anything, but the way things worked out later, I suppose she must not have minded.

After supper, as soon as Elias went to drive Piper home, I came up to Cade in his bedroom and asked him, "Now, what was the meaning of all that nonsense?"

He knew what I was talking about. Cade was never one to play dumb. "She's not his girlfriend or anything. We're both friends with her."

"Let him be, Cade." He was sitting cross-legged on his bed with a schoolbook open on his lap, that big old American flag pinned to the wall behind him, and looking at me with his defiant eyes. I remember thinking, *Son, Eli's never going to have all that you do. Leave this town for him and you can have the rest of the world. Do him that one kindness.*

"It's a free country," Cade said. "Women have equal rights here. It isn't like he won her at a farm auction."

"Just give him a chance. That's all I'm saying to you. Things aren't as easy to him as they are to you."

He laughed. "Piper isn't easy," he said, which wasn't what I meant and he knew it. Then he said, "Whatever," which was the thing he always said to put his foot down on a conversation. It could make me so mad when he said that, because you knew nothing was ever a *whatever* to Cade, no matter what he said. It just meant he didn't want to listen to your part anymore.

It wasn't too long after that when Piper started coming

around with Cade instead. Elias didn't react one way or another when he saw them, but I knew that way of being, too.
On Eve's birthday every year, nobody had ever looked at me
and furrowed their brow and sensed something was wrong,
or asked if I was feeling poorly. So I knew Eli might be dying
inside and never show a soul. Or he might be all right and
here I was just pushing my own feelings onto one of my children, like the kind of mother who can't see the break between
herself and her young ones, or admit that they might be better and stronger than she is. I just couldn't tell which it was.

If I had it to do over again, I would have flat-out told Cade
he wasn't welcome to bring that girl home. For Eli's sake I
would turn on her the way Eddy turned on Randy, cast her
out with all that prejudice, and take my punishment from God
for my cruelty when it was time. I would never have made
Eli look at all that, if I'd known for certain. But I didn't, and
the fact was, I didn't want to lose my chance to have her as
a daughter-in-law someday. I think that was in the back of
my mind, that I just couldn't quite let that girl go. Whatever
Cade's guilt is in everything that happened, it's my guilt, too.
It's a sadness and a shame, the things loneliness can do to you.

Chapter 11

JILL

That night, after my morning with Leela in the craft room, I lay awake feeling the baby tumble and kick inside me, jabbing its little feet against my diaphragm muscle in a slow jog. From downstairs I heard the clicks of a magazine being pushed into a gun, then the slide pulling back. Elias was up and settling into his routine. Sometimes when I heard him downstairs I'd think about how lonely I'd felt in the dark living room of Stan's apartment, long after Cade had come and gone from his daily visit to me, lying there listening to the gentle clatter of the vertical blinds above the air vent, their movement letting in shards of harsh light from the courtyard lamps. If Stan was asleep in the bedroom alone, somehow the loneliness seemed to echo. I felt right only when he'd come out and sit beside me, channel surfing with the volume down low as I drifted off to sleep, resting his big heavy hand on my shoulder. It wasn't Stan that I wanted, not especially; it was just the presence of another human being. The touch of one.

Go down and say hello, I thought. *Make an excuse. You promised Scooter.* I slipped out of bed and crept down the stairs, letting the boards creak once I reached the bottom two. I was 98 percent sure Elias wouldn't do anything hasty with that gun, but that 2 percent gave me pause. He glanced over and nodded as I reached the landing.

I murmured a hello and got to work searching through the cupboards. I'd decided to make us a batch of Fudgies—a camp treat made up mostly of rolled oats, which we'd kept around in Olmstead-sized quantities, along with peanut butter and the scraps of chocolate from s'mores-making. In the kitchen I found no chocolate chips, but stuffed in the back of a cabinet was a stash of miniature Hershey bars; they might be Candy's private hoard, but if so, I could claim ignorance later. As I moved ingredients to the kitchen island I caught the sound of a familiar voice from the television: *Just be breezy, y'know?* Abruptly I laughed, and Elias whipped his head around to look at me.

"Sorry," I said. "I like Kendra. She's funny."

"You about startled the piss out of me."

"I'm sorry. I didn't mean to." I abandoned the ingredients and came around his chair to watch the segment. "This is the one where she gets into the fight with the girl in the chow hall. I've seen it, like, twelve times."

"I was just channel surfing. I hate this show."

"Oh, really? That's too bad. I love it. My mom and I used to watch it together all the time."

"Your mom?" He shot a quick glance at me. "Never even heard you mention your mom before. I figured you didn't get along."

I shook my head. "She died four years ago this October. I try not to bring her up too much. People get uncomfortable hearing stories about people who are gone."

"That they do." He set down the remote, as if changing his mind about switching to a better channel. "How'd she die?"

"In a plane crash."

"A plane crash? *Shit.*" He was quiet for a minute as I watched the show, leaning on one arm against his chair. "That's why you moved in with us instead of your own people, then, huh?"

"Yeah. I don't have 'people.' Her parents were alcoholics. I'm sure they died years ago, but anyway, I haven't seen them since I was four."

"Shit," he said again.

I shuffled back into the kitchen and began peeling the waxed paper from a stick of butter. "We all have our traumas."

"That we do. But most people's don't involve plane crashes. You get some kind of extra credit for that one. How old were you, then?"

"Eighteen. Too old to be an orphan, so no extra credit for me." I set down my work for a moment and leaned toward him in a conspiratorial way, my hands resting on the edge of the kitchen island. "You want to hear the weird thing? I saw the clip on the TV at school while I was on my way to class—the wreckage of these two planes, they'd flown into each other—and I didn't give it a second thought. I looked *right at it*. You'd think you'd get some kind of gut feeling when you see something like that, right? Or you'd have some sense of dread or that uneasy feeling that something isn't right. But I got none of that. I just went about my business, clueless the entire day. That really screwed me up for a while."

"Wasn't your fault. So you're not a psychic, so what."

"I know, but since then I overcompensate a little. I see things like that on the news and I can't shake the feeling that it must be personal until I can prove otherwise. One time, there was this avalanche near Deep Creek Lake, which is near the camp where I worked, and these two hikers died. I couldn't get in touch with my friend Dave, the camp leader, so I drove all the way out there to check on him. Three and a half hours each way."

He replied with a low, sympathetic laugh. "Are you serious?"

I nodded. "He thought I was nuts. But I was in college, and it was a Friday, so I had the time to spare. It turned out to be a good excuse to see him."

Elias fell silent again, but there was an expectant feeling within the quiet, as if he wanted to keep the conversation going yet didn't know what to say. I measured oats and peanut butter into a bowl, added in the butter softened in the microwave. After a minute or two he said, "You know it's midnight?"

"Yeah, I know. I'm hungry. I've been eating like it's going out of style."

"You don't show it. It's all baby."

"I hope so." I watched as he cracked open another can of beer with one hand and took a sip from it. "What's the shield tattoo for?"

"It's my unit patch."

"Were you pretty close with those guys?"

"Of course. You can't not be."

"You ever talk to them these days?"

He didn't reply. The TV flickered with the scene in the chow hall. I said, "You know, you could probably meet people like that at the VFW, if you miss spending time with them."

His voice was scornful. "I know that, Jill."

"Sorry." I dropped Fudgie mix by the spoonful onto a piece of waxed paper and slid the tray into the fridge. "My mom was a big advocate of group support like that. She was an AA sponsor."

"That means she was an alcoholic, right?"

"One who didn't drink anymore. She'd done her step work." I nodded toward the beer can on the side table. "She would tell you not to mix that with Prozac."

His laugh came out as a single note—a bark of surprise. "Guess you were the one who hung the bag on my door, then."

"It's no big deal. I was on it for a while myself."

"I just started it a couple months ago. Scooter picks it up, since I don't drive anymore, and he won't say anything to Dodge. If Dodge found out he'd start razzing me about it, and that'd work my nerves, and it wouldn't end so well."

"I get that. But mixing alcohol with antidepressants won't end so well, either."

"Eh, who cares. I'm okay so far. And I'm already a shitbag, so just put it on my tab."

"Why do you say you're a shitbag? Nobody thinks that about you."

He took another drink of his beer. "That's the term. It's an army thing. People who can't hack it, can't pull their weight. I wasn't feeling so hot by the halfway point of my last tour, but no way in hell I was going to come out of there labeled a shitbag. It's funny, though—over there, I could make it work. I could push through it. Back here, not so much."

"How come?"

"Because I'm supposed to *relax*. There, it's normal to be on edge 24/7. You hear a sudden noise, you can aim a rifle at it. You're *supposed* to be suspicious of everyone you don't know. Try any of that over here. You just can't get used to it." He broke his focus on the TV and met my eyes, his gaze frank and clear. "You know why I had to stop driving? Fucking *bicyclists*. They come pedaling up alongside my Jeep out of nowhere and I'm ready to kill somebody. And other stuff, too. Motorcycles, road work. The noise. It's like chaos-noise. It doesn't match up with what my brain tells me it is."

I nodded.

He exhaled smoke away from me. "So I stopped driving.

Fine. I put my ass in this seat and stay here. And then Candy's kids come up behind me and try to scare me, or they jump up and down and say the same thing over and over again, or they shriek—you know, the stuff kids do. And I feel like I'm going to beat the living shit out of them."

"Me, too."

He laughed a little. "No, but I really *am* going to beat the living shit out of them. I can feel my muscles pumping up for it. One time, John—the littlest one—came by and knocked over my beer. And I grabbed him by the shoulder and smacked him across the side of the head with my hand. He went running back to Candy crying, 'Uncle Elias hit me, he hit me.' She spanked him and told him to leave me alone." He picked up the beer can again. "That's when I got my ass to a doctor."

"Did they tell you it was post-traumatic stress disorder?"

"Nope. Combat stress."

I frowned. "That's not what it sounds like to me. My mom knew some Vietnam vets who—"

"Well, I don't know about Vietnam. But here, now, you pretty much have to point your weapon at your commanding officer for them to decide it's PTSD. The Prozac helps, though. I don't feel like hitting the kids anymore. The downside is, I don't feel *anything*." He shrugged and dropped his cigarette into his beer can. "No panic, no excitement. I'm like a ghost. But at least I'm not killing anyone."

"Maybe they can change your medication. Or your dosage."

"Maybe. That would require going back to the doctor." He stretched his leg out and brought it back, gingerly, as though testing it for pain. "I just want everyone to leave me alone. You're okay, though. If you think I'm a shitbag, it's no skin off my nose, because I know what you went and did." He nodded at my belly.

I laughed. "Hey, now. Your mom has declared me Cade's true wife."

"Yeah. You're his biblical wife because he knows you in the biblical sense. Sorry to break it to you, but if that's true, then your boyfriend's a polygamist."

"At college they just called him a man-whore."

He shot me half a grin. "Fair enough. Say, can you pass me that heating pad over there?"

"Sure." I handed it to him. "What hurts?"

"My leg and my shoulders. They always hurt."

I moved behind the chair and let my hands rest on his shoulders. His muscles tightened, but he didn't flinch, and so I began rubbing them slowly, rhythmically, working my way across his neck and upper back. He let his head drop forward, and so I worked my thumbs along his spine and down to massage his shoulder blades. He groaned, and I smiled.

"Is that better?" I asked.

"Oh, yes. Damn, that's way better."

He sat upright again and sighed. Softly I rubbed his temples, the sides of his jaw, his scalp. I scratched his forehead along his hairline, and stroked my fingers back through his buzz-cut hair. He tipped his head upward, eyes closed, smiling.

"Fudgies are probably ready," I told him. "You want some?"

Without opening his eyes, he asked, "What the hell's a Fudgie?"

"Chocolate and peanut butter comfort food."

"Fuck, yeah."

I laughed and patted him on the shoulders. "I hope you like them. I'm not the most awesome in the kitchen."

"I have faith," he said.

The next morning I awoke, groggy and exhausted from interrupted sleep, to the sound of bacon sizzling in the skillet downstairs. The smell of it wafted into the room, and I was out of bed and dressed in no time. Pregnancy had made me a serious carnivore. In my ordinary life my staples were bread and fruit, but lately I found myself snacking on strips of leftover flank steak, cold from the fridge. I hoped it was helping build the baby's brain.

Scooter was already in the kitchen, dressed in a white crew-neck undershirt, a Patriots ball cap and a pair of Levi's thirty-inch-waist extra-longs. He was chugging chocolate milk from a Coca-Cola glass. The beagles licked bacon grease from the floor around Candy's feet. I could hear Cade washing up in the bathroom, and Dodge sat at the table with his arms folded in front of him, looking more alert than anyone ought to be at 6:00 a.m. He met my eye but offered no greeting. I wondered if Scooter could sense the tension.

"Mornin', Jill," said Scooter. He had a milk mustache.

"You guys doing a clean-out today?"

"Nope. The AC's not cooling the place down like it ought to. Got to try to fix it."

"It's at eighty-five in there right now," said Dodge.

Candy raised the skillet high and carried it to the kitchen island, sending the beagles scrambling. Dodge asked, "You think Elias knows anything about HVAC work?"

Cade walked in from the hallway. "He doesn't."

"That sucks. Would make the sumbitch good for something this morning."

"Easy," said Cade.

"I *am* being easy." Dodge moved his hands to the sides to make room for the plate Candy was setting in front of him, casting a meaningful glance at me before finishing his thoughts. "Boy needs a drill sergeant. Get him to come out and *work*. Or one of those trainers like on TV, make him run on the treadmill till his ass falls off."

"He could have run circles around you a year ago," Cade told him.

"A year ago. Now all he runs circles around is that island right there. Relay races with a box of Ho-Hos." He dug into his eggs, and I glanced at Scooter, who looked away. "We're gonna get him *straight*."

Cade kissed me goodbye at the door, but I followed him out to the car anyway. The Saturn wasn't looking its best these days. The white paint above its wheel wells showed splatters of mud, and the backseat was a mess of crumpled sandwich wrappers and soda cups, unwashed laundry and boxes from the copy center filled with résumés. As Cade climbed in I said, "You've got to get Dodge to stop saying that crap about Elias. He's a bully, your brother-in-law."

"Don't make a melodrama out of it. It's just Dodge being Dodge. He's trying to get Elias working to keep his mind busy, so he means well. I'll give him *that* much credit."

I scowled. Glancing quickly at the house, I said in a low voice, "I think you ought to talk Elias into going back in to get his meds adjusted and to get some counseling. I can't believe they'd just hand him a prescription and let him go home without any other treatment. He's twenty-four years old and all he does is sit there all day. I don't like Dodge trash-talking him, but he needs to get *up,* at least."

Cade's expression had grown peevish. He was in a hurry to leave, and I knew it. "Give the guy a break. He spent three years fighting the Taliban. It's okay for him to sit down and watch TV for a while. You and Dodge both need to realize that."

"If you think he's acting like that because he just wants to *relax,* you're off in la-la land."

He cocked an eyebrow at me. "What I think," he began, and his voice was cold, "is that people ought to back off and let the guy *be*. Elias has always been a couch potato. Just give him some space, and stop playing into it by lavishing attention all over him for being lazy. Don't think he doesn't *love* that shit. He knows how to play it. Girls love it when he whips out his Eeyore impression." He turned the key in the ignition and slammed the door. The window scrolled down, and he added, "I'll try to talk him into coming with us when we do the gun-club thing with Dodge, okay? Get him to come out and socialize a little. Even with those idiots, it would be an improvement."

"Sure, you can try, but he won't go."

"You forget where my skill set lies. If I can get college students out to the polls, you'd better be damn sure I can get my brother to walk into the backyard."

"If you say so."

"I say so." He leaned a little out the window, and I kissed him on the mouth. Then he reversed out of the driveway and spun out onto the road, disappearing past the trees in a blue-gray haze of burning oil.

Another week passed before the gun club met again, and Dodge managed to hassle Cade into coming along. Cade was already in a bad mood. The ten résumés he had sent to various offices in D.C. two weeks before had resulted in no phone calls at all, and what was worse, the news had gotten back to him that Drew Fielder had taken a permanent position on Mark Bylina's staff. The previous night Cade had been downright morose. He had drunk an entire six-pack of beer in front of the TV, slept for two hours and then was up half the night cursing at the clothes dryer he had suddenly decided to repair. He had looked like death when he woke up at four-thirty in the morning, but that afternoon he returned from work in the chipper mood I recognized from his days of

campaign volunteering. It was one-dimensional and decep-
tively shallow, but he could muscle through a bad day with a
smile on his face as long as he kept moving.

As Dodge packed his cooler and ammo into the truck, Cade
approached Elias and nudged his shoulder. "Hey," he said
good-naturedly. "C'mon. Don't make me do this on my own."

Elias looked at his brother over his shoulder, barely raising
an eyebrow. "I don't think so."

"Just this once. I don't want it to just be me and those dip-
shits."

"Jill's going."

"Yeah, but they'll leave her alone. I'm the one they'll be
giving all the shit to." He barraged the back of Elias's shoulder with pokes of his index fingers. "*C'mon.* Back me up."

Elias sighed heavily and stood up, and Cade clapped him
on the back. As he headed out the door behind Cade, I felt
impressed with Cade's work. Maybe he was right about his
brother after all; maybe Elias just needed more encourage-
ment.

Dodge drove his truck up the slim dirt road that snaked into
the woods, but the rest of us walked. As I followed Cade and
Elias up the trail I saw the trees clear into an opening that revealed the closest thing to a party I had seen since my arrival.
An ancient boom box blasted an '80s heavy-metal sound track;
the fresh piney air carried the smoke from the grill, filling
the clearing with the scent of hamburgers. On a series of tree
stumps surrounding an ashy fire pit, the men of the club sat
drinking beer from bottles shiny with condensation. As they
drank they chatted and cleaned their guns with loving care.

"Your old hangout," Dodge announced to Cade and Elias,
climbing out of the cab of his truck. "You know you missed
it."

Elias looked over the scene before him. "Not really."

Dodge chucked the package of paper targets onto a fallen log. Cade reached into a cooler and retrieved two beers, offering one to Elias, who held up his hand to decline it. Even Candy had come along; she stood at a card table removing sheets of plastic wrap from bowls of pasta and potato salad, scooping a spoon down into each one. Scooter looked expectant, standing on the sidelines squinting at us through his little glasses, arms crossed over his chest, displaying the oversize tattoo winding around his biceps. Beside him squatted Matthew, balancing his small weight against the butt of his rifle pressed against the ground. He had received the gun for his eighth birthday, Candy had told me, and he often shot birds and squirrels with it in the woods behind the house. According to Candy he did this only with Dodge's supervision, but that seemed to be a flexible rule. He wore it slung on his back at every opportunity, regardless of whether his father was home.

The other men moved easily around the space, but Elias stood more or less where Cade had left him, holding the uncomfortable posture of a new kid approaching the high school cafeteria. I got him a cheeseburger from the grill and carried it over, offering it to him on a paper plate with a flourish and a friendly smile.

"Keep it for now," he said. He looked around the perimeter of the clearing, eyes steady. "Know what, I don't think this was a great idea. Why don't you walk me back to the house."

"No, you don't," called Dodge. "It's a beautiful day and we're about to get started. Leave now and you'll miss all the fun."

Somebody pulled back the slide on a handgun, and at the click of it Elias shook his head. "No. I don't like this."

"I'll walk him back," I called over to Dodge. "It's not a problem."

Cade planted a foot against the fallen log beside him.

"Come over here and sit down, Eli. I'll hang out with you until my turn comes up."

Elias looked at Cade's earnest face, then at the log, and brushed past me to where his brother stood. He eased himself down beside Cade, but at the metallic clunk of a magazine being locked into a rifle his arms twitched, and I watched as he pushed a hand back across his hair to make the sudden jerk of his muscles look natural.

Dodge was standing at one of the wooden posts wedged into the dirt, unwrapping the pack of targets. I sidled up to him, turning my back to Elias and Cade. "Hey, I think Elias ought to go home," I said. "I think he's too nervous for this."

He picked up his staple gun and glanced at me as he fastened a target against a post. "I think he can be the judge of his own self. How about you stick to cutting the balls off the poultry and let Elias keep his for the time being."

I breathed in deeply through my nose, not eager to create a scene that would make it obvious to Elias that I had been talking about him. As I retreated toward the grill, Dodge barked, "Jill. Cade. You two get to go first."

He handed a .22 to me and another to Cade, then rattled off a list of rules that appeared to be for Matthew's benefit. When I racked my rifle, Cade snickered and shook his head. "I'm so screwed," he said. "You're probably a hundred times better than me at this."

"Probably."

He grinned, and I focused on the target and sighted in. Candy laughed and said, "A pregnant lady shooting a rifle. If that isn't the doggone funniest thing I've ever seen."

Dodge gave the signal, and we both fired. When I glanced over at Elias his shoulders had relaxed, and he watched us with more engagement in his eyes than I had ever seen when he sat in front of the television. *This turned out to be a good idea after all*, I thought, lining up my second shot. Even Cade looked happy, and with only a few shots left to go, he said in a cheerful voice, "You are indeed kicking my ass."

"I try."

"I had no idea they'd trained you so well at militia camp."

"It's not militia camp, it's homesteading camp."

"Or so Dave claims. Looks to me like—"

A loud cry from Matthew snapped my attention to the sidelines. As I lowered the rifle I saw the boy hurrying toward his father with his arms extended, a black plastic zip tie tight around his wrists. "Now, what in the hell did you do to yourself?" demanded Dodge.

"I was just playing. I pulled it with my mouth."

"Well, that's not a good way to play, is it?"

He whipped out his buck knife from its case on his belt and set to work trying to convince his son that he wouldn't cut off his hand at the wrist in the process of removing the tie. I rolled my eyes and unloaded my rifle. Beside me, Cade grinned and did the same. "Game over," he said, and only then did I focus past the tussle between Matthew and Dodge to see Elias doubled over behind them. Candy was rubbing his back, her long hair falling forward as she leaned down to talk to him.

"Hey, I think Elias is sick," I said.

I hung back while Cade rushed over. Even from a distance I could hear Elias's gasping, stilted breathing, see him nodding rapidly at the soft things his siblings said to him. Sweat trickled down his temples in slow, broad droplets. "Matthew's fine," Cade was assuring him. "It wasn't even all that tight."

"I know. I know."

"So don't worry about it. Just breathe."

Candy fluttered around him for a few more minutes, and finally Elias rose to stand, taking unsteady steps toward the path as Cade draped his arm around his brother's shoulders. I watched them until they vanished beyond the trees.

"All right, enough of that drama," shouted Dodge. He snapped the buck knife closed and patted his son on the back, sending him running back to the food table. "Who's up next?"

"Apparently he just doesn't like the sight of zip ties," said Cade. We were speeding down the road toward Liberty Gorge, a spontaneous excursion Cade had announced as soon as I walked in the door from the gun-club get-together. I understood exactly why: tonight he couldn't abide another family dinner, sitting across the table from Dodge as he offered a postgame analysis of the gathering. I'd offered to go with him, gladly.

"That's a little strange," I said.

"Sounded like he had to use them on people before, so it really bugged him to see his nephew bound up like that. I only ever saw him like that once before, over Christmas. We drove into town to see a movie, and once we got there he saw a piece of trash in the parking lot and freaked out. We ended up going back to the car and driving home."

"Over a piece of *trash?*"

He flipped his visor down against the lowering sun. "Yeah, well, apparently over there people hide IEDs under pieces of trash along the roadways. And he'd just gotten back, so I understood he was still in soldier mode and all that."

"Yeah, but I don't think freaking out at trash is 'soldier mode.'"

"Maybe not. I dunno. Makes more sense now why he never wants to leave the house, though. I figured he was over all that." We approached a turnoff marked by a mailbox—a simple dirt path that led through a field. "You know what, let's go to the quarry. I've been wanting to show it to you anyway."

I braced myself for the sharp turn. "So are you going to talk to him about going back to the doctor now?"

"Yeah, I suppose so. That's got to be embarrassing, what happened to him today. If it was me, I wouldn't want to be going around like that." He parked on the scrubby grass beneath a tree. "This is it. Our old parking spot and everything. Hasn't changed a bit, except there's no water. Which was kind of the whole point."

I looked out over the jagged expanse of rock. It was a long way down. Cade left his sunglasses in the car, and as we approached the gaping, empty space, he stopped and peered up at the sky, squinting. High cirrus clouds marked the clear and solid blue, and the sunlight shone down through the trees as sharply as if thrown. He said, "I haven't been back here since they drained it. It's disorienting."

"Sounds kind of like it was an old swimming hole, like in *Tom Sawyer*."

"Yeah, and in the winter you could skate on it. We used to come out here all the time—winter, summer, anytime except when it was raining. Every year at Christmastime all the kids who'd gone away to school would have a reunion up here. Me and Elias and a lot of the other guys, we'd play hockey here once it was good and frozen. You see that spot?" He gestured toward the center of the empty space. "That was the no-go zone. It didn't freeze hard enough over there, so if your puck went that way you were just screwed. One winter we lost so many pucks, we took to making them out of firewood dipped in beeswax just so they wouldn't be worth anything. It didn't work very well. We thought the beeswax would make them slicker, but it knocked off real fast once we started banging on them with the sticks."

"So why'd they drain it?"

"Somebody drowned. One of the Vogels' daughters from the next farm over. It was during the winter."

I looked out over the canyon the rock formed, at all its precipitous ledges and sharp, loose boulders. Filled with water it must have been idyllic, but beneath the surface, dangerous as hell. "That's awful."

He kicked a few rocks over the edge. "Yeah. She was a friend of Candy's. She'd been at one of the reunion games but nobody else knew her real well, so we were all just...talking to each other and not much to her, I guess. She must have been skating like everybody else, and at some point she went through the ice and nobody noticed. I didn't hear anything about all that until later. Me and Elias had already left, so we missed the whole thing."

"Candy must have been devastated."

"She was in shock about it, I guess. Candy's funny about stuff like that. It's hard to say her faith comforts her. It's more like she uses it to work out the logic of why everything happens. If something good happens she goes on about how it's a reward for obedience or an answer to a prayer, and if things go wrong she says it's a test of faith or a punishment. It's almost like karma with her. I think it drives my mom nuts." He sat down on a smooth stretch of rock. "This is the old sunbathing stone. In August, anytime you came here, there'd be a bunch of girls in their swimsuits stretched out here trying to get a tan."

I moved to sit down beside him, and he reached for my arm to ease my way down. "I can't stand it when people try to explain random tragedies. You wouldn't believe how many people have said to me that small planes are dangerous and my mom never should have been in one in the first place. As if I'm going to say, 'Oh, I feel much better about losing her now that you've explained why it was her own fault.'"

"Yeah, you and Candy are going to be the best of friends."

I laughed and turned onto my back, resting my head in Cade's lap. The sky was a more appealing sight than the jagged gap of the quarry; the high clouds moved through it slowly, their trailing edges thin as contrails. Cade stroked my hair back from my forehead in an idle way, and said, "I wish you could see this place the way it was before. I feel like there's this part of me I can't even show you because it doesn't exist anymore."

"It's pretty much the same, though, right? It's just the water that's missing."

"It's just the people that're missing," he said.

I turned sideways so I could look out at what he was seeing: the ledges where his friends had once stood, the knotted yellow rope hanging from a tree, the scrubby and pebble-strewn grass that must have been the site of a hundred tailgate parties. I wondered if Elias missed it the same way. The Olmstead home seemed riddled with broken connections—to their extended family, to their way to gather as a community and even to each other, for the atmosphere of the house felt heavy with brooding thoughts that nobody talked about. It was no wonder Cade hated coming home. I had never imagined, in all my time growing up with just my mother, how hard it might be to live in a family. From the outside it had looked like the easiest and most natural thing.

Maybe it'll be different after the baby gets here, I thought. The common work of caring for a newborn might bind the family together once again; a christening might even be an opportunity to reach out to Randy's family and put a stop to the enmity from Dodge's side. It might even give Elias a sense of renewal and purpose, and a distraction from all he had going on in his head. These are the thoughts I had, heady and optimistic, as Cade tried to make sense of the lost quarry lake.

After all, my mother had never hesitated to share her burning testimony that it's never too late to start over. My mother, however, was not an Olmstead. It was a lesson I would learn, again and again, in the months ahead.

Chapter 12

JILL

The first blow came with the letter from the university, telling Cade that he had been cut from the work-study program due to a missed filing deadline. He started out bewildered, then grew angrier and angrier as he paced the back porch with his phone against his ear, pleading with the people in Financial Aid. I sat in the chair beside Elias and folded the freshly washed hand-me-down baby clothes slowly into a basket, lying low but listening in. At last he came in and slapped the phone down on the table in disgust.

"April 25," he barked. "That was the deadline. You know what I had going on April 25?"

"I can't remember."

He jabbed the air with his index finger, gesturing toward my belly. "Junior there. School during the day, work in the afternoon, Stan's in the evening, five hours of sleep. Bylina's office any spare minute I got. You puking your guts out until they had to stick an IV in you. Like I'm supposed to remember financial aid paperwork in the middle of *that*."

"I don't know what to tell you, Cade."

"Nothing *to* tell me. We're not going—I can't—" He couldn't bring himself to say it. He stopped in midpace and glared at the wall for a long moment, then kicked a box of

Leela's stars across the floor with the bottom of his boot. It skidded to the fireplace and hit the tools, knocking the poker to the floor with a clatter. "Goddamn it to hell."

"Well, I guess you file again and hope for the spring."

He ignored that. "All these months, since even before we left, I thought we were going back for the fall. They let me register and everything. And all this time, there's been no hope."

"That sucks, bro," said Elias in a monotone. "I'd transfer you my GI Bill credit if I could, but they don't let you."

Cade set his hands on his hips and looked at the basket of clothes at my feet. "I'll get a job down there, is what I'll do. Just have to try harder. Because I am *not* fucking staying here. Not for thirty seconds longer than necessary."

"Can't blame you," said Elias. But Cade was already heading out the back door, throwing it open so brusquely that the walls trembled. I rose from the chair, tugging my shirt down to cover my cumbersome belly, and made my way outside, taking my time to let him cool off a little. I found Cade leaning against the shed, smoking a cigarette and glaring into the middle distance. He didn't so much as glance at me as I approached, yet once I had set my own back against the shed in a little gesture of solidarity, he started speaking.

"We gotta get out of here, Jill," he said. "I never would have moved back up here if I'd thought it would cut my ties this badly. I thought it was strategic, you know? Saving money so that in the fall everything would go smooth. And it's not working out like that at all."

"I'm sorry about the work-study." I turned my head to see him in profile: still so handsome, still the golden boy, but with a restless, hollow look around his eyes that hadn't been there a few months before. "Isn't there any way around it?"

"No." He flicked the cigarette away half-smoked, as if he

was embarrassed to be caught by me. "I'm so pissed. *So* pissed. Everybody and everything I worked for is frickin' leaving me behind. That's supposed to be my life's work back there. It's not here, that's for sure. I was *never* meant to be here. You know how I didn't want to bring you here on Christmas? You see why now? It's like an echo chamber of craziness here, and they're taking me out with them."

He slid his back down the side of the shed until he sat crouched in the scrubby grass, his knees pulled up tight against him. "That baby," he said. "It'll all be worth it, right? This'll all make sense once it gets here."

"That's what everybody says," I agreed. To make him smile, I added, "Candy says so. This one and the next twenty after it."

He rewarded me with a grin that looked genuine, if a little tired. "Soon as you get better from having the baby, we're gone. I promise I'll have a job by then. And I know I need to focus on getting that appointment for Elias, too. It's just so weird that they built him up into this big brave guy and now he flips out at the drop of a hat."

I knew Cade meant well, but it wasn't Eli's bouts of anxiety that had me so worried. It ate at me, this sense that Elias was the type of person who would sit there calmly smoking and watching TV until the day Dodge made one comment too many; he would finish off the pack of cigarettes, or let the movie run to the credits, then walk over to the Powell house and shoot everyone in their sleep. Cade might think I was being fantastical and morbid, but things like that happened. They happened all the time. When I thought about my mother's story about the almond trees—how she had found herself in just the right place at just the right time to see the light shine down on a truth that would change our lives— I couldn't help but believe there was a purpose to our being here. Maybe we were the only two people in the world who could contain a disaster, here in this place, here at this time.

"He needs to go see a regular doctor, too," Cade added. "Go in and get the come-to-Jesus talk about his weight. Because, seriously, it can't be good for you to get that fat, that fast. I'd be glad to take him out running so he can look a little better, but I can't until he backs off eating like it's a state fair contest."

I grinned—not at the insult, but at how unsurprising it was for Cade to think Elias would be happier if he made himself more attractive. I said, "I'll coax him into going if you make him the appointment."

"Deal. I'll make it tomorrow." He sighed and rubbed the heels of his hands against his eyes. "Right after I send out thirty more résumés."

The next day, as promised, Cade called the VA hospital and made an appointment for Elias on the next available date, which wasn't for two weeks. As soon as it was booked, I started looking for a natural opportunity to bring it up with Elias. The first one came on an evening when Dodge had left for the range with his gun-club buddies and the rest of the family, except for a dozing Eddy, were at midweek church. Cade made himself scarce when he saw me hovering around Elias. He knew how to take a hint.

As soon as I sat down beside him, Elias switched the channel to *Lockup: Raleigh*. "Kendra's probation hearing is coming up," he said. "Hearing the boyfriend's victim impact statement ought to be interesting."

"I thought you hated this show."

"It's grown on me. Makes my own family seem normal."

"Yeah, I know what you mean. I always figured that's why my mom liked it, too."

On the screen Kendra was speaking emphatically to the unseen interviewer, explaining why she felt she was ready to be released. *I've been minding all my p's and q's,* she was saying. *If something's poppin', I stay out of it. I'm done with that kind of life.*

"It's sad, you know?" said Elias. "Five years she's burned up in that place. Her kid barely knows her. Looks like about the only skill she's got is surviving prison. Not something you can transfer to civilian life."

"She seems pretty resourceful. She'll probably find a way."

He watched in silence, exhaling a slow trail of smoke. The heating pad rested against his thigh, its little red indicator light aglow. "You know, all that time I was over there, I figured I'd come home and get married pretty quick. I'd have some kids, buy a house maybe down in Liberty Gorge. It seemed easy, like a board game. Get off the plane, roll the die again. Figure out how many spaces you get to move."

"You've only been back for, like, seven months, though. There's plenty of time for all that. Who'd you expect to marry?"

"No particular person. I figured it would just sort of happen, the way everything else does. The natural progression. But I guess everything looks easier from a distance. Unless you're Cade." He rolled his shoulders and rested his head back against the chair, gazing up at the ceiling. "If you're Cade, you can just skate straight on through all of it."

"You know that's not true. Cade and I wouldn't be here if it was."

"It's a minor glitch. It's not the first one he's had. He flounces and cries and thinks the world's going to end, and after you shower him with pity he ends up walking out of it without a bruise. It's the way he is. Sometimes I envy it so bad I want to knock him out. I could live a long time on just a taste of that kind of life."

The television showed a clip from a boisterous *Lockup* segment coming up after the commercial, but Elias's gaze seemed far away. "Cade wants things to be better for you, too," I said. "He made you an appointment at the VA hospital on Wednesday. Just a follow-up."

He shot the quickest of glances at me. His eyes flashed surprise. "I'm not going."

"Why not? It's no big deal. I'll drive. You'll get some better meds, I'll get a chance to get out of Frasier for a few hours—we both win. I'll buy you lunch. Get you something other than Candy's grilled cheese."

"No chance."

"It's not until next Wednesday. Sleep on it. We'll see how you feel once it rolls around."

"I'm going to feel like shit once it rolls around," he replied, his voice getting tighter. "Same as every day. Dodge had the nerve to say he's taking me to work at the U-Store-It next week so I can stop 'freeloading.' Asshole. *He's* gonna talk about freeloading, living in a glorified shed behind his in-laws' place. Guy needs to be knocked out."

"Just ignore him. Everybody else does."

Elias grunted a reply. I stood up and rubbed his tense shoulders, and after a few moments he released a deep, slow breath.

"Your muscles cramp up when you stay in one position for too long," I told him. "I think that's why your back hurts so much. Maybe we could go for a walk once a day, huh? Just up and down the street a little. Loosen you up."

"With you pregnant out to here."

"Ah, so what. I could use the exercise, too. I'm sick of not being able to run." I kneaded his muscles, first one side and then the other, working my hands in tandem. He rolled his neck, then took a final drag of his cigarette and crushed it in the ashtray. The sallow light from the lamp beside him illuminated only one side of his face, leaving the other in shadow. The memory of him lying on his back on Stan's futon came back to me just then. He had seemed like a stone wall, nothing but muscles and uniform and an elaborate set of fighting reflexes ready to go. Now it seemed as though all of that had pulled inward, like blood retreating toward the heart when one is in danger of freezing. But pride still guarded the perimeter of his mind from invaders like me.

"We'll go," I affirmed, letting his silence be his answer. "You and me."

"Sure." He let his head drop back against the easy chair. "You always smell like Starbursts."

I laughed and scratched gently along his hairline, and he cocked his head like a dog getting its ears scratched. Candy had cut his hair in the kitchen the other day, buzzing him with the clippers after she'd trimmed each of her boys. The white of his scalp showed through clearly beneath his dark brown hair. He smiled, and I rested my hands on his shoulders. Eyes closed, he crossed his arms over his chest and laid his big hands over mine. "You kill me, Jill," he said. "You really do."

I headed upstairs to my bedroom and curled up around Cade, who had propped himself up on the pillows to work on his laptop. He draped his arm lazily across my back and continued to peck at the keyboard with his left hand.

"How'd it go?" he asked.

"Okay. He said he'd go."

"That's good. You must be persuasive."

I burrowed my head beneath his arm and breathed out a sigh against his chest. Guilt gnawed deep in my belly, and I wasn't entirely sure why. I thought back to the evenings I had spent with Stan, and how even as his arms had comforted me, I knew where the boundaries lay—where I belonged, and with whom. I had felt so lonely then, but my kind of loneliness was nothing more than physical separation from the one I loved. It was nothing next to Elias's kind—to be broken and sick, shell-shocked, lost inside his own mind that could never quite come home.

I told myself I meant no harm by it. That I carried no intention of touching him in any way that wasn't chaste. And if he liked it a little more than he should, then perhaps he would remember that he was a twenty-four-year-old man, and he would get up from his easy chair and go out in search of a woman who could offer him more. One who wasn't pregnant with his brother's child.

If it had worked even a little, then it would have been worth the world.

Instead, it didn't work at all.

The following Wednesday morning Elias climbed into the Jeep without any apparent nervousness. He said almost nothing for the long drive, taking charge of changing out the CDs at intervals, and that was all. At home he never listened to music, but on the floor behind the passenger seat he had a padded black case packed full of CDs arranged in little plastic sleeves, and his taste in music disarmed me. All of his selections were women with sweet soprano voices—Alison Krauss and Faith Hill and Kate Bush. It was a world apart from the music that blasted from the stereo at gun-club meetings. But it seemed to soothe him, and he gazed out at the scenery the whole way, chain-smoking with the window rolled down.

At the VA hospital we settled into the waiting room for a little while, and when they took him back I opened a magazine and prepared for a long wait. But within fifteen minutes he was back again, a pink form and a prescription in one hand, looking satisfied.

"That's it?" I asked.

"That's it. They're taking me off the Prozac and putting me on something else." He held up the paperwork. "I told them I just wanted something to calm me down, and didn't need all this antidepressant shit that screws with my body. So that's that."

"So what they gave you isn't an antidepressant?"

"No, it's just some sort of anti-anxiety medication. Pretty cool. It sounds a lot simpler. And they gave me better pain meds, too. You were right."

"What about counseling or support groups or anything like that?"

He shook his head. "I don't need any of that. Sit around with a bunch of other loads and talk about the past? No thanks."

I got up from the chair, accepting the hand he offered to help pull me to standing. "It's not like that, though. I'm telling you, those groups can make all the difference in the world. My mom swore by them." I glanced at the pamphlet display on the wall. "They must have *something*."

"Don't worry about it, Jill. This'll do me. Come on."

He started out the door, and I followed him. I wished Cade were here with me, able to back me up, because Cade believed as much as I did that Elias needed to reconnect with people—old friends, other soldiers, anybody who didn't live in our one little household. Elias had lived in this town all his life—surely those people were all around us, the friends he had grown up with, the women he must have loved. And yet he seemed like someone lingering just outside the doorway of a school dance, unsure how to make his entrance, or if stepping into the crowd would only amplify the loneliness inside him.

As we climbed into the Jeep he didn't say anything more, and I turned my attention to the drive. Partway back, as Alison Krauss sang "Two Highways," I cocked an ear to the harmony and realized Elias was singing along, his rough voice quiet and crooning. I reached over and patted his hand, and as if by reflex he flared his fingers the way a man would to interlace them with his lover's, before letting his hand drop against the seat once again.

Chapter 13

ELIAS

The little girl always unnerved him. She lived in the mud hut at the end of the road, a dust-caked old crapheap not fit to store a broken lawn mower, but her eyes were green. Green, like a regular person's; faceted, luminous and edged all around with deep black kohl, even though she was only seven or eight years old. A tiny whore. Elias knew it was normal, all that eyeliner, that Pashtun kids wore it all the time. Many of the men in their families, heterosexual or so they claimed, used it, too. More than three years in the country, in and out, living in the grit and smelling their sweat and eating some of the shit they called food, and he still didn't get these people. Savages all. Scrabbling to survive, living in the Stone Age. The children wore rags and threw rocks at dogs. They had their strange and vengeful God, their mothers whose hands fluttered to cover their faces with swaths of black, like caped vampires. More than anything, Elias wanted to get the fuck out of there. More than anything, he believed he had fallen through the quicksand of Pashtun country and into some sort of nightmare gnome hole where the bright upper world would never look the same again.

The green-eyed girl wore bracelets—bangles that clinked when she played—and a ratty teal skirt too short by half a foot.

Her auburn hair had a blaring reddish sheen that he would have thought was fake if he hadn't known better, too rock-and-roll to be real, but nevertheless it was hers. It was thick and longish and blunt cut above those eyes. There was a permanent crust under the girl's nose. She ran back and forth from her family's place to the market, or to her aunt's or cousins', because everybody here was related to everybody else and deep in the night on patrol it made your skin crawl to think of all those ancient people plotting against you, jabber-whispering in their strange language, and all those relatives fucking.

The problem with intel was that everybody knew things and nobody could document a single one of them. In the military there were the intel people, those whose job it was to fish for information and get it all square and pass it up to the right people, and then there were the guys on the ground, the ones in Elias's unit, who saw things and heard them but whose knowledge was met with shrugs. Little crumbs of intelligence. Piled up together, they meant something. But nobody cared what the grunts knew. They were there to protect the Afghans, not that the Afghans gave a shit.

He saw the girl every day before Wharton died. He saw her every day after. She was one of the multitudes, but among all those other raven-haired, sand-colored children he couldn't shake the sense that she was a plant. A crusty-nosed spy from his own tribe of real people, sent to report back about whether he performed with bravery and valor. He knew there was nothing too strange about her coloring. The region was like the hallway bathroom of the high school we call the Earth, where all the paper spitwads of every delinquent passing through merged to form a rippling topography born of every race, color and creed, and betraying none specifically. She wasn't the only one who looked like she could have been his own mixed-blood cousin. It was the kohl that drove the point home. *Look at my eyes,* said her face. Taunting.

The rumor—and it came at first as one of those crumbs—was that one of the hajjis, a young man who drifted between the various homes of his kinsmen, had funneled explosives to the ones who killed Wharton. Probably it was true. The guy came and went from the town as he pleased, never collecting enough bad associations to get himself arrested or his house raided, but they knew what he was up to just the same. It ate at Elias for months, knowing that this was the one sure guy on whom he could pin the death of his brother-in-arms, and still the man walked free as a bird. Finally word came that the man was suspected in another grenade attack in the next town over, and they got orders to arrest him. On that morning, as soon as the hajji had wandered from one house to another that was easier to secure, they formed a four-man stack at the door and rushed in. Elias knew this drill. He knew his part, knew the skills so well that they were not conscious thought so much as a dance between his optic nerve and the fibers of his muscles. His eyes transmitted orders across the web of his nerves like a cyborg, and in the moment of it he felt not pride, not competence, but like a most excellent machine. Evolved above his own humanity to something better, specialized exactly, humming along its own perfect code.

They, the squad, were order in the chaos. That was to be expected. The two men in the house jumped up and started yelling, and the woman screamed. A pack of kids ran out the back into the courtyard. A shot rang out, and the older man flew backward into the mud wall beside the black barrel stove, his white caftan blooming with blood, before he slid down, slumped. The woman dropped to the floor, her body lost in a black *salwar kameez* curling like a snail shell over the baby. Her jeweled shoes stuck out the other side. He aimed his gun at her.

The hajji was already zip-tied and collared. He shrieked in high-pitched pussy Pashto. The words, which Elias could understand to a certain degree, rolled through his mind interpreted but ignored. The baby wailed its haggard newborn scream, and the woman, shaking, peeked out at Elias through the hijab she had pulled across her face defensively. They were Pac-Man ghosts, these women. Eyes floating down the street, loose and disembodied, but don't be fooled, they're after you. The pissed-off baby started crying with everything it had, choking and strangling on the end of every sob, like it was pulling that last bit of sound from the bottom of its intestines before jerking down another gulp of oxygen. Elias heard the *clunk-clunk-zzzzzzzt* of her shoes falling off and somebody zip-tying her ankles. She mumbled something to Elias in pleading, miserable Pashto, but it was muffled by the hijab. He looked at her eyes and thought about those mouthless ghosts, how they ran from you one minute, turned on you the next.

Another soldier secured the woman's wrists and dragged her out to the courtyard with the hajji, leaving the baby on the carpet. A couple of the children had made it over the high mud walls around the garden, but three remained, huddling in a corner. They did not look as frightened as Elias thought they should. There was a boy of about ten and two girls, one dark, the other with her lined green eyes and crusted nose. The staff sergeant barked a few textbook phrases at the man, trying to milk him for information. From inside the house the baby's cry drifted out, but listlessly, and the situation started to feel organized and under control. The hajji would implicate himself as an insurgent, killing the man in the house would be justified and they could move forward with tracking down every last bastard responsible for Wharton's death. *I have no notion of being hanged for half treason,* a great patriot once said. The pure notes of this rang in Elias like the first chord of a song, not because he would commit treason either in half or in full, but because the army had shaped in his soul the belief in being *all in,* and in his life there would be no more half-assing. Since childhood he had fought the bugaboo of his own lethargy, that and the timidness he liked to cover up with one cocked, ironic brow—but no longer. Gone was the fat-ass kid forever getting shouldered into lockers and bleachers, who could laugh it off, who fantasized extensively about going down on the girls who struck his fancy but could not ever bridge the gap that would make it happen. Now he was the real Elias, the soldier with the M16, backed by the full faith and credit of the U.S. government and sporting abdominal muscles you could bounce a quarter off. His center of gravity was low and stable, he did not laugh it off and once he got out of this sand trap and into a place where sex was legal, he would make it happen. Oh yes.

The staff sergeant, still shouting, jabbed his rifle into the ribs of the hajji. Elias scanned the top of the wall. It all happened very fast. The boy in the corner, the kid, let out a *Braveheart* cry and rushed toward the staff sergeant, head down, arms pumping. And Elias dropped him. Just like that, he aimed and fired, and the kid fell to the ground like a duck. The woman in the hijab howled, then shrieked, stretching out her zip-tied wrists toward the boy. She flopped sideways in the dirt and began inchworming rapidly toward him, ignoring the shouts of the soldiers to *wadrega, wadrega, wadrega.* Then another shot snapped the air—that would be Kitson, who easily freaked—and the woman finally stopped as ordered, but not of her own volition.

The baby began to cry again.

Something inside Elias's head, a place apart from the instinct that saw threat in the kid's run and squeezed the trigger by reflex, began to whir like an airplane engine. Reflection was a horror. By the light of it he knew—of course he knew, it was obvious—that his shot had been unnecessary. The kid could easily have been stopped by a large adult hand or a solid kick. He was unarmed. He could have been restrained with a thin piece of plastic. The two girls huddled in the corner and he was making a grand show of being brave for them. That was all. And now the woman was dead, too. None of this was right, it was unraveling, the signals getting tangled and jammed. If you didn't have control, you had nothing. No safety. No authority. You were just a pack of fuckers shooting people for no specific reason.

The sister, she stood shouting in the corner, her eyes covered by the other girl's hands. *Manan, Manan,* she called at the boy in a sharp voice, as though she expected her brother to get back up; she must not know yet that her mother was dead. He looked at her shouting mouth, the hands cupped over her eyes like the bulging closed lids of a lizard, then behind her to the other girl. The green-eyed girl stared back at him, her pupils tight against the light, the kohl thick and unsmudged. She was a plant. She knew he was Elias from New Hampshire, slumming in the land of the savages, faking at being an American badass. The difference between cyborg and savage lies in a single shot.

It was an accident.

He could absolve himself for each he had killed as a machine of war.

He could never forgive himself for a human failure, for that was something he owned alone.

It was one of the things he shoved down, and locked away, and carried home.

Chapter 14
CADE

The first Sunday I had off, I drove down to the U-Store-It and rolled up the door on that storage unit where Elias used to lift weights. All of the customer's crap was still there, exactly how we'd left it years ago. Gradually, taking my time about it, I moved the whole weight bench and most of the weights into the Saturn. I had to go into the office and find a bolt wrench to get the bench apart. Dodge would have kicked my ass if he'd seen me making off with that customer's stuff, even if he knew the reason, so I couldn't exactly ask for help. Once I got it back to the house I had to repeat the whole process, carrying it all down to the cellar and reassembling everything. It was possible Dodge would come downstairs at some point and ask why the hell we had a weight bench, but probably he wouldn't have put together where it came from. Most people's first reaction when they see you with something new is not to ask where you stole it from. And anyway, I felt justified. If we couldn't get Elias to leave the house without having a nervous breakdown, I could at least give him something worthwhile to do at home.

While Candy and Jill were cooking supper, I coaxed Eli downstairs. It didn't take a whole lot to do it; nothing ever changes around there, so even a hint of anything different

gets those people all hot and bothered. Once he was standing at the bottom of the stairs he looked straight at the weight
bench and said, "You crazy son of a bitch."

I grinned. "Hey, everybody needs a hobby."

"You actually went and stole that guy's equipment."

"I *borrowed* it. He hasn't been back to look in what, five
years? He'll never know it's missing."

Elias walked up to it as if it was an unfamiliar dog. Touched
the weight I'd already set on the bar, ran a hand along the top
of the bench. I said, "Try it."

He sat down and slid beneath the bar, braced his hands on
it and lifted. Three times, up and down, and that wasn't any
small amount of weight, either. "Hoo-ah," I said. "That's the
spirit. Knew you had it in you."

"It's nothing. At Bagram I was lifting twice this much, sets
of ten reps, all damn day." He did two more and then let it
rest in the frame. "Guess I'm out of shape, though."

"We'll get you back into it. We're gonna get you *laid,*
buddy."

He laughed. "Never had a lot of luck with that in Frasier.
No reason to think it'll change now."

"You don't know that. Get back in shape and see what happens. Even Jill thought you were pretty hot last fall."

He'd lifted the barbell again, but shifted his head to glance
at me. "Shut up."

"I'm serious. If Jill thinks so, you know she wasn't the
only one."

He shook his head and worked through a set of five. "We'll
see about that."

"How's the new medicine working out for you?"

"I hate it."

That was not the expected answer. I said, "Huh?"

"I told Jill the old stuff made me feel like a ghost. Just numb and lethargic. I couldn't even jack off half the time." I laughed, but he shot me a reproachful look. "I'm serious. It makes it so you can't, and if you think that's funny, *you* try living like that for six months. Now I'm off that, and they gave me Xanax instead, which is supposed to just stop anxiety. Fine." He sat up on the bench and shrugged his shoulders around a little to loosen them. "I figured I'd just take it when I needed it. But it doesn't work like that. It's like I was standing in a canyon, turned around and saw a wall of water coming toward me. All the stuff I wasn't feeling while I was on the first drug, it came right at me. The happy, the sad. Loss. Anger. Wanting things." He rubbed his forearms, the way people do when they're cold. "It's too much."

"But that's good, though, right? That's the human experience."

He chuckled. "Man, fuck the human experience. Don't even give me that line. Here we are, right? The day I sat on this bench and you sat across from me and told me you'd knocked up Miss Piper, don't tell me you were all jazzed up about the human experience. You just wanted to crawl into a hole and disappear."

"Yeah. But it worked out. Everything always does."

"Didn't work out for that baby."

I had nothing to say to that. It kind of pissed me off that he said it, even. I shrugged, and when Elias stood up I slid onto the bench. The remark irritated me enough that I figured I could probably match him with the lifting. Hostility is good for things like that.

"Feelings are overrated," Elias concluded. He stood with his arms folded, his skin marked up like the margins of a high schooler's notebook. "I'm done with 'em. Wouldn't mind getting laid, though. Not fair only one of us is getting all the fun."

★ ★ ★

I briefed Jill about the whole thing the next day, once I'd more or less stopped stewing over what my brother had said. When I found her, she was reading some kind of parenting book by the small lamp in the living room. The rest of the lights were off for Candy's kids, who sat in front of the TV watching cartoons and eating Potato Pearls out of a giant metal can. They stuffed their hands down in it and scooped them out while the Looney Tunes flickered over their faces. Potato Pearls kept falling out of their hands and bouncing across the floor like plastic BBs. The beagles were on alert, chasing down every one that went astray.

Once I got her attention, Jill followed me out back and heard me out. I'd backtracked to talking about my weight-lifting idea when she interrupted me.

"I don't care where you got the bench from," she said, "but did you say he's on *Xanax?*"

"I think that's what he said, yeah."

She looked alarmed, and laughed without any humor at all. "That's not good. You definitely don't give that drug to someone with a drinking problem. It's a benzo. I wonder if they even asked him about that or if they just wrote the scrip and stuffed it in his hand before they kicked him out the door."

"Elias doesn't have a drinking problem."

"Of course he does. When have you ever seen him go to sleep on less than six beers? You don't call that a problem?"

Beats the hell out of me, I thought. I just stared at her.

"Make him another appointment," she said. "Make it for *soon.* Like, next week. This time I'll actually go back to the examining room with him. And if they try to kick me out I'll tell them they're idiots. My mom would freak if she heard this. It's one of those basic questions they should have asked automatically."

"I don't think he'll go. I think he'd rather be on nothing at all."

"That's not a good idea at all. Cade, this is getting more and more stupid. You know what I think?" I hated it when Jill said that, because she didn't actually care whether you wanted to know or not; you were going to hear it, either way. "I think I should call up Dave and see if he'll let us live down there for a couple months. You, me and Elias, I mean, once the baby gets here. He might, and you'd be closer to all your interviews."

I was shaking my head before she was even finished. "At that camp you worked at? No way."

"Why not? We've both got enough skills that we could pitch in and teach. And Dave's a great guy. He's got the space, and I'm pretty sure he'll let us all stay. We need to get Elias out of this house, away from Candy and Dodge and that damn TV. He needs a fresh start, and there's no better one than Southridge. Believe me, I know."

Any words of explanation that came to mind would only make me sound petty. I was remembering the picture I'd seen of her and Dave standing together in the woods, his arm thrown around her shoulders, both of them leaning toward each other and smiling for the camera. He was older for sure, but not by a significant margin—ten years, maybe twelve. It was the kind of age difference that would have been huge when she was fourteen or fifteen, but wouldn't be all that noteworthy now. And I'd been in the room when she called him to tell him she wouldn't be back this summer. At the end of the call she said, quiet but matter-of-fact, *I love you,* as if that was just something she always said. There had been a pause after it, and my brain filled in his voice saying *I love you, too.* No way would I take my girl and my new baby and go live next to the other guy she loved, owing him favors, letting him be my boss. Screw *that.*

"It's the most therapeutic thing," she said. Her hands were slicing the air, as if she had this whole thing specced out on a grid. "I'm telling you. Dave used to be an army ranger—well, he was almost one. Elias could relate to him, and it'd be way better than leaving him up here with Dodge and Candy."

"Not going to happen," I told her. "I've already got a plan. It'll work. You just have to have a little faith in me."

She tipped her head, and her hands went still in midair. "I've got all the faith in the world in you. But we need to act *soon* with him. Dave will help us, and sometimes you just have to accept help when it's offered. Admitting you need it isn't a weakness. It's a sign of strength."

This was something Jill did a lot. When she was talking about moving in with Stan or what my dad needed these days or anything where someone was having a hard time, she started sounding like she was running an AA meeting. I wouldn't have rolled my eyes at her, but I sure wanted to some days. So I let it go. I told her we'd figure it out once the baby got here. And I guess I just ignored the obvious, which was that if I was really a good judge of my capabilities, we wouldn't have been stuck in fucking Frasier in the first place.

Chapter 15

CANDY

The jungle-camo jacket pulled tight across her brother's back as he lay in the dirt with his eye up against the AR-15's iron sight, trying to get a bead on the paper target's red center. The scuffed bottoms of his boots faced Candy. Their father crouched beside him, rattling off instructions in a voice that had the crack of a rifle in it, so sharply did it cut the air. In response Elias squeezed the grip and the bipod in turn, as if he was milking a cow, or crushing one of the foam stress balls they gave out at the hardware store.

Pop. Pop. The second one was hesitant. *Pop.* She squinted, tightened her arms across her jacket, prayed for him. They had been here for three hours, in this clearing in the heart of the woods, long after their father's friends had packed up and gone home. It was their job to run back and forth to the house in search of additional ammo, beer, gun-cleaning equipment, bags of corn chips or whatever else their father might order. In between, Candy drew letters in the dust, quizzing Elias on his alphabet. He was only in the first grade; she was in the third. When he grew tired of that she placed acorn caps and bits of gravel in each of his palms and asked him to find the sums. It gave her a good feeling to teach him this way, a tender and grown-up feeling, and sometimes when he got an answer right she felt the urge to pull him into her arms and rock him like a baby doll. But he would never tolerate that.

It had been all right until their father called Elias over to try his hand at the AR-15—calculated, Candy could see, to show off for their friends—and Elias had missed every shot at the target. Their dad, inspired by three or four beers' worth of overconfidence, had been embarrassed by his son's incompetence, his forgetfulness about even the most basic elements of loading and handling a rifle. The failure had won Elias an hour of remedial training, and their father's frustration escalated with every missed shot.

"No," he said, incredulous. "No, no and no. Why's your hand shaking? Stop that. Just *look*. It's *red*. Just line 'em up."

Pop.

Candy winced. Their father's arm flew out at Elias, attempting to cuff him on the side of the head, but he dodged it. Quickly he made a second grab, this time for the back of Elias's jacket, which bunched up like the neck of a kitten. Without letting go, he cupped his other big hand around the back of Elias's head and, with a steady, deliberate rhythm, knocked his forehead into the leveled stump on which the rifle rested.

"What's rule one."

"Point it in a safe direction."

"What's rule two."

"Finger off the trigger."

"What's rule three."

"Know what you're shooting at."

"Then why don't you, you worthless fucking turd."

He dropped his clutch of jacket and Elias slumped against the ground. After a moment Candy skittered over, gathering up a clinking armful of empties to be sure she looked useful, and ushered Elias out of the woods. Their father ignored them, staying behind, unloading his rifle alone.

Once home, Elias clunked straight up the stairs and climbed into bed. Candy followed at half his pace. His bedroom door creaked a little on its hinges when she pushed it open, but his closed eyelids didn't flutter. He only curled into a harder ball beneath the blanket, like a potato bug showered with light. Above the blanket, the bridge of his nose and his forehead were sheeted with the pale brown grit of the clearing.

She stepped into the room and softly shut the door behind her. Without even removing her shoes, she climbed into bed behind him. She draped a hesitant hand against his shoulder; then, when he didn't move, she wrapped her arm across his chest. His solid body beneath the blanket was radiant and warm. Carefully she rested her forehead against the bristled back of his head. She could feel her own humid breath double back to her as it hit his neck. His heartbeat against her wrist seemed to stoke the furnace of his body, pushing out heat and more heat, unrelenting and as constant as a star. The regret she felt for him, enormous though it was, had no good word, no solid shape. It was only a reaching out, a formless but abject remorse. She would stay with him until he awoke. Only through her steadfastness would he know the depth of her loyalty, her alignment with him.

In the cocoon of her brother's warmth, she fell asleep.

She was awakened by a steel grip at the back of her dress, pulling its collar tight against her throat, jerking her puppet-like from the bed. She knew it was her father, and so she gritted her teeth and held down the impulse to scream. He was shouting, *You leave him alone, you don't coddle him, he doesn't need you.* Her shin scraped the edge of the bed, but then she was on her feet, stumbling backward, tugging the lace of her collar away from her neck. Elias's eyes were wide open, but he hadn't moved.

"You get down there and you help your mother with the dishes," her father shouted.

"He was just asleep," she said, her voice low and shaking, pleading in its tones for calm. "Already asleep."

His large rough hand hustled her out the door. Downstairs in the kitchen she could hear his ragged shouting, his voice coming through the ceiling like sound through water, all vowels. She pictured the earnest effort on her brother's face earlier as she drew letters in the dust: *A. O. E for Eli.* As she floated the plates in the hot water beneath a tower of brittle suds, she remembered how snug his warmth had been beneath the woven blanket, how her arm across his chest made her feel like she could lash them together like the logs of a raft, keeping them adrift until it was over.

Chapter 16

LEELA

Things between me and Candy weren't always so strained. There was a range of time—between when she was ten and thirteen years old, say—that I thought she might turn out like a regular daughter anyway. She grew real interested in homemaking arts around that age, wanting me to teach her sewing and how to make peach pies and such. It felt a little like a game, but I went along with it. For a while she had a hutch of rabbits in the backyard, white ones, and the babies came out so tiny and sweet you couldn't help but love them like they were kittens. But then Eddy said they weren't worth keeping unless we used them for food, and then once a week or so Candy'd go out back with Eddy's .22 pistol and shoot a few for supper. I've lived on a farm all my life, and still I couldn't stand the sight of her skinning those things on the counter. They were the same little creatures she'd been loving on just the day before. I couldn't abide it, so they had to go.

Back then we still got along fine with Randy, and we all spent time together often. Randy's wife, Lucia, she was in my kitchen three or four days a week, and we traded and lent and borrowed things like our two houses were really one, just broke in half and dropped ten miles apart. She had her two little girls then and they tagged along everywhere with her, bobbing along with their pigtails and their dresses made from the same fabric as hers. I had to work not to envy her. Candy was getting ready to turn twelve, and I was feeling the loss of her childhood. Lucia's daughters were just toddlers then and I kept thinking she still had all those years ahead with them, all that potential for happy memories, and here she was pregnant with the next one, too. But this is just exactly why the Lord tells us not to covet things, not once but twice. Because envy will eat at your soul if you let it, and it'll take you to a place inside yourself where you'll have the things of this world at whatever cost. So I tried to push it all down deep, because the truth is when I tried to give it up to the Lord, it seemed like even He didn't want it.

One afternoon, when Lucia was sitting at my kitchen table drinking herb tea as we watched Cade chase her little girls around in the backyard, I let it slip a little bit. I said, "Even though he's almost seven years old, sometimes I think about having one more. Don't know if I'm ready to say goodbye to those baby days just yet."

And she said, "I wouldn't with Eddy."

Well, I just stared at her then. There she sat with her hand on her mama belly, with all her long hair swept back just so, that mug of lemony tea in her other hand. She was watching her girls, and looked so much at peace. And yet that statement had just come matter-of-factly right out of her mouth. I said, "I beg your pardon."

She shrugged her shoulders and kept watching her girls a minute. Then she turned her eyes on me, and I steeled myself inside, because I knew Lucia was one to say what she was thinking when she looked like that. She said, "If Eddy were my kids' father, the way he's been acting, I wouldn't want to bear another one of his. I'd just say no thank you. Because you know what, Leela—and don't you look at me that way, because I'm telling you the truth. The Lord commands us to raise them up in righteousness. And there's no point in bringing them down from heaven in the first place if that's a covenant you can't keep."

I said, "I think you ought to be leaving now."

"Oh, it's no reflection on you," she said. "But something's gone dark inside that man and you know it. It seems like he's always grinding on the edge of that temper like a blade. You didn't do anything to deserve that, and I'll tell you what, neither did Elias. Randy said next time he sees his brother pin that boy against the wall, it's going to be the last time."

I stood up, and once I did, she pulled herself up, too. "Well, I guess I'll fetch my girls," she said.

After that I didn't say one more word to her. I didn't have the kind of words inside me that could talk about those kind of feelings. I'm not a violent person in any way, but as soon as she walked out the door I felt like kicking it and slamming on it with both fists. All I had inside me was a scream, and it seemed to fill me up like a tongue of flame. I was made of rage. I don't think I really understood until then why we need redemption. I knew why we need strength from the Lord, sure, and his help in carrying our burdens. But it wasn't until right then that I could understand how even a good-hearted person, a God-fearing person, could break every commandment in her heart, shatter them all like a mirror falling off a wall.

I never told Eddy what she said. He saw I had a cold shoulder for Lucia after that, but he chalked it up to women's bickering. It was a few months later that I found out I was expecting again, and I took that news with joy, even as a small part of me guarded itself a little. I could feel that baby's spirit hovering around me, and I knew who she was. It was different from with Candy. I remembered this spirit from the first time, with Eve, like when a good friend walks up behind you and without even looking you know who's standing there. It was a welcoming feeling, as if inside my heart I was saying, *Oh, hello there.*

You know, I remember, when I was a child, how some mornings my mother would pull up the shade as she was waking me for chores, and I'd turn and see the light so bright that I had turn back to face the wall. And other times, when it was pig-slaughtering season, I'd watch them string up the hog, but once they slashed it open I'd grimace and look at my father instead. And this was one of those things. When I woke up one morning and found my sheet thick with blood, my heart couldn't bear to look upon it. Instead I just pictured Lucia, sitting there filled up with her son and all her sanctimony, telling me why I didn't deserve to bring down another soul from heaven, or to give a second chance to the one I'd lost the first time. Why my family wasn't good enough for Eve.

A lot of women might pat my hand over that, and say, oh, Leela, those are the thoughts of a grieving mother. You'll be forgiven of all that anger. But if you want to know the truth of it, I don't want that forgiveness so much as I want an answer to my question. If the Lord wants to grant us our righteous desires, then I want to know why he kept taking her back from me. Because you can't fault a woman for the man she married. God knows we go in with the best of intentions. I think Lucia was wrong about that, and if she wasn't, well, the Lord and I have some things we need to work over. I can take on the burdens of my children's failings, but not those of my man. It's too much to ask, and I don't say that too often.

Chapter 17

JILL

My due date was three weeks away. I could hardly eat a thing anymore, with my stomach crowded out by the baby; also, I got winded easily, and my bladder had been shoved aside to make room for somebody's head. I got up two or three times every night to pee, and that might not have been so bad except that the August heat—tolerable during the day, this being New Hampshire—seemed to settle over our bedroom at night. This made falling back to sleep an arduous task. We slept with our door closed, for privacy, and our windows open, for circulation, but it did little good.

And so, after using the bathroom one night, I trekked down the stairs to sleep on the sofa, where the air was cooler and Cade's warm body would not be beside me. As I arranged the pillows I noticed an unusual sight over in the addition: Elias was awake, sitting in his old chair just the way he used to. I walked over to where he sat and said, "Hey. You all right?"

He grunted a yes and didn't look away from the television.

"Haven't seen you up at night in a long time."

"No." He exhaled a cloud of smoke and glanced at me. "I didn't take my meds today."

"Why not?"

"Because." He seemed to toy with leaving that as his only

answer, then spoke again. "I've been taking more than I'm supposed to."

"Uh-oh."

"Yeah." He wouldn't meet my eyes. "I'm an idiot. When my leg starts to hurt I always pile on the Tylenol, you know— like, 'kill it with fire,' and it takes the edge off in no time. That doesn't work so great with Xanax. And then you run low, and guess what? You got two weeks before you're allowed to refill." He sighed deeply and rubbed the bridge of his nose between his thumb and forefinger. "I ought to know better."

My heart ached for him, but I knew he would be ashamed for me to make a show of it. I nodded. "I'll make you another appointment, okay? I'll see what I can do to get a sooner one this time. They must have *some* way to fast-track them."

A dullness descended over his gaze. "No. I don't need people making special exceptions for me like I'm a friggin' invalid. I'll work it out. I'll probably take one in an hour or two so I can get some sleep. Right now I'm just trying to remind my body who's boss."

I hesitated, but then reached out and stroked his forehead. It was beaded with sweat. "I'm sorry, Elias," I said.

"Fuck, don't be sorry for me. Jesus, Jill. You know that's the last thing I want to hear anybody say." He laid his head back against the chair and allowed me to stroke the sweat back from his forehead, massage his scalp with my fingertips. "This sucks," he said. "I wish I'd stayed on the other stuff."

"I'll take you back to the doctor. They'll straighten it out."

"No. I'm starting to feel like a goddamn science fair project. Forget that. I'm just gonna get myself off this stuff and go back to what I know. It's not worth it."

"There's got to be something that'll work better than what you had before."

"I don't even care. I can live with that. I just don't want to be like this."

I rubbed his shoulders reassuringly, but when he didn't lean forward as he normally did, I ran my hands down to his arms and kneaded the muscles there. "I love it when you do that," he said. Then he laughed a little and said, "I totally fucking hate it."

My hands froze in place, then retreated. "I'm sorry."

"No, don't stop. *God.*"

I began again, but hesitantly, feeling the sudden rangy energy his body was putting forth. He tolerated it for a few moments, then threw my hands off with a flail of his arms that was almost violent.

I took two steps back. He rose from the chair and walked around it to the refrigerator, retrieving a beer from the produce drawer. As he cracked it open and drank, I watched him from a distance. He wore a T-shirt that was large even for him, shorts that hit below his knees and, despite the fact that it was the middle of the night, a pair of battered running shoes. Elias was never without shoes. He slept in his sneakers. Now, for the first time since I had moved in, he looked as though he might need them to escape the house.

"I'm sorry," I said again, my timing awkward, my voice small. "You can be hard to read, Eli."

"I know it." He sounded calm and ordinary. The refrigerator door closed, and the kitchen went dark again. "You didn't do anything wrong. I'm just bugged out about the medicine."

"We'll take care of that next week, okay? Or as soon as we can get you in to the doctor, anyway."

He leaned back against the kitchen island. "I'll figure it out. Are you headed back to bed?"

"Sort of. I came down to sleep on the sofa. It's too hot up there. Right now I'm so tired I'm dizzy."

He set down his beer and held out his arms. It was the first time he had ever done that. I walked into the hug, and despite the complication of my giant belly, he found a way to pull me close with his arms around my shoulders. The bulk of him was too much for my arms to encircle, but I did the best I could. When he buried his face in my hair, his bristly crew cut scratched my cheek.

"It's good you're here, Jill," he said.

I nodded, but I felt so exhausted and light-headed I couldn't really reply. Unsteadily in the dark, I made my way over to the sofa and curled up on my side beneath the lightest afghan. In the cool and the white noise I fell asleep quickly. And then—I don't know quite how much later—I was vaguely aware of Elias's shadow passing over me, leaning in. Somewhere in the core of my mind I recognized the weight of his steps against the floor, the scent of his body. But that was all, until I vaguely heard the vibrato of someone yelling in the distance, over and over, and I could not tell whether it was Cade or Elias because the voice carried the pure raspy note of the Olmstead men, the common song of all of them, the one my son would sing someday.

Chapter 18

CADE

The screaming woke me from a dead sleep. By reflex I clutched for Jill, but her side of the bed was empty. I scrambled over the bed to the stairs, barefoot and shirtless. The voice was my brother's. From the landing I could see Elias's silhouette: broad back, thuglike neck, arms out just slightly at his sides as if he had tried to react but got frozen in place. Over his shoulder I could make out Jill's face as she rested on the sofa, sleeping peacefully through his raw, haggard screams.

I rushed down the steps and started toward Elias. Only then did I see that the lower half of Jill's body—my boxer shorts that she'd slept in, her legs entangled in the afghan—was soaked in blood. It streaked her legs to the knee and seeped into the bottom edge of her T-shirt.

"Jesus Christ," I shouted. I shoved Elias aside and tried to shake Jill awake, calling her name, but she wouldn't wake up. Faintly, she breathed. I yelled for Dodge, but of course he was in his own house, too far away to hear me. Elias's screaming kept on in a gravel monotone, an alarm that wouldn't goddamn quit. I looked at him and shouted, "What did you do to her?"

Elias just kept on yelling.

My mom had appeared at the top of the stairs, clutching at the neck of her nightgown. "Get Dodge," I ordered her.

I tried to loop my arm beneath Jill's knees, but her legs were too slippery from blood to let me get a solid grip. The blanket beneath her was too bloody to use. To Elias I yelled, "Get me a different blanket, quick."

Elias didn't budge. That never-ending Tarzan yell was more than I could take. I crossed the room to where he was standing and shoved him in the chest. "Stop it. *Stop* it. Tell me what you did to her. What did you fucking *do* to her?"

The screaming stopped, and Elias panted but said nothing. I shoved him again, but he was too heavy for it to move him or even register. I was losing time. I wrapped the bloody afghan around Jill's legs and hoisted her up. My mother scuttled past Elias and opened the door, and I rushed outside into the warm night air.

The porch light cut through the blackness, but only far enough to get me partway across the lawn. Dodge was sprinting across the grass toward me. I could hear his ring of keys clinking on his belt. When he came into view he was dressed in his jeans as if he kept them fully outfitted beside his bed like a minuteman. "What happened?"

"Jill's hurt. There's blood everywhere. Open the car door."

Dodge pulled open the passenger door of the Saturn and put his arms behind Jill's shoulders to help ease her in. I got her legs onto the seat, then stopped and said, *"Fuck."*

"What?"

"I don't have enough gas. I don't get paid until tomorrow."

Dodge nodded toward his SUV. "Take mine."

"You're blocked in. Get her in the Jeep."

"I'll drive."

"No, you better stay here with Elias. I don't know what

the hell he did to her, but we can't leave everybody else here with the goddamn psycho."

He shouted to my mother to bring me the keys while we maneuvered Jill into the back of the Jeep. As I started the car he laid a hand on the windshield to stop me. I rolled down the window, and he said, "Take her to the firehouse. They can get her to the hospital faster."

"Right. Yeah, okay."

When I spun out of the driveway onto the pitch-dark road and the car lurched between gears, I felt nothing but afraid. Jill was the one who would know what to do in this situation. She would know how to stop the bleeding, how to prevent shock, how to change gears without leaving the goddamn transmission in the middle of the road. I should have let Dodge drive after all. I had overestimated myself once again, as I always did, because I was so used to being golden that I had missed the fact that in the face of gritty reality I was less than nothing.

The dense forest broke and the small clear lights of Liberty Gorge appeared. I made a quick left turn and followed the street to where the old hose tower rose up high above the small shops around it. At the curb I lurched the Jeep to a stop and ran in through the open bay doors. Four guys in dark blue uniforms were playing poker around a table. I barely got three words out before they rushed past me, instantly to work. The lights of the ambulance whirled on. Then the siren chirped, and I stood aside as three of the men eased Jill onto a gurney, stanching the blood and wheeling her to safety all at the same time.

I leaned against the rear of the Jeep, let my head drop back and felt relief and shame wash over me. She would be all right. She was in the hands of men who knew what they were doing. Men who were not me.

★ ★ ★

The baby's cry was a strangled, wet little sound. It punctured the air of the white waiting room like the yowl of a cat. I'd been staring at the ceiling, slumped into an ergonomically curved plastic chair, and when the sound came I looked up in surprise. It had happened so fast. One minute they were wheeling her into surgery, fending me off with waving hands shrouded in plastic gloves, and the next—almost literally the next—came the cry. But it seemed a good long time before the door swung open and a small crib clunked through it, pushed by a nurse. On the center of the white mattress, like a seashell nested in cotton, lay the baby, all wrapped up with just its head sticking out. Its skin was dusky pink. Its eyes were closed but with eyebrows raised, head turned to the side as though listening to a distant hum.

"It's a boy," said the nurse, all cheerful, as though this whole thing were normal.

So this was the price I had paid. This was the six pounds that had crushed me like it was the weight of the whole world. I had to catch myself before I laughed. All of a sudden I felt like such an embarrassing whiner. For months I'd been carrying on like nature's original jackass, and here was this baby who was—and there's just no other word for it—cute. I'd never held a baby in my life, not even one of Candy's, but I reached in and scooped him up. It was like picking up a soda can you think is going to be full but turns out to be empty. They had him wrapped up so tight, he was like a very delicate football.

"Is Jill going to be all right?" I asked.

"She lost some blood, but she'll be fine once she recovers. Why didn't you tell us she had placenta previa?"

"What's placenta previa?"

She explained it to me, but the words went over my head,

and I shrugged. The nurse asked, "Did she get *any* prenatal care?"

"We couldn't afford it."

She scowled at me. "It's a potentially fatal condition for both mother and child. A simple sonogram would have detected it."

"Oh." I looked down at the baby. "Do I need to sign him out or anything?"

She gave me a funny look. "He's going to the nursery. What did you think, you can just walk out the door with him?"

"Well—Jill can't take care of him, right? She's sick and all."

"That's what the nursery is for. He hasn't even been bathed yet." She took the baby from my hands as if he was a prize she'd decided I hadn't earned after all. "Sit tight. As soon as your wife gets into a room, I'll let you know."

My wife. When the nurse said that I felt ashamed that she was wrong. It was yet another thing I'd dropped the ball on, like the prenatal care and getting a better job, keeping the fences in good repair and getting Elias taken care of before he turned into a raving lunatic at the sight of somebody bleeding.

It was a relief, at least, that Elias had nothing to do with why she was bleeding. I felt kind of bad about that, the more it sank in. If he hadn't started screaming, Jill would have bled out right there on the sofa and nobody would have realized it until it was too late. It was such a weird response for him. The guy had seen carnage on a level I could never imagine. He'd seen dead Afghan people by the score, kids even, and he'd told me about some of those, mutilated or partially eaten by animals. He'd seen his own buddy blown apart into a dozen pieces by an IED. In those situations he had acted decisively, and we knew that for a fact because he'd lived and come home, a Purple Heart veteran, honorably discharged. And then in his own house he acted as if his legs were stuck in concrete, screaming as though a truck was barreling down on him. Those anti-anxiety pills he was taking weren't doing a damn thing. I made a mental note to talk to him about that.

But it might not be anytime soon. I had a son to look after now, and that son had a mother I needed to watch out for, too. At least we knew now that under pressure Elias didn't lash out—he froze. That made the whole thing a little less urgent. At least he wasn't a danger to anybody.

I wish it had been that simple.

Chapter 19

JILL

It was seven in the evening when the painkillers wore off. My eyes slit open to the view of a faded pink wall fractured by the beige plastic bars of my bed. On the little cabinet there sat the incidental items of an ordinary birth—an opened package of blue trauma pads, a stack of tiny diapers, a kidney-shaped dish, a glass jar of Hershey's Kisses with a single balloon tied to its neck—but I knew the birth had not been ordinary. I tried to roll over onto my back, but a slice of pain seared through my abdomen. I winced and eased over more gently. Not long after I'd awoken from the surgery, in a busy room washed in a greenish light and the beeping of many machines, I had laid a cautious hand on my belly and felt the incision, a vertical one, the same as my mother's. The surprise of it had filled me with an odd sense of peace. *Her experience is yours now,* I had thought. *She came through it, and so will you.*

I reached for the call button, but as I did my door swung open and a bassinet rattled through it, pushed slowly by a nurse.

"Here he is," she said. "Chewing on his fists. Let me give you your meds and then you can feed him."

I looked up to see Leela craning her neck to peek around the doorway. Strands of her gray hair, bunched up in its usual bun, had worked themselves out to form a disheveled halo around her face. "Oh, good, Jill, you're awake now."

The room was dim, the stiff green drapes drawn tight across the windows, and Leela didn't offer to turn on the lights. When the nurse left she lifted the baby with competent ease and handed him down to me. I hadn't seen him for hours, and already he seemed older, his round little face evenly pink and the tips of his ears unfolded from their squashed state. I pulled up the sheet for modesty while I nursed him, and Leela said, "Oh, don't worry about that. Goodness. How do you feel?"

"I'm okay." The baby was so warm, his body soft and as radiant as a coal. I couldn't help but think of Elias then, how dry and heated his skin always felt when I massaged his shoulders, like a clay dish lifted from the oven. My gaze caught on the little index card at the end of the clear bassinet. On it was the cheerful image of a blue teddy bear beside a name blocked in thick marker: "OLMSTEAD, Thomas Jefferson." "I thought it would be a girl," I told Leela.

She settled into a chair beside my bed and patted my arm. I expected her to murmur a platitude that perhaps the next one would be or that God liked to surprise us, but instead she said nothing. The sudden quiet felt almost like a moment of silence for someone lost. I stole a glance at her and wondered if she had hoped for one, too.

"I guess I expected a girl," I continued, "because I'd know how to raise one. With a boy I don't have the first clue. So I thought obviously it would be a girl, since my mom used to always tell people that God doesn't give you more than you can handle."

Leela uttered a small but disparaging laugh. "Well, *that* isn't true, is it?"

I turned to her, feeling my eyes tighten with confusion.

"God gives people more than they can handle all the time,"

she said, her voice lilting with the obviousness of her words. "Shoot, babies in the Third World aren't dying because they just didn't try hard enough. You'd be a fool to try and predict how God will hand out pain. We all just love the world enough that we want to stay in it. See the day through to a better day past it."

"But you believe in God."

"Of course I do. But I believe in hunkering down till life gets better, too. And it does. You're here, after all." The baby's cap had slipped, and she slid it back over his head. "Besides, your child might surprise you. Maybe he'll love chasing the hens around the yard and helping people in little quiet ways that make them happy, and he won't care a thing about power or influence. You just never know. He might be a mama's boy."

"I'm sure Cade wouldn't like that."

Her mouth went tight and, even as she touched my arm in a soft way, her voice was firm. "You let him be who he is, no matter what Cade or anybody else says or thinks. In the end he isn't either of you. You remember that. He's himself. If I could go back and do just one thing over again as a mother, I'd hold tight to that and never let anybody make me feel bad for it."

But Cade is his own person, I thought. I looked down at the baby, batting his loosened fist against my chest, and stroked his brow that was creased high by the effort of his nursing. I tried out the idea that I might one day see elements of myself in him after all, and the thought of it cheered me. But most of what Leela said was beyond me then. I filed it away for later, not even realizing that she had not been speaking of Cade at all, but of Elias.

I stayed in the hospital for nearly a week. Once TJ and I finally came home—walking in under a paper banner made by

Candy's boys and treated to a celebratory dinner of roast beef and buttery Potato Pearls with a messily frosted cake for dessert—we found ourselves carried in by the tide of a household that had been taken over by hunting season. Men from the gun club gathered on a nightly basis to clean their weapons, discuss strategies and trade tall tales about their past successes. Eddy sat in his recliner in the midst of all this, nodding and making approving comments, looking deeply pleased to be, for once, at the center of a social gathering. As they spread out their equipment all over the living room, I retreated to the chair beside Elias's to nurse TJ in front of the TV. But Elias was almost never there anymore. He stayed in his room constantly, either to detox himself, get away from the crying baby or avoid the pressure to participate in the hunting expeditions. It could have been any one of those things, but I was too exhausted to give it much thought. For once I was distracted from my annual dread of the upcoming month of October. It was difficult to reflect on the events of four years ago while caring for someone whose needs kept me lodged in the present moment, and I didn't mind at all.

Once bear season officially started, the men mostly vanished, and even at mealtimes we saw little of Dodge. He and Scooter spent nearly every evening, deep into the night, sitting in a tree stand watching for bears. They dressed head to toe in camouflage, sprayed themselves down with scent-eliminating chemicals and wore their rifles slung on their backs like jungle commandos. Matthew copied his father, dressing in his own miniature set of fatigues and carrying his rifle around the house in a similar fashion, even during his dining-table school lessons. Candy thought this was adorable.

"Look at him, Eli," Candy prompted one afternoon, nudging Elias as she served him a sandwich during one of his rare awake hours. "Looks just like you at that age. Remember you used to get dressed up and chase me around with that BB gun of yours?"

"Mmm-hmm."

"Always the soldier even then. What do you think, Matty? You going to be a soldier like Uncle Elias?"

Matthew grinned. "Uh-huh."

"You hear that?" Candy smiled at her brother. "Remember? Those were some good times, huh? Running around like a bunch of ninnies, crawling around under the porch getting filthy dirty. Kids don't hardly ever play like that anymore. All they want to do is watch TV and fool around on the internet."

"They ought to be playing with their cousins," said Elias.

The room went silent. Dodge, who had been sitting in a dining chair pulling on his boots, shot Elias a sharp look and let the stare linger. Candy set down the plate beside Elias with a muted thunk, and even Matthew cast a nervous gaze between his parents. Elias, for his part, didn't shift his gaze from the television. On it, Rachael Ray sprinkled pepper flakes into a pot of chili, her wooden spoon moving energetically to match her voice.

"They don't have any cousins," said Dodge.

Elias's expression didn't change. When he spoke, his voice had a shrug to it. "Family's family."

Dodge slung his gun over his shoulder and left. Candy had retreated to the kitchen, where she tidied up from the sandwich-making in chilly silence. From my nest in the chair nearest his, a cotton blanket thrown over my shoulder and the baby nursing beneath it, I watched him steadily. My eyes implored him to look at me, but he only shifted in his seat, flicking the ash from his cigarette without even looking to see if he'd hit the glass ashtray. I missed the sense of connection I'd once had with him—the rolled eyes when Candy misspelled a word on her lesson chalkboard, the shadowy smirks at the corner of his mouth when Dodge said something even more ignorant than usual. But now he seemed to have turned inward, not bothering to send those subtle messages. His mind was as impenetrable to me now as it had been the day I met him. And speaking his mind about Randy made me wonder all the more what was going on in there.

Maybe he's angry at you, I thought. The idea caused anxiety to well up inside me, but I knew I couldn't blame him if he was. In the five weeks since the baby's birth I had paid little attention to him, easy enough to do when he was almost never awake. The more time I spent apart from him, the more unnerving details wormed their way into my memories of the hours before TJ's birth. I remembered the power I felt in Elias's arms when he threw my hands off him, and the muted electric thrill it stirred in me. When he hugged me and pressed his face into my hair, I heard him inhale deeply. All along there had been so many solid walls that made our friendship safe: our filial relationship, my growing pregnancy, his heavy and hurting body, the complete lack of privacy. I had meant no harm, but I loved him in a way that wasn't fair to him. It was so easy for me to share my affection generously, knowing at the close of each day I would lie down with Cade and offer him the best of it. But Elias spent each night alone, and there was no place for him to channel whatever feelings welled inside him. Without ever meaning to, I had been cruel.

Now that TJ was here, I felt chagrined by it all. I needed to learn to live beside Elias in a way that would not hurt, or tempt, either of us. I needed to get over my judgment of Candy and look to her as a model for how to be with Elias. She knew how to care for her brother without adding complications to his already overburdened mind.

On the afternoon after his comment to Dodge, I caught up with him sitting on the back porch, looking out over the backyard from his mother's white wooden rocking chair. He wasn't smoking, wasn't drinking and wasn't asleep, so it was immediately noteworthy.

"Jill," he said, "I've been meaning to apologize to you."

I laughed in surprise. "For what?"

"For not doing anything to help when you were bleeding out on the sofa. It just got to me, and I felt frozen by it. I'm sorry for standing there screaming like a little girl."

"But you *did* help," I pointed out. "Cade said I would have been dead by the morning if you hadn't alerted everyone."

Elias's expression changed. He seemed to be considering that. Then he shook his head. "I'm trained in field medicine. There's a lot I could have done besides watch Cade throw you in the car. If you'd died, it would have been on me. I'm the one in the house who knows how to handle that. But I *couldn't* handle it."

"And I'm not dead. So there's nothing to worry about."

He sighed and rubbed the bridge of his nose in his weary way. "Just accept my apology, all right?"

"No. I don't accept that you have anything to apologize for in the first place, so I can't."

He frowned. "I really wish you would."

"You were trying to wean yourself off the medicine," I said. "Nobody would have expected you to do anything differently. I'm sorry I've been preoccupied these last few weeks. I'll get Cade to make you another appointment, okay? And you and I can drive down together, like last time."

He shook his head. The chair's wooden rockers creaked in rhythm, and he gazed out over the yard. "I already know what they'll tell me. They'll lower my dosage and I'll just take twice as many. I can see it coming. Every time I try, I just binge on it the next day. They can't stop me from doing that, and neither can I."

I touched his shoulder, but he shrugged my hand off. "Maybe they have an inpatient program," I said.

"Detox, you mean?"

"Maybe."

He chuckled. "Put it on my tombstone," he said, and drew a hand slowly in front of him as if envisioning the sign. "'This man was a shitbag. May he rest in peace.'"

"Elias, come on. You'd hardly be the first veteran to deal with that. They can't all be shitbags."

He shook his head again, and I sighed. "Eli," I said, "would you like to hold the baby?"

"Sure."

I handed TJ to him. He took him easily, nestling him into his arm, and looked down at his face. At first it surprised me how easily he handled the baby, but then I remembered he had been here through the births of all three of Candy's sons.

"He looks just like Cade," he said.

"Yeah, I think so, too."

"Got that arrogant li'l mouth." He leaned back against the chair, looked out at the yard again, and rocked.

"You want me to take him back?"

"No, he's fine."

I walked off to get some lunch, pleased for the opportunity to eat without having to keep an eye or a hand on the baby. And when I came out to the porch to take TJ again, he was still asleep in the crook of Elias's arm, and Elias, for all that his face was ever unreadable, looked almost content.

That night Dodge and Scooter joined the rest of the family for supper before hiking out into the woods to sit in their hunting spot. Elias happened to be awake, so he joined everyone, too, then returned to his room. The house was quiet and cool, and when Cade came in to undress for bed, he glanced at TJ asleep in the laundry basket and threw me a pleading look. We made love for the first time since the birth, very carefully. Cade seemed almost apologetic, and grateful; only afterward did I realize how much we had needed it to take away the feeling that as a couple we were fragmenting, becoming two employees of the same baby rather than a man and a woman irresistibly attracted to each other.

TJ slept well that night. Not until two o'clock in the morning did I awake to the muted report of a gunshot from outside that I realized must be Dodge and Scooter having finally crossed paths with a bear. The noise woke TJ, and regretfully I pulled myself away from Cade's warm bare chest and lifted the baby from his basket.

I pulled him to my breast and eased back into bed, arranging the covers over myself and the lower half of TJ's body. Cade had left the door ajar, and the night-light from the bathroom was the only illumination in the darkness. The baby's nursing was slow and rhythmic, and I closed my eyes in deep fatigue. When I opened them, Elias was standing in the doorway, looking at me with his plain, unreadable eyes.

I pulled up the edge of the quilt immediately, self-conscious to be caught nursing the baby bare chested in front of him. When he didn't react, I held up a finger to let him know I would be with him in a minute. I looked down at the baby, and when I glanced up again, Elias was gone.

After a while TJ fell back asleep at my breast, and I laid him softly in the basket. I pulled on one of Cade's T-shirts and a pair of pajama pants and tiptoed down the stairs. The entire house was dark; both televisions were off, and the lamp that always burned beside Elias's chair when he was awake had been snapped off, as well. I checked the porch rocker and found it empty, then headed back up to my room. Only then did I notice Elias's door was closed, and I knew he must have grown tired of waiting for me to finish nursing the baby and had gone off to bed. For that, I felt a little sorry. Elias and I needed to talk. He had put his arms out to me. That was progress. If he would do that much, maybe he would open up to me about how the rest of us could help him, too. And we could all move forward.

I slipped back under the covers and slept until four-thirty, when TJ woke to nurse again and Cade got out of bed to attend to the day's chores. And then I drifted back to sleep for a while, until I heard Cade yelling from the barn, and then Candy's scream, and I realized it had not been Dodge's gun that went off that night, but Elias's.

It was Dodge who stopped me at the door of the barn with both hands held up and out, his face a warning that he meant business, that there was no chance I would find a way to push past him. I screamed for Cade, but Cade didn't even turn in the direction of my voice. I could see him crouched on the floor of the barn, with Elias's legs jutting out to the side, sneakers on as always, but both he and Cade were in shadow. Candy came and went, her long hair flying behind her as she ran between the main house and the barn, then down the driveway to meet the ambulance. From the upper window came the sound of TJ squalling with increasing vehemence, but my own newborn's crying had become a distraction from the primary event. After a while Leela appeared with TJ on her shoulder and her face bone-white, and then red and blue flashing lights twirled in the driveway, accompanied by the staticky clatter of radios. Only then did Cade reappear from the barn, both of his hands and the front of his T-shirt covered with thick red blood. His expression was stoic, and he met my eyes before pointing to the house and saying in a voice that was not to be argued with, "Get inside."

I took the wailing baby from Leela and trailed into the house, sitting in a dining chair near the window and setting him to nurse. Instantly he went quiet. The window offered no good angle on the barn and driveway. After the sirens chirped to life, I caught sight of Cade stalking over to the shed. He pulled off his shirt and stuffed it into the trash, then squatted by the garden spigot and rinsed off his hands. I let out a shaky sigh and switched TJ to the other breast. There was nothing to do but wait for Cade.

He came back into the house and jerked open the bifold door of the laundry closet, then opened the dryer, spilling out clean clothes onto the floor as he searched for a fresh T-shirt. I asked, "Are you going with him?"

"I'm driving down there now. They wouldn't let anyone come in the ambulance. Said we needed to follow in a car. Dodge is already on the way, with Dad."

"What happened? Is he going to be all right?"

He pulled a shirt over his head and looked at me as though I had asked the stupidest possible question. "He shot himself in the head, Jill."

"Okay, but do you think they can save him?"

"Of course they can't save him. He's dead. You think a guy like Elias doesn't know how to pull off something like that? Did you see my hands?" He felt in the pockets of his jeans. "Damn it, where are my keys?"

"But I *saw* him. I just saw him first thing this morning. I know I did."

"Well, I just saw him, too. Jesus Christ." He pulled off his watch and dropped it onto the counter. Smears of blood marked both the countertop and his skin. "Get rid of all that, will you? My mom's going to have a nervous breakdown if she sees it, and I gotta go."

I tore off a paper towel. "Do you want me to come with

you? I can leave TJ with Candy. Maybe they *can* save him. You won't know until they get him there."

"He's *dead,* Jill. And no, you can't come. It'll be hours and hours. I'll have to help Dad figure out where to send him and how to fill out all the paperwork. And when the hospital files their report, I want them to know every last detail. I want them to know who's accountable."

I set TJ on my shoulder to burp him. "What do you mean, who's accountable? Nobody's going to think it was you or Dodge."

"I mean so they know it's the army that did it. So it's on the record that they broke this poor bastard and then ignored him and blew him off, and when he tried to get help they threw some pills at him, and then he shot himself because they'd turned him into a drug addict." The volume of his voice ramped up gradually with each sentence, until he was nearly shouting. "I want it to be on that last line on his death certificate. 'Cause of death: homicide.'"

"Cade...they're not going to do that."

"They'd better. It's criminal. You don't agree with me? You don't think they royally screwed him over?"

"I never said I didn't agree. I just said there's no recourse."

"It's my opinion," Cade began, leaning toward me with his hands against the kitchen island, "that people are endowed by their Creator with certain unalienable rights, namely life, liberty and the pursuit of happiness."

"Nobody's arguing with you."

"And whenever any form of government becomes destructive to these ends, it's the right of the people to alter or abolish it. That's my right and my duty."

I stood up and joggled TJ on my shoulder. "Cade, don't go in there with your sleeves rolled up quoting the Declaration of Independence. They'll think you're a nut job. The important thing is to get Elias taken care of."

Cade threw his arms in the air. "He's *dead!*"

"I just saw him!" I shouted back again, and in the moment I felt so passionately correct that nothing would ever have convinced me otherwise. "I bled a lot, too, and here I am! So don't you write him off until someone with a degree who knows what they're talking about tells you different!"

He swore at me, grabbed his keys from the hook and slammed the front door.

It would be many hours before I saw him again. And by the time he walked back in the door, dry-eyed and grim and smelling of cigarette smoke, I'd had much more time to consider all that had been said.

I felt sorry for what I'd said about hearing it from a person with a degree. I knew that must have been salt in the wound for Cade, that only a person who had finished college was qualified to judge what he himself had seen.

I believed, finally, that Elias was dead.

And I thought, where the army was concerned, Cade might be right. Maybe it *was* the army's fault for throwing him back into the world when he returned from war, woefully ill equipped to make his way through the battlefield of normalcy. Maybe it was their fault for nurturing a culture in which he couldn't admit need without acknowledging failure.

But also came the terrible thought that it was my fault, too. For not listening to my mother's voice that had whispered to me so insistently over these past months, warning me that what we were doing for Elias was not enough—never enough. For not recognizing, the previous afternoon, that Elias was trying to make his peace with me and Cade. And worst of all was not what I had failed to do, but what I *had* done: how I, with the best of intentions, had led him to love me. Deep in my heart I had known for months that his fondness for me was not sisterly, but in spite of that I laid my hands on his shoulders and my son in his arms and expected him to find it a comfort and not a burden.

For a long time after the funeral it seemed always to be on my mind—the constant question of whether my friendship with Elias played a role in his death. He left no note, no letters, no explanation. In the infinite stretch of time that followed, some days I told myself it was egotistical to assume I had a part in it at all. He was addicted, in pain, mentally ill. None of those things had anything to do with me. But I couldn't get away from the belief, down in the core of me, that it was true. Elias's mind was a crowded room of people he could never get his arms around: not to hold, not to carry, not to save. And so he put a bullet in it, and in doing so joined most of them, and left only one behind.

Chapter 20

ELIAS

Today is the day I will die. The words scrolled through his mind every morning as he awoke, like the news ticker on CNN, steady and plain. With his arms still tucked beneath his pillow, his face pushed into its foam, he would mull on the thought until he had accepted it. Some days it was easy, especially if the previous patrol shift had gone very well or very badly. A good day meant he was ready to die. A bad day meant he might as well.

He rolled out of bed and followed the smell to the bathroom. Above the urinal was a message scrawled in thick marker: VALOR HONOR DUTY QUIT WHINING, followed by a second message scratched beneath it in ballpoint pen, in shaded block letters to make up for the wimpier medium—FUCK YOU SIR.

Get dressed. First smoke of the day. Three doughnuts and an omelet. And it was time to go on patrol.

Before he'd deployed, Candy had given him a book of daily devotionals to take with him. Each day had a Bible verse and inspiring story and ended with some kind of affirmation, like "I know that my redeemer lives" or "I dedicate this day to you, Lord." After a while it got to be too much to lug around, and he gave it away. The skills of being a soldier were straightforward, but the brain game was a paradox. He never prayed for his own safety, because it somehow felt cowardly, but the whole day became a long rosary for every soldier who crossed his path: *Protect him today, Lord. And him. And her.* And even though he began every day with an affirmation that he would die, he knew that wasn't the struggle; there were harder things to reconcile. At the end of it all, you die whether or not you're prepared to. But he still couldn't bring himself to think upon awakening, *Today is the day I'll kill somebody.*

His patrol shift was set to end at seven. The day had been slow, hot and boring; they had spent the shift driving around the desert in the Cougar—an imposing hulk of a vehicle, solid as a safe at Fort Knox, with Elias in the machine-gun turret at the top. Now the sun was setting behind the western stretch of land not marked by any mountains, and bands of tangerine and gold streaked the sky. *Sunkist,* Elias thought. The sky looked like the soft-drink can, and the small fireball of a sun completed the image. The suffocating heat was starting to dissipate ever so slightly; the sweat that trickled to his jaw felt cool. This side of the landscape was disorienting to him, so flat and singularly pale, a planet other than his own. He could sense his pupils contract and open again as he looked at it, like they couldn't figure out what they were seeing or determine whether to gaze close or far. He was tired.

Elias pushed the sweat from one eye with the heel of his hand and scanned the perimeter. All at once—it was unmistakable—he saw the figure of a man disappearing into a ditch. A crumpled sheet of plastic lay on the other side of the road: the hallmark of a hidden IED. Without hesitation he swung the gun into position and fired on the man, rattling out a volley of bullets at the ditch. The staff sergeant shouted his orders to him quickly: "Don't kill." He was an insurgent, and the captain wanted him brought in for interrogation. "Shoot near him until the Buffalo gets here to neutralize it. Keep him down, but keep him alive."

"He's wounded already," Elias called back, but the answer was the same.

The man's dark head appeared at the edge of the ditch, and Elias greeted it with a fresh round of rifle fire. Minutes stretched on in silence. The sun drifted lower; the sky was a Sunkist can no longer. Darkness was falling over the desert like a hand descending. Elias fired again, watching the bullets skim the sand like flat stones across the quarry lake.

An hour passed.

Two.

The desert around him was black as blindness. He watched the man now through night-vision goggles, which cast the landscape in *Ghostbusters* green. Now and then the radio crackled, promising the Buffalo to relieve them in short order; his stomach growled protests that he ignored. The man kept peeking out at intervals, eyes frantic and forlorn, and each time Elias shot over him again. Beneath the starlit sky he felt all the exposure of a stage. Darkness and isolation caused paranoia to rear up inside him, and as time wore on he began to feel jumpy on the trigger, desperate for resolution. *Just kill him, Elias* came the voice in his mind. *End this thing. Kill him and you can get back in the Cougar. Chill out and wait for dinner.*

But that wasn't the order.

The ghoulish palms and scrub trees rustled in the wind. In the strange glow of the goggles the desert offered up the starlight with a sheen that looked like ice. Fatigue and hunger wore at him, and some irritating corner of his brain, exhausted to the point of delirium, had decided that the desert was the

quarry lake in winter. Each time the man ducked back into
the ditch it seemed as though he were slipping underwater;
strange thoughts invaded Elias's mind, whispers that didn't
follow logically. *You can't shoot here on private property. He would
have drowned by now anyway.* And then the man's eyes would
glow deerlike above the ridge again and Elias would barrage
the sand in reply. Because it *was* sand, he reminded himself.
Even at home, the lake wasn't there anymore. The county
had drained it when the Vogel girl went under. He thought
back to the sight of the girl skating on wobbly ankles across
the open ice, her arms out at a low angle for balance. To the
way his sister's eyes had followed her all afternoon in the manner one watches a kitchen fly, calculating where it will land.

From the ditch he heard a few broken phrases, weakly
shouted. None of it was intelligible. Most likely the man had
looked up at the stars, considered his wounds and his odds,
and decided to talk, but they couldn't be sure. They couldn't
leave the vehicle until the ordnance was disposed of, and
they couldn't give the enemy the chance to get away. A hand
clawed at the ground above the ditch, then vanished at the
clatter of the rifle.

Why didn't you help her? he had asked Candy late that evening, once it was all over. Only in his mind had he asked the
real question: *How could you just stand there and do nothing when
you know somebody's dying?*

I did, she had replied. *I called for help.*

The third hour turned over, and at last the Buffalo rumbled
into sight. "Good job, soldier," the staff sergeant said to him
as he ambled down the turret and collapsed onto the bench.
Somebody handed him a Red Bull, and it kept him awake
long enough to get back to the barracks.

The air conditioners greeted him with a blast of wet cool
air and all their incessant grinding. He squirted some peanut

butter onto a packet of crackers from field rations, smoked his last cigarette of the day and stripped down to his undershirt and boxers. At the urinal he recycled his Red Bull—VALOR HONOR DUTY QUIT WHINING—before falling into his bunk and pressing his face into his pillow. He was still alive.

With his sleep came his dreams. He dreamed of kneeling on the rifle range with his father beside him as he shot and missed, shot and missed. Everybody was watching. With each shot the helplessness doubled in his belly and doubled again, infused every moment with the dread of the inevitable. He dreamed of the man's dry hand against his skull, pounding his forehead against the stump—not of the pain so much as the humiliation of his sister watching it all and knowing her brother had failed, feeling pity for him. He dreamed of her curling up behind him, offering him her love as he feigned sleep to ease the embarrassment of accepting it.

And when he awoke the next morning, the dream dissolving with the light, he understood the man in the ditch had felt just as he had—helpless, desperate, abandoned—but no, a hundred times worse, and without the glimmer of love to comfort him at the end of what he had endured. Elias pushed this away and forced a new thought, a dependable thought: *Today is the day I will die.* And it was easy to accept that morning, because he knew, in a small way, he already had.

Chapter 21

CADE

The funeral was held on a Sunday, the first day the air smelled like fall instead of summer. An American flag draped the blond-wood casket. I really wasn't cool with that. As I fell in line behind Dodge and gripped the handle to carry it to the grave, the flag seemed less like an honor than an affront.

I did not look left or right. The mourners were a blur, anyway. I caught a line of mottled green—camouflage uniforms, probably people my brother had served alongside. Somewhere to the right of me, Candy was crying. My parents were the gray heads at the front. It was a kind of relief that my dad was too broken-down to serve as a pallbearer. Not a father's job to bury his son.

I knew he felt awful. Elias and Candy always swore I was the favorite, but my parents didn't run like that. They loved Candy for being their daughter and a good Christian. I was the smart one who was going to break out and make it in the world. But Elias, he was what they'd envisioned when they first got married and tried to picture what their son would be like. Happy to be their kid, happy in New Hampshire, aspiring to do okay in school, and serve his country, and come home to marry some local girl and keep the land in the family. Even after he came back as screwed up as he was, they never imagined for a second that he would deviate from the larger plan. Nobody thought he would except maybe Jill, and that was just because Jill didn't understand what Elias was supposed to do.

I stepped back from the casket, folded my hands and looked at her across the aisle. Her eyes were dry, and she hoisted TJ to her shoulder with a competent shrug that was so like her. I didn't know how she could be so goddamn stoic. Once she finally got it through her mind that Elias was really dead, she slipped right back into her cool, quiet, unflappable Jill mode. Normally I admired her for being like that, but now it made me uneasy as hell. I couldn't shake the feeling that behind it all was a big "I told you so."

Past her shoulder stood a solid, heavily built man in a dark suit, close enough that he could touch her. I glanced at his face and almost reeled back from pure shock. The guy was my uncle Randy. Right away I looked at my father to see if he had noticed, but my dad only stared at the ground, shrunken inside his dark blue suit. Dodge would be the real measure of whether Randy's presence would be a problem. But Dodge was standing right next to me, and there was no way I could check his expression without being obvious.

Candy's minister was conducting the service. Once we got to the sermon part he got all evangelical, which I thought was distasteful. The rest of my family wasn't like that, and Elias hated that kind of shit. But it brought Candy to tears, big gulping sobs that had her clutching at tissues and her sons and Dodge as if she was slipping on a patch of ice. I knew that her mind divided up the world into two neat categories of "saved" and "damned," and it had to be crumbling with the effort of figuring out where Elias fit. *Cognitive dissonance,* my professors would have called it. She had loved Elias with a depth I doubted any of us could quite match. I felt a shiver in my shoulders when I wondered how she would reconcile the brother she loved with something as blasphemous as suicide.

Without being obvious, I looked again at Randy. I hadn't seen him in ten years, maybe twelve, but he didn't look any different now than he had when I was a kid. That was crazy, because my father's brother was younger than him by only eight years, and in the past decade my dad had aged at what seemed like double the speed of ordinary time. But Randy was still fit and dark haired, with the cowboy glower I remembered well. I tried to decide whether it was nice that he had come to pay his respects, or so insulting that somebody ought to shoot him where he stood.

The bugler was playing "Taps." Two of the soldiers in uniform folded the flag, and one handed it to my mom. The casket was lowered into the grave and the mourners began to throw handfuls of dirt onto it, but by now I felt weary of the whole thing. I wanted to go home and curl up on the sofa with TJ on my chest. Drink a beer. Watch the Patriots play the Steelers.

I breathed a sigh through my teeth and waited it out. As I took my place in the line to thank the mourners, I watched Randy shake hands with the minister, speak to him briefly and then saunter back up the hill without a word to any of us. At that point I figured "shoot him where he stood" would have been the right way to go, but it was too late now.

"Hi, Cade."

I focused on the woman who had stepped in front of me and, for the second time in half an hour, almost fell backward with shock. It was Piper. Her hair was short now, tucked behind her ears in a way that gave her a slick, professional look. She was as skinny as ever, and it really showed in her face. Her eyes looked huge. She held her hand out to me, and I shook it. What I really felt like doing was throwing my arms around her and pulling her off her feet. I was that glad to see somebody who hadn't pissed me off lately.

"Hey, you," I said, and began to smile, but then I realized the greeting was way too familiar for a funeral, besides which that Michael guy—the one she'd been with back at Christmas—was standing right behind her shoulder. Her eyes glinted as if she were laughing at me. I straightened up and said, "Thanks for coming. It would mean a lot to Elias that you're here."

"I'm so sorry, Cade."

I nodded. I had no idea what to do with pity, but the offering of it made me feel weak. Being weak made me angry. None of those were good feelings when it came to Piper.

She loosened her grip on my hand, and I knew she was about to move on. I asked, "Where are you going to school now?"

"At the University of Vermont. Graduating in May."

"That's cool." The rest of the people in the line were beginning to look annoyed, so I knew I had to let her go. "Thanks again."

Driving home, Jill was quiet. After a while she asked, "How are you doing?"

I shrugged. "I just want to get this crap over with. He's gone. There's no point in standing on ceremony."

"It doesn't give you any sense of closure?"

It was all I could do not to laugh outright. "Hell, no."

"It was nice to see all the people who cared about him. I thought you'd have more extended family there. Seemed like it was just you guys."

"Pretty much. I saw Randy there." I stopped and signaled my turn. "*That* was a surprise."

"Are you serious? Boy, he'd better hope Dodge didn't see

him. There would have been a brawl in the middle of the funeral. Or worse."

"It's possible Dodge saw him and just ignored him. He knows how torn-up Candy is, so this might be the one occasion when he knows he's full of shit and so he lets it lie for his wife's sake. That'd be good to see for once." There was a tractor in front of me, and I let my hands rest on the bottom of the steering wheel as I followed it slowly. "She's not going to take this well."

"Candy?"

"Yeah. In her world, a person doesn't do something like this. It offends Jesus. She's either going to be really angry at Elias for what he did, or really angry at God. In her way of thinking, Elias is screwed. He's damned."

"Maybe it'll soften up her approach to the God business."

"No chance of that. Candy's nature is to take a hard line. Which one she'll take, I don't know."

"What about you?" she asked. "Are you worried about his soul?"

"No. Not like I could do anything about it anyway. What I should have been more worried about was his mind. But I didn't take it seriously enough, and here we are."

"It wasn't your fault, Cade."

I can't tell you how many times she said that to me over the next few months. All I can tell you is how many of those times I believed her. None.

The day after the funeral I drove down to the tattoo parlor in town and got Elias's unit insignia inked on my forearm. Jill was opposed to the idea, telling me I was letting grief make me impulsive, but I went anyway and took Scooter with me. The tattoo guy was a buddy of his, the same one who'd done the tribal design on his arm. The needle hurt more than I expected. The truth was, physical pain had not been a big part of my life. I'd never even broken a bone. The worst I'd ever suffered was some painful road rash falling off my bike, and this hurt way more than that. But Scooter looked unimpressed by the size of the design and the blood that wept from the needle's line across my skin while the artist worked, and so I kept my mouth shut and my face blank. Gradually the underside of my forearm took on the large black shield that Elias had worn. It was depressing and satisfying at the same time to watch it take form. This was the standard Elias had carried into battle, and now that he had fallen, it was my job to carry it the rest of the way.

The concept was easier in thought than in practice. I'd gone back to work the day after Elias died, only taking off for the day of the funeral, and that hadn't been such a great idea. I needed to get away from that damned house for a few days. Every morning when I approached the barn door to milk the cows, my heart rate would start to accelerate. Fresh straw had been spread around inside, but when I cleaned up I could easily see the dark brown stain of his blood on the hard-packed earth. Inside the house, seeing his empty chair was killing me. I did what I could—went out back with the chain saw and cut down the rest of that oak tree he'd hacked up, disassembled the weight bench and took it back to the U-Store-It—but none of it gave me any of the closure I was looking for. Instead it seemed to make it all worse, as if my brother was getting further and further away. I guess Jill could tell how strung out I was getting, because she started encouraging me to take some time off work, and she freaked out about money as much as I did. So I took four days off work and told everyone I was going camping, which was the polite way of saying I needed to go live in the woods for a while or my head was going to explode. Jill approved. She packed me a week's worth of clothes, with extra socks and moleskin for hiking.

The night before, I felt Dodge watching me while I packed the cooler. When I started packing up my car, he wandered out to the porch and just stood there. After a while he said, "Your car's not going to make it if you run into bad conditions."

"It'll be fine."

"Uh-uh. As much as you complain about it overheating? You really want to be an hour away from civilization if that happens again?"

I shrugged. "I've got my phone," I told him, which was a stupid answer because in our part of New Hampshire you might as well send smoke signals half the time. Where I was going, the only good my phone would do me would be to knock out a rabbit if I was starving and my aim was good. But the truth was I didn't care. I just needed to get away.

"What would you say to making it a fishing trip?" he asked. "I could stand to go on one of those."

I smirked, sort of laughed a little. "I hate fishing."

"Fine, I'll fish, you sit on your ass and think your thoughts. Either way, there'll be dependable transportation."

It wasn't his big behemoth of an SUV that won me over. My car wasn't safe and I was okay with that, but the other thing that wasn't safe was *me*. I was going to go crazy if I didn't get some peace in my head, but being alone with my thoughts for a few days wasn't necessarily a route to peace. Having Dodge there as a sort of spotter in case my brain started slipping off the edge wasn't such a bad idea. And I figured he'd be tolerable. Dodge was an idiot around the house, but he wasn't as bad when he was alone.

We left for the fishing trip the next morning as soon as dawn broke. It wasn't too long before we crossed the border into Maine and, the better part of an hour later, found the lake he'd had in mind. Together we pitched the tent in near silence. True to form, away from the family his obnoxious edge was all but gone. He pulled a six-pack of longnecks from the cooler and handed me one, then set to work getting the fishing tackle in order while I cleared space for a campfire. It was pretty clear that Dodge's plan was to keep us busy and slightly drunk. It seemed like an inspired idea.

Still, the way he acted threw me for a loop. Most of my life I had hated Dodge. From the beginning he had embodied everything I hoped not to be, and the older I got, the deeper grew my antipathy for him. But recent events had shown him in a different light from what I was used to. When Jill was bleeding to death, Dodge was the one fast on his feet, helping me get her in the car. When I found Elias in the barn, it was Dodge who didn't get hysterical but instead called for emergency services—something we *never* did around here—stayed calm and kept the women back from his body. At every turn Dodge commanded a sense of order and authority.

And it was a damn good thing, because under stress all I could see were the ways I had failed in the task of becoming a man. My failure as a provider had nearly cost Jill and TJ their lives. In the chaos of it, I blamed Elias but showed no leadership. And then on the terrible morning when I found my brother laid out on the filth-covered floor of the barn, his limp arms and missing face making him look like a scarecrow made of blood, what was the first thing I had done? I admitted defeat, and shouted for Dodge.

I sat on the hard dirt outside the campfire ring and rested my back against a fallen tree. The lake glittered just ahead. It was amazing to look at—a flat silver pool set deep into the black earth that crumbled at its edges like cake. I shoved the hair out of my eyes and sighed from the bottom of my lungs.

After a minute, Dodge came over and sat down beside me. He wore a ball cap with a fishing hook looped into the brim. His dirt-worn jeans were slung low and held up by a leather belt that had seen better days, but still carried an army of items at the ready: keys, buck knife, Leatherman tool.

"Fishing's gonna be good," he said. "I can feel it in the air. They'll be jumping."

I nodded and twisted a green stick until it split open into threads.

"It's gotta beat my last big fishing trip, for sure."

"How do you know?"

Dodge grinned. Beneath the brim of his ball cap his eyes crinkled up at the corners, and his missing side tooth exposed a dark hole. "Told Candy I was coming up here and then took my ass straight to the clinic. Got snipped, checked into a motel, spent three days with an ice pack on my balls and drove home. Bought some fish at the market on the way back and stuck 'em in the cooler for her. Done and done."

I took a moment to process all this, then burst into a laugh. "You got a *vasectomy?*"

"Sure did. I got all the kids I can handle. Don't you ever tell her, though. She'd shit a brick."

"No kidding. She's always telling Jill how we need to have this 'full clip of babies' or something."

"Quiver-full family. She can want it all damn day, but somebody's got to pay for it. The day I tap my maple trees and money runs out like the slots in Atlantic City, then me and God will have a talk. Till then, he can want me to have thirty kids, and I can want a nice camping trailer, and he and I can call it even."

I laughed hard. "Well, your secret's safe with me."

"You ready to do some fishing?"

"Yeah, sure. I warn you, I'm not very good at it."

Dodge clapped me on the back. "Comes as no surprise, boy."

I kept in good spirits through the time spent fishing and into the night, but over the next couple of days my thoughts got bleaker and bleaker. Dodge seemed to sense this, but it also didn't seem to surprise him—after all, that was the whole reason we were here in the woods. My brother had died. I needed to grieve. I'd get it all out of my system and return home ready to face life without Elias. I wasn't sure how that was possible, but it was the goal.

On our second-last night there, we ran out of beer. The next morning after breakfast Dodge set out to replenish the supply. After he drove off I scraped the skillet from breakfast and buried the food scraps to keep animals away. I pulled off my dirty T-shirt and exchanged it for the one I'd left drying on the clothesline overnight, then tucked my nose into the collar to gauge how badly I needed a shower. The test confirmed what I'd suspected—despite the field hygiene, I stank, and yet the fact of it bothered me only a little. The first few days of the trip had felt like the welcome escape I had hoped for, but now, with the last full day mostly over, I felt a measure of panic at the thought of going back. Real life awaited: the shitty job that took only a laughable stab at my expenses, my girl who could shed half her blood and still be twice as tough as I was, my little bud of a son for whom I was the model of manhood. It was what didn't await me that gnawed at me most. My brother, who had died because he had burned out his usefulness to the country he had served, and also because I was an idiot.

I ducked into the tent to retrieve a fresh pack of cigarettes—the last from Elias's carton. Since moving back I'd limited myself to two or three a week, mainly because it really pissed off Jill when she saw me smoking. But Jill wasn't on the camping trip, and so I'd tossed the half-full carton into the SUV before we left. I'd smoked a whole pack each day of the trip. It felt decadent. I was using Elias's lighter, which they had given me in the hospital along with the rest of the personal effects from his pockets. Dodge had last used it to kindle the fire at breakfast and hadn't given it back. After a quick hunt around the campsite, I found it sitting on a stump in a pile of things Dodge must have emptied out of the SUV before he left: a copy of *Sports Illustrated,* a foil packet of freeze-dried chili, the lighter, a spool of fishing line and a handgun.

It was not Dodge's gun; I could tell that right away. Dodge owned a 9 mm Glock. I knew that for a fact because I'd seen it a zillion times since we started shooting lessons months ago. This was an M9 Beretta, almost new, and I knew exactly where it had come from. It was Elias's.

I picked it up and looked over the matte black metal. Dodge had cleaned it, wiped it down at least, thank God. I supposed he had intended to sell it to a dealer, which would explain why he had put it in his SUV and left the magazine in it. That made Dodge a scuzzbag, because he had no right to pawn Elias's possessions—but then, for all I knew, he had run it past my father already. Both of them still thought I was basically an idiot when it came to guns and probably wouldn't ask my opinion.

I sat on the fallen tree and turned it over in my hands. The sight of it took me back to that morning. The expanding triangle of light moving from the barn doorway across Elias's sprawled legs. The way his body, heavy and dense as wet sand, had refused to be shaken back to consciousness, no matter how I tried. And all the blood, vast mucking quantities of blood that slicked my hands and shirt and just kept coming, a pornographic excess of the stuff that felt like a screaming confession of just how much Elias had inside him, how much life, how much of a god-awful mess.

The dark. The nervous animals who could smell death in their midst, looking at me above the stall doors with their oversize eyes. My own raw scream for Elias, and then for God, and then for Dodge, in order of their authority to fix this, and yet nobody could. The mistakes had already been made, turning Elias into a slowly ticking time bomb who had meant well and loved us all and then tucked himself away to detonate.

I rested my elbow against my knee and pressed the barrel against my right temple. The metal felt cool, like an ice pack. I pulled back and racked it, then returned it to the space above my ear. To obliterate oneself: mind and face all at once, smudged from the great class photo as though by a pencil eraser. I could take care of my miserable disappointing half-assed existence in one click.

But I had chosen to carry the standard. I had etched it into my arm. There was no point in having hauled it up from its falling place only to pick myself off a week later. The insignia was still raw around the edges, achy and itchy like a new thing still stretching into its nerves. I would not be Elias's collateral damage. I would be my brother's avenger.

I turned the gun around and looked for a target. At the peaked space above the open tent flaps was a white label with a flag in its center and words underneath: "PROUDLY MADE IN THE USA." I sighted in on it, precisely on the field of stars, and fired.

My aim was off by half an inch, hitting the red and white bars, but it was still a respectable shot. For once.

I returned the Beretta to its place on the stump and, at long last, lit up my smoke.

★ ★ ★

Dodge returned about an hour later. He brought back a pair of cheesesteak sandwiches and a greasy bag of French fries, in addition to the beer.

"Got tired of eating all that campfire cooking," Dodge explained. "Roughing it is good for a while, but it wears off."

"Good call. It's greasy as hell, though."

"You've just stopped being used to it. You're gonna be shitting in the woods all night."

I laughed. I'd kicked up the fire while Dodge was gone, and we ate near it for the warmth. Once we were done, I rounded up all the trash and locked it in the truck to keep away bears, then lit a cigarette with an ember from the fire.

"You're gettin' to be as bad as Elias," Dodge said. "Better slow it down or the little woman isn't gonna be happy."

"She'll live."

"Guess she doesn't have much choice in the matter."

As I cleaned up around the fire, Dodge picked up the pile of objects from the stump and began to move it toward the SUV. Suddenly he stopped, paused and set down everything but the Beretta. He ran a finger across the muzzle and held the hand near his face. I met his stare.

"What did you shoot?" asked Dodge.

"The tent."

Dodge's head swung slowly in the other direction. He looked at the tent for a long moment, his gaze locking on the hole in the label before he ducked to see the exit hole. Then he looked at me again.

"Why in the blue hell would you shoot the tent?"

I shrugged and exhaled loosely.

Dodge returned his gaze to the tent. Then he turned back toward me. Looked as if he was considering what to say. It took him a while.

"You know what," he finally said, "everybody's pissed about what happened to Elias. I know I am. But probably you most of all."

"Maybe."

For a long moment Dodge said nothing further. He looked at the SUV and then up at the trees, as if they might shed some light on the situation. It was dead quiet.

"I don't know what they taught you down in Washington, D.C." Dodge began. "I don't know if they sold you all that Oprah crap about being in touch with your feelings. I know you went down there with the notion that they would all kiss your golden-boy ass because that's what your mama told you—"

"Whatever."

"Don't 'whatever' me. You sure didn't come back thinking any different, so I suppose they didn't relieve you of that notion. But I'm gonna school you a little bit, Cade." At the sound of my name, I looked up at him. "You need to man up. You might think I'm a redneck piece of shit, but I get by. Your brother, he was a good soul, but you won't see me putting a bullet in *my* head."

"Shut the fuck up," I said, but it lacked any aggression. I was tired, and my stomach already hurt from the grease.

"And you sure as hell better not pull that stunt on my watch. You made that baby and you got that woman to put her trust in you. Don't ever let it be said about you that you took the coward's way out because life's not fair and you were boo-hooing about your brother."

I said nothing.

Dodge walked over to the tent and examined the bullet hole. "You better hope it doesn't rain tonight, boy. If it does, I guarantee you you'll be sleeping in the wet spot. And don't think for a second I won't tell the whole family exactly that."

★ ★ ★

Dodge was right. I spent half the night shitting in the woods. Next morning we woke up and broke camp, and Dodge made a bunch of noise at me again about the tent. I didn't care. On the drive home I put up with his country music station without saying a word. At the New Hampshire border we stopped to get lunch, and I caught sight of another shop I wanted to stop at in the strip mall.

"Not in any hurry, are we?" I asked Dodge.

"Not really, why?"

We stopped in at the pawnshop. In the glass case they had a lot of different wedding rings and engagement rings. I picked out a narrow gold band that would bottom out the last of my money until payday. Dodge said, "Your timing's a little funny."

"No time like the present."

"You think she'll go along with it?"

"Beats me. I got nothing to lose."

He chuckled as if he wasn't sure that was true.

"You know what," I said slowly as the clerk wrapped up the box. "Yesterday I was one second away from splattering my brains all over a pine tree. Even if she says no, life could be worse."

The clerk, who'd been pretending he wasn't listening, for a split second looked up at me uneasily.

Dodge said, "That would have been a stupid-ass thing to do."

"I didn't do it, did I?"

"No. You think maybe you ought to take a little more time to get your head together before you ask her?"

"*Now* who's on *Oprah?*"

"Just a thought."

I took the bag and headed next door to the tattoo shop.

Dodge looked amused while I explained to the guy what I wanted. Half an hour later I walked back out with a new motto in puffy black letters that curved around the insignia: *Fiat justitia ruat caelum.*

"Where the hell'd you get *that* from?" asked Dodge.

"John Quincy Adams. It's Latin. 'Let justice be done though the heavens should fall.'"

Dodge smirked and gave a quick laugh like a bull snorting. "You make a lot of noise, Cade."

I said, "I'm not just making noise anymore."

Chapter 22

LEELA

Maybe a month or so after I lost Eve, there I was sitting at the breakfast table in my mother's house, waiting for my tea to steep, and I had a revelation. It was very early, and the sunlight came through the window almost sideways, colored like pollen. The fields outside were cast in that haze. Easter had just passed, and where the table pushed up against the windowsill there was a basket made out of that plastic canvas stuff threaded with yarn, with the face of a bucktoothed rabbit on the front. In the bottom lay a few small chocolate eggs wrapped in foil, the dregs of that year's candy she kept around for guests and neighbor children. It made for a poor and paltry scene, but I had my revelation even so.

I thought about the blind man in the Gospel, the one they bring to Jesus to test him. They say to him, so, was this man born blind because of his own sin, or because of what his parents did? Because everybody thought it had to be one or the other. But Jesus, he said no, this man was born blind so the glory of God could be revealed in him. And then he touched that man's eyes and healed his sight. It made me think, maybe there's a purpose for this sadness that I just can't figure out, the way that man lived his whole life up until Jesus came along with everyone having the wrong ideas about why he was blind. Maybe someday I'll come to find a purpose to this. And it wasn't much, but it was just enough to cast a little sallow light on my heart, give me enough to feel around by. It would be a lie to say that made me feel better, but at least it made me feel like I could live.

Much later on, when Lucia came to me with that foolishness of hers, I thought about that again. I had the righteousness of knowing Jesus taught that the Lord doesn't curse children for the sins of their parents. And even though I never received the witness for why that angel came down twice and swooped back each time, I had the comfort of knowing our hands were clean of it.

I don't want to talk about what happened to Eli. We owe him the dignity of not speaking of that. Because it's the truth, at wakes and memorials and such, that all the talk begins to turn a life into a set of tall tales. Somebody will tell a story, and when their friend laughs or sighs they'll add a bit, or leave off the part that makes the deceased person look a little bit bad. At the end of it all, the real life dies back little by little, and in its place you have only a bunch of make-believe stories about the person who lived it. If you want to keep the flame of a life burning, you simply don't speak of it. Something that isn't talked about never changes. And that, I can tell you for a fact, is God's honest truth.

I'd prefer to talk about Eddy.

That last spring we were all together—before school and the army took the boys away—Eddy's face had been real, real red all the time. He'd begun to sweat so much that he took to carrying around a kerchief in his pocket that he used to wipe away the beads of perspiration that popped up like pearls on his forehead. Always he had been a hot-tempered man, but lately he reminded me of those cartoon thermometers they show on the television weather reports on the hottest summer days, with the red pushing against the top and droplets flying out like the whole thing is melting. Well, there wasn't any telling that man that he ought to see a doctor. Unless you wanted the upbraiding of your life, you just left him alone. We all knew the art of that.

One evening, he and I were sitting in the den next to the kitchen, watching television. Eddy was sitting in the plaid chair that later turned into Elias's, and I sat in the other one, crocheting on a blanket for Candy's John, I suppose. He would have been the baby then. It was an April night, and it wasn't warm, but Eddy mopped down his face and leaned forward to see the TV better. It was some program on The History Channel, some war thing. All of a sudden I guess he got fed up with whatever they were saying, because he picked up the remote and said something in a disgusted voice and changed the channel. That was all right, except I didn't understand a word he was saying.

"Come again?" I asked him.

He looked me in the eye and he babbled off something different this time. It was a normal conversation voice he was using, but it was like baby words coming from his mouth, just nonsense. He shook his head, then tried again, but the words still didn't come out right. I kept my face steady so he wouldn't get mad at me and think I was mocking him. But I thought that was awful strange. Sometimes if he was drinking he didn't make a lot of sense, but at least the words he used would string together all right, even if the thoughts didn't.

That happened another time maybe a week later, at dinner. He was correcting Matthew on his manners, pointing a finger at him, when halfway through the sentence it all turned into gibberish. From the look on his face you could tell he knew, and it didn't make any more sense to him than to the rest of us. Everybody looked around at each other, but nobody said a word about it. By then I'd looked it up in *The Merck Manual* we kept in the side table in the front room. It was an old one, but then, so was Eddy. From that I knew that if a person had speech problems that come out of nowhere, it might be a stroke. I watched him as we ate, saw the confusion behind his eyes, and I confess I felt a hard kernel inside me—almost an excitement, or maybe gloating. All those times he'd yelled at me when I told him he ought to get a physical, all those years he'd spent trading on this idea of himself as a hard-tempered man who'd scrap with anyone for anything—perhaps now, here at this dinner table, we'd arrived at the spoils of it. You know, deep down in the heart of hearts—no matter how Christian a person is or how much they say they forgive their enemy—everybody wants to see the justice of God. It would be like pure clear water on a hot day, to have lived with an injustice for so long, to have stood by watching as somebody with a bad soul got a good life, and then to suddenly see the payment come due for that person. Not revenge—I don't mean revenge. I mean fairness. It's a pleasure as true as any other of the body or soul, because believing in a fair world is the only thing that makes life livable.

Yet dinner went by, and Eddy was all right, and the next day he woke up just the same as always. Elias was in the front room, cleaning out the fireplace from the winter. He had a plastic sheet spread out over part of the room, with the grate and the poker sitting on it, and himself halfway up in the chimney trying to knock out all the wood ash. Well, Eddy came downstairs, took one look at Eli and said, "Boy, what in the hell are you doing?"

Elias crouched down to look out at his father and said, "What does it look like I'm doing?"

That made Eddy turn that plum-red color of his. "Don't you start smart-mouthing. You see all that ash you're getting all over the furniture? The floor? You didn't think to drape anything?"

Elias ran a hand under his nose, leaving a streak of lighter gray. "Like anyone'll be able to tell anyway. I'll vacuum after I'm done."

"Come here."

"I'm working."

"I told you to come here."

Elias ducked out from the fireplace and came over. He wasn't even all the way to his father when Eddy grabbed a big bunch of the front of his shirt and got right up in his face. Oh, and then the yelling started. Eddy in that barking voice shouting about how he'd paid for all this and Elias was lazy and didn't care to do a job right, that's why he was a failure—all that manner of hollering. My son, he just stood there and took it. He and his father were the same height and built alike, though his father wasn't as heavy. Then Eddy shoved him in the chest, back toward the fireplace, and Elias shuffled back over and started to get back to work. But when he knelt down again Eddy shoved him in the hip with his boot, starting that yelling all over again, pushing Elias's head with the flat of his hand. Elias, I guess he got fed up, because he said, "Knock it off," though with another word in there I won't say. Eddy shouted at him not to curse at him, but then when he bent over to get in Elias's face again, he staggered to the side and fell into a chair.

At first neither Elias nor I moved to help him. We both just watched, like rabbits in their holes watching a mad dog get taken down. Eddy tried to stand up, but fell farther down instead, and slumped there on the floor. It wasn't in his vocabulary to try and call for help. His body was powdered with ash down one side, where he'd slid onto the plastic sheeting, and there was a streak of it across his cheekbone. He pulled himself to the middle of the floor on his left arm, while his right just hung there. I wasn't stupid, now. I knew what was happening. But half an Eddy, especially when angry, was still powerful. He was a mad dog wounded.

"Dad, what's the matter?" asked Elias. Eddy just lay there, breathing in a stuttering sort of way. Elias looked at him, then at me. "What should I do? You think I should drive him to the hospital or something?"

"If he'll go."

Neither of us proposed calling 911. All the fuss Eddy had made over the years about how we don't call 911, nobody was going to even float that idea right then, when he was still conscious and maybe up to making us pay for it. So Elias got on one side of him and I got on the other, and together we hoisted him into the Jeep and took him down to the hospital that way. It cost him a lot of time. Elias didn't really realize how serious it was, and I didn't say much. Probably I should have, but that kernel was back inside me again and it gave me a sense of calm. This didn't feel like an emergency. It only felt like what was inevitable, like a harvest.

My first thought, when the doctor confirmed to us that he'd had a stroke, was *Praise God, he'll never hit my son again.* That is God's honest truth, too.

But Elias left for boot camp just a couple of months after that. It turned out he'd had that in the works for months. That surprised me, because Eli and the army didn't sound like a very good mix. That boy already had enough holes in his spirit from the drill sergeant who sat across from him at the dinner table; last thing he needed was to have a stranger shoot him full of more of those, especially when the world had finally turned a little more fair and cut him the break he needed. But he was an adult and could do what he liked, and he wanted to go.

Sometimes I think I should have insisted he stay home. I should have said, son, I know you, and I don't think you're cut out for this. Had I pushed at that, maybe we wouldn't have fallen into all this trouble. But I was afraid to be like Eddy or Dodge, always telling Eli that he wasn't good enough to do a thing, that he was too weak. And so I let him go. Some days I have such a sore regret about that, I can barely face the day. I feel like I ought to be ashamed to show my face to the sunrise, knowing if I'd done differently Eli might be here to see it, too.

Exactly one week after that awful day, I got a letter in the mail with an unfamiliar handwriting on the envelope. It was from Harold, the first man I married, telling me he had seen the obituary and extending his condolences. He wrote, "I am certain Specialist Olmstead was fortunate to have a mother such as you." That was a bittersweet thing to read. It caused me to think of how young I was when I walked out on him, how I didn't understand at all about how hard life would get, and how maybe he acted hard-hearted about Eve because he was too sorry to know what to say or do. My father was a gentle man and that wasn't his way. I suppose I expected every man to be just like him. Well, I would learn. I'd learn the hard way. And seeing Harold refer to me as "Mrs. Olmstead" filled my eyes up with tears, because it's the sorriest thing to know that what you've left behind, you can never go back to get it.

But with Eddy, I never did stir up any regret about how I handled all of that. I never felt one bit of guilt. That right side of him still doesn't work too well, and feeling the weakness of his body has taken all the fight out of him. And I'll tell you, if ever there was a weakness that manifests the glory of God, it's that one. He finally sent the rest of us a measure of peace and harmony in our home. Perhaps it's cold for me to believe that, but if it is, so be it. If I have to glean in the fields for a little of the fairness of life, don't begrudge me what I find.

Chapter 23

CANDY

He was always her victim. Not Cade, because he was too small. Always Elias. He would chase her screaming through the backyard, around the henhouse and shed, through the mud-rutted horse corral where her house with Dodge would someday stand, between the rows of cabbages in the garden and finally under the porch. Cornered between the lattice and the moldering wood, she would scream with the exhilaration of being trapped and helpless, shivering with it as he combat-crawled toward her on his belly. Even then he had a set of jungle BDUs from the thrift store, black work boots and a T-shirt that said "Marines." His belt was loaded like a cop's: his Boy Scout knife, his BB gun, make-believe clips of ammo made from Mike and Ike candy boxes wrapped in electrical tape, and his trick handcuffs. He had the BB gun out as he crawled, pointed at her once she ran out of space to run. Probably it wasn't loaded. But you never knew.

"Gotcha, you goddamn VC," he always said, drawling, imitating the men from the gun club. He was nine years old. She felt the thrill of the words he wasn't supposed to say, profanity and blasphemy at once. His hair was short as the bristles of a currycomb. He grabbed for her ankle, but that was all he could do. At twelve she was almost too old for this game,

and she fought too hard for him to subdue her without turning her into the sort of mess that enraged their mother. The
game was supposed to end there, but it never did.

He was not lithe like Cade. He maneuvered on his elbows
to turn toward the exit, cumbersome, working against his
belly. And she pounced, springing from her corner to land on
his back, asnatched the cuffs from his belt. He cried *awwww*
in defeat, and she slapped them on his wrists pulled behind
his back as he writhed against the earth. Above him her body
rocked as if on a boat. Sometimes she grabbed him by the
front of his hair, what she could grasp of it, and pulled his
head back to see him wince. Sometimes she scrambled away
and left him to flick his thumbs against the levers in hope
they would release.

It wasn't this that started it. It was already there: the particular, pinpoint thrill, one that came with the amorphous sense
that she should not talk about it. That the pleasure of over-
powering him was far disproportionate to what it ought to be.
She thought about it often. On the stereo in their station
wagon there was a knob for the volume and a sliding control
that deepened the bass. If she slid it lower, even the lightest
song on the inspirational-rock station developed a palpable
throb. Made it vibrate in her bones. Her predilection was the
same way. No matter how sweet the song inside her, if they
drove past a traffic stop and saw a man being taken into cus-
tody, or if in the church coatroom a man struggled to get out
of the sleeves of his coat, the bass lever in her throttled downward. By thirteen she knew it was shameful. Anything that
made your thoughts go that way was a shame on you, by its
very nature. *Get thee back, Satan.* It was almost certainly what
the apostle Paul had meant when he wrote about the thorn in
his side. The church, her pastor said, was a hospital for sin-

ners, not a museum for saints. And so there she was, more and more often, and *that* was not shameful.

Then she was fourteen, and there came the day of the Easter passion play. She wore a smock made of sackcloth and a thin crown of flowers. She was part of the Hallelujah chorus. The man playing Jesus, naked but for a rag wrapped around his hips, hauled his cross through the street that led to the church's front yard. The Romans hoisted him onto the cross and, because the Jesus of their play was a real man and not a martyr, bound him to it with lengths of rope. His head lolled back, the tendons in his neck thrust and trembled against the thin skin, his hands contorted. She felt dizzy with the thrill and the horror. She was certainly damned.

When Dodge started coming around, drinking beer with her dad in the living room and inviting her to talk to him about school, she welcomed his attention with an almost frantic enthusiasm. When he asked if she would ride with him over to the sport shop to pick up a new vest for hunting season, her father gave his permission. They fucked in the front seat of his truck, and she was grateful. She was damned now for a specific, common thing. She would be in hell for a crime she could name. To see Dodge helpless with desire for her was empowering. And to take pleasure from him—for he offered it effusively—was surely nowhere near as evil as taking it alone, with thoughts as aberrant as hers.

She was a good woman now, and she lived a good life. She knew she was forgiven of her sins, although she could never quite believe that a payment would not be extracted from her sometime in the future. A reckoning, not for her sins, which were forgiven, but for her nature, which she carried inside her through her Christian life like a swallowed balloon full of heroin.

She told herself she needed to put her faith in God and know her fears were unfounded.

And then Elias shot himself in the head.

Chapter 24

JILL

In the days between Elias's death and his funeral, Leela cooked. She abandoned her workroom and spent what seemed like all day in the kitchen, making casseroles and long pans full of green beans seasoned with bacon, scooping precise balls of cookie dough onto baking sheets. Whatever wouldn't fit into her own refrigerator she stored in Candy's, and when space ran out in that, she cleared out the big chest freezer and laid down trays in that. On the dining-room table, in a long row down the middle, sat seven or eight family-sized chunks of defrosting meat. Each sat in an enamel pan, slowly dripping icy water around the edges of its plastic wrap. These were the former occupants of the chest freezer, and I supposed she intended to cook them, too.

It was all for the funeral. She seemed to be expecting the whole world to join her in mourning. She sent Cade to a catering supply store in Liberty Gorge to buy disposable aluminum cookware for buffets. The kitchen island was cluttered with giant cans from the cellar storage, Freeze-Dried Chicken and Corn Bread Mix and Milk. Once, as she added a second layer of cardboard-textured dried potato discs to an au gratin casserole, Candy snapped at her, "Stop using up all our food storage. We might need that, you know." Leela said nothing, kept at what she was doing, but I knew what she was think-ing: the end of the world had already arrived.

Once the funeral was over, the food all eaten, she retired to her workroom and didn't really come out. I knew she was still making her stars, because Dodge would come downstairs with an armful of boxes marked up for priority mail. When Cade came back from his camping trip with Dodge and she didn't even come down to greet him, I went up myself to check in on her.

"They're back," I said. "Dodge and Cade. Them and about twenty pounds of stinky laundry and you'll never guess what else."

She shook her head. She was painting a stripe across a star. Her eyes weren't puffy or red, and the room was tidy as ever. My heart ached for her, and I thought, not for the first time, that it would be so much easier to offer her comfort if she would make a show of her grief—to grow hysterical, scream and rant, allow her environment and personal habits to fall apart in a sort of tableau of what was going on in her head. But her dignity made me shy, and the gulf between us seemed to grow wider with each day that passed.

"Cade got a tattoo," I told her. "He got it last week, but I don't think he's shown it to you yet. It's a tribute, I suppose you'd call it. I don't know. He seems more upbeat. I guess being out in the woods did him good. It always does, for peo-ple." I leaned against the door frame and watched her paint for a minute. "You want to go for a walk or something? The river's real pretty right now."

Her voice sounded weary. "I don't think so, Jill."

"Just a quick one? How about a trade? Come out with me for a little while, and when we get back I'll help you paint. Or package them up, or whatever you want."

She looked up briefly. "I could use the help, that's for sure. I'm trying to get seventy extra all ready for a craft show."

This caught me entirely by surprise. "A craft show?"

"Yes. In Concord." She swirled the brush in the water and uncapped a new bottle of paint. "For one thing, we could use the money. That death benefit by itself isn't going to pay the costs of the funeral. And for another, it's good to have something to do."

"To stay busy, you mean?"

"Yes. A project. And this is mine. Can you hand me that brush right there? The very, very thin one." I found it on the shelf above her table and handed it to her, and she added, "I'll try to get Candy working, too. She can paint, a little. And she can drive, so that's a help in itself, since I don't."

"I don't mind watching her boys so she can do that."

"Good. My girl's got a brittle mind, like ice on a pond. Needs to always press forward in case the ground won't hold her."

"Cade's just angry."

She unfolded the magnifying lens that hung on a chain around her neck and peered through it at the field of stars, eyebrows up, focusing. In a voice like a stone skipping across the water, she said, "Men always get angry. It's what they do."

To help Leela, I took over the aspect of her barn-stars business that she just couldn't handle these days: painting soldiers' names on the inside backs or on wooden banners that hung from the bottom, at the request of the families who ordered them. They might have been active duty, or veterans, or killed in action; we had no way to tell. And what Leela needed right now was mechanical work, something she could churn out without thinking very hard, not a task that would force her to reflect and wonder. Every day, outside her craft-room door,

I collected a box of stars and a square of notebook paper detailing the day's orders. I took them down to the porch and worked alone, because I knew she needed the silent time far away from everyone else.

In the midst of the morning's work, I heard squawking in the barnyard and looked out toward the henhouse. Ben Franklin's green wings went up, flaring and thumping the air before he tumbled a large white bird into the dust, using his thick-clawed feet to make the lesson hurt. I didn't have to look closer to know who the unfortunate bird was. One of the capons had gotten scrappy lately, tussling with Ben Franklin a dozen times a day, and all the hits he took didn't seem to be teaching him who was boss. After the first few fights, Dodge had named him Mojo. "Sure doesn't act like he got his balls taken out," he'd commented, watching Mojo goading Ben Franklin into another go-round among the hens.

That was the problem, and I knew it. Castrating the roosters in the kitchen that day, I'd felt eager to prove my worth, but I was inexpert with the details. In the confusion I must have missed something, and now the sexless rooster was proving to not be so sexless after all. Mojo was maturing into a beautiful bird, pure white in his body with black-and-white feathering up his neck, crowned with a red comb. A flash of green-black tail feathers swayed when he strutted, and his feet bore tufts of white down, like marabou slippers. But he wasn't supposed to turn out like that. His alpha-male rooster characteristics never should have developed. We had eaten his brothers months ago, but I wasn't sure what to do with Mojo. He wouldn't be any good to eat, none of the families around us needed another rooster and I hated to kill him without purpose. Dodge liked him, too. He enjoyed watching the impromptu cockfighting.

"They going at it again?" asked Dodge. He had come out to the porch at the sound of the squabbling.

I nodded and said, "I think we need to build Mojo his own enclosure."

"No way. Let the best man win. Or bird, I suppose."

"It's not safe for the hens, though. To have all those claws flying."

Dodge shrugged. "Get Cade to do it. If he's got time to mope, he's got time to work. So God knows he's got it to spare."

This was true. When Cade had first announced he was going on a camping trip to get his head together, I had thought we were on the path to healing. He came home with some of the old fire to him, having had the epiphany that in the past year he had spent too much time sulking and not enough showing leadership. *Showing leadership:* that was his new pet phrase, and it encompassed everything from not working harder to get help for Elias, to his contentment about staying in a crummy job, to the fact that he and I were still not married. Two weeks after Cade returned from the woods, we drove to the courthouse and were married by the justice of the peace. It was all subdued and almost casual. Had I been the type of girl who'd dreamed of the wedding she would have one day, I would have been terribly disappointed, but I was not that girl. I wanted Cade to have the sense of control he craved in the face of chaos, and I wasn't in much of a mood to celebrate. I was mourning Elias, too.

I understood Cade's hurt. I understood his mother's stoicism. It was Candy who puzzled and worried me. Since Elias's death she had gone nearly silent, slapping down paper and pencils for her children at the dining table each morning after breakfast, offering a few perfunctory lessons from a math or grammar book before sending them outside to play for the rest of the day. The meals she made were strange. For supper one night she served three canned vegetables and nothing else; the next she put together an elaborate feast of all of Elias's favorite foods. Leela worked to engage her in the craft show project, bringing down boxes of half-sewn garden flags patterned like the Stars and Stripes, a concession to Candy's crafting preferences; she would tell her daughter in a firm tone that they needed to be completed by a certain date. Candy, who had set up the sewing machine at one end of the dining table, would hammer them all out in an hour, working at a sweatshop pace, then toss the pile back into the box and hand it over. She took not an ounce of pleasure in the work, and her frenetic energy set me on edge. I gave her a wide berth, working apart from her as much as possible.

One morning, as I was on my knees in Candy's garden, I saw a truck coming from a long way down the road, a small shimmering shape growing larger against the mountains that had gone blaze-orange below the tree line. At first I thought it might be Dodge's, until it came close enough that its dark green color was apparent. I rose from my task—pulling the last of the carrots from the ground before snow buried the garden—and shaded my eyes with my hand, trying to discern the driver. When the strange truck pulled into the driveway and a child climbed out, I stayed to look but didn't go over right away. A few feet away from me, TJ napped in the laundry basket, bundled in a thick sweater and shaded by a quilt pulled half over the top. I didn't feel comfortable walking away from him, as small as he was. A pioneer woman might have, but my pioneer skills didn't extend that far.

As the child from the car approached, I saw that both of the little boy's hands were occupied with a giant plate covered in aluminum foil that reflected piercing rays of the sun. He looked up at the house in an uncertain way, then started toward it. Hurriedly I waved him over. With Candy's boys where once I had reported them to her for their obnoxious behaviors, I didn't dare now. They had begun flinching when she even reached over their shoulders to gesture how to do a math problem or find a state on a map. It was still silly to think she'd manhandle a neighbor's child, but keeping kids away from her had turned into a gut instinct for me.

The little boy was perfectly combed, in a neat flannel shirt and corduroys. He handed over the heavy plate and said, "This is for you, Mrs. Powell."

"Oh, I'm not Mrs. Powell. But I'll make sure she gets it. Okay, buddy?"

He nodded and squinted in the sunlight. "Are you kin to her?"

"Kin? Yeah...well, I'm her sister-in-law. Her brother's wife." The boy nodded again, though I was sure he was too small to make sense of the connections. "Thanks."

He glanced back toward the truck. In a reedy little voice he rattled out, "Our family would like to express our sincere condolences at the loss of your son and brother who valiantly served our nation. The Bible says, 'Greater love hath no man than this, that a man lay down his life for his friends.' John Chapter fifteen, verse thirteen."

I stared at him.

"We have you on our family prayer list for every morning."

"Thank you."

Abruptly he turned and walked back to the truck. There appeared to be a woman in the driver's seat. I waved, and she returned it with a vague wave of her own. The boy climbed in, and she followed the half-circle drive around before going back down the road in the direction from which she had come.

A folded note taped to the top of the aluminum foil fluttered in the breeze. I opened it and read the handwriting.

Dear Olmsteads and Powells,

Our sincere condolences at the loss of your son and brother. While it has been years since we last saw Elias, we grieve with you just the same. He brought honor to our family. Without regard to our past differences we would like to extend the offer of any assistance you might need in this time of grieving. Lucia and I hope you won't hesitate to call on us. God's blessings on your family.

Sincerely,

Randy Olmstead

Lucia, Michael, Lydia, Amy, Brent, Junior, Ellie

I peeked under the foil on my way into the house. Cookies, mostly chocolate chip, but also sugar and molasses, with a loaf of banana bread in the middle of the arrangement. It crossed my mind that this was the family Dodge had been openly threatening to us for months now, but in the weeks since Elias's death he had dropped the subject entirely. I had assumed that he must have seen Randy at the funeral and realized the man bore his family no ill will; and while Dodge would never admit to being wrong, it made sense that Randy's show of respect had shamed Dodge into silence. Whatever the reason, I was glad to have that particular worry gone, and pleased at the prospect of their mending the rift. In the kitchen I handed the plate over to Candy, who regarded it with suspicion.

"A kid dropped by with all this," I told her. "Junior or Brent, I suppose."

She raised an eyebrow, then opened and read the note. Without hesitation she opened the cabinet door under the sink and began dumping the contents of the plate into the trash.

"Whoa, hey," I snapped at her. "Hold on. I think it was pretty nice of her, don't you? Did you read that note at all?"

"Sure I did."

She kept shoveling cookies into the trash. The plate was much too large for her to maneuver into the space, and the beagles snuffled around eagerly, gulping down cookies that missed the trash can. I slid around her and slammed the cabinet door shut, and she stood up straight to cast a dark glare on me. Her shoulders were as wide as Cade's. Her long curly hair fanned behind them like a cape. I lifted my chin and held her gaze, willing myself not to let her call my bluff.

Leela came around the landing and into the kitchen. "What's the—oh, my. Candy?"

I could feel Candy's breath against my forehead. "Randy Olmstead's family brought by some cookies," I explained. "Candy's not happy about it."

For a long moment Leela said nothing. Then she said, "Well, Candy, if Jill wants the cookies, let her have 'em."

"*Mom,*" I said, and both Candy and Leela looked at me in surprise. It had just been the word that came out of my mouth, and it surprised me, too, but I didn't betray that. "They sent over a nice note and said they want to help if they can. There's no need to be petty about it."

"Can't imagine the moment when we'd ever need their kind of help," said Candy. "Somebody'd have to be dead or dying for those people ever to cross this threshold."

"Somebody *did* die," I pointed out. "Maybe it's time to reconsider, then, huh?"

"Not on my watch."

I looked to Leela, who shrugged. A wave of frustration rippled through me, and I wished for Cade to be there so he could talk some sense into these people. He didn't seem to bear his uncle's family any particular ill will. But he wasn't home, and if I had learned one thing by living there so far, it was that Cade's family held a kind of sway over him that dwarfed his otherwise strong will. I wouldn't be wise to test it.

Instead, I wrote a thank-you note to Randy's family and put it in the mail the next day. I signed only my own name to it, but it was something, at least. A declaration that I was above the rest of the family's squabbling. It felt good to write it—liberating—and it seemed like the reasonable, sane thing to do in the face of Candy's erratic behavior and Leela's stony silence. Sanity seemed like an especially valuable thing right now, one I ought to store away in case of a family shortage, like evaporated milk or Potato Pearls.

The ax broke. That was the problem that led me into the shed that day. It was a frigid morning and I couldn't get warm; the furnace, I suspected, was failing, doing little more than blowing around the air heated by the living-room fireplace. For a long time I sat in front of the fire, watching TJ bat around toys on his play mat rigged with arches that suspended his rattles above his head. Since the night before, he had been tugging at his ear, the now-familiar sign of an impending ear infection. *Not again,* I'd thought with a sense of dread, and nursed him twice as often in an effort to clear all the fragile little passageways. But the chances that would work were slim, and I knew now. I pulled the cuffs of my sweater over my hands and held my fingertips to the flames until they began to die down, and then I decided, for TJ's sake and mine, we needed more wood.

Winter had been colder than expected and, where the woodpile was concerned, we were down to the bottom third of the cord, which Cade had not split properly. Such had been the theme of the past five months: chores were done carelessly, the remnants of tasks often trailing into the next day or week, as we found ourselves too distractible or disheartened to summon a good work ethic. Cade had it the worst of all. In November he had given away the two remaining cows to the Vogels, unable to continue venturing into the barn to milk them twice a day. Now he slept in until seven each morning, but he wasn't any better rested for it. Often when I awoke to nurse TJ I found his side of the bed empty, and it worried me awfully, this evidence that his sense of work and routines and clear paths through the madness was faltering. *If only he could run, he'd be all right,* I thought, but you can't run in New Hampshire in the winter. All you can do is stay put and try to stay warm. He'd been using the shed as his getaway place, the cave where he could retreat from the rest of us and maybe find a few moments of peace.

Laying TJ in the playpen, safely out of licking range of the beagles, I strapped on my boots and ventured out into the deep snow intent on splitting just enough wood to get us through Cade's workday. I found the ax and wedge embedded in a section of tree sitting on a larger stump, all powdered with snow, and I cursed quietly. Cade was the worst in the world at putting away tools. When I tried to jerk the ax from the wood, the handle rattled in the fitting and then pulled out, leaving the ax head where Cade had left it.

"Winter and tools, Cade," I muttered. "They don't mix."

I sighed. My breath whirled into the air like white smoke. I shoved my jeans deeper into my boots and began the trek through the snow to the shed. Dodge had conscientiously shoveled paths from his house to both main house and shed, forming two sides of a triangle, and so I headed toward the space he had cleared. Once at the shed I shoved its sliding door open and faced the mess Cade had left behind. At least the tools he neglected to put away indoors wouldn't be damaged by the weather, but the place was still a disaster. In the center of the room was an enormous worktable littered with saws, hammers, boxes of nails, pliers in all sizes, rolls of tape and crumpled bags of barbecue-flavor potato chips. Beer cans were stacked in a short pyramid at one end, as though he'd had the idea to build a wall of them, frat-party style, but lacked enough material.

The walls were covered with nails and braces for hanging all sorts of tools, but there was no ax to be found. I did a cursory survey of the buckets clustered on the floor, then began sliding out boxes from the shelf suspended beneath the worktable. The first held a jumble of old drill batteries, the second a few half-filled cans of paint. Losing hope, I pulled out the last box in the row. Inside it were six lengths of thick metal pipe, neatly stacked.

There was something oddly tidy and uniform about the pipes—it didn't fit with the mess of the rest of the shed. I lifted out one of them—nearly a foot long and heavier than expected, pinched closed on each end, with a length of wiry cord protruding—and turned it over. *It sort of looks like a bomb,* I thought. And then it dawned on me: *It is.*

I controlled the impulse to drop it and bolt from the shed. *Softly now.* I set it back in with the others, then eased the box back onto the shelf before hurrying outside, leaving the door ajar and the latch swinging on its hinge. From the henhouse came the fluttery sounds of the birds, their gentle clucking conversations. The sky was hidden beneath a thick cataract of white clouds. Squinting at the haze of light that filtered past them, I peered up at the top floor of the house—those four neat windows high above the back-porch roof, the rusted grate of the attic fan disturbing their symmetry. Somewhere up there, Leela worked. She was the one I needed to talk to.

I climbed the stairs to the top floor and knocked softly at her door. When she opened it, her kind face wore a businesslike, somewhat irritated expression. The magnifying lens on its dull yellow cord rested against her chest. It came back to me right then, the way she had looked when Candy dumped Lucia's cookies in the trash, her gaze stoic and impenetrable. She was one of them, after all. They had cast off a brother forever, simply because he disagreed with them on a point that, to me, barely warranted a bump in a conversation. I loved Leela and I believed she loved me, too, but if I asked her a question that challenged the uprightness of her family, she would align with them, not me.

"I think TJ's getting another ear infection," I said. Her face softened, and I added, "And we're out of wood, and it's cold, and I can't split any because I can't find the right tools. I think the furnace is broken."

She reached out and cupped my chin. Her face had gone blurry. "Well, there, don't cry about it. Dodge'll be back in a bit, and we'll get him to look at it. Surely we've got some of those fire-starter logs in the cellar. Did you take a look?"

I rubbed my cuff beneath my nose, and she pulled me to her. Her hug pushed my face against her shoulder, and I choked a sob. "I know, I know. It's hard when your baby's sick. He'll be all right, now."

I nodded and pulled in a shaky breath. It made me so terribly weary, this business of having family that I loved but could so easily lose. Whatever I had seen in their shed wasn't worth a rift with Leela. *Nothing would be worth it,* I thought, *except TJ,* and I tried not to think about how it might come to that, the way things worked in this family.

It was three-fifteen in the morning when Cade and I loaded TJ into the Saturn and drove to the emergency room, navigating the pitch-dark roads to the furious soundtrack of TJ's squalling. In an hour his fever had spiked to 103, and Cade, bouncing the purple-faced baby against his chest, had cast ever-more-frequent glances at the road beyond the front window before asking me, in a defeated and vaguely frantic tone, to bring him the car seat. Now he raked his fingers back through his hair with his left hand, flexed his right against the steering wheel and mumbled that he was going to lose his mind if the kid didn't quit screaming.

"He's in pain," I reminded him. I had to speak up to be heard above the baby. "He's not doing it to be obnoxious."

"I know, but God. It's as bad as the night he was born. Remember?"

"No. I was unconscious when he was born."

"I mean Eli. Well, you wouldn't remember that, either. The way he just kept screaming and screaming until I was ready to punch him in the face just to make the noise stop."

I glanced at him. Only half-seriously, I said, "Okay, well, don't punch the baby."

"I'm not going to punch the baby. Jeez, Jill. I feel sorry for the poor kid."

He pulled into the circular drive of the hospital and I carried TJ inside. By the time Cade had parked and followed us in, TJ was nursing desperately at my breast in a plastic chair in the hallway, awaiting a promised shot of antibiotics. Cade sank into the chair beside me with weary grace, letting his head drop back against the wall so that his ball cap popped partway off, and stared up at the acoustic tile of the ceiling.

"I'm so freakin' tired I can't see straight," he said. "And I gotta get up for work in two hours."

"Call in sick."

"I can't. Not after what this hospital visit is gonna cost."

"The state has a program for—"

"Fuck the state. C'mon, Jill. You know we don't do stuff like that."

I looked away. TJ gulped noisily, but at least he sounded

contented. I pulled his feverish body more tightly against me, less for his comfort than for mine.

"What's the matter?" he asked.

"You sound like Dodge."

"Oh, please. Not everyone wants to sponge off the government, is all. Dodge didn't invent that concept himself."

"Maybe not, but it annoys me when you agree with him. You never used to."

"That's because his ideas used to be dumber."

I turned to look at him again. He sat with his knees splayed wide, bootlaces half-undone, pulling his Terps cap down over his eyes and then pushing it up again in an idle way. The copy of Elias's tattoo was too dark against his pale arm; his brother's complexion had been swarthier, and Cade couldn't pull off the look. Seeing him now was like looking into a chrysalis to see Cade's half-formed, new incarnation: from the elbows up he was still his old self, but below that, he was turning into Dodge.

"Maybe his ideas are as lousy as ever," I proposed.

Cade glanced at me and cracked a grin. "*I'm* getting dumber, huh? Maybe so."

"Whose stuff is that in the shed?"

His grin evaporated. "What stuff?"

"You know what I'm talking about."

The nurse padded over with a loaded syringe on a tray. I sat TJ up to allow him to get his shot, setting off a new round of hysterics. Cade took him from my arms and lifted him to his shoulder, settling into the same bounce that had failed to lull him an hour before.

"You don't understand how it is around here," said Cade. "We used to blow stuff up at the quarry all the time, just for the hell of it. What else are we going to do around here, play croquet? There's nothing to do on a weekend except drink, fish and screw. And I don't like fishing."

I kept my own gaze locked with his, trying to gauge the honesty of his words. He looked at his shoulder, where the baby had just spit up milk on his T-shirt. "Nice," he said.

I tried not to smile. "So you're telling me it's all leftover stuff from high school?"

"Yeah. I can get rid of all that. Do you have a burp rag in your bag there? This smells disgusting."

I handed him the cloth from the diaper bag and watched him mop himself up. As he did, a doctor stopped short beside us, looked at his clipboard and then at our baby, and asked, "Thomas Olmstead?"

"That's him," said Cade. "The one who just puked on me."

The doctor's smile was stiff. "Can I have a word with both of you in the exam room?"

Chapter 25

CADE

The day Maryland beat Wake Forest in the ACC tournament, I stood up and cheered. No joke: when the team scored the final two points I jumped up from the recliner and did this cowboy yell, both fists in the air. Jill, who was lying on the sofa half-asleep with the baby corralled between her knees, almost jumped out of her skin. "Good Lord, Cade," she said.

But I was wired. Down in College Park I knew they were going crazy in the streets. Normally I would have felt bad about missing the celebration, but at that moment I was exhilarated just to be part of the tribe. My team was going up against Duke, our archrival, and had every chance of advancing to the NCAA tournament. It was a great day.

For the month of March, watching basketball was pretty much all I did. At work I could get away with switching the TV channel from local news to basketball, and every chance I got I kept an eye on the play-offs. On game nights you couldn't budge me from that television for love or money. Even Dodge got in on it. He started buying the beer. For the first half I'd have TJ lie on my chest while I watched. Ever since the day we took him to the E.R., when they told us he had to have this ear surgery that would require general anesthesia, we were both especially freaked out about the baby. It was as if we felt that at any moment someone might come knocking on the door and tell us it was time to return him like an overdue DVD, and so one of us was carrying him around every second. But as agitated as I got during these games, I needed to hand him off to Jill after a while. The kid would have gone flying.

It all made me nostalgic for college, and not in a good, glory-days way. It ached. I thought about the street hockey games in front of the White House, how good it felt to sail over the pavement on my skates, fighting for the ball, everybody yelling and cheering. Police and security people, uniformed and armed, were everywhere, and none of them stopped us, because we were permitted. The white marble buildings and monuments gleamed in the sunlight. In my pocket I had an ID card that allowed me into the halls where the legislators met. I had a good haircut and I was in shape. That card felt like a golden ticket, an infinite VIP pass. It wasn't, but it sure felt like it then.

I kept thinking about all that—the person I'd been back then, the person I was now. I kept telling myself I needed to reapply for work-study, hit the deadline this time, but I couldn't find the heart to do it. Every time I sat down to work on it I pictured a thin letter declining my application, something with "Dear Applicant" at the top, and I'd push the whole thing away like a plate of food I couldn't eat. If my school rejected me now, I knew I'd lose it. I wasn't even sure that I hadn't lost it already.

One weekend—it was a Saturday, the day we played Memphis—I gathered up all the stuff from the box in the shed and drove it out to the quarry, just as I'd promised Jill. I hadn't been exactly honest with her when I told her it was all leftovers from high school. It was true we used to set off fireworks there a lot, but that wasn't what she'd asked. I didn't want to tell her I'd been experimenting with a few ideas, in the beginning as a challenge to Dodge. He had all these screwy, amateurish concepts of how to blow things up, notions he'd come up with from listening to those gun-club idiots tell thirdhand stories to each other. I'd look them up on Google to affirm they were misinformation, and they always were, but along the way I'd come across things that *might* work and get curious to try them. And then, as I worked, I'd find myself thinking about people who had it coming—people who had wronged us, like that stupid doctor who'd written Elias the Xanax scrip, or Fielder taking credit for the work I'd done. When the work in the shed went well I felt like some kind of mad scientist in there, *competent* at something again, finally, and I'd start to imagine that Fielder was sitting there in the corner all tied up and whimpering, watching me ace a project he wouldn't have the chance to claim as his own. It wasn't serious, just an idle sort of going through the motions, a way to make me feel I could do something if I wanted to. Visualization: it was something they always talked to us about in public speaking classes and how-to-succeed seminars. You envision yourself being articulate and powerful and wowing the crowd, and then it's way easier to walk out there as if you own the place and make it all happen. It always worked pretty well for me when I was knocking on doors for candidates. But fantasies aside, I'd made a promise to Jill. What mattered was that I was dumping it all now, and I meant well.

I parked in the same place Elias always used to, beneath the trees, and opened the pipes up one at a time with the bolt cutters. I shook out the nails and powder into the grass and watered it all down with two gallon jugs I'd stashed in my trunk, to neutralize all the powder. *There,* I thought as the water drained down into the earth. *Clean slate.* There was more than one way to vindicate Elias's death. I'd get a haircut on my way back to the house, work on my résumé while

I watched the game and Sunday drive down to D.C. to put out some feelers. Watching all that basketball had filled me up with that miserable feeling of being estranged from the place where I belonged, and wanting to get back there felt like the most important thing in the whole world right then. More important even than what I'd sworn to do.

Jill was super-enthusiastic about me driving down to D.C., even volunteering to call me in sick at work so I didn't need to be bothered. The Terps had lost the second-round game by then, but once I got down there I was so happy to see College Park that I didn't even care. That first night, rolling into town at 9:00 p.m., I got a room at a motel up the road from campus—a place called the Mustang Inn. An orange horseshoe-shaped sign marked it from the road, and it had a reputation, which is how I knew it would be the one place I could afford to stay. I kicked off my sneakers and stretched out on the bed, had a cigarette and mulled some things over. I was back, *finally,* but I was an outsider now. In my absence this place had kept moving, and if I wanted my membership back I was going to have to fight my way back in.

Next morning, I cleaned up as best as I could under the lukewarm shower and took the Metro down to Capitol Hill, carrying my messenger bag full of résumés. All morning I talked to front-desk people and managers, and all morning I fought frustration that my game seemed off somehow. Before, it had been easy to talk my way into meeting with people much higher up the food chain than these. Lunchtime rolled around, and I ducked into a fast-food place to take a leak. While I washed my hands I stole glances at myself in the mirror, trying to figure out the problem. I was all ready to blame the usual things—lack of a tan, small-town haircut—when I realized what it was: I looked desperate. They could see it in my body language and in my eyes, hear it in my voice. Realizing that, I felt disgusted. How many times had I snickered at people like that myself—men talking to the candidate, trying to sound cocksure but coming off hopeful and needy; women who sidled up acting flirtatious but showing the wrong kind of hunger in their eyes. I couldn't stand thinking that had been me all morning.

I bought a cup of coffee and was about to walk back out when I saw a group of people heading into the deli across the street. There were five of them: a guy from my old street hockey group, a campaign volunteer named Kelly I'd hooked up with after I drove her home from the office one night, a guy and girl I didn't know, and Drew Fielder. It was the deli where we normally got lunch most days, all of us on Bylina's staff. I watched them all walk in and gradually sit down at a big table by the window, leaving two of the guys up front to order. Fielder sat down with the girls, who were laughing and chatting together about who knows what. The hollow feeling I'd fended off the night before came back full-bore. The old-Cade part of me itched to walk across the street and say hello—schmooze and network, ask about job openings, establish connections. But I couldn't do it. I'd just seen what I looked like right then, and I didn't want them to see it, too, Fielder especially. He'd give me shit about where'd my tan go, was that cow barn he smelled, how was the little woman these days and had I heard how Stan was doing lately.

My stomach growled. I hadn't eaten since the drive down and knew I had to be hungry, but I didn't feel like eating, and anyway I barely had enough cash to get a cheeseburger. So I just watched them through the window for a couple minutes, then slid out the door and hurried back up the street to the offices I hadn't hit yet. I tried to psych myself up to project confidence, but my heart wasn't in it anymore. And after another hour of that I got back in my car and headed back toward 295 North. God knows I didn't want to go back to New Hampshire, but it was obvious enough I didn't have a life in D.C. anymore. Everyone I knew had moved on, and here I'd vanished from their minds without a trace, as if I'd never even mattered to begin with.

It wasn't any mystery how I'd gotten to this point, and it didn't all have to do with Elias. Even after Jill and I moved in with my folks, even after TJ was born, I was completely bound and determined to come back to school the next year. And then TJ got the first ear infection. And the second. And the third. Every time it happened we had to throw another wheelbarrow full of money onto it, as if it wasn't bad enough already that we had the bills from his birth. I'd gotten some money out of my folks to pay for that, but I couldn't keep asking them, and then they dropped the bomb on us about the surgery. Driving away from D.C., I thought about it nonstop, and the whole thing made me feel gloomy as all holy hell. Between the debt I was carrying and how shitty I'd felt since my brother died, it seemed impossible that I would ever pull it together enough that I could come back to where I belonged. I'd try to distract myself thinking about something different, but every time I drifted back, my brain wanted to crawl off to the corner and curl up in a ball. So I turned my mind to the subject I'd tried to keep it off lately, ever since I'd cleaned out the shed and tried to make good on my promises to Jill. I started thinking about Piper.

At the funeral she'd told me she was at the University of Vermont. A little bit of internet searching had informed me she was the president of a service group that did Christmas in April and Harvest for the Hungry and those types of things. It gave me a pang to see that, knowing that she might be impressed with the career of service I had ahead of me, if I'd

still had it. At first I told myself I was just curious what she'd
been up to, but in no time at all she had taken over my brain.
At work, when I wasn't watching basketball, I daydreamed
conversations with her. Driving through Frasier, past all the
familiar spots, I mused over the high school memories. And
more and more, my thoughts had been drifting to her when
I was with Jill. It wasn't personal and it wasn't even deliberate. I'd be making love to Jill, letting my mind wander to
buy some time, and then Piper would get in there like smoke
drifting in around a door.

As I came off the New Jersey Turnpike onto 95, I batted
around which way to go, then took the exit toward Vermont.
I didn't think too hard or too deeply about it, just merged
right. And then I kicked the radio volume up and didn't think
about much at all for the next few hours. It was as if I was
finally able to turn my brain off, maybe because it had gone
into total shutdown mode, like nuclear power plants do when
a catastrophe is looming.

It was late evening when I pulled up in front of Piper's
dorm building. I knew it was hers because I'd stopped in the
Student Union and looked her up in the student directory at
the front desk. That's where I was that day: desperate in the
job search, a stalker in my downtime. *You're really hitting rock
bottom today, Cade,* I'd told myself as I flipped through the directory, but of course I still had a long way to go.

Sitting there outside that old stone building, I knew she
might not even be in there at all. But I didn't care that much.
Didn't get out of the car and try to hunt her down. All I
wanted to do was sit there and look at the things that were familiar to her. The giant oak. The light pole with the Ramones
bumper sticker plastered to it. The fat guy in a trench coat
with a head of wild, curly hair, walking out of her building

and then, later, back in with a plastic grocery bag. I wedged my knee against the dash and smoked my last few cigarettes one after the other, watching for her, drinking in her world. Men walked by, and I wondered if any of them knew her. I kept picturing her face the way she'd looked at the funeral, her eyes all big and somber and seeming to hold a complete knowledge of what I'd lost. But watching the students come and go from the dorms made me think about Jill and me, too. I looked up at the lights in those windows and thought about the people who must be up there together, careless and whiling away the time as if it was nothing. Jill and I had been that way once, and not all that long ago, either. Almost as soon as I met her, I fell so hard for her. I knew I still loved her the same way now, but I felt as though I'd set my feelings for her down somewhere and forgotten where I'd left them.

Sometime after midnight I put the Saturn back in gear and drove the rest of the way home. When I finally crawled into my own bed, thanking God that TJ was in the laundry basket and not all sprawled out on my side, Jill wiggled backward and nestled herself against me. I kissed her on her shoulder and she made a contented purr.

"How'd it go?" she whispered.

"Fine."

"I'm sure it did," she said. "You're still the most handsome bastard in the world."

I managed to smile, and she slid her bare foot down my leg. As I made love to her, very quietly and with the last little bits of energy I had left after that bitch of a drive, I thought about the extra hours I'd spent away from her and TJ and all the extra money I'd burned up on gas. I felt lousy about it, but I was glad I still had enough of a human soul to recognize when I was being a selfish asshole. Little rags of it seemed to be getting sucked away into the black hole that had opened up in me after Elias died. I didn't know how much longer what I had left would last me.

The next night, after TJ and Jill had gone to bed, I got back to work in the shed. Now that I could forget going back to Maryland anytime soon—forget ever doing anything but scrape along enough to maybe stay just ahead of all the bills—there was no reason to hold on to the fantasy that I could lobby for change like a real person. I was never going to raise my hockey stick over my head while everybody cheered, coasting along on my skates under that blue sky, not ever again. That alone was a sore, open wound, and I was one shallow bastard that I felt that way.

But where Elias had been screwed over—that was something that mattered. It was a mission I had—to state unequivocally that what had been done to him was unconscionable and corrupt and morally wrong. The fact that the fire of it still burned in me was a sign that I still had a human soul, too. And I wasn't cheating on anybody in my heart when I kept that flame alive. On the contrary, I was keeping the faith.

Fiat justitia ruat caelum.

Chapter 26

JILL

A couple of weeks before the craft fair, Leela asked me to take her down to Henderson, south of where Cade worked, to buy supplies. Scooter, who had just come in the door from helping Dodge repair the rental house's faulty dishwasher once again, asked if he could hitch a ride. Before I'd arrived in Frasier he'd had free use of Elias's Jeep, and now he was reduced to bumming rides from all of us. I tried to be a good sport about it. He never complained about his circumstances, but I knew it was a tough life for him—reluctant to move too far from his grandparents' nursing home, but unable to scrape together much of a living alone in this small town. He was lonely, and sometimes, watching him work with Dodge, I suspected he maintained the tenuous friendship more out of desperation than actual fellow feeling.

He was quiet for the whole ride down, tipping little puffed apple crackers into his palm for TJ to pick up one at a time. Glancing at him in the rearview mirror—at his impassive face, at the light that glinted off his glasses and obscured his eyes— I mused over whether I dared to ask him if he knew what, exactly, my husband was up to these days. Ever since his last trip to Maryland, Cade had begun hiding in the shed again, night after night. Just a day earlier, as I cleaned out his jeans pockets before doing the wash, I closed my hand around a dozen aluminum nails. I had stood there in front of the washing machine, staring at them in my palm, and wondered if I even *wanted* to know. My mother had always said that denial was the most powerful force after God, and I felt the undertow of it then, trying to drag the unnerving suspicions from my consciousness and tuck them away in a nice dark spot where they belonged. It was like the pull of sleep.

I dropped Leela off at the craft store, then rounded the corner and pulled up at the storefront for the mom-and-pop hardware store housed on the first floor of a crumbling Victorian building. Before he could get out, I said, "Come sit by me a second. I need to ask you something."

Cooperatively—in his easy Scooter way—he climbed out and then back into the Jeep, settling into the passenger seat Leela had just vacated. I cut the engine and turned to face him, and he eyed me back warily.

"You remember when we painted the porch that day?" I began. "How you told me you were worried about Elias?"

He nodded.

"And it turned out you were right. And you came to me because you didn't think the rest of the family was picking up on it."

"I remember."

"Well, now I'm coming to you. I'm worried about what's going on with Cade. He promised me he wasn't building bombs, and now he's back in the shed again all the time. Just like after Elias died."

He hesitated. "Did you look in the shed yourself?"

"He's started using the padlock. I don't know the code."

Scooter shifted in the seat. He glanced back at TJ hammering against the seat back with the soles of his tiny sneakers.

"He and Dodge have been talking a lot," he said. "I think they've got something planned."

His words should have come as no surprise, but I felt the squeeze in my chest even so. "Like what?"

"I don't know. They talk about all kinds of things. Cade's so pissed about Elias, and Dodge just feeds it and feeds it. I don't even think Dodge feels that bad about what happened, truth be told. I think he just likes that he can puppet Cade by talking about it. But he still talks real big about how it was an injustice done to him and they need to settle the debt."

"But what are they *doing*? What does that even mean?" I made a helpless sound, a humorless half laugh. "Should I grab my kid and run? Or what?"

He shrugged. "I couldn't tell you. Olmsteads are never real clear on what they're actually up to. Trust me, I hear stories from the Vogels."

"Well, will you tell me if you do hear anything? Promise me you will." He looked uneasy, and so I leaned in closer, dropped my voice. "I promise not to lay blame on you. And if you trusted me back then, I ought to be able to trust you now."

He replied with a slow nod. Then he said, "If you need to get away from the house, go to the other Olmsteads. Randy and Lucia. You can trust them. They're good people."

I squinted at him in surprise. "How would you know?"

"They're no strangers to me. I went to church with them growing up. I don't see them too often now, but I know what kind of stock they are. They're taking the blame for what the renters said to Dodge, and he's spreading that around all over, and they don't say a word in their own defense. It wasn't them at all."

"I know. Dodge is paranoid."

"No, I mean, it was me. I got creeped out hearing all the remarks Dodge made about their daughter and I said something to them privately. I'm sure the other Olmsteads know it came from me, but they're church people, they wouldn't snitch on me about it. And of course Dodge thinks it's Randy because he thinks everything's Randy." He cracked his knuckles one at a time, his gaze focused past my shoulder at the town scene around us. "The only reason I can trust you with all that is I've seen you can keep a secret. You've got integrity. I'm counting on you, same as you are on me."

"What secret?"

"About Elias. That he didn't love you like a sister-in-law. That time we were all working at the house, painting and whatnot, the way he looked at you." I opened my mouth to protest, but Scooter shook his head. "A person would have had to've been an idiot not to see it. He took it to his grave, and you never stirred up contention over it. It was smart you kept that quiet. Candy didn't like people who interfered with her brother too much."

My voice seemed caught in the trap of his accusation. I looked away, and into the awkward silence he said, "Well, I'm going to go buy a hammer. You can pick Leela up and then swing back around to get me."

The door slammed. After a moment I turned the key in the ignition and radio music filled the car: Alison Krauss, "Two Highways." Beneath the notes of it I could almost hear Elias's harmony, but I knew it was just a trick of my memory, filling in what we all had lost.

I dropped Leela off back at the house, then Scooter at the Vogels', but from there I turned the Jeep east and kept on driving. A year ago, when Elias was struggling, I had considered calling Dave to ask his advice, but I shied away from doing so because I didn't want to confess to an outsider that there was a problem in my family. Now it shamed me, the pride that had stopped me from seeking help. How many times had I heard my mother speak of the importance of humbling oneself and admitting when a situation had spiraled beyond one's control? I owed it to her, and to Elias, not to make the same mistake twice.

I needed no map to find Randy's place. As soon as I had read their address on the card Lucia had slipped in with the cookies, I knew it would be a place on the main highway just across the border in Maine. I'd guessed the house would be large, and I was right: it was a sprawling Cape Cod–style place, with a sloping second story on top of a ground floor sided in rough-hewn stone, attractive and not very old. From the porch a large American flag flapped in the April wind, and a sturdy wooden swing set in the front yard was crowded with shouting children. When I shut off the Jeep and opened my door, the children all turned to stare at me. Lucia leaned out of a window of the second story above the garage; after a moment she waved to me, then noisily clanged a bell attached to the siding. The children rushed back inside through the open garage door.

I unclipped TJ from his car seat and slammed the door, drawing a shaky breath. As I approached the house I could hear a woman's voice calling to someone inside. In a moment the front door opened, and there stood Lucia in a blouse and long skirt, her hair arranged in a heavy braid that fell to the small of her back. "Jill Olmstead," she said.

"Yes."

"I can tell that's Cade's baby."

She gestured me inside, and I stepped into the entryway. In the living room a woodstove blazed, and its gleaming light seemed to gild the camel-colored furniture and red rugs. It was a lovely house, tidy and clean and welcoming. A fresh scent of burning wood brightened the air. Photographs of the children hung from every wall. "Scooter told me it would be okay to talk to you," I began.

"Of course it's fine."

"I was hoping I could speak to Randy. I want to talk to him about Cade."

She led me into a large and open kitchen, where a tall man was rising from the table. His hair was dark, but his face was not unlike Cade's: angular and handsome, though roughened by age and years of working in the sun. I said, "I came to see you because I have a concern about the family."

"Do you, now."

"I wouldn't come to you if I had an idea of where else to go. Since Elias died things have been in sort of a downward spiral." I forced myself to focus on the task at hand, not to allow my emotions to well. Randy Olmstead didn't look like the sort of man who would appreciate a strange woman sniveling in his kitchen. "I thought they'd get better, but some people in the family aren't dealing with their grief very well."

"Scooter's told us about that."

I nodded. "Cade took it particularly hard. He's angry. He was having a rough year even before it happened, so it's that much worse after. And he takes Dodge so much more seriously these days, and you know Dodge. He's—his ideas are—"

"He doesn't always look at things from every angle."

"That's one way to put it." TJ was squirming in my arms. Lucia scooped him up and carried him to another room, leaving me alone with Randy. I gnawed my lip, worrying over how much I should reveal. "Listen, Elias trusted you. I think Cade would, too, but he's so angry—he needs somebody to talk him down, desperately. He seems confused to me, like he doesn't know how to honor his brother and also let go of what happened. And I'm worried that he's going to do something—stupid. As a result."

Randy tipped his head to the side a bit. The look he gave me was a measuring one. "What do you mean by 'stupid'?"

"That he's going to try to take revenge on somebody for Elias not getting enough help. Cade's not a violent person, he really isn't. But he's... grandiose. And with Dodge in the mix, I don't know what that could mean." I shrugged helplessly. "I don't understand people like this. You do. I can tell him all day long that he needs to deal with his feelings, but that means nothing to him. He's a man, he's an Olmstead—he's Cade. You can talk to him in a way he'll understand."

Randy's jaw shifted in a pondering way. Then he moved forward, and I stepped out of his path as he walked around the kitchen table to a brightly lit spot where a wooden rifle lay flat beneath a round, mounted hobby mirror. Beside it a wood-burning pen sat in its holder, the source of one note of the woodsy smell. Randy took his seat and pulled the mirror into place above the rifle stock. He rested his forearms against the table and looked up at me.

"What I say to you stays between you and me and the walls of this house," he said. "You give me your word on that."

"You have it. You have my word."

He picked up the wood-burning pen and turned his attention to the rifle stock beneath the magnifier. From where I stood I could see he was burning in a picture of a deer leaping through trees and brush, with script curving above and below the image. A thin stream of smoke came up from the pen as he touched it to the wood.

"Those Olmsteads," he began, "and I'll count the Powells, too, for sake of discussion. For a long, long time now, they've been coming up with ways to justify things an ordinary man would have a hard time reconciling. For my own part, between you and me, I don't know how you set down into a feud that divides your own family about some petty difference of opinion. Or how a grown man finds it in himself to take an interest in a fourteen-year-old girl, or how a father gives a blessing on that."

"Candy was sixteen, wasn't she?"

He blew against the wood. "He didn't *marry* her until she was sixteen, and I don't suppose they consummated it until then, because she's a Christian girl. But it was wrong just the same. I didn't hold with him even giving that thought an audience in his mind. And when you look at how it corrupted her, you can't help but lay that blame on her father's shoulders, as well. A girl that age ought to be thinking about how she can grow up to be a worthy young lady, not how she can gratify some grown man's appetites."

"Corrupted her?"

He looked up fleetingly from his work, but I caught the grimness of his gaze. "I'm referring to the accident at the lake. You can make of that what you will." He shifted the rifle beneath the magnifier. "My heart goes out to my sister-in-law in all she's suffered. Leela raised those children as best she could. I believe in the traditional family, but there wasn't a day that went by when those children were young that it didn't cross my mind how much better off they'd be if my brother had a hunting accident."

My eyes widened, and the gaze he cast on me was challenging. "Tell me I'm wrong."

"I never knew Eddy then."

"You knew Elias, so you knew Eddy. Elias was what happens when the Lord makes a fine young soul and entrusts it to the likes of Eddy Olmstead."

I watched as he pressed the tip of the pen to the engraving of a tree, buzzing it over all the little leaves. Then he set down the pen and pushed the magnifier to the side. "But you came here to talk about Cade. I can offer you shelter for you and your son. You're as welcome here as any of the children of my blood. But if Cade wants to speak to me, he'll have to approach me on his own. Coax him into coming to me if you like, but I can't go chasing him down."

"All right," I said. But my throat felt tense with frustration, and in rapid speech I continued, "But what if he won't listen to me? Won't you call him, at least? He's a good person, really he is. He's just grieving, and his grief has gotten the better of him. He listens to all the stupid stuff Dodge says and it's like he's lost his perspective. If he could just be snapped back in line by somebody he respects—"

"I have no reason to think he respects me."

"I know he will. He's so angry, that's all, and he won't listen to reason from me. He's only twenty-two, Randy. He needs a father figure to lay down the law for him. He'll listen, if you speak to his conscience."

"He's a grown man old enough to have a child and old enough to make his own calls about things, for good or for evil. And as much as you may not like it, this may *be* his conscience. Maybe the truth is he's not as different from Dodge as you'd hoped, and if that proves true, Lord knows there's not a thing that can be done for him." He set down his tools and came around the table to stand before me. "I have a guest room in the basement with its own bath. You're welcome anytime you need it, and you might. You can take it right now if you like."

Without warning, tears began trickling down my face. "I can't do that. I'm not going to leave him just because he's grieving. I'd never do that to him."

"That's fine. But if the day ever comes that you decide his son is paying too dear a price for his father's grief, the offer stands."

I nodded and scrubbed my cheek with my sleeve, and Randy laid his big hand on my shoulder.

Once I got home from Randy's, I put TJ straight down for a nap and lay down on the bed in the dark room, watching him squirm in the laundry basket. The exhaustion I felt was bone deep; my mind, more than any other part of me, demanded rest. I needed time to think about all that Scooter and Randy had said, time to mull over how I would move forward from here, what I would say to Cade or demand of him. But in my current state, every thought popped like a bubble as soon as it rose to the surface of my mind.

I closed my eyes and let the peace of my weariness overtake me. Yet not more than a few minutes passed before I heard rapid footsteps on the attic stairs and then Leela's voice, sharp and sure. "Outside, Jill," she ordered. "Candy, Jill, outside!"

I bolted from the bed and hurried to follow her. She was hustling down the staircase ahead of me, her magnifying lens bouncing against her chest and her skirt bunched up in one hand. She shouted Candy's name again, but her daughter wasn't to be found. As we passed through the screened porch I heard a frantic rustling outside, a fluttery, broken noise accompanied by the noisy squawking of chickens. Leela rushed over to the side of the shed and turned on the garden hose. It had an old-style nozzle on its end, and water gushed out in uneven bursts as she ran with it toward the chicken coop. At first glance the swirl of wings was both green and white, but just before the water hit the birds the white ones wilted down. Ben Franklin's powerful wings beat the air hard, and then he squawked indignantly, strutting backward from Mojo's wet and docile corpse.

"You get back from there," Leela barked at him. "You blasted bird."

In the excitement Candy had emerged from the Powell house, her home-sewn dress protected by an apron spattered with paint. She peered around me and Leela to better see the chicken enclosure, then uttered a sharp laugh. "Old Ben finally did it," she said. "I told you that other one still had his balls."

I steeled Candy with a look. "I messed it up. That's why he's supposed to be in his own enclosure."

"Chewed right through his *own enclosure,* looks like," she observed, making sure to mimic my tone and accent. And I saw she was right—the wire had been picked apart at the base where it connected to the wood frame, allowing Mojo to squeeze through onto Ben Franklin's side. I supposed he was after the hens.

"Well, let's get him out and trash him," Candy said. "He's no good to eat, after all."

High above our heads, a strident little voice rang out. "Who goes there!"

We all looked up, and I caught sight of Matthew standing at an attic window with his rifle pointed at me. "Matthew!" Leela scolded. "You put that away!"

"Give me liberty or give me death!" he shouted. "No king but King Jesus!"

"Matthew!"

He ducked out of the window, no doubt inspired by the expression on his mother's face, but his little eyes reappeared just below in the venting slats for the attic fan. As Candy headed into the house to corner him, Leela said, "I pity him."

"Matthew or Mojo?"

My question was a serious one, but she replied with a tired laugh. "Matthew," she said, "although Mojo, too, I suppose, dumb bird that he was. Ask for trouble and you're sure to find it. That goes for the both of them."

She shooed the hens and Ben Franklin into the henhouse, and we stepped through the gate to retrieve Mojo's body. "Got to get him out before Old Ben gets to pecking him," Leela said. "They develop a taste for blood real easy. Then he'll be pecking at the hens and anybody who comes near."

"That's the last time I ever try to keep a second rooster. I should have killed him earlier like Candy said."

"Nah." Leela made threatening noises at Ben Franklin as I dragged Mojo out through the gate. "You meant well by it. Can't nobody ever fault you for meaning well. And it's Mojo's fault in any case. He was the one always picking a fight. Old Ben's just stronger and scrappier."

The rooster was heavy. I stopped for a minute and set him on the grass. His long throat had been torn open by Ben's savage talons, splattering the gray-and-white down of his beautiful Brahma coat with clotting blood. I had failed to desex him properly, failed to keep his fence in good repair. The signs had been in front of me the whole time, and I'd shrugged them off. My mother never would have.

Leela saw the tears I fought. In the most sympathetic voice, she said, "Don't worry about it, Jill. It's only their nature."

"It's my fault. I screwed it up."

"Well, you didn't mean to. You've had a lot on your shoulders lately. Can't expect you to keep an eye on every last little thing."

"Yeah, but I knew about it. I just didn't bother to think it all the way through. Damn it." I picked Mojo back up again by his feet and resumed my walk toward the trash pile.

"Nobody does every time," said Leela. "You think it's just you? Least you're young. Take a look at my life sometime if you want to know about someone who can't see the train coming."

She was bent over picking up twigs and half-rotted leaves

from the yard as she followed me, working around the trail of blood from Mojo. I said, "That's not true."

"It's true enough. We do what we need to do to get by, Jill, especially when we're busy and our choices aren't many. You've got the will to speak up, at least. And the will to move on if it gets that bad." She straightened and gave me a mild smile.

"Nothing would ever be so bad that I'd leave my family," I told her. "Not Cade, and not the rest of you, either."

"Life can get funny," she said. "You never can be too sure about it. Any decision you make, I'd love you just the same. No matter who you leave or where you live."

I stopped where I stood and turned to her, searching her eyes for meaning. And what I found, I couldn't doubt: that she knew everything I knew, and that she loved me like a real mother does, without fear of loss or pain.

Chapter 27

CADE

Dad wasn't doing well. He didn't eat much and he slept all the time. Sometimes when I caught sight of him in the recliner, knocked out, he looked so pale and still that I had freak-out moments thinking he was dead. He'd gotten worse since Elias died and everybody figured he was depressed, but now I was starting to think something was really wrong with him. He wore sweaters even when it was hot inside. He'd always been built Irish like my grandmother's family, short in the legs and thick around the chest. Now he looked withered, like an old man. I wouldn't have guessed my father could even get that skinny.

His body wasn't the only thing falling to crap around here. The wood siding on the north side of the house was starting to rot where it hadn't been painted for years, and we had a roof leak in Elias's room. Mom had put down an old canning kettle in there to catch the drips, and the stain spread like a coffee ring on the ceiling. I went in there once to clean up the papers that had gotten soggy on the floor before we realized about the leak. The water had trickled under the bed, and under there I found a little stack of porno magazines and also a photo of me and Jill. The colors were washed out where the water had gotten to it. I wasn't sure what to think, exactly, about the fact that it was there. It could have just been a coincidence that he had it in his room, like maybe he kept it around the way people do with family photos all the time. At the same time, the thought sort of wormed its way into my head that it was his way of keeping a photo of Jill in his room but excusing it because I was in it, too. I thought about him putting his thumb over my face to make me disappear and then I shoved that thought out of my head before it got any worse.

Also, there was the Saturn. On top of the usual problems, every time I braked it felt as if I'd just pulled onto gravel. I handed it over to Dodge so he could figure out what the problem was. Sometimes with a car you get a sense when it's going to be a cheap repair and other times you can feel in your gut that the fix is going to cost you an assload of money. This was one of the latter situations.

"It's your rotors," Dodge said once he got back from the very short test drive. He dangled my keys in the air and I pocketed them. "Feels like you've got bags of marbles where the brakes ought to be. I wouldn't drive it."

"I got no choice."

"We got the Jeep, right? Just use the Jeep."

I shook my head. I hated driving the Jeep. Jill could drive that thing and shift like a NASCAR driver, and I still dropped gears every time between second and third. It was the hesitation that got me, and I knew it, but I couldn't seem to overcome it.

"Well, you got a choice," Dodge said patiently. "Drive the Jeep, or get your ass killed. Pick one."

I got in the Saturn and slammed the door. Dodge just shook his head at me. Thunder, the larger of Dodge's beagles, jumped against the door and bayed, scrabbling his nails against the paint. I opened the door again and he hopped in. His tail smacked my face as he climbed straight into the back looking for fast-food wrappers. I figured he was better off with me than getting kicked around the house by Candy.

"Don't you get my dog killed," Dodge shouted. I gave him a thumbs-up and backed out of the driveway.

I kept the car at fifty-five so I wouldn't have to brake suddenly for speed traps. On the open road, I rolled down the window. The violent throttle of the wind was satisfying. It was only a couple of miles to Piper's house. It was set far back from the road at the top of a little rise, a battered Victorian with a new American flag on a pole in front of it. Two cars sat in the driveway and I didn't know if either of them was hers. I steered the car into the gravel pull-off right in front of it, stopping just behind the little shack where they used to sell produce in season. The signs were faded but still nailed up: Fine Fresh Lemonade. I shut off the ignition and eased the seat back so I could look past that shack to the house. Thunder climbed into my lap and rested his muzzle on my leg. After a minute I cut the engine back and turned my Dave Matthews CD on low. If the car was about to shit the bed anyhow, it didn't matter much if I ran the battery down. And the music made me think about better days, high school and college both.

Piper had had this hat from Guatemala, knitted, with earflaps and strings that hung down to about her elbows. She had mittens that sort of matched. They were made from about four hundred colors of yarn and she started wearing the hat as soon as the weather got cool. That fall when we were both seventeen, I'd get on the school bus in the morning and see that hat pointing up above the green vinyl seat and I'd go over and sit next to her. We were an item then and she expected it. She was always huddled over whatever book was assigned to her for English, reading like a madwoman. *Of Mice and*

Men, The Great Gatsby, The Scarlet Letter—she plowed through them at light speed. The catching-up was necessary because neither of us was getting a lot of homework done. Halfway between her house and mine there was this house we biked to in the afternoons. In my part of New Hampshire there are a lot of broken-down buildings—old motels, lodges, cottages too small for more than one person and a skinny cat—along the side of the road. Abandoned, and nobody comes back to pay the taxes or fix them up, and so they just rot back into the earth. This one house between ours, it was a Victorian that still had most of its shutters and the original gingerbread along the porch, but the roof had rotted out in the back and so water had gotten into what had once been the veranda. It was essentially a ruin, but it was also a shelter, and one where nobody was going to bust in to milk the cows or watch TV. That's a priceless thing when you're seventeen.

Most distinctly I remember the feeling of biking there—pedaling as if the cops were chasing me, tires crackling through the leaves, the trees arching overhead and throwing sunlight at me like javelins. Most of the time her bike was already there, white but hidden beside the encroaching woods. She was still afraid to go in without me—bad men always ranged near the forest, so they said. We were done exploring the house. We knew the crumbling plaster in the bedrooms upstairs, the gutted kitchen, the fireplace all walnut splendor and filthy black ash. What we weren't done with was each other.

Before it happened there wasn't any real anticipation. We'd brought in a couple of old quilts during the summer, but we didn't discuss what we did on them or what we might do later. One afternoon, fooling around, we kept getting closer and closer. The intent was to ride the edge of it, to drink down how tantalizing it was to be *this close,* but at a certain point a million years of evolution kicks in and starts giving really loud instructions. The thing I remember best—not just in my brain, but along my nerves when I think about it—is the feeling of unbelievable pleasure when I pushed into her, at exactly the same moment her voice in my ear shivered a long, rising scream of pain.

Not long after that, the weather got too cold to use that place anymore. We switched to the shed behind my folks' place, because from the main house it's pretty hard to see people coming in and out of it, and I could block the door from the inside with the circular saw. There was light and even a little space heater. For about a month we met there all the time, three or four days a week probably. I spent 97 percent of my waking hours thinking about being with her. The other 3 percent, we were in the shed.

Then Dodge got wise to it. He made eye contact when we were coming out of the shed one day. I didn't think he'd say anything, because he was a guy, even if he was also an asshole, and I figured he'd have my back. And he didn't say a word. Instead he took up this major project building new cabinets for his kitchen all of a sudden—the kitchen in their house that they didn't use for anything except making cereal. Every day, all afternoon, he'd be in that shed sawing and staining wood, screwing stuff together, pulling out tools that hadn't seen the light of day since I was in elementary school. God, did it ever piss me off.

And then came that lunch hour when Piper pulled me aside and told me she thought she was pregnant. The whole weight of how careless I'd been crashed down on me all at once. Even after the whole scare was over I couldn't get past the feeling of being estranged from her; I could barely even look her in the eye, let alone go out with her. For five months we were each other's whole world, and then in no time each of us shriveled to nothing.

In the end I regretted everything about it. I regretted not knowing how to hold on to her, not knowing what to say to her, not preventing that situation from happening at all. I got older, and spent time with more women, and regretted what a crappy lover I'd been to her, now that I knew how to be a good one. TJ came into the world, and sometimes I'd look at him and wonder whether Piper and I really had conceived a child together back then, and felt awe and remorse welling up in me at the same time. It felt like something I'd never be able to fully put to rest, the way I'd both loved her and hated everything that happened between us.

And so I sat in front of her house and stared at it like a beagle at a prairie dog hole. There were a million things I wanted to say to Piper now. It seemed crucially important to tell her I was sorry for being a dick to her back then, but that wasn't the only thing. I wanted to talk to her about Jill and why it always happened to me that this shell grew over me when things weren't going my way, even when I loved the girl. I felt that maybe if she looked me in the eye and told me how it was—said the things I had a hunch she'd thought about me for years—it might snap me out of it. I wanted to hear her talk about Elias again, as someone who'd lived in our world and knew what he'd been like before the war. I'd tell her about how since he died I felt I was walking around with a cannonball-sized hole in my chest you could see clear through, stick your hand right in there and have it pop out the other side, like surrealist art. And while I was at it, I wanted to tell her I was sorry for being such a shitty lover, and we'd laugh about it, and between us we'd understand that I could own up to everything I'd done wrong because I knew better now.

But she didn't come out. I rolled down the window and lit a cigarette, then sat there scratching the dog behind his ears while I watched the house. The sun was starting to go down behind the mountain. The flag flapped in the wind, and on the tree out front, the dark leaves rustled all at once like bats flying out of a barn.

Once dusk came I threw the car back in gear and drove home. I didn't have to touch the brakes once the whole way. I was feeling like a pro, as if I'd beaten the Saturn at its own game. And then, right as I was coming up the road with the house in view, my headlights swooped across the yard and a deer took off from Candy's goddamn vegetable garden. It burst across the road in front of me, and I slammed on the brakes. They made an awful grinding noise, but beneath my foot the pedal felt like it was just poofing on a bottle of perfume. The deer thudded against my windshield. Glass shattered like a spiderweb, the dog thumped against the door and yelped, and finally the deer tumbled to the road and the car came to a stop.

I opened the door and climbed out. Thunder slunk out behind me and sniffed at the deer, then bayed. The Saturn was *destroyed*. The windshield was in a million tiny pieces, the hood caved in, the bumper dented where the car had finally stopped against the deer. I stood there looking at it, half my brain whimpering *my car, my car*, the other half an absolute blank. The blank half won out, and I reached back in across the driver's side to get my cigarettes and lighter from the passenger seat. Thunder was still sniffing at the deer, wagging his tail and doing his obnoxious beagle bark, getting all excited at the chance to hunt the roadkill. From the house I heard Lightning start yapping back, and then the door slammed and footsteps, human ones, started hurrying across the lawn.

"You dumb son of a bitch!" Dodge said. "Didn't I tell you this would happen?"

"The car was trashed anyway." I exhaled smoke and looked down at the deer. Dodge was still looking at me in incredulous silence. After a minute or so I said, "We ought to field dress it and butcher it once we get it in the house."

"God*damn*, Cade." Dodge was staring at me as though I'd lost my mind. "There's better ways to hunt a deer than to slam into it with your car."

Lightning came tearing across the lawn with Jill and Candy close behind her. "Holy crap," said Jill.

I looked at Dodge. "Guess I'm driving the Jeep now."

Jill stroked down my arm. "Are you hurt or anything?"

I shook my head.

"Cade," she said.

I couldn't even look at her. I knew it wasn't her fault. I swear to God I knew. But it was as if the whole thing was past her now. It was like hearing Piper cry out that first time I was with her—you can love somebody and they can love you back, but when they suffer or you do, the pain stays where it started. You can say, wow, that sounds like it must have hurt, but you don't actually feel it one bit. In fact, in the midst of it, you're free to go ahead and feel something exactly opposite. Love tricks you into believing that together you complete a circuit, that everything flows between the two of you in a current, that the two become one flesh. And that's bull even in the metaphorical sense. Jill couldn't feel what I felt about Elias, and so she wasn't responsible for it. By extension, she wasn't responsible for anything I would do with it. She was free of all of that, and I didn't begrudge her for it. Not at all. I was glad.

Chapter 28

JILL

Candy slashed the deer's throat with a single clean cut, and the blood poured onto the ground with a lush splashing sound. Dodge had strung it up from the tree nearest the garden, where Candy thought the smell of its blood in the earth would drive away others of its species. Belatedly, Dodge thrust a bucket beneath the carcass. The sound was identical to that of flowing water. Candy slapped the deer on its flank and said, "This baby's gonna feed us all winter long."

From around the front of the house I could hear a loud metallic banging, then the sound of shattering glass. Walking over, I found Cade standing next to his Saturn with a sledge-hammer, beating the crap out of the hood. The windshield was smashed, and glass littered the driver's seat. For a couple of minutes I just stood there, watching him destroy the car. When he worked his way around to the back windshield, I asked, "Do you want to talk about it?"

He took aim at one of his taillights and whanged it with the hammer. "Talk about what?"

"Your accident. Your brother. How angry you are and where you're going with it."

"Pretty broad range of subjects."

"Cade."

He looked up at me with the defiant expression of a young man called to the principal's office. A riot of small scratches from the glass and metal covered his arms.

"This is not what you do with grief," I said. "Stop it. You're better than this, Cade. If anybody can take what happened to Elias and make something positive come out of it, it's you. But look where you're at right now. You need to—"

"Save your intervention for somebody who cares," he said. His voice took on a jeering note. "Life isn't a fucking AA meeting, Jill. Not everybody wants to sit around talking about how powerless they are and how they turned it all over to God. 'Aggressive fighting for the right is the noblest sport the world affords.'"

"So that's where you're going with this, then? You're not going to try to get over what happened to Elias at all. You're just going to keep beating and beating against that wall until somebody pays."

"Somebody owes." He whacked the back windshield. "I'm the collection agency."

I knew right then that I was going to leave him. There was no redemption to be had here, no moment of clarity when Cade would realize it was time to pull it together. Months ago, TJ's birth had shown me that I could be as strong as my mother when I needed to be; what she had endured, I could get through, as well. I couldn't remember that day we stopped in the almond orchard, and yet here I was again, standing in her place this time, knowing it was time to leave this family behind.

I would leave as soon as TJ recovered from his ear surgery. I owed my son that much, not to delay his medical treatment so I could get away from the dead end of Cade. If I could make it with him this long, I could tolerate him a little longer. And then, with the same sudden surety of knowing I was leaving, I knew my destination: not Randy's, but Southridge, the place where I'd belonged all this time. *You've got a home, and it's here,* Dave had assured me. I hoped he meant it, because I was about to show up on his doorstep either way.

I watched Cade for another minute, standing clear of the shattering glass and plastic. Then I slipped into the house, and as I made my quiet way up the stairs to check on my sleeping son, it struck me that this was exactly how my mother had done it: to walk away from my father because she saw no place for him in her future with me. I wondered if she had once loved him as I had loved Cade. Always, he had seemed so remote from my mother that I'd felt as though I was, and always had been, hers alone. I mused on whether TJ would one day feel that way, too, indifferent to who his father had been or the love that had created him. And as I lifted him from the laundry basket and cuddled him awake, I wondered if that was a victory or a loss.

Eddy was sick as a dog. On the morning Cade drove Leela down to Concord for the craft fair, when I came in with Eddy's coffee, I could not wake him up. He breathed, and behind his lids his eyes fluttered, but the usual soft shaking and calling his name did nothing to rouse him. His skin bruised so easily that I was afraid to shake him any harder. All of a sudden I felt very nervous.

"Eddy," I said more loudly, almost a reprimand. I laid my hand on his bristled cheek and patted it firmly. A crust of drool traced a line from his mouth down his chin, like a ventriloquist's dummy. I left his coffee beside the bed and called for Candy from the landing.

She thumped up the staircase and brushed past me into the bedroom. With a jaded gaze she glared down at him, ruffled the sheets a bit and said, "He's fine. He's tired, is all."

"He won't wake up."

"He just needs his rest. Leave him alone. He doesn't need your damn coffee."

She started toward the door. "Candy, stop," I pleaded. "It isn't normal for him to be like this. Don't you think we ought to call an ambulance or something?"

The corner of her mouth lifted in a smirk that was unlike her. "We don't call 911," she said, imitating Dodge. "And the phone's out anyway."

This was true. Eddy had been the one who paid the phone bill, and since he had gotten so ill, no one had bothered with it. Dodge and Candy's house had no landline, and Dodge and Cade made do with their cell phones. But Candy didn't have one, and I'd let mine go long before, when money got too tight.

"I can walk over to the Vogels' and call from there," I challenged her. "Or we can take him to the firehouse. We can't just leave him like this. What if he doesn't wake up?"

"He'll wake up once he's had his *rest*. Jeezum, Jill, let the man *be*. Don't need to call out the National Guard 'cause an old man's sleeping."

She hustled down the stairs. In the silence of the little room I looked at Eddy for a long moment, then flicked at his cheek gently with my fingers. "Wake up, Eddy," I said. "Hey. Coffee."

His breath sputtered, but his eyes stayed closed. Neither of the Vogels would challenge Candy, that much I was sure about. They were old-school New Englanders, reticent and respectful of their neighbors' privacy. *Get Scooter,* I thought, but I couldn't be sure he would stand up to Candy; if she chased him off, I would just lose time. What I needed was someone strong enough both to defy Candy and help me get help for

Eddy. I looked out the window toward the mountains. I could think of nothing to do but one thing.

Without a word to Candy, I lifted TJ from the high chair and slipped out of the house, pulling away quickly in Elias's Jeep. Gravel crackled like popcorn beneath the tires, and I knew she would hear me, but at least I could keep her guessing about where I was going. It was a burst of luck that the Jeep was even there; Cade had been using it to commute to work ever since he wrecked the Saturn, leaving me carless, but he had taken Leela down to Concord in his father's truck because there were so many crafts to carry. From the backseat came the gentle sounds of TJ playing with the rattles that hung from the bar of his infant car seat. Knowing he was safe with me calmed my nerves, but only very slightly.

The road wound east through the dark summer woods. The farther I drove, the narrower it grew, until my tires seemed barely to straddle the asphalt while skimming the dust on either side. At long last Randy's house came into view along the side of the road, the stacked stone rising like a fortress above the green hill of the lawn.

Lucia answered the door, flanked by a pair of her younger children. When I explained to her that Eddy was ill, she simply nodded, instructed her nearest teenage daughter to watch the little ones and hitched her purse to her shoulder. I recognized her truck, the green pickup with mud above its tire wells, from when she had dropped off the plate of cookies months before. She stayed close in my rearview mirror the whole way back to Frasier.

Candy stood at the storm door, defiant. Her long, wavy hair expanded across the breadth of her shoulders, thick as a plank. Before Lucia was five steps from her car, Candy shouted across the yard, "You're not coming in here."

Lucia said nothing. Over her shoulder was the strap of a blue duffel bag she had retrieved from the backseat of her truck. She trekked steadily across the soft yard to the porch and climbed its four stairs. Then she stopped and looked at Candy.

"Not in here," Candy repeated. "Turn right around and go back where you came from."

"One Christian woman to another," said Lucia, "if you'll please let me in, Candy."

"No chance of that."

The boys had gathered behind her. Matthew craned his neck to peer over the arm she used to block the doorway, while John came closer, nestling his head against the bulk of her hip. Mark watched from the other side of the doorway, wearing his green army helmet with the crack in it. I could hear the faint clatter of the objects on his belt hitting one another.

"I never did you a wrong," said Lucia.

"Randy did."

"Well, I'm not Randy. Come on, now. This isn't about him. This is about your father."

Candy's gaze drifted over Lucia's shoulder. She was watching, I knew, for Dodge. Then she closed the door in Lucia's face.

Lucia and I looked at each other. "I live here, too," I said. "So let me in."

Almost fearfully, I jammed my key in the door and pushed it open. My gaze darted around—I was half expecting to see Candy standing there with a shotgun. Instead I heard the water running in the kitchen, and the normal sounds of the boys horsing around near their mother. Candy was pretending she had nothing to do with Lucia and her intrusion. Willfully oblivious.

I set TJ against my shoulder, and Lucia followed me up the

stairs. A line formed between her eyebrows as soon as she saw Eddy. She set her bag at the end of the bed, like a country doctor, and gave him a quick examination with her eyes and hands. "How long has he been asleep?"

"Since around seven last night."

She pulled back the covers and felt around on the mattress. "Dry."

"That's good, right? That he still has control of his bladder and all."

Her head gave a slight shake. "No. It's kidney failure." She braced her hands beneath his arms and looked to me to grab his ankles. As I did, I saw the fabric of her skirt pull tight across her belly and realized she was pregnant.

"No," I said. "You can't carry him."

"I carry wood every day. Don't concern yourself about it."

I hesitated, then looked toward the steep and narrow stairs. For one long, uneasy moment I tried to accept her reassurance, but all I could think about was the moment I'd come across the plastic hospital-issue bag with my clothes in it from the night TJ was born, the fabric dark and stiffened with blood. One slip of Lucia's foot could end in a calamity I couldn't bear. "No way," I repeated. "If you have a phone, we should call an ambulance."

"No time for that. Go get Scooter." I raised an eyebrow, and she said, "Well, he lives right over there. He'll help, Jill. This isn't the time for petty loyalties. He'll know that."

"All right. Can you handle Candy if she comes in?"

"Of course I can handle Candy. Candy isn't anything."

I passed TJ over to her. As she shifted him to her hip with her capable hands, I ran down the stairs and out the door toward the Vogels' farm. Scooter lived in the walk-out basement, one with a door that was never locked because this was Frasier. My pulse pounded in my ears as I raced across the gray asphalt road and through the overgrown grass, past Sara Vogel's neat vegetable patch with its pie tins rattling on stakes and strings, to Scooter's rain-beaten basement door.

Without a knock, I pushed it open and shouted his name. He looked up from where he lay on a battered sofa, playing Atari games on a television three times his age. A few words about Eddy's state were all I said, and in an instant he had shoved his feet into his boots and was rushing past me out the door, flying across the lawn in his untied boots and unbelted jeans. By the time I arrived back on our property I could hear Candy shouting from inside, and Scooter was shuffling out the front door with Dad over his shoulder in a fireman's lift. Lucia followed close behind, TJ on her hip.

"Sorry," said Scooter, edging toward the porch stairs. "Tried to wait for you, but Candy was making a scene. Which car?"

Lucia opened the rear door of her truck, and I helped ease Eddy onto the seat. "I hope he's all right," said Scooter. "Poor old dude."

"Say a prayer," said Lucia. She passed me TJ and climbed into the cab of her truck, gunning the engine.

"Wait," I said. "I need the diaper bag. It's just inside the front door."

Scooter shook his head. "Stay here and I'll go with her. I know all his information. You call Cade, get him to come to the hospital."

His idea made more sense than mine. I couldn't give proper attention to Eddy's needs with a baby in my arms, and there was no chance I would leave TJ with an unstable Candy. I stepped back and Scooter climbed into the passenger seat, barely pulling the door closed before Lucia backed out of the driveway.

From inside I heard Candy yelling at one of her boys. I took a deep, shaky breath, then loaded my son back into the

Jeep. I could call Cade from the U–Store–It office and give him the news about his dad, then stay there for a while until Candy had a chance to calm down. No way was I about to go back inside. She frightened me now.

Chapter 29

LEELA

When the Vogel girl first started coming around, I didn't pay her too much mind. She knew Candy from church, and I wasn't all that keen on that church of theirs. I go with her now, but mainly to get out of this house for a bit, since I never did learn how to drive, and being inside all the time gives me cabin fever something fierce. And I like to sing. I keep the songs going in my head while the pastor is talking, so that way I can get through the whole service.

That Vogel girl—her name was Lindsay—she was younger than Candy by a couple of years, and unmarried. Despite that they were friends, and I felt torn about that situation. On the one hand I remembered what it felt like to be a child-less woman in a room full of mothers, how they elbowed me out without even knowing they were doing it, and so it was kind of Candy to reach out to her in friendship. But on the other hand this was Candy, and something in me hated for that vulnerable, sheltered Vogel girl to get wrapped up in my daughter. Sometimes they'd be talking at the table, the way Lucia and I used to, and I'd picture Candy standing at that rabbit hutch with her back to me, the suppressor on the .22 reducing each shot to a distant firework. Maybe I thought if I was cool to Lindsay, she'd soon enough be safely on her way.

It was the season when both of my sons went away and then came back. Cade went off to college that fall, and Elias had been away at basic training and infantry school. It had taken him an extra month. He had written to me that he got "recycled," which is the army way of saying you couldn't do enough push-ups or run fast enough, so they make you train all over again. But when he walked in that door after all of that—more than four months after last I saw him—he looked ever so much better. Hardly had any stomach on him at all, and his arms looked strong. It was like I could finally exhale—after all those years of reassuring him he was just fine the way God had made him, finally God had granted him a reprieve from being a butterball.

As soon as Cade got home, too, the two of them went out together to meet some old friends down at the quarry. I guess they had a snowball fight, because when they got back both of those ninnies were covered in snow, with big splotches of it on their backs. I made them turn right around at the door and come in through the back porch. Once they shook off their coats and wraps, they came inside laughing, with hands and cheeks rose-red from the cold. Candy and Lindsay were sitting at the table with their coffee, and Candy jumped right up to pour some for the boys. She poured lots of sugar and milk in Eli's, the way he liked it, and he reached for that mug like he was holding his hands up to a campfire. Even though he looked like a soldier now, I could still so easily see the little boy in him. He'd rather have a cup of cocoa and we both knew it, but he was a man now and it would be coffee for him.

Candy was bustling around the coffee machine, and when I looked at Lindsay I saw she was staring right at Elias, smiling in this shy, surprised way. She was a plain-looking girl, with a heart-shaped face and hair that had never been cut, and she wore those smocky flowered dresses like Candy and the other church women. Elias didn't seem to notice. He was still bantering with Cade, the two of them joking over who had gotten in the best shots of the snowball fight. Lindsay Vogel was his same age, had lived up the road all his life, but her family had homeschooled her and so he hardly knew her at all. When I saw the look she was giving him I thought about Piper, with her straightened hair and model figure, her made-up eyes, and I thought Lindsay might as well march that notion right back out of her head as fast as it had come in.

Candy turned around with the coffeepot and opened her mouth to ask her friend if she wanted more, but stopped before a word came out. She looked from Lindsay to Elias and back again. Then, with a noisy clatter, she set the pot down and called her children over to say hello to their uncles. John was just a baby, pushing his cereal pieces around on the high-chair tray, but the other two came barreling over and threw themselves at their uncles' knees. Lindsay took a lemon cookie from the plate at the center of the table and waved it in front of John's face, playing with him a little before she let him have it. I went upstairs after that, and so that's the way I remember seeing Lindsay Vogel: waving that cookie around for my grandbaby, maybe—or maybe not—putting on a show for Elias of how nice she was with babies. And she *was* a nice girl, even if she never would have been his sort of girl. Anyone could look upon Elias then and see that now he was turning into the type of man who might be able to get a Piper Larsen to give him a second or a third look. And Lindsay—well, she only had three days left in this world. So whether or not she caught Eli's eye didn't really matter anyway.

Because it was three days after that when all the kids in town—the mostly grown ones included—went down to the quarry for their after-Christmas hockey game. For as long as

I could remember it had been like a reunion, when the college and moved-away kids would get together just for a few hours and play like they had in years gone by. I stayed home with John, but Candy brought Mark and Matthew down to watch Cade and Eli play. The quarry lake was so big that all the girls usually brought their figure skates, and they'd amuse themselves that way when they got tired of watching hockey. When my boys got back that day, Cade was so generous in his praise of his brother, bragging about how well Elias was skating and how he'd made two goals. Elias brushed it off, but I knew he was proud. His confidence was like a bud popping out on a tree. It was still fragile, but I believed it would grow. I wondered if Piper was home from school, and if he would see her before he shipped out on the first of January.

It was hours before Candy came home. She didn't have any kind of cellular phone, and as night fell I started to get worried. So did Dodge. He left the house and started driving around town, asking people if they had seen her or the boys. And it was on that drive that he learned what had happened—that during the last hockey game of the day, one of the girls who was off figure skating had cracked through the ice where it was thinnest beneath the overhanging trees, and the others hadn't been able to get her out. As soon as I heard that, I knew it had been Lindsay Vogel. She had been so sheltered, kept away from socializing with the other town kids so much, that she didn't know the quarry ice very well. I guess they all thought she was old enough to know what she was doing, so nobody noticed when she got into trouble. By the time they managed to pull her out, she was gone. Candy was the only one who saw her go through, the one who called to everybody else for help. She told me her boys hadn't seen any of it, that she'd kept them and the other little children away while the other young people tried to get her out. I suppose that's a mercy, that they never saw such an awful thing. For all that Candy seems calloused up against brutality, at least she didn't let them see that.

Chapter 30

JILL

Lucia was right. Eddy was in renal failure, and the afternoon turned into a mad scramble to get Cade down to the hospital to make decisions on behalf of his mother, whom Dodge was bringing back from Concord. His father would need dialysis, and even if he got well enough to be released, coming home wasn't a viable option for the immediate future. Cade didn't know what to do about that, and so, like so many other things these days, he could only patch up a temporary solution: to set up Leela in a motel adjacent to the hospital so she could come and go easily for the duration. He got home at 11:00 p.m., exhausted both physically and mentally. But the next morning, once he came in after the chores were done and found Candy cooking up breakfast as if everything were normal, he tore into her.

"What the hell were you *thinking?*" he barked at her. "He almost died up there in his own goddamn bed with his own daughter *right there.* You don't have the two brain cells' worth of common sense it would take to see how sick he was?"

"Maybe I would have if *she* hadn't gone dancing off to bring over Lucia. You want to talk about sense—and you never had the sense to tell her we don't deal with those people?"

"*You* don't deal with those people. I couldn't care less. And

Jill did the right thing. I'd much rather bring Randy and his whole damn militia to my door than let Dad just keel over and die. Jesus."

Candy shrugged loosely and plated a scrambled egg. "Better to die on your feet than live on your knees."

The corner of Cade's lip curled upward. "So courageous of you to make that decision on behalf of somebody else."

Casually Candy pointed her spatula in my direction. "Ask your wife about the decision *she* made for us. Now Dad's stuck in a hospital, probably all delirious and saying whatever pops into his mind. There's some things around here you better hope he doesn't start talking about."

"That's ridiculous," Cade said. But Dodge didn't agree, and whatever he said to Cade about it later seemed to convince him, as well. From that night onward they instituted a system of nighttime watch shifts, switching off every few hours and bringing in Scooter to take a shift as well, imagining the government was about to swoop in over some unregistered guns. At any hour of the night, when I woke to nurse TJ, I could hear their slow, heavy-booted footsteps creaking the hardwood floors, walking the inside perimeter. Cade kept Elias's gun holstered on his belt all the time now when he was home. The only time he took it off was when he lay down with TJ, and then he would set it on the fireplace mantel, never more than a few paces away.

A few days into this arrangement, I awoke to the clunk of Cade's gun against the nightstand, followed by the soft, rumpled sound of clothes dropping to the floor. I squinted awake: the clock read 2:00 a.m. Cade climbed in beneath the covers and ran his hand up against my belly. "Hey, you," he said with affection, and rolled me onto my back. Despite the late hour he was buzzing with energy. The estrangement I felt from him in my heart should have made it easier to push him away at times like this, but instead it only made it harder. In spite of everything, I still yearned to be close to him, to feel once again the kind of intimacy we had shared in the beginning and store it away as a memory. Soon I would be gone, and who knew how long it would be before I would feel that human touch again, or feel even that tenuous sense of connection? Each time with him now the thought would flutter through my mind—*this could be the last time*—and for a few minutes everything I had grown to resent and disdain and even fear about him seemed to fall away, leaving only the beauty of him, which was the one sure thing he had held on to.

After he was sated, he slumped his arm across me and fell asleep. I never could get used to that unit patch tattoo, identical to the one I had traced on Elias's skin in moments only he and I had shared. For a while I lay there awake and curled with my back against Cade's chest, holding his arm with both hands. But the urge to cry grew stronger and stronger, and finally I unwound myself from his embrace and pulled my clothes on quietly, then tiptoed out of the room so I would not wake him with my snuffling.

From the stair landing I could see the light on beside Elias's chair, a dim star. Downstairs I heard that slow heel-toe double-thump, working its way from the foyer to the living room and around to the addition. I walked on the outside edge of the stairs so as not to let them creak. Scooter looked up as I came down, at first in alarm, then with a somber wave of his hand.

"Hey, Jill," he said, keeping his voice low.

"Hey." I walked up to the front window, pushed the curtain aside and peered out in defiance of the paranoia. Nobody was there. The dark was absolute, broken only by the lacy line of the treetops and the jagged silhouette of the mountains, contrasting black against deeper black. I let the curtain drop and went to the kitchen to run myself a glass of water from the sink. The TV was off. When Cade or Dodge kept watch they left it on—muted, but with the picture on nonetheless, like a sort of electronic eternal flame lit for Elias. Yet Scooter had no such sentimentality, and so the only light came from the reading lamp beside the chair.

"Hope I didn't wake you up," Scooter said. "I try not to walk too loud."

"It's not you. I just couldn't sleep."

"I know what you mean." He had made his way to the dining room now, gazing through each window at the backyard, or at least what he could see of it through the screen porch. A handgun was tucked into the back of his jeans, bunching his shirt at the small of his back. "I'm looking forward to the end of all this."

I drank down my water. "Won't be till Eddy gets home, I guess. And who knows how long they'll keep it up after that. It's the most paranoid thing I've ever heard of, thinking an old man's going to start mumbling about his unregistered guns in his sleep."

Scooter shook his head slowly. His gaze drifted up to the second-floor landing, then returned to bore into me. In a lower voice he asked, "Is that what they told you?"

He sat down in a kitchen chair, then leaned forward to tug the gun from the back of his pants and set it on the table. His face was so young, but those wire-rimmed glasses gave him an owlish look. With his pale skin and high-and-tight haircut, he had the earnest look of a missionary. I said nothing. I could only hold his gaze and wait for him to go on.

"Now's a good time to get out, Jill," he said. His voice had grown so quiet that the low syllables bumped against each other like marbles, but his meaning was clear enough. "Remember what I said to you about Randy."

Fear prickled at the back of my neck. "What's going on?"

"If I knew I'd tell you. I figured you knew more than I did. You live here." He glanced up at the landing again. "I don't think they trust me enough anymore to say. But I know they're not watching the property twenty-four-seven because they're worried over Eddy. That never even came up."

I felt panic tightening my chest as I pictured TJ fast asleep in the laundry basket beside the bed, clad only in a diaper and a thin white undershirt, and the keys to the Jeep in the pocket of Cade's dirty jeans. I had waited much too long to make my escape plans, as if this moment would never come, when all along I knew it would. "Well, what *did* they say?" I demanded. "How much time do I have?"

"It has to do with getting retribution for Elias, that's all I know. If I knew details none of us would be here now. Maybe I would have turned him in already." At the sight of my fearful gaze he lowered his voice to a conciliatory whisper. "I'm sure they won't do anything till after your kid gets his ear thing done. Cade loves his son and all. I know he's planning to be around for that. But if I were you I would go straight to Randy's from there. I wouldn't mess around."

"Have you said anything to anyone? The police?"

"No, they wouldn't do anything. There's plenty of people up here who make that same kind of noise. I'd get thrown under the bus for it, and they'd think it was nothing special. Except Cade always wants to be the special one. That's the one difference, I guess."

I sat down wearily in the chair closest to his and rested my temple against my hand, gazing out the window at the Jeep. Crescents of moonlight reflected off the curve around its headlights, a sharp glint against the darkness. *If only it weren't for TJ.* I wished desperately that I could call upon my mother to get us out of here, give us shelter, frame up the step-by-step plan to untangle our circumstances. But that was nothing more than an idle wish. There was only me.

"I understood it at first," said Scooter. "When the government isn't just, people *ought* to rise up. But the cloak-and-dagger stuff, it doesn't feel right. It isn't the way to honor Elias. He was a soldier. He fought in a uniform. He didn't deceive anybody."

In my life I haven't felt a great deal of regret, but I felt it then. It was like a dissolving in the pit of my stomach, a sense of waste and lost time. The seam of my shorts felt damp from Cade, and again I pictured him dozing upstairs, peaceful and complacent with no right to be so, draped half over my side of the bed. As the regret moved through me I felt it trailed by a fresh burst of anger: at what a stooge he had made me, how easily I had mistaken his ambition for character, and how now I would have to scrap this life and cobble together a new one, again—but this time with a child who deserved better. The thoughts twisted together into a tight bundle of rage. But I needed to push that down for now. Throwing my energy into the chaos of anger would only make things harder for my son.

"Thanks, Scooter," I said. I looked away from the window and into his eyes, nervous and grave as they were. "I can't tell you how much it means to me that you trust me like this."

He shrugged his narrow shoulders and rubbed at a smudge on his gun. "You know what, Jill, I hate feeling like a snitch. The rights and the wrongs here run together until I don't know for sure which is which anymore. But the one thing I know is, the whole reason Elias was in Afghanistan was to fight the ones who brought down buildings full of innocent people on 9/11. So if somebody says they're going to go and do that same kind of thing in Elias's name, I'm going to speak

up. If I follow that way through it, doing what seems right
and logical, I guess I can feel okay when it's over."

I nodded, but more than anything I wondered what those
last three words would mean.

As the sun rose the following morning I lay quietly beside Cade, listening to the peaceful rhythm of his breathing.
I wondered how I was going to get through the next days,
living alongside him knowing all that Scooter had told me,
wondering every moment if my words or actions would give
away my plan to leave him. I felt my mind shuttling itself into
survival mode—locking its doors, sealing its windows with
tape, filling up the bathtub with water to last the duration—
doing whatever would help it press through the day ahead,
accomplishing what needed to be done without incurring further damage. Once Cade had left for work, I loaded TJ into
his car seat and drove over to the U-Store-It. Any calls I made
from the little office would be listed on the phone bill, but I
figured by the time the family received it, I would be gone.

I let myself in with my key, and dialed. Dave picked up on
the third ring.

"Jill," he said, and even over the fuzzy connection I heard
happiness in the way his voice lifted. "Been wondering how
you've been. What's going on?"

My laugh was short and hard. "Things with Cade aren't
going so great. I need to get out. Like, Wednesday."

"Oh, jeez. Well, you know you can come here whenever
you need. Come now if you want."

Silently I started to cry. My throat grew too tight to speak,
and I moved the receiver away from my mouth so he wouldn't
hear my breathing. TJ twisted the long, curling cord between
his fists, catching my hair in his grasp and pulling painfully,

but I didn't care. I could go home now. There was an end to this, and it was Wednesday.

"Can you get down here?" he asked into my silence. "You need gas money or anything? I can wire it to you. Where are you, New Hampshire?"

"Yeah." I forced an even breath, then said, "My son is having surgery on Wednesday. I can't leave till after that, but it's outpatient. Cade will get a ride in to work once it's over so I can keep the car in case there's any complications later and I need to take him back in. But my plan is to leave straight from the hospital and just keep driving."

"Wow. Sounds like things are pretty bad over there."

I blurted a quick, humorless laugh at the understatement. "I can't even tell you, Dave."

"Is he beating you? What is it?"

I couldn't let Dave know the details—not this way, over the phone. If I told him what Scooter had said to me he would probably leave Southridge before the call had ended and show up at my door, throwing everything into disorder. So I only said, "I'll explain when I get there."

There was a long silence across the phone line. Then Dave said, "Jill, let me come up and get you. I don't like the sound of all this. Sounds like you could use a backup in case something goes wrong."

"No, don't go to all that trouble. Just be at camp when I get there."

"Uh-uh. No. The most dangerous time for a woman in your position is when you try to leave. That's when people get killed." I heard drawers opening and slamming shut. "I got a pen. Give me an address where to meet you."

I thought about the tires on the Jeep, worn almost bald. It was a long way down the state, through all the long stretches of woods and past so many abandoned houses and motels, miles between towns. If I broke down and he came looking for me, I'd have no place to go. I said, "The hospital."

"Where your kid's having his surgery, you mean?"

"Yeah, in Laconia. I'll meet you in front of the emergency room. I'll try to be there at noon. We should be done by then."

He wrote down the information I offered him, asking for specifics about the door I'd come out from and what the family members looked like, just in case. As I spoke I saw Dodge's long black truck pull up in front of the office. I slammed down the phone and moved toward the door, holding TJ across my chest with his head cradled in my hand. Dodge sauntered toward the door, keys in hand, with Scooter close behind him.

"Didn't expect to find anybody here," he said. "Something going on?"

"No. Just using the phone. The pharmacy got TJ's prescription all mixed up. Had to call the doc."

Dodge's gaze was cool and narrow. I hiked TJ higher on my shoulder and asked, "You need any help, as long as I'm here?"

"Thought you needed to go to the pharmacy."

"Well, they won't have it ready for half an hour. I can work."

He pondered that, then shook his head. "Just replacing some lightbulbs and a lock."

I nodded and slipped past him out the door. As I clipped TJ's car seat into place in the back of the Jeep, I could see him in my peripheral vision standing steady at the window, watching me. I figured he knew then that something was up. Anxiety buzzed in my veins like a swarm of bees. *You can climb in this car and drive south and never come back,* I told myself. But that would mean starting from scratch with TJ, with a new doctor and a new set of paperwork to get medical care from the state. It would set us back by months. That time meant pain, and infection, and all the risks that had convinced me

to overrule Cade in the first place to get the state's aid for TJ.
I had made this decision already. It was too late to second-
guess myself.

It was only a few more days. We could make it.

I got home shortly before lunch. Candy was preparing mac-
aroni and cheese from a box and ignoring the slapstick fighting
her sons were doing all over the dining room. I settled TJ into
his high chair with a bowl of rehydrated peas and hoped he
would survive the older boys while I went looking for Cade.

It was Saturday, and normally at this hour on a weekend
he would be catching up on lost sleep, having returned to
bed after finishing his morning shift. Now, though, his sleep
schedule was particularly skewed by the night watches, and I
found our bed empty. Returning to the first floor, I caught
sight of him through the broad windows of the screen porch,
standing at a table set up outside the shed. I headed out across
the yard, and as I approached I felt a wave of dread at the realization that he was working on another pipe bomb right
out in the open air, not even attempting to conceal himself.
So Scooter wasn't exaggerating, I thought. I moved toward him
cautiously, wondering if he had assumed I was away from
the house and would startle at seeing me. But instead he only
looked up and raised his hand in a wave.

I called him in to lunch, and he took his time, finishing
up the details of the bomb and making small talk with me
without any hint of apology or shame. As he spoke I watched
his hands—those palms beautiful and square, his fingers as
strong as a pianist's and firm in a handshake. I thought about
how it had felt when he cupped my face, kissing me for the
first time, enveloping my jaw in his warmth. He had so much
potential then, so much skill. And here he was now.

"You know what we need?" he asked, and when he spoke

my name it shocked me back to the moment at hand. "A week-end away. No whining kids, no animals to feed, no parents in the next room keeping things all quiet and inhibited. No sitting watch at three in the morning like we're the goddamn Branch Davidians. Just you and me in a motel room some-place, getting friendly."

I supposed that was his way of telling me the strain of it was getting to him, too. I supposed that, like the government jobs he still applied for and the college-class schedules he still composed before each semester, this was his way of reaching out to touch the Cade he had been before Elias died. *That* Cade just needed a break from the daily grind, and nothing in his life was so overwhelming that an afternoon of good sex couldn't knock it back into perspective. He wanted so much to believe that, deep down, he was still the same guy. And for better or worse, I suspected that was true.

"There's an alumni weekend at our alma mater next month," I said sarcastically. "We could go to that, if you haven't blown yourself up by then."

He snickered and came around to kiss me. "'Let justice be done though the heavens should fall.'"

So this is how it is now, I thought. I imagined the freedom to work under the light of day must have felt pretty good to him. The arrogance of it filled me with a rush of bitterness, but I tried to ride it out and let it go. I wasn't going to be here much longer. And his trust in me, now, was unfounded. As soon as TJ came out of his surgery, I had phone calls I would make.

Cade brushed the dust from his arms and walked over to the spigot to wash his hands. As the dirt fell away, he men-tioned, "I'm heading down to D.C. on Monday."

"To blow stuff up?"

"No," he said, in a voice that suggested I was being ridiculous. "Gonna put out some résumés. Homeland Security, the Veterans Administration. See if I can get any nibbles."

"You're kidding, right?" He wiped his hands on his jeans and glanced up at me, and I continued, "You really think you could pass a background check right now? Seriously?"

"Sure I could. My record's clean."

"Cade."

He stood and shrugged. "Everybody's gotta have a plan A and a plan B. I've been on Plan B ever since we moved here, but I'm still amenable to Plan A. In fact, I'd prefer it. Whether or not they give me a fair shake is their call. In the meantime, I can multitask."

I shook my head. "That's insane."

"No," he said right away, his tone strident. "What's insane is the state of this country, and the state of the VA in particular. It's shameful and it's a dishonor to the people who served. I've never wanted to do anything with my life except make this country better, and through the proper channels. But whenever any form of government becomes destructive to these ends, it's the right of the people—"

"Yeah, yeah, yeah. To alter or abolish it. You've said."

He shot me a reprimanding look and began walking toward the house.

"TJ's surgery is Wednesday," I said, falling in step just behind him.

"That's okay, I'll be back Tuesday night. I wouldn't miss his surgery. Dodge and I will go down in his truck and I'll leave you the Jeep. I doubt the Jeep would make it that far anyway, with the tires the way they are." He stepped through the porch door and waved to TJ. "Hey there, little buddy."

At the sight of his father TJ slapped the high-chair tray with both hands and arched back with a grin of utter delight. Nothing could make me feel more awful than that. In the long run, though, maybe it was healthier—for my son to come away with some deep core memory of a father who loved him, and to imagine the idealized man he might have been. Because I often wished I'd stopped there, too.

Chapter 31

CADE

It was tiring, sitting watch every night, trading off with Dodge and Scooter every couple of hours. The baby woke up what felt like every ten minutes even when I *was* in bed, and after a few weeks of that, the sleep deprivation was killer. Scooter moved in for the duration. We set up an air mattress in the cellar and threw a blanket on it, and that was where he slept.

Dodge came into the shed one evening while I was working on the project. The solder gun was out and a bunch of circuitry maps were spread out all over the worktable. He leaned against the table for a while and watched. Out of nowhere he said, "Scooter's a government plant."

"Huh?"

"You don't think?"

I set down the roll of solder and the gun. "Of course not. How would he be a plant? He didn't just pop up out of no place. He's local. And he just got out of high school, like, a year ago."

"Sure seems like one to me. Never takes any initiative of his own. Always just does what we tell him."

"That's because he's not too bright."

"He helped Randy's wife that one day. Didn't bat an eye."

I gave him a dirty look. "He helped get my dad to the hospital when Candy decided she was going to act like a small-minded bat-shit moron and let him die in his bed. That's the only reason Jill brought Lucia over. Because *your* wife wouldn't help her."

"What's Jill doing consorting with Randy, anyway? How does she even know him?"

"From the funeral."

"So she says. I ran into her at the U-Store-It, all alone, making a phone call from the office. Said she was calling the kid's doctor. What do you figure the odds are of that?"

"Oh, for Christ's sake." I picked up the soldering tools again. "Jill's not a plant either, all right? That I'm sure about."

"You don't think people sell out when somebody makes them an offer, huh?"

"Not Jill and not Scooter. Get a grip."

Dodge was quiet for a couple of minutes. He stood there watching me work. Then he said, "One of these days you're gonna work up the respect due to me. Once you grow up some and come to see things my way."

"Whatever."

"There you go again. Fact is, even when you know I'm right you won't admit it. Too goddamn arrogant."

"The problem's not that I'm arrogant. It's that you shove your nose into my business way too often. You've got to med-dle in everything, whether it involves you or not."

He was leaning on his arms against the bench, but at that he looked up at me with a gleam in his eye beneath his trucker cap. "Oh, I get it. You're still sore about my cabinet project in here, all those years ago. When you were using this place as your little love nest."

I kept soldering and didn't say anything.

"Yep," he said. "Cade sees it Cade's way, through Cadey's big blue eyes. Tell you what, I got tired of seeing the look on your brother's face every time he knew you were in here messing around with that girl. You wouldn't have seen that, though, would you?"

He waited to see if I'd reply, but I stayed silent. All I could think was I hated him more for saying that than I ever had for running me and Piper out of the shed.

"If I were Elias," he went on, "I wouldn't have been able to tolerate that shit. The way you treated him over that—I'd have had a mind to put a stop to it once and for all, any way it took. But nobody ever could get a rage out of Elias, and don't ask me why. God knows I tried. Would have done him good, and God knows you had it coming, Cade."

He held me in a kind of stare-down until I pulled the soldering gun's plug out of the outlet without breaking eye contact. Then he shrugged and straightened up.

"You'll think what you want to think, even when you're wrong and you know you're wrong," he said.

Where Scooter and Jill were concerned I didn't give it a second thought after that, not for a while anyway. Where Piper came in, I put it out of my mind. The project was consuming all my spare time and needed to be my priority. Sitting watch during those long, lonesome hours, watching the night through the window glass and perking up my ears at every sound—all of that made me feel paranoid enough without casting my own people as suspect. Every time I left the house to go anyplace, I felt jumpy. All of this was Dodge's fault. New Hampshire had felt like its own kingdom to me, far apart from the spy-versus-spy political crap in Washington. It's funny how the power of suggestion works like that. Just float the idea that somebody might be watching me, and I'm skittering away from my own shadow.

It wasn't going to slow me down, though, as far as the project went. When I ventured out to the hardware store in

Henderson, I made sure nothing about my appearance would attract attention. Grimy Levi's worn soft and held up by a nicked leather belt, untied work boots, ball cap with the brim rolled tight, three days of beard. My T-shirt had the American Eagle logo across the chest, preppy when I bought it, but the tattered hem and the holes under the arms had long since made it work-shirt material. I looked like any low-wage construction worker who would have every good reason to be buying twelve boxes of nails at once.

I slid the boxes across the counter, told the cashier to add a pack of cigarettes and tugged my wallet out of my back pocket. As she rang me up, another customer plunked her purchase down at the end of the counter. In a quiet voice I knew right away, she said, "Hi, Cade."

There stood Piper, looking at me with an embarrassed smile. Her hair was in a short ponytail sticking out the back of her cap, and her shirt had spatters of white paint all over it.

"Hey," I said.

"What are you doing all the way down here?"

"Just...shopping. I was in the neighborhood." I handed a twenty to the cashier. "You?"

"I live here now." She pushed her one item forward: a toilet flush valve. "I got my own place after graduation. It needs a little work."

"Paint and plumbing, huh?"

"How'd you guess." She laughed quickly and handed over her credit card. "I've got the paint part down. I just need to figure out how to install this thing."

"It's not that hard. You've got to turn off the main water, and then once you drain it there's two bolts at the bottom—" Her mouth had twisted upward with amusement. I said, "It doesn't take long. You want me to do it?"

She lived near enough that she had walked over. She

climbed into the passenger seat of the Jeep to give me directions to her apartment. The drive was so brief I barely got a moment to consider the irony of it. Here I'd been mooning over the girl for months, stalking her even, and now here she turns up at the hardware store and jumps into my car minutes later. But when it happened like that, it just felt ordinary in spite of it all. It was only Piper, whom I'd known since I was born. She was just the girl in the crazy hat reading *Of Mice and Men* on the school bus, the one who sold ice-cold watermelons by the side of the road.

Her flat was on the top floor of an old brick garden apartment building, three stories above the street. My boots clunked loudly against the stairs as I followed her. The apartment smelled like fresh paint, but I could tell it was all coming from the bedroom. The living room was simple but all in order: an old sofa and a couple of museum posters on the walls, and a little dinette table with two wildly painted chairs. She led me to the bathroom in the hallway, and I flicked on the light. The dotted shower curtain and pink rug had been shoved away from the toilet with its missing lid, obviously a project abandoned by someone confounded by it.

I got to work. She had the right tools around, just no idea of how to use them. As I worked she talked to me from the doorway, filling me in about all the details of her life the past few years. I could have predicted nearly all of it: a backpacking trip through France, a broken engagement, a chemistry degree, grad school on the horizon. She asked about my parents, then started on the rest of the family.

"How's your son?"

"He's fine."

"And your girlfriend?"

Even the mention of Jill unnerved me. I didn't like Piper conjuring her at all. "Don't ask," I said, brusque to the point of being rude. The chagrin of it made me realize the answer implied a breakup, but I wasn't about to bring it back up to correct myself.

"I'm sorry," Piper said. "I didn't mean to pry. That's the same answer I always give people when they ask about Michael."

"You two split up?"

"We had different goals," was all she said.

I flushed the toilet and watched the mechanism work, then slid the lid back on with a hollow clunk. "Fixed."

"Thanks so much." As I washed my hands, she added, "It's hard to believe it was almost a year ago that I saw you last. We keep meeting under strange circumstances."

"This isn't as bad as last time."

"Certainly not, no. I'm so sorry about Elias—really, Cade, I am. I was as shocked as anybody when I heard. How are you doing?"

I toweled off my hands. "I'm all right. Good days and bad days."

"I see you got a tattoo. What does it say?" I held up my arm, and she read aloud clumsily, "'*Fiat justitia ruat caelum.*' What does that mean?"

"'Let justice be done though the heavens should fall.'" When her forehead creased up with confusion, I added, "John Adams said it during the Revolution."

She smiled. "You're so wonky, Cade. Even when you rebel, you're wonky. But it's sexy."

I grinned.

"Well, do you want the grand tour? Or do you need to get back to work?"

"I'll take the tour."

"It's not very grand, really. You already saw the living room.

There's the kitchen." She pointed to a little galley kitchen on the right. "And here's my room. Under construction."

I leaned against the doorway and looked in. The dresser was still shoved against an unpainted wall, but the bed had been pushed to the center of the room and piled up with pillows and a white duvet. Blue painter's tape lined the carpet where it met the walls. The light was off, but the room was bright from the sunshine coming in through the blinds.

"Not a lot of personality to it yet," she said. "The landlord paid for the paint, but said it had to be white. I've got all my posters in the closet. Maybe I'll call you when it's done. I can do better than this, *really*. It's kind of embarrassing. I don't like leaving it half-finished."

I laughed at the way she said that. It summed up my thoughts exactly, but on a different subject. She shot me a quizzical look. And then I did the natural thing—the thing that came naturally because I'd rehearsed it in my mind a thousand times in the past few months. I laced my fingers into her hair and went in to kiss her.

She kissed me back. The way her mouth tasted put a lonesome ache in the pit of my stomach from the familiarity of it, from how far away the memory seemed. But that passed quickly, and the excitement of being there with her ramped up second by second. Time had taken a U-turn, at long last admitting it had gone way off the fucking highway, and now I could whiz past all my mistakes and regrets and the specific moments when I became more and more of an asshole and into my sublime original life, which began with the beautiful girl who singled me out to kiss her in the quarry lake. Me above all the others.

I held her face in both hands and leaned back against the door frame. She slid her palms up my stomach to my chest. Every nerve along their path flared on like a gas burner. I knew it was wrong to do this to Jill. She was my wife, the mother of my son, who was the only decent thing my life had to show for itself, and my regrets and mistakes weren't her fault. I knew I ought to stop, but I didn't want to stop. I tried pelting my guilt with a dozen justifications. It didn't count if it was a girl I had been with years before Jill ever came along. It didn't count because I was just horny, and in that sense it wasn't personal against Jill but strictly biological. And it didn't count when the girl was the one Elias had loved, and I had appointed myself Elias's proxy on earth. In fact, this would be the first time it had *ever* been all right to sleep with Piper, because for once I wasn't being a piece of shit to my brother by lying down with her.

But I knew every bit of that was a lie. It counted. Not only did it count, but it was the biggest fuck-you I could give to Jill, because I'd had plenty of chances to walk myself through this scenario in my head and end up choosing the right. And even as I kissed Piper I knew the thing that tempted me most was the opportunity to shake off the embarrassment of my former ineptitude and pleasure the hell out of her, so she'd remember that instead. Even in my compromised state I could perceive what a jackass I was to think that. Jill had taken enough hits for my ego already. She didn't need to take Piper's hits, too.

The challenge was to get my body to cooperate with the ruling of my brain. Piper was murmuring in my ear that she had missed me, how much she loved my body, how much she loved it in really specific ways, and when she felt my erection with one hand and undid my belt with the other one, I knew I couldn't stop but that I had to.

I set my hands against her upper arms and pushed her back gently. Her face got that perplexed look again, and so very deliberately I buckled my belt, checked my zipper, pursed my lips and exhaled slowly.

"I'd love to," I told her, "but I really can't. I can't."

She blinked once and looked away, toward the window. Her long throat caught the light. Shadows played against the tendons, fell into the small hollows at the base. "See you around, then," she said.

"Don't be mad. It isn't personal. I got married, Piper."

She nodded. "Then you're a giant asshole."

I tried to laugh, but it came out as a hard sigh. "Believe me, nobody knows that better than I do."

The night I drove down to D.C. with Dodge, I put TJ to bed before I left and watched him for a long time. Elias always said he looked like me, and there in the dark, with his face all serious, I could definitely see it. He had the same type of hair I had as a kid, the really shiny kind of blond that means your mother's always touching your head to check if it's greasy. His first birthday was coming up, and he was right on the verge of walking. When Jill let him down from his high chair and set him on the rug, he'd pull up on Elias's chair and stand there holding on with one hand, the other one out like a little wing, looking as if he was making up his mind about whether it was worth his time to take a step forward. Jill kept saying we needed to get him a new bed, that it wouldn't be safe to let him sleep in the laundry basket any longer, but I kept procrastinating because I knew the truth. I wasn't going to be there for the next stage with him. I wanted his baby days to be like a closed room or the inside of an egg. Whatever was beyond it, I couldn't think about that.

Once he was sound asleep I grabbed my messenger bag and went out to the truck where Dodge was waiting. On my way out I heard Jill moving around in the kitchen, talking to Scooter, whom Dodge had assigned to the night watch. I didn't say goodbye or anything. I tossed the bag onto the seat behind me, and Dodge said, "Easy," and then he backed out of the driveway and we were off.

It's hard to describe how freeing it felt at first. We drove past the turnoff to the quarry, past the empty lot strewn with bricks that had once been the house where I lost my virginity, past the fruit stand and the hill where Piper's house stood. The road took us by the motel in Liberty Gorge that had been sanding down my soul for the past year and a half, and through Henderson, where the hardware store's security lights glowed through the old windows. I was like a comet flying past these things, burning through all of it on a singular path. It wasn't until we crossed the border into Massachusetts that the shallow exhilaration wore off. I started getting restless, and thinking about too many things, until finally I took the wheel from Dodge so I'd have something else to focus on. He fell asleep as if it was nothing, and I drove for hours and hours and hours.

Here's what was in my messenger bag, sitting on that seat right behind him. A couple of crumpled brochures from Bylina's last campaign. A package of mints, kind of grubby at this point, left over from that same time period. Five letters, stamped and addressed, to the *Washington Post* and the *New York Times,* to Stan and Jill, and one to the Vogels, our neighbor up the road. The picture of Elias in his body armor, in case I started to forget what I was here for. And just to twist the irony, fifteen copies of my résumé. In the event that Dodge decided to scuttle this whole thing, I didn't want a trip into D.C. to be pointless. It was a long drive, after all, and I hadn't been lying to Jill when I said I was still amenable to plan A.

It was dawn when I merged onto the New Jersey Turnpike. The sky was streaked pink and orange, but my eyes had gotten so bleary by that point that it was all running together like a wet painting. I pulled into the first rest stop to take a leak and buy some Red Bull. In the men's room there was this guy helping his kid change clothes—I guess the kid had spilled a drink on himself or gotten carsick or something—and the boy was crying and crying, just beside himself, standing there in his shirt and socks and a pair of diapers. You could tell he was exhausted. The dad was talking to him real softly, saying things like "One-two-three!" as he lifted the kid's shirt over his head, wiping down his chest with a wet paper towel. That about killed me to watch. I couldn't pee fast enough. I hated thinking about how I was never going to be there for TJ like that, hated it like death. The thought crept into my mind then: *Maybe this isn't worth it.* If it had just been me driving down there, to be perfectly honest, I probably would have turned around at that point and driven home. But this wasn't just about me, and it was crucial that I remember that. I was already shut out of every way I knew to work the system, and it wasn't acceptable to just roll over and let my brother be a victim of the government's indifference. At the end of this I wanted somebody up there to sincerely regret that they had brushed off Elias Olmstead, and there was no other option but action. So I got back in the truck, and Dodge drove the rest of the way.

Just outside the D.C. line we stopped at a Starbucks and I ran in to change clothes in the bathroom. Starbucks always has these big single-toilet bathrooms, no stalls, so you can lock the door and get all that space to yourself. I ruffled up the front of my hair a little bit, left a collar button undone, tried to look the way I always did. Casual but polished. It made people comfortable. As I smoothed on some aftershave I looked at my reflection in the mirror over the sink and tried to psych myself up a little. *The Most Handsome Bastard in the World.* Never had any trouble winning people over to my side. *Turn it on, Cade,* I thought, and hustled back out to the truck.

First we drove down to the National Mall and Dodge dropped me off at the curb. I had my messenger bag with me and also a plastic shopping bag, in which was a box containing one of the pipe bombs I'd built. It was a crappy little thing and chances were fair that it wouldn't even go off. I didn't care, since the object of it was to draw every emergency vehicle and cop in the city to this one little corner, not to be the big event. I jogged down the stairs into the Metro station, left the box next to a bench, then jumped on the train to Union Station. All over every Metro station are these signs that read, If You See Something, Say Something, and I had my fingers crossed that somebody would. Otherwise the day was going to involve a whole lot of waiting.

In Union Station I dropped all my letters in the mailbox and stopped at the Au Bon Pain to get coffee and a croissant and kill some time. Standing there in front of the bakery rack, looking at the chocolate croissants, I had this automatic thought that I ought to pick out something healthier. The irony—even in the midst of a plan to blow up a Senate building and off myself in the process, the fear of developing love handles was still as pure as ever. I got the plain croissant anyway just on principle of staying true to what I believed in, right down to the last minute, and went outside to sit on a planter and watch for signs of chaos. Dodge was circling the block, listening to the handheld police scanner for news to call me about, and every time his truck passed by I felt a little edgier. This was the plan: I'd walk over to the usual lunch spot and wait for Fielder to show up, act surprised to see him, tell him I was in town for a job interview, then mention I still had some of Bylina's campaign binders in my car that I ought to give to him. That was the kind of stuff that needed to be locked up or shredded, so he'd want them back for sure. Once at the truck, Dodge would pull him in, and that would allow

me to take his badge and get past security—they'd still recognize me, and so as long as I had the badge I could breeze
through—and set off the chemical bombs packed in Coke
bottles in my bag. They were powerful things, way more effective than anything Jill had seen me working on. Dodge
and I had tested them down at the quarry last week, and those
things went off like napalm.

But that was only the part of the plan Dodge knew. His
job was to get rid of Fielder, and he still harbored this crazy
fantasy that once this was finished we'd drive straight west
and live off the grid somewhere in the deep woods of another
state, most likely with some of his contacts in Montana. Eventually we'd bring our families out, and it would be cool because Jill knew how to live that way and liked it. He'd floated
that idea during the planning stages and I hadn't contradicted
him, even though anybody who really knew me would have
known I'd rather die than live in that kind of isolation, hiding from everybody and pretending not to be myself. What
I knew was that, one way or another, I wasn't going to make
it out of this event alive. If I fled the building and made it
back to the car, well, I had Elias's gun under the passenger
seat. Because once all of this was finished, it wasn't only Elias
who would be reckoned for. In a few days my letter would
arrive at the Vogels' house, and they would finally know that
Candy had admitted it to me and Elias, that very night. How
she watched Lindsay slip and then slide across that ice, crack
and break through, and how the girl had reached her hands
out toward her, met her eye, before she went under. And
how Candy had just stood there for one minute, two, maybe
as many as five, before she yelled to everyone else. Letting
the seconds tick by, holding her own breath like a gauge. She
told us in a voice so calm that we didn't really believe her,
not then. At the time I thought she was only trying to attach

herself to the attention the whole sad story was getting, but I don't think that anymore. I know her better than that now.

I don't know what you do with knowledge like that as long as you're living. You just carry it, I suppose. But if I was going down, I sure as hell wasn't going to leave this world and take that with me. If this whole thing was about accountability, and Dodge agreed with me on that one, then so be it. Because Candy had her part in this, too, adding that burden to all the other ones Elias had to carry, stacking on her part of that crushing weight. Dodge would not be pleased, not one bit, but that wouldn't affect me.

Now I could hear the sirens in the distance, plenty of them. I brushed the crumbs off my fingers and sauntered up to the curb to climb in when Dodge came by again. Back in the truck, he asked me, "You ready to do this thing?"

I popped one of the mints into my mouth. "'The tree of liberty must be refreshed from time to time with the blood of patriots and tyrants,'" I told him. I was quoting Jefferson. "'It is its natural manure.'"

"Just do it right the first time," he said. He was driving slowly, scanning the street. "And don't let it be any of your own blood. We don't need any complications."

It was twelve-thirty. I looked out the window and saw, right there, Fielder walking down the sidewalk in the sea of people leaving the building for lunch, hair flouncing up and down from his forehead. He had his laptop bag slung over his shoulder and was holding the strap with both hands. "Stop here," I said, and as he swerved to the curb I felt that same gut feeling as when a plane is landing, the forward motion, the wheels suddenly grinding against the ground.

☆ ☆ ☆ ☆ ☆

Chapter 32

JILL

I packed while Cade was in Maryland. Into the diaper bag I sorted the simplest and most necessary elements of what I had carried with me into the Olmstead house only the year before. Nearly everything was TJ's—his toys and clothes, the blanket that Leela had crocheted, sized to fit around him in the laundry basket. On the surface of our dresser, in a modest display, rested the small tokens of my romance with Cade: the tickets from our first football game, a Valentine card he had given me, a pressed rose from our wedding day. All these things I left behind.

I zipped the bag and set it heavily on the bed. When Cade had first told me he was going to Maryland, a red flag had snapped up in my mind, but he had said he wouldn't miss the surgery, and I believed him. No matter how angry he was about Elias or what he was plotting, Cade loved his son. Knowing that would add to my grief and guilt, a day from now, when I would call the police from the hospital and turn him in.

I wished I could call Leela, or see her one last time. Even though I couldn't tell her that I was leaving, I wished I could hear her voice again, asking me how the garden was doing or chuckling over TJ's baby mischief. She was a good woman. For a long time after I figured that out, I had puzzled over why a person as clear minded as her had tolerated a life with people like Dodge and the younger Eddy. But I couldn't judge her; I had tolerated so much from Cade in the name of keeping the peace and hoping, through my faith in him, that things would turn around. I might have kept on doing that forever had Cade not lost sight of the difference between a patriot and a traitor. It reminded me that some lines might blur but others stand surely apart, and one can't be a good mother and also a coward.

In the laundry basket, on top of a folded wool blanket, TJ slept. For the remainder of the day I could give him no food, only breast milk, in preparation for the next day's surgery, and I dreaded the struggle when he awoke expecting dinner. I watched him from the corner of my eye, attuned to signs of wakefulness, as I quietly packed our bag. Gray shadows from the window fluttered against his chest, which rose and fell in a rhythm so drowsy and content that it soothed me, even in my agitated state. His cheeks moved to suckle, his fists clenched and loosened. The shape of his brow was just like Cade's. I wondered if he would hate me one day, looking into the mirror through his own eyes and seeing his father's reflected back at him. *I gave all I could,* I thought. I would have to be the most perfect mother, because only the existing parent is real. The other is made all out of myths.

I stepped into the hallway and then, with a tentative turn of the knob, into Elias's room. The bed, stripped to its white sheet, lay stark along one wall; the blue desk with its hutch empty, its chair slightly askew to face me, seemed to expect a visitor. The air felt cooler than on the rest of the floor, and the stillness and silence of it gave it the feeling of a grotto. I ran my hand along the dresser; it was clean of dust. Candy must have been in recently. I wanted a memento of some kind to take with me, but saw none. In a way that seemed fitting.

What I could really use, I thought, *is his phone.* Elias had owned the kind you could restock with minutes from phone cards, and on this day, with escape so imminent and the need so great, I would have gladly spent the money and run the small risk someone would discover I was carrying one. But I had no idea where it had gone. Earlier in the day, before TJ's pre-op checkup down in Liberty Gorge, I had searched our bedroom high and low to see if I could find where Cade had stashed it, after he had been given Elias's personal effects at the hospital. But not a thing had turned up, and his room was the only remaining place it might be.

I opened Elias's dresser drawers and rooted around a little. His clothes were still there, folded neatly. They smelled like him, in a tidy, muted sort of way. Finding nothing else, I decided to brave a search through his old army duffel, slouched in the room's far corner. But all it contained was a set of pressed BDUs, an old Bible with his name inscribed on the cover, an army-issue folding knife and a plastic wallet insert filled with photos of his family and a girl in a multicolored ski hat. No sign of the phone, not even a charger.

I sighed. That morning I'd called Dave from the pediatrician's office phone under the pretense that I needed to reach my husband. Dave was already in Laconia. *Ready when you are,* he had said. My sense of gratitude to him was so profound that it twisted into discomfort deep in my gut. I didn't like feeling so beholden to anyone, not for a favor so immense. But I had to get through this first so I could have choices again.

In the next room, TJ stirred, fussed. A sudden sleepy cry broke the air. I walked backward out of Elias's room and shut the door silently, as though his spirit resided there and was owed absolute peace. Wherever he was, I hoped he had found a full measure of that.

The sound of the truck pulling into the gravel driveway woke me from a light sleep. Beside me TJ lay sprawled on his back in his diaper and undershirt, his plump cheeks moving in a faint rhythm as though dreaming of milk. The clock beside me said it was three-thirty in the morning. A car door slammed; beside me TJ shifted at the noise, but did not open his eyes. I felt relieved they had come home before morning, just as Cade had promised. I hated the thought of taking TJ away for good without seeing his father one last time.

I turned over and attempted to fall back to sleep, but within a couple of minutes the front door creaked open and I heard the heavy footfalls of Dodge's boots, then the sound of something being dragged. Cade's voice came in low and clipped. Dodge muttered a reply, and the dragging sound was replaced by grunts that indicated a heavy object being hoisted by both men.

I rolled over and lay still, my mind attuned to the puzzle of noise from downstairs. Perhaps they had hit a deer, like the day Cade had wrecked his car and Candy had butchered the doe in the front yard. But if that were the case, why would they have brought it inside in one piece? I lay there a while longer, listening. Then I eased myself past TJ and tiptoed down the stairs.

The front door was still open, the screen door propped with a brick, but the porch light was off. Dodge and Cade were both outside, unloading the truck. I looked around the downstairs. The only light came from the lamp next to Elias's chair that we typically left on all night no matter what. I wandered toward the darkened kitchen. No blood or soil, no sign of whatever they had carried. A basket on the kitchen island

overflowed with sweet corn. The beagles' food bowls sat beside each other on the counter awaiting the day's breakfast.
On a slate square above the stove hung a tole painting of a
house with a curl of smoke emerging from the chimney, beside
a quote in country-primitive script: "He restoreth my soul,
Psalms 23:3." I could read it by the narrow band of light that
blazed beneath the tightly closed door of the cellar. I looked
at that door for a moment, considering. Then I threw it open
and ventured down the stairs.

In the center of the room, tied with bungee cord to Eddy's
good Windsor chair, sat Drew Fielder. Above the strip of duct
tape that covered his mouth he looked out at me with hollow,
doomed eyes. The sleeves of his blue pin-striped oxford shirt
were pushed above his elbows; his wrists were bound behind
his back, and one leg of his khaki pants was slashed with a
dark wet stain that appeared to be urine. Drew's ankles were
bound to the legs of the chair with tape, and his shoes were
gone. Above his head the metal cord of the lightbulb swung
slowly, like a pendulum marking time with great cans of milk
powder and freeze-dried meats.

I screamed and, by instinct, jerked the tape from his mouth.
He spit out a wadded paper towel and gasped in a deep breath
of air. "Jill," he said, "get me out of here."

Already I could hear the rapid footsteps of the men returning to the house. "That had to be Jill," I heard Cade saying.
At the sound of his voice Drew strained his shoulders toward
me, bumping his head against my arm, and I skittered back
from his desperate touch. Cade's boots and Dodge's were quick
and hollow against the stairs. Before I could turn I backed into
Cade, who clapped his hand over my mouth when I startled,
whispering a shushing noise like the one he used with TJ.

"Goddamn it," Dodge muttered, coming down the stairs

behind Cade. "*You* better not scream, boy. We don't got neighbors anyhow."

"Cade," Drew said. "What the *fuck,* man."

Cade let me go, and I turned to him with a look of mute shock. "Don't, Jill," he said. "The guy's had it coming for three years now. He's alive, so chill."

"Call the cops, Jill," Drew said.

Dodge pointed at him. "You, shut up."

"You better pick your loyalties wisely right now," Drew told me. "They'll be here by tonight, busting down his door."

"In your dreams," said Cade.

Drew looked him in the eye. "Watch and wait. You're already on the shit list, man. You made a bad, bad move."

Dodge grabbed the chair by its sides and dragged it backward toward the wall, tipping Drew back. The legs scraped the concrete with a broken and dissonant squeal before Dodge roughly righted it again and set to work securing it to the wall with a length of chain. I turned to Cade, who was moving his baseball cap up and down with a nervousness that belied his glowering expression. *This wasn't his idea,* I knew all at once, knowing from that gesture that he was on the edge of a panic he couldn't reveal. "Will one of you tell me what's going on?" I demanded.

"We're on plan C," he informed me in a curt voice. Dodge tossed him a pack of zip ties pulled from his back pocket, and as Cade caught it I saw Elias suddenly clear in my mind's eye, the way he was in the woods that day—the bulk of his curled shoulders, the sweat on his temples, the dreadful distance in his gaze. Cade pocketed the bag as if it meant nothing to him, and said to Drew, "I'm not on any shit list anywhere. So sit tight."

"The hell you aren't. Why do you think you didn't get my job?" Cade looked at him sharply, his hand stilled for a moment on the brim of his cap. To Dodge, Drew said, "Are you the Powell guy? Richard or something? Yeah, he's the guy on the watch list. The antigovernment nut job. No chance Bylina's guys were ever going to clear you for my job when your family runs with this guy."

"Shut up," he said, but Dodge fixed the chain against a second hook and rose grinning. I stopped at the base of the stairs and looked at Drew, momentarily halting my effort to leave. If Drew already knew about Cade's family, we were all in more trouble than I could have imagined. For all these months I had written off Dodge's claims as paranoia, but if they were true, then I was already an accessory. I had known so much and said so little, and whatever agency knew Dodge's name might also know about me and my silence. The fact that I had reasons for it wouldn't matter. People always did.

"They got me on a watch list, huh?" he said, ignoring Cade's scowl.

"Gag that asshole back up," said Cade.

"Why? Let him talk. I'm interested."

Cade gave a shake of his head and moved toward Drew, but the sharpness of my voice stopped him. "This matters, Cade. Let him say what he knows."

The way Drew's arms were fixed behind his back made it impossible to fully raise his head, but he looked up as best he could and trained his glance on me. "Call them, Jill. They're coming anyway, and you've got a lot to lose."

"She's not on your side, little buddy," said Dodge.

"Is that true, Jill?" asked Drew. His voice was plaintive. "You really on the side of this yuck-a-puck and your jack-ass baby daddy? I always thought you were better than that."

"I'm on my son's side. Tell me what watch list you're talking about."

"Will you help me if I do?"

"She can't do a damn thing for you," said Cade. He looked

to Dodge and asked, "What do you want to do about the truck?"

"I'll go clean it out once we've got him situated. You can hold down the fort."

"We can get Scooter to do it. He should be over any minute now. I texted him from the road."

Drew's piercing eye contact kept drawing me back in. "C'mon, Jill, don't be a bitch right now," he said, and what sympathy I had built for him turned sour. "Who kept you company on Christmas? When this guy abandoned you for his *real* family. Who bought you dinner when he left you behind?"

That evening flashed into my mind. "I paid for my own dinner. And then you tried to get me to go to bed with you."

Cade looked at him sharply. His face turned pink. Dodge made a noise that sounded like the yowl of a cat, all the while tightening the bungee cords that Cade had secured too loosely for his taste.

"Sorry," said Drew. "My bad. I got mixed signals. I thought we had a bond. Sorta like the one you had with Stan when you were fucking him all that time you lived in his apartment."

My heart went cold. *"What?"*

Dodge and Cade exchanged a glance. "Where's the duct tape?" Cade asked Dodge, but his voice had a nervous waver.

"In the truck. I'll grab it."

"Yeah, you know what I'm talking about," Drew said to me. Looking at Cade, he said, "Slept in his bed every damn night. I saw it myself."

"Bullshit," said Cade.

"No bullshit. Tell him, Jill. No surprise you didn't tell this white-supremacist SOB you were taking it from the big black dude. How'd the baby turn out?"

Cade grabbed the broom beside the gun safe and whacked him across the face with the handle. His mouth started to bleed, and he rolled his lips to suck back some of the blood. Beyond that, he didn't react. "Don't hit *me,* asshole," he said. "Hit your nigger-loving girlfriend. Not my fault the soul brother's too beaucoup."

Cade thrust his palm against Drew's forehead, making his head whip back and then forward. Streaks of blood poured down either side of Drew's chin, vampirelike. "Shut up," Cade shouted in his face. From the second floor came the drowsy cry of the baby. "Shut up. *Shut up.*"

Drew spit a mouthful of blood into Cade's face, and Cade recoiled.

"You better let me out of here *now,*" Drew shouted back. "You're gonna go to jail for the rest of your goddamn *life.* Best you show some mercy so they don't hang you. Guys are gonna be bending you over in the shower till you grow a vagina. You fucked up for real, Cade. If I were you I'd let me go and run like hell to Guatemala. They know who you are. You'll be lucky if they're not here by sunrise."

By now Dodge was back, tearing a noisy strip from the roll of tape. He slapped it over Drew's mouth and Drew ceased to even try to talk. He just glared at me, trickling blood from around the bottom of the tape and now from his nose, as well. The baby's cry had risen to an insistent howl. I broke with Drew's stare and hurried up the steps to TJ.

He was sitting upright on the bed, red-faced and squalling, the top of his little bare chest shiny with tears and drool. I lifted him and pulled him against me to nurse, the tension in my throat growing tighter by the second. His small fists pounded my chest with frustration when my anxiety slowed the milk letting down. Downstairs I heard the cellar door bang shut, and at that a sob burst from me, a choking, helpless sound that startled TJ and set his arms waving. I gasped back the second sob and tried to breathe normally.

Cade's footsteps clunked against the stairs. I backed up into the corner beside the window. The door swung open and Cade stepped in, looking first at me and then to TJ. For the first time since his return I noticed his clothes were grimy and his eyes exhausted. His tattooed forearm was smeared with blood where he had wiped Drew's spit from his face. He was overdue for a haircut, and with his baseball cap off the lank strands hung around his face in a dirty, formless mess.

"What have you done, Cade," I cried. At the dread in my voice he threw me the uneasiest of glances, reaching into the hamper for a washcloth to wipe his forearm. "Tell me how you're going to get out of this one. Tell me now, and then get me and TJ out of this house before they come to arrest you."

He tossed the washcloth back into the basket. "Nobody's coming. We're all on our own here. And nobody's leaving until we figure out what to do next."

The weight of that notion was almost physical. The house, this drafty and rattling old place, seemed to snug around me as if shrunk tight by Cade's determination. I clutched TJ tighter against my body to steady the shivers that rippled through my muscles, but it didn't work. "How could you do this to us," I stammered, my voice at a whisper, without any hope that he would offer an answer. "If you were going to do something this awful you never should have come home."

"I didn't intend to," he snapped. "I'm not *that* stupid. The idea was to lure him into the truck and hold him while I went into the building with his ID. And then I walked over and the entire office building went on lockdown out of 'an abundance of caution' because of a bomb on the Metro. So I panicked. I didn't know what to do. I just told Dodge to drive and we'd figure the rest of it out once we got here. He was acting like I was supposed to have all the answers, and hell if I know how to cover our tracks."

I waved a hand wildly toward the door. "Well, what are you going to do with him *now?*"

He squinted in a peevish way. "*I* don't know, Jill. Fucking bury him in the backyard. I'm driving back to D.C. tomorrow. I'll think about it on the way down."

I started to cry again.

"Jill, knock it the hell off. It has to be this way. The tree of liberty must be refreshed by the blood of patriots and tyrants, and if it has to be mine and his, then so be it. I'm not just going to let Elias die for nothing. Let them stick a toe tag on him and shove him into their freezer."

"He wouldn't want you to do this. And it isn't going to work. They'll connect this to you in no time. You heard what Drew said. He knew who Dodge is."

"Well, I wasn't expecting that. It wasn't supposed to be like this. And you know why it all is." He pointed savagely at TJ drowsing in my arms. When he spoke again, his voice sank to an aggressive hiss. "Why my life's fucked up. Why Fielder's downstairs. Why you're stuck in this shithole, and why Elias is dead."

"TJ's got nothing to do with Elias."

"Bull*shit* he doesn't. Elias killed himself because I had you and he didn't and he couldn't stand it. Let's just put it out there, all right? Let's lay it all on the table. He came home from the Sandbox and he was doing okay in spite of it all—"

"No, he wasn't."

"Don't cut me off! He was doing okay until I brought *you* home. I thought about this shit the whole way back from D.C., and there's no point now in pretending it doesn't exist. The VA had no business putting him on all those goddamn drugs and making it impossible for him to get up off his ass and get his life together. The fact that he couldn't handle life anymore falls square on *their* shoulders. But just for the sake of argument, let's say what it was that pushed him over the edge. It was him seeing that baby and knowing he was never, ever going to get a chance with you."

"No," I protested. But I knew it was probably true.

"And I love that kid with everything in me," he continued. "I'd give him the world and it's a damn good thing, because that's about what he's costing me. My freedom, my brother, my future, my loyalty to you—"

"*That's* not TJ's fault," I snapped. "Back off the poor kid and take some responsibility."

"That's all I ever do anymore is take responsibility," he shouted. "I've given all I goddamn can, and it's time for the people who owe me to pay up."

"Your son and I owe you nothing," I yelled back raggedly. TJ, who had been almost asleep at my breast, awoke all at once and turned his head to look at his father, eyes baleful and mouth agape. "And we're the ones who are going to be paying."

Cade scowled at me. "'Let justice be done though the heavens should fall.'"

Leave, the instinctive part of my mind commanded me. *Leave now. It's time.* Whether or not I would be implicated with the rest of them, there would be no avoiding the consequence either way, and for TJ's sake I needed to press forward without fear. With my son clutched against my chest with one arm, I snatched up the diaper bag from the bed and, before Cade could step into my path, hustled down the stairs. As I reached the landing Cade grabbed my shoulder, sending the bag sliding down my arm and disrupting my balance. I spun toward the wall to compensate, and then Dodge was in front of me, blocking off the bottom of the stairs.

"Oh, no you don't," Dodge said. "Don't you even think about going anywhere."

"I'm taking TJ to the hospital for his surgery. Whatever it is you're doing here has nothing to do with me. I don't know a thing about it."

"Get back upstairs."

I met Dodge's eyes. Cade's hand gripped my shoulder again, and I shrugged hard, but he didn't let go. "It's easier for you if we're gone," I told him. "Babies need too many things. Let me out the door now and I won't say a word to anyone."

"It's too late for that," said Dodge. "They're all around the house. Agents. FBI probably. Scooter, he was on his way over here and saw them coming up the road. Called to warn us—"

Not us, I thought. *Me.* All the pieces snapped into place in my mind: that when Cade texted him, he realized he had been all wrong in his prediction that they would wait until after TJ's surgery. He had turned them in, most likely in a panic, and only realized after the fact that TJ and I were about to be caught in the net with the rest of them. He had tried to do the right thing, but it was too late and too complicated.

"Fuck my life," Cade said. He let go of my shoulder and pushed past me into the living room. *"Fuck!"* he shouted toward the front wall.

"And they arrested him, or so it sounded like. Now they got people outside every door. And we're just waiting."

Dodge stopped speaking and looked toward the living-room window, but its dusty drapes had been drawn tightly against the night. Cade leaned back against the wall and gazed toward the ceiling with an empty expression, as though looking to God for instructions. I asked, "Waiting for what?"

"For them to make contact."

I looked impatiently at Cade. The door was right there; everything within me pulled me toward it, and irritation was rapidly replacing my fear and disbelief. "Well, why don't you take out your damn phone and call them yourself? It's all over anyway, right? And your son needs to get to the hospital."

Cade didn't respond. He looked stricken. In the silence, Dodge spoke up again. "I told you Scooter was a plant. Like hell he just happened to walk into that one. Arranged to disappear before he got trapped in the house with us is more like it."

"Shut up, Dodge," Cade said peevishly. "It could have been anybody. Someone who saw your truck, someone who works with Bylina—Uncle Randy, even—"

Dodge cocked his head in rueful agreement. "Randy, yeah, it could be. Thanks to Miss Busybody over here."

I scowled at him. "Why don't you quit listening to yourself talk for five minutes and get the police on the phone so we can get out of this? Where's Candy?"

"Downstairs watching our guest. She set the boys up in Grandma's workroom. Cade'll take you upstairs, too. Got to have someone keep them kids away from the windows."

"No chance. I'm not babysitting so you can bicker back and forth with the police. Cade, give me your phone."

He gave me a long, guarded look, as if he was considering it. Dodge said, "Goddamn, Cade, your little woman needs to see the back of someone's hand."

But right then, it rang. I took a step back from him and shifted TJ to the other hip, and Dodge took advantage of Cade's distraction and mine to take me firmly by the upper arm and pull me out into the hallway. "Up the stairs," he ordered.

I shook him off. "Don't you dare."

"Fine. Walk." When I balked, he met my eye with a gaze widened by impatience. "You want to be down here if they bust in, huh? You think that's such a smart idea? Best you and your boy be up at the top of the house, away from the people they want. And don't think they're going to give us any warning."

As much as I hated him, there was a logic to what he said. I stepped onto the first stair and he nudged me forward. On the second floor the shades were all drawn. I held TJ firmly against me as I navigated the narrow staircase to the attic. In Leela's workroom, the three little boys sat hunched around Dodge's laptop from which came the tinny dialogue of a children's show about George Washington. Despite the early hour, John's face was a mess of red lollipop residue; Matthew, seated in the middle, wore his birthday rifle slung on his back as always. The little square of electrical tape over the webcam curled outward at its top edge.

"Tell Cade to tell them I need to leave," I told Dodge. "That ought to be his priority."

Dodge grunted a reply and thumped back down the stairs.

I set TJ down on the floor and shut the door. "Matthew, give me your rifle."

He shook his head slowly, not raising his gaze from the screen. "'This is my rifle,'" he quoted. "'There are many like it, but this one is mine.'"

"Not right now, it isn't. Hand it over."

"No." He began babbling a half-coherent version of the Rifleman's Creed. "I will ever guard it against the ravinges of weatherman damage—"

I walked up behind him and lifted it off his back, ignoring his indignant *hey,* and unloaded it before securing it in the craft closet that was safely outside the door. Crouching on the floor, I peeked out through the thin gap between the bottom of the shade and the window. I squinted against the sudden swirling lights, red and blue, that pulsed in rhythm against the dark sky. Out on the main road sat two ambulances, three fire trucks, several other boxy emergency vehicles and a white van from which sprouted a satellite dish perched atop a long pole. At the end of the driveway, glinting beneath the moonlight and partially obscured by the trees, a large black truck blocked the exit. I sighed from deep in my chest. There was still the chance they would let me walk out with TJ and take us to the hospital if Cade put his son ahead of himself. *He might,* I told myself. None of this had been a part of his original plan. Surely he wanted his son to have this surgery as much as I did.

I sat with my back against the wall beneath the window and waited out the long minutes, watching the backs of the three little boys hunched over the laptop, the wanderings of TJ as he crawled across the rug. All of a sudden I had an idea. "Boys," I said, and they startled at the sharpness of my voice. "Let me see that computer a minute."

I took it from Matthew's hands and checked the network connection. Our phones had been cut off long ago, but Dodge had kept up payments on the satellite internet to keep his eBay sales going. Relief washed over me at the sight of the little icon of expanding rays. I logged in to my email and sent off a quick message.

Dave—complication. We're in trouble here at the house in Frasier. SWAT teams or FBI outside. Might not get to hospital but am trying. Help if poss.—Jill

I turned off the WiFi connection and handed the computer back to Matthew, who snapped the video back on. "TJ stinks," he said as an afterthought. Sure enough, the baby needed a diaper change, and I had left the bag downstairs. I carried TJ down the narrow steps to change him in my room, where we kept extra diapers next to the laundry basket where he slept. As I laid him down on the bed, working hard to keep my touch gentle in spite of my anxiety, Cade stepped into the darkened room behind me. "Jill, Fielder's lying about you and Stan, isn't he?"

I looked over my shoulder and shot him a perplexed look. *Of all the things he could be worrying about right now.* "Of course he is."

"I thought so." He rested his back against the wall and looked toward the hallway, dimly lit from what little daylight was now creeping in around the shades. For the first time in all this I noticed the handgun holstered on his belt, just behind his right arm. "But he said—he said he saw you himself."

I closed up the diaper and lifted TJ to my hip. "He saw that I slept in Stan's bed sometimes, but never when Stan was home. It's that simple."

"I thought you were sleeping in the living room."

"When he was home, yes, but his mattress was more comfortable and I was pregnant and my back hurt, so when he wasn't there I didn't see the harm in sleeping there. Come *on,* Cade. Drew's just exaggerating to distract you, and it's working. It's ridiculous that's even in your head at a time like this."

"If everything was so up-and-up, then why didn't I know about this before?"

"Because there wasn't anything to say. Seriously, if it was like that between me and Stan, do you think I would have taken *this* as my best option in life?" My voice was rising. TJ thumped his fist against my chest and squirmed, but I lacked the restraint to lower my voice. "If I haven't proven by now that I'm loyal to you, then God help me, Cade. Nothing would make you believe it."

He broke eye contact grudgingly and looked toward the hallway again. Light splintered down in a broken pattern against the stairs, like kindling for a fire. "You know what, Jill—" he began, and the quaver in his voice was strange. "My old girlfriend, Piper...I almost slept with her about a week ago. I ran into her and it almost happened. Wait, no. That's not the whole story." He faced me, his eyes freakishly bright. I realized with astonishment that they were wet, almost overflowing with tears. "I was *trying* to find her. I couldn't, though. And then I just stumbled into her, and one thing led to another, and I kissed her."

I had no idea what to say. This was a fresh affront, this knowledge that I had stood through all of this beside a man who was chasing his ex-girlfriend in his spare time. I gave a short, sharp bark of a laugh and said, "That's not cool."

"I know. I *stopped*. I felt terrible. I'm such a piece of shit, babe. I'm going down so hard. I swear to God I thought I was going to die yesterday, once I walked into the office building with the stuff in my bag. I never planned to walk back out, no matter what Dodge thought. 'The tree of liberty must be refreshed—'"

Impatience and boredom filled my voice. "'With the blood of patriots and tyrants.'"

"Right, yeah. And now what am I supposed to do? Go to jail? What the fuck would *I* do in jail?" His voice was rising. "I'm too goddamn smart to be in jail."

"I don't have any idea what you'll do," I snapped. "I guess you should have thought about that several months ago."

He leaned against the door frame, his head against the darkly stained trim, weary. His gaze caught the middle distance. "This is all Dodge's baby," he said. "He's the one who knows. The man with the plan."

"Dodge is a first-class moron. And you've *always* thought so. Do the right thing, Cade," I pleaded. "If you love us, find a way to get us out of here."

His phone rang, and he scrambled to answer it. "Yes," he said as he hurried out of the room, skipping down the stairs toward Dodge. "This is Cade Olmstead."

I sat down hard on the mattress and turned TJ around in
my lap so his face pressed against my chest. He gnawed his fist,
still so hungry, and submitted to my desperate cuddling with
placid ease. I breathed shallowly, straining to hear his father's
words from far away. When I failed, I rested my cheek against
his small downy head and, with dense, choking sobs, cried.

"There's no reason for me to do that if you're not going to
let him get to the hospital anyway," Cade was saying into his
phone. I had strapped TJ against my hip in the baby sling and
cautiously ventured downstairs. Despite all of Dodge's warn-
ings, an hour had passed and nothing had happened yet; it
seemed harder to believe we were in imminent danger of a
SWAT team invasion. "You're not following what I'm saying
here. He's got surgery at eight a.m. My wife's not involved in
this. She just wants to take him down to the hospital in Laconia and get it done."

He saw me standing at the door of the pantry and waved
me away, but I only moved a single step back. The last of
my loyalty to him had melted away with his confession, and
even in the midst of far greater concerns I seethed from the
insult of it. From the corner between the cellar door and the
kitchen, Dodge stood watching the local news on the living-
room television, using the remote to switch between channels.
Of course our house was the central image on every station,
either a straight-on shot from the road or an aerial from the
helicopter I had been hearing overhead. The memory of my
mother's plane on the red desert floor unfolded itself in my
mind, and a shudder flickered down my spine as I wrapped
a protective arm around TJ. Our story wasn't going to end
the way hers had. It couldn't. I was here and aware, moving
about that house on the screen, and I wouldn't let that happen.

"Well, just move your damned vans for half a second,"

Cade said. "Or have somebody take her down there, even. When you say 'I'm sorry, that's not possible,' you know how that sounds to me? Because it's really the only thing I want to talk to you about."

There was a long silence, and then Cade rolled his eyes. "Fine, never mind, then," he said, his voice taking on a sarcastic, bitchy edge. "Then how about you call me back when you actually want to negotiate instead of just try to fuck with me? Because that's not going to go real well."

He clicked off the phone. "Did you really just hang up on them?" I asked. "You can't do that. You have to talk. TJ and I need to leave."

"They'll let you leave. They just won't let him get his surgery."

"Well, fine, then. Just let us walk out and we'll worry about that later."

Cade laughed as if I'd made a joke. "Yeah, right. *Then* what incentive would they have not to break down the door and take me with them? We're a family. Nobody's leaving. If he can't get the surgery there's no point anyway."

I looked incredulously at Cade, then at Dodge, who had eased himself down onto the sofa with one arm behind his head and his gun resting on his belly like a bag of chips, eyes still fixed on the TV. "You can't hold us *hostage,* Cade."

"I'm not holding you hostage. We're married. We're sticking together, that's all. Like always."

He raised his eyebrows in an imploring way, a puppy-dog look, but distraction shifted his gaze to the television. His phone buzzed again, but rested ignored against his hip as he watched the live helicopter shots. Its incessant vibration stirred a memory of one of our first nights together, when he kissed me with escalating passion against a shadowed stadium wall after a football game, his BlackBerry vibrating against my thigh the entire time. Once upon a time I had wished the damn thing would go silent just for a little while. Now I desperately hoped he would answer it.

"I'm getting impatient with all their back-and-forth chitter-chattering," Dodge said in response to the sound. "Shit or get off the pot, that's what I say. One of us ought to go out there and stir something up. Give 'em some real incentive."

"Shut up, Dodge," Cade said, but he sounded listless this time. From the cellar, I heard Candy's syrupy voice speaking, smooth and level. Drew was moaning. I cast a long, measuring look on Cade, then bolted across the living room to the door.

"Stop her!" Dodge barked, but he was already up and grabbing at me, his arm folding across my chest as I scrambled with the locks. TJ howled and gripped at my shirt. As Dodge dragged me backward I felt a small cold impact at the back of my head: his gun. I braced one arm around TJ and clawed at Dodge's arm with the other, twisting and struggling, too overwhelmed by purpose to feel afraid. The arm only tightened, and TJ squalled with fury.

"Sweet Jesus," Cade said. Dodge's balance swerved, and the feeling of the hard steel went away. Cade's voice ramped up louder, tense as the springs of a trap. "Christ, let her go already."

"Take her back upstairs."

He released me roughly, and I pulled TJ against my chest to try to calm him. He screamed to the end of the air in his lungs, his round face inflamed with rage. "Give me the baby," said Cade. His voice was conciliatory.

"Not on your life."

"C'mon, Jill. Let me talk to them some more before you go running out there and get you and TJ shot up. It isn't going to be much longer."

I looked past him to Dodge, who met my gaze with a

pointed glare. He slid his gun back into his shoulder holster, slowly. Cade prodded my waist, and I tramped back up the stairs.

Back in the attic room, Candy's boys were still riveted on the laptop screen. *The devil's third eye,* Dodge always called it. I took it back from Matthew and tried to set up the network connection again, but it wouldn't work. "Damn it," I muttered.

"Aunt Jilly said a bad word," intoned Mark.

I set the laptop back in their eager hands and gnawed my nails, gazing out the window at the trucks that seemed to have doubled in number. The broken thunder of the news helicopter vibrated the glass. My hands shook, and the memory of Dodge's gun planted behind my ear loomed so large in my mind that all my strategic thoughts of escape seemed to have shriveled. That was the goal, I supposed—to intimidate me into obedience, to keep me quiet and scared. As I sat against the wall and pulled TJ against me to nurse, I pictured Dave standing in a hospital corridor, watching the clock, and I felt the anger inside me rise to a boil. They were destroying my plan to escape. All this time I had held out for TJ's sake, and now they were making all those miserable weeks pointless. Now perhaps I would be charged as an accessory, because I had known things I should have reported, tried and failed to hedge my bets about Cade's conscience and his sanity. At the very least the coming weeks would be a mess of lawyers, two-way mirrors—possibly even foster care for our son. I could lose my child. He would become motherless, just like me, but it would be so much worse for him. He would be shucked into a system whose goal was merely to keep him alive.

That's unproductive thinking, Jill. I heard the shadow of my mother's voice behind the thought. *Calm down. Remember, don't quit five minutes before the miracle happens.*

"Aunt Jilly, I'm hungry," said John.

"Let me see if Grandma's got any snacks up here," I replied, doubtful. TJ had fallen asleep at my breast, and I eased him back into the sling before rising awkwardly from the floor. There would be nothing in the craft room, but perhaps there was some food squirreled away on the shelves on the landing. I closed the craft-room door behind me to soften the laptop's hearty chime of "Yankee Doodle" and began rifling through the clutter on the bookshelf. Three stories down there was enough food to feed all of Frasier for a year, but nobody had thought to hand up so much as a box of graham crackers before they confined us to the attic. *Sixty thousand dollars,* I remembered Cade saying as I looked over the basement in wonder. He had mocked his family then, so sure he was nothing like any of them.

The bookshelf search turned up nothing, and I wasn't eager to return to tell John he would have to go hungry. My back aching from TJ's weight, I walked with a gentle sway to my gait to keep him asleep, back and forth in front of the attic fan. Then, as I approached it once again, my eye caught a movement just beyond its slats. I stopped and peered through the mesh and past the slats. Two men in black SWAT gear were moving around behind a truck that blocked the driveway. My heart pounded, and TJ, as if sensing my surge of adrenaline, raised his eyebrows high above his closed eyes and stirred. I rushed to the craft closet and pulled out a torn length of white sheet to drape from the window. But as I unsnapped the grimy closures and braced my hands against the sash, another motion caught my gaze. The window below mine opened and the lean black silhouette of an automatic rifle appeared, then Dodge, easing his upper body out the window to sight in.

I glanced at the closed door of the craft room, then at the closet still wide open beside it. In a few efficient movements I grabbed Matthew's rifle from the closet, reloaded it and took aim through the venting slats for the fan. The pop of the gun cut the air; I felt the flail of TJ's arm against my back, and then Dodge slumped half out the window. The rifle fell from his hands and clattered against the porch roof. Blood bloomed on the back of his head, long streaks of it unfurling like a lily.

Someone screamed. A man. I guessed it was Cade.

I shoved the gun back into Leela's closet and buried it beneath the bolts of cloth. "What the *fuck!*" I heard him shouting from the second floor. "What the *fuck!*"

I slipped back into the workroom and locked the door behind me with the old key that jutted from the lock. Matthew stared at me as I hurried in. He asked, "Did Uncle Cade go and shoot himself?"

"Maybe."

"That's what happens. My dad says so. That's what happens when you don't know your target."

I nodded and peeked out the shade.

"Uncle Cade's sort of stupid with guns."

"He sure is."

Cade's howling had turned into a wail. After a few moments a long shrill sound from Candy rose up, as well. I heard the sound of the attic door being thrown open, and my heart thumped in my ears, a double thud that resonated like being underwater. I felt as though I could feel all four chambers pumping, each distinct. TJ, sensing my anxiety, pulled up his legs inside the sling and twisted against my side. But he did not awaken.

"The *hell* you didn't!" Cade shouted, and without a reply from Candy I had to assume he was talking on the phone. "Then why the fuck is my brother-in-law hanging dead out my window?"

Candy began to sob in a messy, noisy way, punctuated with

fresh wails. "All right, all right," Cade said. "All of them, yeah. Take 'em all."

Relief flooded through me. I wrapped my arms around TJ and stood just inside the attic door, prepared to rush out as soon as Cade opened it. But when he did, he blocked my exit with his arm. "Not you. Candy's boys."

All the relief I had felt turned abruptly to dread. The boys ducked beneath his arm and raced down the stairs like water down a drain. I tried to push past, but he shifted to stand in my path. His face was pale, eyes frantic. "Stay there, Jill."

"What? Why?"

"It's not safe for you to go out. They shot Dodge. Candy wants her boys, fine, but you're not going anywhere. Not as long as they've got a sniper on us."

So that was what he believed. I had no problem playing along. "But they're not going to shoot us. It's safer for everybody if TJ and I go, too. Why would you want your son to stay here if there's a sniper on the roof? Just let us go, Cade. If they see you're willing to be reasonable, they're less likely to rush in on you."

"And there's less to stop them from shooting me if they do." I looked at him in dismay, and he combed both hands back through his hair. "Sorry, Jill, but that's where it's at right now. You know I'm out of cigarettes? Fine frickin' time for *that* to happen."

Just leave anyway, I thought. *Shove past him and run.* But I looked at the gun on his hip and thought better of it. I didn't think he would hurt me or TJ, but I had never thought he would hold Drew Fielder hostage, either. "If I go, maybe I can negotiate for you better than anybody else can," I suggested. "I've got more sympathy for you."

He glanced toward me. I kept my expression neutral, but in the effort to do so I realized I wasn't lying. More than anger,

I felt pity for him. He could have been something wonderful, but here he was, whiling down the minutes that would
end in him losing everything. Prison was going to be ugly
for Cade. He was too good-looking and too easily cowed by
another man's will.

His phone buzzed. He looked at it, then handed it to me
and sat on the floor, leaning back against the craft closet. I
stared at the phone and then at him, and asked, "What am I
supposed to do, answer it?"

"Yeah. I'm tired."

I turned it on. "This is Jill."

"Jill!"

The sound of Dave's voice bewildered me. I hurried into
the workroom and turned away from Cade. I couldn't utter
a response. Dave's voice came on again. "Is that you, really? I
thought I was going to talk to Cade. Are you doing all right?"

Glancing back at Cade, I gauged his reaction, but he only
stared at the wall in a passive way. "I don't understand," I replied carefully.

"They've had me talking to him for a couple hours now,"
Dave explained. "I got your email and then I saw the news,
and so I called the police. They said sometimes it helps if
someone with a connection to the family tries to help broker
a truce, so they put me on. I'm trying to get you out of there.
Is the baby all right? Are you?"

"We're both here. We're not hurt. Cade's trying to process
whatever just happened."

"Yeah. They say they need him to be clear on the fact that
they don't know what the situation is with Dodge Powell,
and they're investigating it, but they don't believe it was one
of their men. They say they're not in a position to retrieve the
body. Do you know the condition of the hostage?"

"I'm not sure. I've been up in the attic all this time." At

this Cade scowled at me. "What Cade wants...is to talk to a lawyer who will put together a good case for him."

"Am I on speaker? Can he hear me?"

"No."

"Good. What Cade *really* wants is for everybody to go home and forget this ever happened. In the end the choices are going to be that either he comes out or the SWAT team comes in. It's a lot better for everyone, especially him, if he picks the first one. Tell me what it's going to take to make that happen."

I thought about the things Cade wanted. Not one of them sounded like anything that anyone could provide any longer. "I don't know, Dave," I replied. "If I did I'd tell you. He's just tired."

"Is that why he had you take the call? He's still armed, though, right?"

"Yeah." I looked at Cade again. "He could use some cigarettes. I think that's what he wants."

Cade gave me a listless thumbs-up.

Dave snorted with irritation. "Duly noted. Put him on the phone."

I handed it to Cade, who clicked it off. Draping his arms loosely over his bent knees, he gazed up at the small round window, looking thoughtful and faraway. My stomach tightened with the fear that he was putting together how Dodge might have been shot just below that window. His back pressed against the door of the closet where the rifle still lay hidden.

He said, "Lay him down."

"You mean TJ?"

"Yeah. He's asleep anyway."

I looked around the room as though seeking out a place to set him, but I was buying time, trying to discern Cade's purpose. "I can't," I told him. "He'll wake up if I take him off my back."

Cade got up from the floor and, with gentle hands, braced TJ in the sling. I fumbled at the closure and loosened it enough that Cade could lift him. When he opened the closet door with his free hand, I caught my breath. But he pulled out a crocheted blanket from the shelf below the fabric bolts, shook it open and dropped it on the floor where he had just been sitting. Onto its folds he laid TJ, who didn't stir. Then he stepped into the workroom, where I still stood, and closed the door so softly that the click of its latch made barely any sound.

"C'mere, Jill," he said.

I didn't move, but he came to me. He kissed me, working my shirt down over my shoulders as he unbuttoned it, letting his head drop to kiss my shoulder, my collarbone. I felt the warmth of his breath, the tip of his tongue, but as if from a great distance.

"You're the most beautiful woman in the world," he said, rasping a whisper. "I love you. And I love our son."

His phone vibrated against the front of my thigh. He lifted me with one arm and set me on the worktable, then eased me onto my back. The worn wood pressed against the back of my skull and my tailbone, but that felt distant, too. From my neck to my thigh he ran his hands down my body, touching me as a blind man touches the face of a loved one, as if yearning to burn it into his memory. *Give him whatever he wants,* I thought. *He doesn't care about getting out of here alive. You do.*

His voice rose in frustration. "C'mon, Jill. Don't be cold to me. I don't want to feel like I'm raping you or something."

My laugh was short and sharp. "I don't know how I'm supposed to relax. Do you?"

He shrugged. His expression was entirely benign. He slapped his phone onto the table, then his gun, before unbuckling his jeans and letting them slide down. "Clear your mind," he suggested.

I diverted my gaze to the space above his shoulder. Leela's barn stars, each painted in a cheerful variation of the Stars and Stripes, marched across the wall just below where the roof vaulted. Here and there yellow bows stiffened by wire and starch curled beneath them, like fossils recalling a battering wind. I remembered, all at once, Elias singing "Two Highways" in quiet harmony, watching out the window as we flew past the deep woods, the last of his cigarette smoldering between two fingers. A terrible ache for him opened in me out of the clear blue. My eyes burned inside and a sob choked into my throat, but I held both at bay. Cade tugged down my shorts by the waistband, and I closed my eyes, but it only made my mind's image of Elias grow sharper and more true.

I thought of how warm and broad his body felt when I rubbed his shoulders. Of the dense wall of muscle deep beneath his skin, and the way his hair bristled along his neck in a line so clean, and the smell of him that changed as I touched him. I remembered how he looked in the apartment that first day, stretched out on the futon. Even though I knew that was not the real Elias, only the perfect one that the real world could not sustain, I couldn't believe the one in the easy chair had been the real Elias, either. I wondered if any of us had ever seen the real one, or if he was all soul, never finding a body to inhabit that could feel like a home to him.

Cade slipped a hand beneath my shoulders and pulled me up to kiss him. I wrapped my arms around his neck and moved willingly to the edge of the table. All the thoughts that my loyalty to Cade had held at a distance now flooded my mind, and that image of Elias fell over Cade's body like a projection onto a screen. I felt no shame from it because we all knew— every member of this family—that the moment Elias died we dropped our shallow and insular battles and turned all our loyalty to Elias: to love and mourn him, to avenge and remember him, to imagine the life he might have lived and to carry it forward like a glowing ember wrapped in a leaf.

Once it was over, Cade breathed hard against my neck, and pressed his temple against mine, and said, "I need to get that guy on the phone."

Opening the door was enough to wake TJ, and I attended to changing him while Cade got back to the business of negotiating with the police. As I fastened TJ's new diaper, the lights suddenly cut out. The sky outside was overcast, and the attic instantly fell into shadow. TJ whipped his head back and forth, regarding his surroundings with large, nervous eyes. I made a few comforting noises and carried him down the stairs.

Cade was taking a seat on the sofa as we walked in, moving things around on the coffee table with a restless energy I didn't like. The holstered gun was back on his belt again. No longer was he attempting to stay away from the windows, and he was smoking a cigarette that looked hand-rolled. A dozen gutted cigarette butts lay scattered across the coffee table, the obvious materials he had used to come up with the one he was smoking now. Across the shaded room he shot me a glance that looked almost resentful.

"Don't know what the hell Candy did to him," Cade said, "but he's not looking real good."

"Drew?"

He grunted assent. I considered asking more questions, then decided my knowing more wouldn't help anyone. I crossed the living room on the way toward the kitchen.

"Where you going?"

"I need food for TJ. I'm all out of the snacks I packed in the diaper bag."

"There's too many open windows along the porch."

"Well, what do you want me to do? The kid needs to eat. All he's done is nurse all day. Everything in the pantry is dried stuff in those giant cans. Same in the cellar—"

"You're not going in the cellar. No way."

"Of course not, but I'm just saying, I need to get to the fridge."

Cade gave the kitchen a long look. Then he said, "I got on the phone with them again—not the guy you know, but the first one. They asked about the condition of the hostage. I went down to take a look so I could tell them correctly."

I waited for him to continue. "And?"

He gave a slow shake of his head, then looked up at me from where he sat. "Jill...this was Dodge's idea. It wasn't mine."

I didn't really believe him, but I nodded.

"If I go upstairs and put this gun in my mouth, you know what that accomplishes?"

"Cade."

"Absolutely nothing. It's the same thing Eli did. It's like I put all this work and time and effort into doing right by him, and the whole time I was just circling the block. I can't make any kind of grand statement now, like I meant to down in D.C. Can't even kill Fielder with any fair reason, because Candy already did most of that job, so far as I can tell. That'd be like shooting puppies in a box."

I winced.

"If I walk out of here with my hands up, they send me to jail. And Fielder, he'll get the last laugh on that one, because I won't make it two days before some big guy makes me his bitch. Basically I've got zero options."

He took his phone out of his pocket. It was buzzing energetically, and turned in a slow spin against the wood once he set it on the coffee table. We both looked at it, and I said, "I think you should choose what's best for TJ."

He nodded. I walked into the kitchen and took an orange from the bottom drawer of the dark refrigerator. I sat TJ on the kitchen island and cut a small piece off the top of the orange with a kitchen knife, then pulled it in two and handed TJ a section before beginning to peel off the skin from the rest. He worked the orange section into his mouth, nursing out the juice, watching with interest as I peeled. His legs swung in a carefree way. It occurred to me that he was as oblivious to my anger and fear and sense of betrayal as I had been to my own mother's suffering that day, but I loved him no less for it. I was glad he didn't know, glad he could sit and eat an orange in the calm of the eye of the storm, and if I could have held things that way for him forever, I would have. For the first time since my mother's death I forgave myself a little for walking past that television. I understood then that if her spirit could have guided me it would have marched me away from that scene, sent me about my business to keep the peace in my soul as long as possible.

And then a gust of air blew across the kitchen, light filtered in and I looked up to see the front door open. Cade racked the gun and stepped outside. The screen banged shut, and as I gathered TJ into my arms with a sense of great caution, several loud pops ripped the air. I dropped to the floor with TJ, holding him against my side as I crawled with the other arm toward the corner beneath the table. Shouts rang out, a chaos of voices peppered with more gunfire. I curled beneath the table, enveloping my son with my body in an embrace that all but crushed him. Boot steps crashed into the house, voices, the sudden sense of exposure and broken boundary. I squeezed my eyes shut tight and breathed in the cold smell of the stone floor, the muscles of my back steeled against the world beyond me.

That this was a rescue did not enter my mind. These were only strangers, Cade's adversaries, invading our home.

A gloved hand fell against my side, and then I was dragged back against the stone, not moving from my position around the baby. TJ, his mouth no longer stilled by my sleeve, twisted his head upward and let loose with a furious cry. So close to my ear, it filled my mind. My thoughts and his scream became one and the same.

It was that cry that shook away my fear and thrust me forward into the next of what life held for me. The cry was the punctuation that acknowledged the terribleness of what had gone before, and gave it a stopping place past which I might believe things would be better.

I got to my feet, planting them against the stone. Someone had me by the arm. I shifted TJ to my hip, and as if to declare the Olmsteads had never claimed me, said, "I'm Jill Wagner."

Chapter 33
CADE

For the past couple hours especially I've had some time to think about my regrets with regard to the current situation. When they put me on the phone with this guy, Dave Robinson, he said to me, "Don't you think Jill's been through enough the past few years, losing her mom and all, without you making threats on your own life now? That's kind of selfish, don't you think?" I gave that some real thought. I knew Dave had her best interests at heart and had helped her a lot previously. Jill had told me all sorts of wild stories about the kinds of people they taught at that camp, crazy paranoid types who live in the woods in their vans, and it irked me to think Dave might think he was dealing with that kind of individual when he was talking to me. I'm not like that at all. I'm a reasonable person. So in talking to him I tried to kind of meet him halfway, because after all this is over I hate thinking he'll be talking to Jill about what happened and have negative things to say about me.

When he said that about her mom, though, what came into my head was this: the thing I pity Jill over, more even than what happened with her mother, is that she's an only child. I mean, every family has its issues, its sad circumstances and crises they never saw coming, but there's also people you can look in the eye and know that they're carrying it with you. Whatever happened in my own family, I could sit with Elias and know he thought the same of it as I did. Candy, she's added her own share to that whole pile, but at least I knew the Olmstead business was her burden, too, whether she liked it or not. Jill never had that. The whole thing with her mother dying, she had to deal with it all on her own. They say no man is an island, but Jill pretty much *is* an island. It's kind of hard to watch, like when you see a woman carrying a really heavy suitcase and she keeps insisting she doesn't want your help in getting it across the airport.

My regret is that it's looking as if I won't get the chance to give my son a brother. I can't really put to words the ache that comes with just thinking about that. If they burst into the house and kill me, or if I do it myself, or if I step out that door and start shooting down the driveway so I at least go out in a battle instead of cornered in my own home—any way this ends, TJ's going to have to carry it, and there's no way around that. Only a brother could make that any lighter.

So I'll put it out there as my final statement, these two messages to those two people I love most.

Thomas Jefferson Olmstead, if you take away one noble thing from the deeds I did on this earth, let it be that I chose to stand in opposition to the full crushing force of the Government of the United States of America—its history and rule of law and sheer power to enforce its will—to right a roaring injustice done to my family. I would have done the same for you. For you I would have stood against the entire world.

And Elias Olmstead, for the wrongs I did you, and for the love I cost you, know that I always believed that among family we struck the bargain with our loyalty. I'm paying up now. And if I see you on the other side of this, I hope you'll call it even.

Epilogue

JILL

Nobody had told me about the magic of a toddler's first spring. Through the long months of winter TJ grew used to the skeletal trees, the fractured shapes they made against the sky, the clearness and plainness of looking up. And then all at once, in April, they burst out into a great banner of shimmering pale green, as suddenly as all the fans in a stadium rising to cheer. At first it frightened him. He stared up distrustfully at the new canopy, listened to the rustle of animals he could no longer see. When we stepped out the door of our little cabin at Southridge, even if only to walk the twenty feet to his grandmother's cabin next door, he hid his face against my shoulder and muttered, over and over, his most powerful word: *no*. He was too young to remember that he had seen all this before, but old enough to feel unsettled by the realization that the world will change without warning.

On the morning I put Leela on a train back to New Hampshire—a week's visit to see her grandsons at Randy's, Eddy at the nursing home and possibly Candy, if she had earned visiting privileges—I decided it was time to take TJ on a hike. I tied his winter cap beneath his chin to block the April wind and strapped him into the backpack carrier Dave had given me as a welcome-home gift. Before Dave could see us, I hurried down the trail behind our cabin and into the woods. I knew he would insist on coming—fearing bears, twisted ankles and all sorts of hazards that might befall a lone hiker with a special burden. But the walk wasn't far, and I wanted TJ to know I was not afraid.

Without a blanket of thick and heavy snow beneath my feet, the journey went much faster. Dry twigs cracked beneath my boots, and the last fall leaves, worn thin and lacy from the storms of winter, shuffled to the edges of the path. TJ chattered about the birds, piping his two-word sentences punctuated with mimicked animal sounds; his feet patted my sides as if coaxing a racehorse. Since his ear surgery the previous fall, he had begun imitating all the sounds around him with an enthusiasm that delighted me. To TJ, Frasier had been a quiet, muffled place, but all the music of this forest belonged to him now.

In a short time we arrived at the clearing, and I stopped near the campfire pit, turning to face the mountains whose ski trails the spring had reclaimed.

"You see that, buddy?" I said. I twisted my neck, looking up to catch a glimpse of my son. "It's *pretty,* huh? You want to get down?"

I eased off the backpack and set TJ loose. For one long moment he stood and surveyed the land around him, taking in the breadth of the space and the height of the trees, cocking his ear toward the rush of the waterfall nearby. Sometimes I was certain he had Cade's mind—analyzing everything he saw, planning his moves one by one, yet not immune to temper tantrums and petulance. I wished I could feel the pride of an ordinary mother who sees the best of her child's father reflected in his spirit, but a bittersweet ambivalence was the best I could do.

From the direction of the trail came the sound of a bounding dog. I scooped up TJ, and a moment later Tess appeared, tail wagging and tongue lolling, with Dave following close behind with a walking stick in hand. "What are you *doing?*" he asked, but his tone was cheerful. "You know there's bears here, right?"

"I have yet to see a bear. In ten years I have never once seen a bear."

"That just means they're good at hiding."

I grinned. "Well, we're fine. I'm trying to help TJ get over his new fear of trees."

Dave nodded and looked out at the mountains. "He's had a lot of change lately. Can't blame the kid for wanting everything to just stand still for five minutes."

TJ squirmed in my arms, and I set him down on the ground once again. As he toddled forward to pet the dog, I remembered the day Dave and I had hiked here—that Christmas afternoon two years or an eon ago—when I first knew of his little life. That day Dave had spoken of his doubts about Cade, and I had ignored him. But even now, after all my son and I had traveled through to return to this place, I wasn't sorry for that. Cade had only been human, with a savage side and a pure-hearted one, the same as everybody else. The same as me, or Leela, or Elias. As good a man as Dave was, even the help he offered me had not been purely selfless. He welcomed the excuse to bring me back, and not just because I was a hard worker, either. I think I had known that, in the packed-away part of my heart, for a long time.

And I could find a way to make room for it. Because grief always gives way eventually and cracks open into something new, the way my mother had once stood beside a highway with me, looking out over a thunderstorm, knowing it was time to usher in a change that would make things better. It was my turn now, and I could do the same—for the sake of my child's life, yes, but also for mine.

It's not too much to ask of a person. It's love, that's all.

★ ★ ★ ★ ★

AUTHOR'S NOTE

★ ☆ ★ ★ ☆

The first stirrings of this story entered my mind over a late-night dinner with a friend at IHOP. The friend and her former husband had both been in the army—she was still on active duty—and had each served in Iraq. Sitting across from me with her hands wrapped around a cup of hot cocoa, she began a slow and heartbreaking reflection on the end of her marriage. As she described her then-husband's transformation from a loving partner to a man who struggled to put his harrowing experiences behind him, and the toll that it all had taken on his psyche and their marriage, the war finally came home for me. I know many people in the military, but very few who are on the ground in a war zone. I'd heard about post-traumatic stress disorder, but overall I had been very insulated from soldiers' experiences and those of their families. Yet as I listened to my friend that day, I started to put together how far-reaching are the effects of PTSD, how devastating and how permanent. There was no optimistic hook to this story, where the soldier ends up running a marathon and becoming a motivational speaker, nor the defining end point of a suicide or line-of-duty death. There was only a quiet and ordinary loss that went on and on and on.

Over 212,000 Iraq and Afghanistan war veterans have been

treated by the Department of Veterans Affairs for PTSD, but because half of vets seek health care elsewhere, the number affected is likely far higher. Soldiers affected by PTSD may experience flashbacks, feel tremendous anxiety and hyper-alertness, and suffer from intense feelings of guilt, all of which make it extremely difficult to function in society the way they did before the war. Recently, greater awareness and greater focus has improved some services for soldiers with PTSD, but many soldiers and their families continue to find the treatments offered to be inadequate or superficial. The suicide rate among combat vets is already alarming, and it is rising. As the drawdown continues and more and more soldiers come home, the United States and its allies will be faced with societies that include more than two million veterans of those wars—and by VA estimates, more than one-quarter of those men and women experience PTSD.

I don't have any illusions that *Heaven Should Fall* represents anything more than my imaginative ideas about one soldier's, and one family's, experience. To do justice to those who served, I researched extensively to be sure Elias's symptoms, his feelings and his experiences of war would be as credible as possible. I spoke to soldiers, read accounts written by those with PTSD, watched videos of patrols in Afghanistan and sought out affirmation of the smallest details, and sometimes made sweeping changes to accommodate some aspect I'd gotten wrong. At the end of it, quite honestly, I loved Elias more than any other character in the book; if I have made any errors in the physical details, I apologize, but I most of all hope the emotional details of his story tell the truth.

I encourage anyone who is moved with compassion for our veterans and their families to support organizations such as Disabled American Veterans, which offers the Veterans Crisis Line in addition to its plethora of other services to wounded soldiers. And in the difficult economic climate that exists at the time of this writing, I hope that our legislators will be mindful of the fact that cuts to community mental health services disproportionately affect veterans and their families.

ACKNOWLEDGMENTS

★ ★ ★ ★ ★

Many thanks, first and foremost, to my agent Stephany Evans, whose hard work allows me the privilege of writing a set of acknowledgments at all. And I am deeply grateful to Susan Swinwood, my editor at Harlequin MIRA, for her wonderful skill and extreme patience.

To a few extraordinary people in the writing community: Ann Hite, Eleanor Brown, Keith Donohue, Carolyn Parkhurst, Alma Katsu, Gary Presley and Rick Bylina, who courteously allowed the use of his surname in this book.

To my friends, en masse, for their extraordinary support. Laura Wilcott, Hillary Myers, Stephanie Cebula, Jalin Sopkowicz, Sarah Thompson, Amanda Miller, Christine Barakat and Elizabeth Gardner; Kathy Gaertner, Erika Schreiber, Laurine Kandare, Laura Carns, Mollie Weiner and Kay. And of course, Vern Roseman, Sara Spivey Roseman and Miranda Poff, for the inspiration (as well as the fuel).

And finally, to my husband, Mike, and to my kids—James, Catherine, Breckan and Luke—thank you ever so much for your patience and your love.

1. Jill's relationship with her mother was a close one, which leads to her sense of anxiety and guilt at not having intuitively known when her mom died. Do you think Jill's feelings about that are irrational or natural?

2. Cade is ambitious and outgoing, and early on he and Jill have a strong relationship. Did you see signs even then that a ruthless element existed in his personality? Did his behavior set off any red flags for you, or did you feel that the change in him was entirely brought on by his grief and circumstances?

3. Jill's mother was a member of Alcoholics Anonymous, and Jill is well versed in their philosophy, which becomes a kind of spirituality that she draws from during difficult times. Have you known anyone in a recovery program, or participated in one? Have you learned

anything from such a program that applies to your life, regardless of whether you are in recovery?

4. At the beginning of the story Cade seems uninterested in his old girlfriend, Piper, but as things deteriorate in his own life he grows obsessed with her. What do you think is behind this change of heart?

5. How do you think Elias's upbringing affects the way he feels about his experiences of war? What do you think is the biggest contributing factor to his suicide—is it his PTSD, or something else?

6. Candy uses religion as a way to see the world as inherently just and, as a result, feels no compassion for others. This backfires on her when Elias dies and she feels punished for her own feelings and misdeeds. What is your opinion of Candy's way of approaching her faith?

7. Even Leela, who is one of the most sympathetic members of the Olmstead family, has moments when she takes a hard-hearted approach to people close to her—Eddy and Lucia in particular. Do you think her callousness toward them is justified?

8. It's implied that Candy had more involvement in Lindsay Vogel's drowning than she owned up to. What do you think her role was, and why?

9. Elias suffers from PTSD, a condition that affects as many as one-quarter of soldiers returning from the wars in Iraq and Afghanistan. What do you think can be done to reach soldiers who struggle to readjust, or who need help but are reluctant to seek it?

10. Cade professes to deeply love his son, his wife and his brother, yet throughout the story he commits acts that violate their trust and risk their safety. Do you believe he truly loves them and is limited by his human flaws, or that he doesn't fully grasp the meaning of love and loyalty in the first place?

11. How did you feel about Jill's actions toward the end of the story? Did you feel she was doing the best she could with what she had, or that she was too complicit in her own problems in the end? Were you satisfied with the way the story was resolved?